PRAISE FOR JIM BUTCHER
AND THE DRESDEN FILES

"Butcher is the dean of contemporary urban fantasy." —*Booklist*

"Think *Buffy the Vampire Slayer* starring Philip Marlowe."
—*Entertainment Weekly*

PRAISE FOR SEANAN McGUIRE

"The plot is strong, the characterization is terrific, the tragedies hurt . . . and McGuire's usual beautiful writing and dark humor are present and accounted for. This has become one of my favorite urban fantasy series." —*Fantasy Literature*

PRAISE FOR KEVIN J. ANDERSON

"Anderson's skill in delivering taut action scenes and creating well-rounded human and alien characters adds depth and variety to a series opener that belongs in most SF collections."
—*Library Journal*

PRAISE FOR ROB THURMAN

"Thurman continues to deliver strong tales of dark urban fantasy."
—*SFRevu*

SHADOWED SOULS

Edited by

JIM BUTCHER
and KERRIE L. HUGHES

ROC
New York

ROC

Published by Berkley

An imprint of Penguin Random House LLC

375 Hudson Street, New York, New York 10014

Library of Congress Cataloging-in-Publication Data

Names: Butcher, Jim, 1971– editor. | Hughes, Kerrie, editor.
Title: Shadowed souls/edited by Jim Butcher, Kerrie L. Hughes.
Description: New York, New York: Roc, 2016.
Identifiers: LCCN 2016025491 (print) | LCCN 2016033135 (ebook) |
ISBN 9780451474995 (paperback) | ISBN 9780698192607 (ebook)
Subjects: LCSH: Fantasy fiction, American. | Science fiction, American. |
American fiction—21st century. | BISAC: FICTION/Fantasy/Urban Life. |
FICTION/Fantasy/Contemporary. | FICTION/Anthologies (multiple authors). |
GSAFD: Fantasy fiction. | Suspense fiction.
Classification: LCC PS648.F3 S49 2016 (print) | LCC PS648.F3 (ebook) |
DDC 813/.0876608—dc23
LC record available at https://lccn.loc.gov/2016025491

First Edition: November 2016

Printed in the United States of America
1 3 5 7 9 10 8 6 4 2

Cover illustration by Chris McGrath

CONTENTS

INTRODUCTION

I love Harry Dresden. Seriously. He's the perfect guy: deep, dark, somewhat handsome but with a geeky streak. He knows all kinds of magick and he stands up for his friends and family. He also has really awesome pets. Mind you, there's always the possibility of becoming collateral damage.

My love for Harry isn't just a crush; I respect his journey in life. He started off as an orphan, learned to fight off bullies, and then became a force to be reckoned with. I also respect that he hasn't become a monster along the way.

Harry might argue, though, that he is a monster. Mainly because of that collateral-damage thing, but what he has slowly come to realize is that many of the people who pretend to be good are not, and the ones who do bad things are often the ones protecting everyone, and that's where the heart of *Shadowed Souls* lies.

I invited the authors to write a story based on the idea that good and evil are just two aspects of a complicated and very human story.

I wanted the plots to play with the concept and invite the reader to explore the edges of their own darkness. I wasn't disappointed.

The stories get dark—some of them get really dark—and a few of the protagonists are truly monsters. I'd still invite them to tea, though, maybe not in my home, but definitely someplace safe— perhaps at Mac's for a beer; I hear he brews some really good stuff.

Welcome to *Shadowed Souls*, and remember something Jim told me: Good isn't always light, and evil isn't always dark.

—Kerrie L. Hughes

FOREWORD

A pack of coyotes circled my house last night.

My little dog is old and sick. His time could be close, and I imagine that they could smell that on the scents he left around the yard. They circled the house, yipping and barking, territorial-challenge barks that were supposed to make him want to come out and defend his territory. Coyote sounds, but maybe an octave deeper than I was used to from coyotes.

It worked. Poor little guy was frantic, pacing back and forth around the house, desperate to do his duty as he had his whole life and go to bark at them and defend the home territory.

Well. I heard three different animals, which probably meant there were more like five of them—some making noise, while others slipped around all sneaky-like. Coyotes are smart like that. But even if there were only three of them—three of the new, larger coyote-dog-wolf hybrids that seem to be emerging, maybe—it seemed an awful lot to ask of a twenty-pound bichon frise. My dog thinks he's darned near a wolf, but I've never had the heart to tell him that he's a bichon.

So I went out to confront them instead. I yelled at them, let them know that this was my territory and their presence was not desired.

They yelled back at me. Louder. Got more excited, enough that I could hear them breathing as they ran in the dark and the woods outside. I'd approached the source of the first sounds boldly and with confidence, the way you're supposed to confront potential predators, to let them know that you're not weak and not afraid of them.

But as I stood there facing the woods, I heard sounds of movement in the woods to my right. And more sounds over in the woods to my left. And I realized that the coyotes were moving into position all around me. I'd seen one of them a few days before—it had approached to within twenty feet of me, golden eyes and a black nose at the edge of the forest. It was big. German shepherd–sized, maybe seventy or eighty pounds. I'd seen a young adult just wandering around my yard a few days before that, definitely a wild creature, but maybe fifty pounds of canine.

And I realized that if I continued acting the way I was, I was in potential danger.

So I fell back to the house while the coyotes continued yelling and barking and trying to taunt my sick old little warrior out to be a meal.

So instead of yelling and screaming, I turned out all the lights in the house. And I slipped outside, very quietly, with a loaded rifle.

And in seconds, all the noise from the coyotes stopped.

Yeah.

That's what I thought.

Within a minute of my coming back inside, the dog had relaxed. He went to sleep and almost immediately had dreams where he was barking and growling very bravely, from the sound of it.

At the time, I was coldly furious with the creatures who were trying to hurt my little buddy. But, looking back on it, I can't really think that I was justified in feeling that way.

Coyotes aren't evil. They're predators, and they're awfully intelligent and very, very good at their jobs. They've thrived even in the face of expanding human civilization. But they aren't monsters. It's their place in the natural world to prey upon the old and weak. It keeps prey species strong, helps prevent the spread of disease, and grants a swift end to creatures that might otherwise linger in pain for days or weeks or months.

As frightened as I was on behalf of my little fuzzy buddy and, for a few seconds, for myself, those creatures weren't monsters. They have a place in the world and a job to do, and they were doing that job faithfully.

In turn, I was doing *my* job as a protector of my dog, and the moment I let them know that I was serious about my position, they honored it and left. They made their intentions clear, and I made mine clear in terms they could respect.

And yet, for a while, I had to be concerned about maybe getting eaten. If you haven't ever had that concern confront you in such a primal and visceral fashion, I highly recommend it. It gives you a whole new perspective on the world.

We all like to think that we'd be the people to fight off the coyotes when they come for ones too weak to defend themselves, but in thinking that, we often miss an important point: Coyotes aren't monsters.

But they are made of shadow.

They live in a part of the world that we don't like to think about or look at—even though the world needs them there, doing that job.

A lot of the people in these stories you're about to read are made of shadow, too. They aren't good. But they aren't necessarily evil, either. They need to be where they are, doing what they do. So come along and take some time to consider the darkness, and those who spend their lives moving in and out of it.

—Jim Butcher

SHADOWED SOULS

COLD CASE

by Jim Butcher

"You understand what you must do," said Mab, the Queen of Air and Darkness.

It wasn't phrased as a question.

I gripped the handrail on the side of the yacht and held on as it *whump*ed and *thump*ed through choppy water on the way toward a bleak shore. "I get it," I told her. "Collect the tribute from the Miksani."

Mab stared at me for a long moment, and that made me uncomfortable. It takes a lot to make that happen. I mean, you should see the stares my mother can give—Charity Carpenter is terrifying. And I got to where I could shake those off like nothing.

"Lady Molly," Mab said. "Regard me."

Not *Look at me*. Oh no. Not nearly dramatic enough.

I looked up at her.

We weren't around any mortals at the moment, but we were technically moving through the mortal world, among the Aleutians, and Mab was dressed in mortal clothing. The Queen of the

Winter Court of the Fey wore white furs and a big, poufy white hat like you might see on a Northern European socialite in an old Bond movie. No mortal alive would have been wearing white heels on the frozen, dripping, bucking deck of the yacht in those seas, in the beginnings of a howling winter storm, but she was Mab. She would take the path of least resistance when practical, but her willingness to tolerate the possible alarm and outrage of the human race extended only so far. She would wear what she felt like wearing. And at the moment, it would seem that she mostly felt like wearing an expression of stern disapproval.

My own clothing, I knew, disappointed her gravely, but I was used to doing that to mother figures. I was dressed in flannel-lined winter jeans and large warm boots, with several layers of sweaters, a heavy bomber jacket, and an old hunter's cap with ear flaps that folded down. Practical, sturdy, and serviceable.

I didn't need them any more than Mab needed the furs, but it seemed like it would be simpler to blend in—to a point, anyway.

"Appearances matter, young lady," Mab said, her voice hard-edged. "First impressions *matter*."

"You never get a second chance to make a first impression," I said, rolling my eyes.

I might have sounded a bit like this guy I know. Maybe a little.

Mab stared at me for a long second before she gave me a wintry smile. "Wisdom wrapped in witless defiance."

"*Witless*," I sputtered.

"I am offering you advice," Queen Mab said. "You have been a Queen of Faerie for less than a week. You would be wise to listen."

The yacht began to slow and then slewed to one side, throwing a wave of icy spray toward the rocky shore. It handled too well to be a mortal craft, but out here, where few eyes could see, the Sidhe who piloted her were only so willing to be inconvenienced by seas that would have daunted experienced mortal captains and advanced mortal vessels.

Not mortal, I told myself sternly, in my inner, reasonable voice. *Human. Human. Just like me.*

"Thanks for that," I said to Mab. "Look, I get it. My predecessor hasn't performed her duties properly for, like, two hundred years. I've got a huge backlog. I've got a lot of work facing me. I understand already."

Mab gave me another long stare before saying, "You do not understand." Then she turned and walked back toward her cabin, the one that was bigger on the inside than it was on the outside. "But you will."

I frowned after her for a second, then glanced at the thrashing twenty yards of sea between myself and the land and asked, "How am I supposed to go ashore?"

Mab moved her eyes in what might have been an impatient glance, if she'd actually moved them all the way to me, and went into her cabin and shut the door behind her without a word.

I was left standing on the pitching deck. I glanced up at the Sidhe piloting the yacht. They were both male, both tall, both dark of hair and eye. Which was not my type. Even a little, dammit. One noticed me and met my gaze boldly, his mouth curling up into a little smirk, and my heart went pitty-pat. Or something did. I mean, he was a damned attractive man.

Except he's not a man. He's one of the Sidhe. He's picked a look he knows you like for his glamour, and he'd cheerfully do things with you no human could possibly be flexible enough to manage, but he wouldn't care.

My reasonable voice sounded a lot like my mom's, which was more than a bit spooky.

Besides, I didn't need him to care. I just needed him to look pretty while I tore his clothes off and . . .

I shook my head and looked away, out at the ocean. Being the Winter Lady brought a host of challenges with it. One of the most annoying was what had happened to my libido, which had never exactly lacked for health. These days, I was like an adolescent boy bunny rabbit. Everything had sex in it, no matter how much it didn't or how hard I tried not to notice it. It was annoying, because I had a job to do.

The two extremely sexy Sidhe stared at me, being all smoldery and distracting, but not doing a damned thing to help me get ashore or prove myself on my first mission for the Queen of Air and Darkness. And since the last Winter Lady who had failed Mab wound up with a bullet in her skull, I figured I'd better not screw it up.

Which is what she'd meant about first impressions. It had been a polite threat, and, as I realized that, my legs felt a little wobbly.

Fine, then.

I called upon Winter. Big-time. I let the endlessly empty cold fill me, subsume me, and winds rose around me as the power of Winter flowed in. I let it freeze everything—my concerns of what would happen if I failed Mab, my curiosity about what was coming next, the lust inspired by the pilots (whom I suddenly realized had probably been placed where they had precisely to test my focus and resolve).

And then I let it out.

All my life, magically speaking, I had been used to being a spinner of cobwebs of illusion and mental magic. I'd always had enormous finesse, and always lacked the kind of power I had seen my mentor wield. I'd forced myself to adjust to the idea that I would always have to be subtle, indirect, manipulative—that that was the magic that was mine to command.

That was no longer true.

There was a thunder crack that thrummed from the surface of the sea as Winter's ice froze the ocean ten feet down for half a mile in every direction. The yacht suddenly locked into place, no longer pitching and rolling.

I'd have to do the math to be sure, but I thought that little trick had taken as much energy to accomplish as fairly large military-grade munitions. The two pilots just stared at me, suddenly uncertain about what they were attempting to play with.

That's right, pretty boys. Mess with me, I'll hit you so hard your children will be born bruised.

I gave them a sunny little smile, vaulted the side rail, and walked to shore through howling winds before the ice started breaking up again.

><><

They actually named the town Unalaska, Alaska. Despite the appeal of an innately oxymoronic name, Unalaska struck me as something closer to a colony on an alien world than as a mortal village. It's a collection of homes and businesses around Dutch Harbor, famous for being the central port for the fishing boats on that show about how dangerous it is to catch crabs.

(Actual crabs. Literal ones, like, in the water. Sheesh, this Winter mantle thing is so childish sometimes, because it's definitely not me.)

The buildings are all squat, sturdy, and on the small side—the better to resist massive winds and snows and rains and frozen ocean spray that turns to coatings of ice when whipped up by a storm. The town was surrounded by looming, steep, formidable mountains devoid of human markings, and clung to the limited flat spaces at their feet like some kind of lichen stubbornly hanging on in the shade of a large stone. The icy sea filled whatever vision was not occupied by the sky or the mountains, cold and uncaring and implacable. The sky overhead was a neutral grey, promising neither sunlight nor storms yet ready to deliver both with an impartial hand and little warning.

It wasn't a place that was inviting, kind, or merciful to mere humanity, and yet there they were.

We were. There we were.

I trudged through freezing winds and half an inch of sleet that had hardened into something between ice and snow and didn't shiver.

Harry Dresden once warned me about lying to myself.

I tried not to think about that too hard as I walked through the endless twilight of an Aleutian autumn and into town. I threw a glamour, nothing fancy, over myself as I went. I muddled my features from stark-boned beauty down to something much plainer. I darkened my hair, my skin, both of which were paler than usual, these days. I added on a few pounds, because I'd never really recovered the weight I'd lost when I was playing grim-dark superhero on the streets of Chicago, when Harry had been mostly dead. Everything about the look said *unremarkable*, and I added on the barest hint of an aura that I was an awfully boring person. It would be easier to move around that way.

Then I opened my senses to try to track down the elusive Fae who lived among the human population in Unalaska.

>—<

The wind was kicking up, with more rain and sleet on the way, and apparently the inhabitants of Unalaska knew it. No one was on the streets, and a few cars moved about furtively, like mice getting out of the way of a predator. I sensed a trickle of quivery energy coming from one low building, a place called the Elbow Room, and I went on in.

I was immediately subsumed in the energy of a crowded, raucous little dive. Music and the scent of beer, seared meat, and smoke flooded into my face, but worse were the sudden emotions that filled my head. There was drunken elation and drunken dread and drunken sullen anger and drunken lust; mainly, though, there were sober versions of all of those emotions as well. Threads of frustration and tension wove through the other emotions—servers, I imagined, overworked and cautious. Wariness rode steadily through the room from one corner, doubtless the bouncer, and cheerful greed hummed tunelessly under the rest, doubtless from the dive's owner.

I'm a wizard and I specialize in delicate magicks. I'm awfully sensitive to people's emotions, and running into this batch was like walking into a wall of none-too-clean water. It took me a moment to get my balance back, adjust, and walk inside.

"Close the door!" someone shouted. I took note of a young man, his face reddened and chapped by frigid wind. "Christ, I been cold enough to freeze my balls off for days!"

"That explains a whole hell of a lot, Clint!" shouted another man from the far side of the bar, to a round of general, rough laughter.

I closed the door behind me and tried to ignore the sullen, swelling anger radiating off Clint. There was something very off about his vibe. When it comes to emotions, people and monsters have a lot in common. It takes a very, very alien mind to feel emotions that are significantly different than those you'd find in human beings—and there's a vast range of them, too. Throw in mind-altering substances, like hormones and drugs, and it's absolutely unreal the variety available.

But I recognized an angry sexual predator when I sensed one.

I faked a few shivers against the cold as I wedged myself in at the bar and nodded to the bartender, a woman who looked as if she might wrestle Kodiaks for fun on her days off, if she ever took a day off. I put down some cash, secured a beer, and felt an ugly presence crawling up my spine.

I took a sip of the beer, some kind of Russian monstrosity that tasted as if it had been brewed from Stalin's sweat and escaped a Soviet gulag, and turned casually to find Clint standing behind me, about three inches too close, and breathing a little too hard.

"I don't know you," he said.

"Wow," I said.

"What?"

"That's got to be the best opening line in history," I said, and swigged some more beer. Hairs probably didn't start popping out on my chest, making little *bing* noises as they did, but I can't swear to it. "Did you want something?"

"I don't know you," he repeated. His breath was coming faster, and there was a kind of glossy film on his eyes I didn't like much. "Everyone knows everyone here. You're new."

"But not interested," I said, and turned away.

He clamped a hand down on my shoulder, painfully hard, and spun me back around. "I'm talking to you."

Once upon a time, that sudden physicality would have made my adrenaline spike and my heart pound with apprehension. Now my whole head suddenly went icy-hot with anger instead. I felt my lips pull back from my teeth. "Oh, pumpkin," I said. "You should walk away. You aren't going to like how this one plays out."

"You need to come with me," Clint said. He started to pull at me. He was strong. Wobbly on his feet, but strong.

"Take your hand off me before I lose my temper," I said, my

voice very sharp, and pitched to carry to everyone in the room, even over the noise and music.

And I got almost no reaction from the room at all.

Now *that* was interesting enough to notice. Places like this were full of your usual blue-collar crowd. You wouldn't find many philosophers or intellectuals here, but there would be plenty of basically decent people who wouldn't think twice about taking a swing at an aggressor.

Except no one was even looking at me. Not one eye in the entire room. Everyone was staring at a tiny TV screen on a wall, playing a sports broadcast so grainy and blurred that I couldn't even tell which game it was. Or they were focused on their drinks. Or at random spots on the wall. And the whole place filled with the sudden, sour psychic stench of fear. I turned my eyes to the two men at the bar next to me, and they only traded a look with the bartender, one that practically screamed out the words, *Oh no, not this again.*

What? Was Clint really *that* scary?

Apparently.

Certainly no help was coming. Which meant it was up to me.

"Let's do this the fun way," I said. "I'm going to count down from three to one, and when I get to one, if you are still touching me, I'm going to put you on a therapist's couch for the rest of your natural life."

"With me," Clint insisted, breathing harder. I'm not even sure he realized I had said anything.

"Three," I said.

"Show you something," Clint growled.

"Two," I replied, drawing out the number, the way Mary Poppins might have to unruly children.

"Yeah," Clint said. "Yeah. Show you something."

"O—" I began to say.

I didn't get to finish the word. A man seized the middle finger of Clint's hand, the one on my shoulder, snagged the other fingers with his other hand, and bent the single finger back. There was a snapping sound like a small tree branch breaking, and Clint let out a scream.

The newcomer moved with calm efficiency. Before Clint could so much as turn to face him, the new guy lifted a foot and drove his heel down hard at a downward angle into the side of Clint's knee. There was a second crack, louder, and Clint dropped to the floor in a heap.

"I don't think the lady likes you doing that," the newcomer said, his voice polite. He was a little over medium height, maybe an inch or two shorter than me, and built like a gymnast, all compact muscle and whipcord. He wore nondescript clothes much like my own, his features were darkly handsome, and his black eyes glittered with a feverish, intelligent heat.

I also knew him. Carlos Ramirez was a wizard, and a Warden of the White Council. He was only a couple of years older than me, and hotter than a boy-band bad boy's mug shot, and I instantly wanted to jump him.

Whoa. Down, girl. Just because you're the Winter Lady doesn't mean you have to behave like your predecessor did. Look where it got her.

"Miss?" he asked me. "Are you all right?"

"Yes, fine," I said.

"I apologize for that," he said. "Some things just shouldn't happen. Excuse me for a moment."

And with that, Carlos reached down, snagged Clint by the back of his coat, and dragged him to the door. Clint started feebly thrashing and swatting at Carlos, but the young wizard didn't seem to notice. He dragged Clint to the door and tossed him out into the sleet. Then he shut the door again and turned back to face the room.

Everyone was staring at him. The jukebox was wailing a song about broken hearts, but the talk in the room had died completely. The fear I'd sensed earlier had ratcheted up a notch. For a frozen moment, no one moved. Then one of the customers reached for his wallet and started counting bills onto his table. Everyone else started following suit.

Within five minutes the place was empty except for us and the bartender.

"What the hell is this about?" Carlos murmured, watching the last patrons depart. He looked over his shoulder at the bartender. "Was that guy the sheriff's kid or something?"

The bartender shook her head and said, "I'm closing. You two need to leave."

Carlos held up a twenty between two fingers. "Beer first?"

The bartender gave him an exasperated look, took a step to her left, and then said, "Do you understand me, mister? *You need to leave. Both of you.*"

"That a pistol or shotgun you got back there?" Carlos asked.

"Stick around. You'll find out," the bartender said.

The fear coming off her was nauseating, a mortal dread. I shook my head and said to Carlos, "Maybe we should."

"Mostly frozen water is falling from the sky, I'm starving, and I haven't had a drink yet," Carlos said. He asked the bartender, "There another place for one?"

"Charlie's," she replied instantly. "Other side of the bay. Green neon sign. Good burgers."

Carlos squinted his eyes and studied the bartender, as if weighing the value of heeding her words versus the personal pleasure he would take in being contrary.

Harry Dresden has had a horrible influence on far too many people, and has much to answer for.

"Okay," he said mildly. "Miss, would you care to join me for a meal?"

"That would be lovely," I said.

>–>–<–<

So we left and started trudging through the sleet.

The sound of it hitting the ground and the sidewalks and roads was a wet rattle. I didn't need to, but I hunched my shoulders as if against the cold and dropped my chin down to my neck as much as I could. "Goodness, this is brisk," I said.

"Is it?" Carlos asked.

"Aren't you cold?"

"Of course I am," Carlos said. "But I figured the Winter Lady would think this was a balmy day."

I stopped in my tracks and stared at him for a moment.

He offered me a sudden, mischievous smile. "Hi, Molly."

I tilted my head to one side. "Mmm. What gave it away?"

He gestured toward his eyelids with two fingertips. "Seeing ointment," he said. "Cuts right through glamour. I've got eyes all over this town. When they spotted a lone young woman walking in from the far side of the island, I figured it was worth taking a peek."

"I see," I said. "Carlos, tell me something."

"What's that?"

"Do you mean to arrest me and take me before the White Council? Because that isn't going to fit into my schedule."

I'd had some issues with the White Council's Laws of Magic in the past. The kind of issues that would have gotten my head hacked off if Harry hadn't interceded on my behalf. But then he mostly died, and I'd been on my own, outside of his aegis. The Wardens, including Carlos Ramirez, had hunted me. I'd evaded them—always moving, always watching, always afraid that one of the grim men and women in gray cloaks would step out of a tear in the fabric of reality right in front of me and smite me. I'd had a recurring nightmare about it, in fact.

But they'd never caught up with me.

"Molly, please," Ramirez said. "If I'd wanted to find you and take you to the Council, I would have found you. Give me that much credit. I even sandbagged a couple of the ops sent to bring you in."

I frowned at him. "Why would you do that?"

"Because Harry liked you," he said simply. "Because he thought it was worth sticking his neck out to help you. Besides, I had my own area to cover, and in the absence of a Warden, you were giving the Fomor hell."

They hadn't been the only ones with a surplus of hell. I hadn't been having much fun, either. "Why didn't the Council appoint a replacement, then?"

"They tried. They couldn't get anyone to volunteer to take Dresden's place as the Warden of the Midwest."

"Why not, I wonder."

"Lots and lots of problems and not enough Wardens," Carlos replied. "With the Fomor going nutballs, we're up to our necks and sinking already. Plus, everyone they asked had a good opinion of Harry, and nobody wanted to inherit the enemies he'd made."

"So, to clarify," I said, "you're not here to bring me in."

"Correct, Miss Carpenter. It would be a little awkward now that you're royalty. And, frankly, I have no intention of crossing Mab if I can possibly help it. Ever."

"Then why *are* you here?" I asked.

A boyish smile flickered over his face, and something inside me did a little quivering barrel roll. "Maybe I just wanted to meet the famous new Queen of the Winter Court," he said.

I fluttered my eyelashes at him and said, "Don't you trust me, Carlos?"

The smile faded a little and then turned wry. "It isn't personal, Molly. But from what I hear, you're a sovereign executive entity of a foreign supernatural nation, one that is on formal and unsteady ground with the White Council."

I felt myself grinning more widely at his mistake. "So it's Council business, then," I said.

His lips pressed into a grimace and he said, "No comment."

"So formal," I said. "What did you think of that scene in the bar?"

"Weird, right?" he said.

"Do you know what I think I'd like to do?"

"Circle back and watch the place to see why everyone was leaving?"

I winked at him. "I was going to say, 'Find a warm spot to make out,' but, sure, we can do that if you'd rather."

Carlos blinked several times.

Actually, I kind of blinked, too.

The past few years had been hard ones. I'd gotten used to walling people away. My libido had shriveled up from lack of use. I'd barely been able to allow Harry to come near me. And now here I was, flirting with the really, exceptionally cute Carlos Ramirez, as if I were a girl who enjoyed flirting.

I remembered that girl. I used to be that girl. Was that also a part of what Mab had done for me when she arranged to have me ascend to be the Winter Lady? Because if it was . . .

I liked it.

Should that be scaring me? I decided that I didn't want to worry about that. It was just such a relief to *feel* that kind of feeling again.

I pursed my lips, blew Carlos a little kiss, and turned to circle back toward the Elbow Room. It took him about five seconds to begin to follow me.

>—<

We found a shadowy spot next to a building within sight of the Elbow Room. I flicked up a veil to make sure we wouldn't be observed, and we settled down to wait.

It didn't take long. Within five or ten minutes, a silent column of men, twenty strong, came down the road, their feet crunching through the half-frozen sleet. Clint was at the head of the column with another man, a very tall, very lean character with a captain's peaked cap, leathery skin, and the dull, flat eyes of a dead fish. They marched up to the Elbow Room and filed inside, neat as a military unit on parade. No one said a word the entire time.

"Huh," Carlos noted. "That's not odd at all."

"No kidding. Dive Bar of the Damned." I frowned. "They look like locals to you?"

"Waterproof boots and coats," he said. "Fishermen, likely."

"Like, Clint's shipmates? Do shipmates come get involved in bar fights for their fellow shipmates?"

"Do I look like somebody who knows something like that? I'm from LA." He scratched his nose. "The question I'm having trouble with is, are there people who are willing to get into a fight for the sake of a jackhole like Clint?" He squinted. "Can I ask you something, Molly?"

I grinned at him. "It's pretty early in the season to entertain any more proposals, Carlos."

In the dark it was hard to tell, but I think his cheeks turned a few shades of color. It was actually kind of adorable. "What are *you* doing here?" he asked.

"Talking to the Miksani," I said, or tried to say. To my intense surprise, what came out was, "Talking to prospective make-out partners."

Carlos grimaced. "I'm serious."

I tried to say, *Miksani,* but what came out was, "So am I."

"Fine," he said, "be that way."

Why the hell would that be happening to me? Unless . . . it was a part of Winter Law.

The Winter Court of Faerie had an iron-clad code of law laid out by Mab herself. It didn't work like mortal law did. If you broke it, you didn't get punished. You didn't break it. Period. You were physically incapable of doing so. When Mab laid down the law, the beings of her Court followed it, whether they wanted to or not. They actually knew the law, on a subconscious level, but it took a real effort to summon it to your conscious mind. I took a slow breath and realized that any of the Hidden Peoples of the Winter Court were entitled to their privacy and could not be outed to the mortals or anyone else without their prior consent.

I let out a breath through my teeth and said, "It's not personal. I can't talk about it."

He frowned at me for a moment and then said, "What about a trade?"

"I'll show you mine if you show me yours?" I asked. "I like the way you think."

"Wow," he said, and now I was certain his cheeks were flaming. "Wow, Molly. That's not . . . It isn't . . . Could you please take this seriously for a minute?"

I smiled at him, and as I did, I realized that a trade changed everything with regard to the law. Bargains had to be balanced in the proper proportions and in similar coin. That, too, was Winter Law. If Carlos told me why he was present, I'd be free to say more about my purpose in kind.

"Deal," I said.

"We got a report from Elaine Mallory through the Paranet," Carlos said, watching the door to the Elbow Room. "Vague descriptions of a strange vibe and unusually odd activity here in Unalaska. People going missing, weird behavior, energy out of whack—that kind of thing. Someone had to check it out."

"Huh," I said.

"Your turn."

"Mab sent me," I said. "I'm here to collect on a debt."

I felt his eyes on me for a moment, and then he said, "You're . . . Mab's bagman?"

"Bagperson," I said. "Though I think it's more like a tax collector."

"They're just bagmen for the government," he replied. "What happened? One of the Miksani piss Mab off?"

I lifted my eyebrows at him. "You know of them?"

"Duh. Wizard," he said. "Jeez, Molly, give me a little credit."

I found myself smiling at him. "It's internal Winter Court business."

He nodded. "It occurs to me that if there is a tribe of Fae here, they probably know a whole lot about strange things happening in their town."

"That does seem reasonable," I said.

"It seems like we both might benefit from mutual coopera-
tion," he said. "If I help you with your job, maybe you could help
me with mine."

Help from a mortal, on my first job? Mab wouldn't like that.

On the other hand, I was pretty sure that when it came to me
filling the role of the Winter Lady, Mab wasn't going to like a lot of
things I did. She might as well get used to it now.

"I think that could work out," I said. "Provided you help me
with my job first."

"Molly," he said, and put his hand on his chest. "You wound
me. Do you think I'd welch on you?"

"Not if we do my job first," I said sweetly. "You know Winter
well enough by now to know that I'll do what I say I will."

"Yes," he said simply. He offered me his hand and said, "Do we
have a deal?"

I reached for his hand, but apparently bargains weren't closed
with handshakes under Winter Law. So I drew him toward me by
his hand, leaned over, and placed a soft kiss on his mouth.

Suddenly there was nothing else in the world that mattered.
Nothing at all. Just the soft heat of his lips on mine, the way he
drew in a sudden, shocked breath, and then an abrupt ardor in
returning the kiss. Something shuddered through me, a frisson of
pleasure like the deep-toned toll of an enormous bell. The kiss
was a symbol. Both parties had to agree to a kiss to make it happen like this one.

After a time, the kiss ended and my lips parted from his, just a
little. I sat there panting, my eyes only half-open, focused on
nothing. My heart was racing and sending bursts of lust running
through my body that began to pool in my hips.

I wasn't sure what the hell was happening to me exactly, but it
felt incredibly . . . *right*.

That probably should have scared me a little.

Carlos opened his eyes, and they were absolutely aflame with intensity.

"We have a deal, wizard," I whispered. Then I shivered and rose, stepping away from him before my mouth decided it needed to taste his again. "Let us begin."

>—<—<

I focused my will, quietly murmured, "Kakusu," and brought up the best veil I could manage—which is to say, world-class. It was one of the first things I learned to do, and I was good at it. The light around us dimmed very slightly, and we vanished from the view of anyone who wasn't going to extreme supernatural measures to spot us. The mix of sleet and rain could be problematic, since anyone who looked closely enough would see it bouncing off an empty hole in the air. But nothing is perfect, is it?

I nodded to Carlos, and we padded quietly across the street to circle the Elbow Room. A building that spends half the year mostly buried in snow doesn't go in for a lot of windows. The only two in the place were side by side, deeply recessed, and high up on the wall, to let in light.

We both reached up and got a grip on the slippery sills, and then quietly pulled ourselves up to peer into the bar.

The fishermen were standing facing the bar in two neat lines. Their scrawny leader in the captain hat was staring at the bartender, who stood behind the bar, gripping a cloth like some kind of useless talisman. Her face had gone pale and was covered in beads of sweat. She trembled so violently that it threatened her balance, and she just kept repeating the same phrase, loudly enough to be heard through the window, over the sleet: "I don't know, I don't know, I don't know, I don't know, I don't know."

Captain Fisherman took a step forward, toward her, and the strain on her face immediately increased, along with the volume and desperation of her voice. "I don't know, I don't know, I don't know!"

"Psychic interrogation," I noted. Invading a human being's mind was a monstrous act. It inflicted untold amounts of horrible damage, not to their brain but to their *mind*. The sensations it could cause were technically known as pain, but the word really doesn't do them justice. If someone went digging in your head long enough, they'd leave you a mindless vegetable, or hopelessly insane.

I knew, because I'd done it. I'd had the noblest intentions in the world, but I'd been younger, dumber, and a lot surer of myself, and people had been hurt.

Carlos let out a growl beneath his breath. "And we have a Third Law violation. And there's no way that's an accident or even badly misguided benevolence."

"Assuming he's mortal," I whispered. "If he isn't, then the laws don't apply to him."

"Either way, his head is coming off."

"Cool," I said. "Who is he?"

"Who cares?"

"What's he doing here?"

"Breaking the laws."

"Uh-huh," I said. "I wonder how many friends he has."

In my peripheral vision, I could see the muscles along Carlos's jaw contract and then relax again. I glanced aside and saw him visibly force down his anger and shake his head a little. "I'm taking him down. Just as soon as I find out exactly who he is, how many buddies he has, and what designs he has on this town."

"Oh," I said innocently. "Is that not what you meant the first time?"

He started to mutter an answer when his fingers slipped on the slickened windowsill and he fell.

He didn't make much noise. A little scrape on the wall and a *thump* as he hit the ground—but the captain's head whipped around in a turn at least forty-five degrees too great to take place on a human neck, his eyes narrowed. He paused for about two seconds, and then spun on a heel and started walking for the door.

"Company," I hissed to Carlos. I dropped down quietly from the window. My feet did not slip on the ice, because, hey, Queen of Winter over here. I moved quickly and crouched over him, putting my hands lightly on his chest. "Stay flat and stay still. I'll keep you covered."

He looked down at my hands and gave me a quick look, then his expression went focused and stoic and he lay back on the sleet-covered ground.

I did everything I could to shore up the veil covering us both. The captain stepped out of the Elbow Room and looked around, and I got a close look at the man for the first time.

There was visibly something wrong with him. At a casual glance, it might have looked like he'd simply been exposed to a little too much cold and ultraviolet radiation and freezing salt water. But the cracks in his skin were a little too sharp edged, the reddened portions a little too brightly colored for that. I got the slow and horrible impression that his skin was trying to contain too much mass, like an overstuffed sausage. There were what looked like the beginnings of cataracts in his eyes—only their edges quivered and wobbled, like living things.

That was pretty weird, even by my standards.

It got absolutely hentai-level weird when the man opened his mouth and then opened it a little wider, and then opened it until his jaw visibly unhinged and a writhing tangle of purplish red tentacles emerged and thrashed wildly at the air, as if grasping for scents.

I felt my mouth stretch into a widening grin. A sleet storm was a terrible place for scent-hunting. I couldn't tell you how I knew that, but I knew it as certainly as I knew that he hadn't noticed the flaws in my veil. This was not the territory of this creature, whatever it was. It was mine.

The tentacles withdrew with a whipping motion, like a frog recovering its tongue. The captain swayed from foot to foot, looking around the night for a moment, and then turned and paced back into the bar. A moment later, the whole weirdly silent column of fisherman freaks, including Clint, marched out of the bar and back down the hill toward the harbor. Clint was walking on his broken knee as if it didn't particularly bother him that it was bent inward like that.

"What the hell?" Carlos breathed as they walked away. "What was *that*?"

"Right?" I asked him. An absolutely mad giggle came wriggling up out of my belly. "That was the most messed-up thing I have ever seen from that close." I looked down at him, put my hand up to my mouth, and made gargling sounds while wiggling my fingers like tentacles.

And suddenly I realized that I was straddling Carlos Ramirez. And that he was staring at me with dark eyes that I felt like I could look at for a good, long while.

"Do you know what I want to do?" I asked him.

He licked his lips and then glanced at the retreating group. "Follow them?"

"Yes, all right," I said, and swallowed. "Follow them. We can also do that." I rose and helped him up.

"Wait—what?"

"I'm flirting with you, dummy," I said, and smiled at him. "What, you can't work and banter at the same time? After all your big talk?"

He lifted a hand, closed his eyes, and pinched the bridge of his nose for a moment. "*Dios.* This . . . is very much not what I was expecting for this evening. And hang on." He ducked back around the corner of the Elbow Room, and a moment later emerged with a small bundle of gear. In a few seconds, he was donning the gray cloak of the Wardens of the White Council and buckling on a weapons belt that bore a sword on one side and a large pistol on the other.

"Swords and guns," I said. "Hot." I picked up a corner of the cloak and wrinkled my nose. "This, though . . . Not."

"Wardens do a lot of good," he said quietly. "It isn't always pretty, what we do, but it needs to be done." He nodded toward the retreating backs of the captain and his crew. "Like those . . . things. Someone has to do something." He smiled faintly as he started walking in their wake. "You and Dresden can't be everywhere."

I watched him for a moment, taking in details. "You're limping," I noted. It was a weakness, and it stood out to me. It might not have before.

"Should have seen me a month ago," he said. "Could barely get out of my chair. Chupacabra kicked me in the back. Come on."

I could see the pain in his movements now, and cataloged them on pure reflex. His back was too rigid, much more so than it had been before. The fall from the window had aggravated injuries that hadn't healed properly. That could be used against him.

I wish thoughts like that didn't come to me so naturally, but after months fighting the Fomor on Chicago's streets, months under the instruction of the Leanansidhe, they were second nature.

I folded my arms against a little chill that had nothing to do with the weather and hurried after the handsome young Warden.

>—<

The weather continued worsening as we reached the waterfront. It wasn't far from the Elbow Room, but *far* was a relative term when a viciously cold wind was driving sleet and icy spray up the slope and into our faces. To me, it was brisk but actually a little bit pleasant. But for the sake of camaraderie, and definitely not because I wanted to conceal my increasing levels of weirdness from Carlos, I emulated him. I bowed my head against the wind and hunched my shoulders while hugging my own stomach.

"Who would live in this?" Carlos growled, shuddering.

"People smart enough to stay indoors during this kind of weather?" I suggested. "Tentacular parasites? Obstinate wizards? You come to Alaska but you don't plan for the cold?"

He couldn't really roll his eyes very well when his lashes were becoming steadily encased in ice, but he came close. "Maybe you'd like it back in your cell, Your Highness."

I flashed him a quick grin, and then we kept on following the captain and his crew. They wasted no time in marching back to a waterfront pier and boarding a ship with the name *Betsy Lee* painted across her stern. They filed up the gangplank, neat as you please, and went belowdecks, all without hesitating or looking back—and all in total silence.

We watched for a moment more, and then Carlos nodded and said, "I'm thinking freak fuel explosion. Boat burns to the water in moments, takes them with it."

"Wow," I said.

"Not yet," he said. "Not until I'm sure it's only them. Just thinking of the shape of things to come."

I looked up and down the waterfront, what I could see of it through the weather, and said, "Well, we're not sitting out here all night and babysitting the boat." And we weren't going to be moving quietly around the *Betsy Lee*, either, not with all that ice on the deck.

But I could.

"I'm going to take a peek around," I said. "Right back."

"Whoa," Carlos said. "What? Molly . . ."

I ignored him and ran lightly over the short distance to the dock and down it, and then leapt lightly out onto the deck of the ship. My feet didn't slip, and a continuous series of rippling shivers ran up and down my spine. I was putting myself in danger, treading into the territory of what was clearly a dangerous predator, and it felt really, really good.

Is that what happened to Maeve? Had she gotten a little too fond of the feeling of danger? I mean, she'd spent years defying freaking *Mab*. Could it get more dangerous than that?

I shook my head and started scouting the ship, relying on my instincts. Harry'd always been a good source of advice about problems. He dealt with them on a continuous basis, after all, and in his studied opinion, if you had one problem, you had a problem. But if you had *multiple* problems, you might also have an opportunity. One problem, he swore, could often be used to solve another, and he had stories about a zombie tyrannosaurus to prove it.

The Miksani had several centuries' worth of a spotless record in paying tribute to Mab. They'd stopped only a few years ago. As diverse and fickle as the beings of Faerie could be, they rarely did things for no reason. And, lo and behold, in this same little town in the middle of more nowhere than any other little town I had ever seen, tentacular weirdo critters were conducting a quiet reign of terror.

Chances that these two facts were unrelated? Probably close to zero.

I didn't want to take my chances in the confined spaces belowdecks—that was a losing proposition for me, if it came to a confrontation. So I conducted a quick survey of the deck, the bridge, and the fishing paraphernalia stored on it, keeping my steps as light and silent as I could. I spotted it just before deciding to leave again: a single dark feather gleaming with opalescence, pinned between two metal frames of what I presumed to be crab cages, stored and ready to drop into the sea.

I felt a little surge of triumph, took it, and leapt lightly back to the deck. I rejoined Carlos a moment later. He was sliding his gun into its holster. He'd been ready to start shooting if I got into trouble. And they say there are no gentlemen anymore.

"What'd you find?"

I held it up, grinning.

"Feather?"

"Not just a feather," I said. "A cormorant feather."

He peered at me. "How do you know that?"

I didn't want to say something like *I Googled it under Winter Law*, but the mantle of power I'd inherited from Maeve knew all about Mab's subjects, and the knowledge it contained flowed through me as certainly as lessons learned in childhood. "How do you think?" I asked instead.

He struck his head lightly with the heel of his hand and said, "Durr. The Miksani."

"Elementary, Watson," I said, and winked at him before I started walking. "I suggest you bring your pistol, just in case."

"Just in case of what?" he asked, turning to follow.

"In case the Miksani decide they aren't in the mood for company."

>—><—<

Iliuliuk Bay is the next-best thing to four miles long, and that makes for a lot of shoreline. We had to walk around the bay to get to the portion of Unalaska that was physically farthest from the dock where the *Betsy Lee* was moored. The weather stopped worsening and held steady at torturously miserable levels. Carlos drew up his cloak's hood and trudged along stoically.

It took time, but we reached a log building on the edge of town that bore a sign that read UNALASKA FISH MARKET. A pair of cormorants—large, dark seabirds—huddled on a protruding log at the building's corner, taking partial shelter from the night beneath the eaves of the building's roof. I could feel their dark, bright eyes on me as I approached the darkened building, but I didn't head for the door. Instead I went straight to the birds.

"Greetings to the Miksani from the mistress of Arctis Tor," I said in formal tones. "I, her appointed representative, have come for the tribute rightfully due the Winter Court. I believe that a meeting with your elders could produce positive results for all parties."

The birds stared at me hard. Then, as one, their eyes swiveled to Carlos.

He lifted a hand and said, "Warden Ramirez of the White Council of Wizardry. I apologize for showing up at the last minute, but I come in peace, and would appreciate a meeting with your elders as well."

The two birds stared at him for a moment and then looked at each other. One winged away into the night.

The other flapped its wings, soared down to the ground not far from us, and shimmered. A second later, the cormorant was gone, and an entirely naked young woman crouched where it had been a moment before. She had the bronze skin and almond eyes of someone with a generous helping of Native American blood in her veins, and her hair was nearly longer than she was, dark and glossy, with faint flickers of opalescence in it. She couldn't have been older than me, and she was built like a swimmer, all supple muscle and muted curves.

Her eyes were agate hard. The anger boiled off her in waves.

"Now?" she demanded of me. "Now you come?"

"I'm kind of new at this," I said. "This was actually my first stop. I'm Molly, the new Winter Lady."

The girl narrowed her eyes, staring a hole in me as she did. She was silent for a full minute before she spat, "Nauja."

"It's nice to meet you, Nauja," I said.

The simple pleasantry got a suspicious look and narrowed eyes in response. Apparently, Maeve had left quite an impression on the locals. That girl had been a real piece of work.

"I have nothing to say to you," Nauja said, her tone carefully neutral. She turned to Carlos and inclined her head in something resembling politeness, only a lot stiffer. "Wizard Ramirez. We have heard of you, even here. You have done much for one so young."

Carlos gave her his easy, confident grin. "Just wait until I'm old enough to get my driver's license."

Nauja stared at him for a second and then looked down sharply, her cheeks turning a few shades pinker. Not that I could really blame her. Carlos was pretty darned cute, and he could *kiss*. My lips tingled faintly in memory, and I folded my arms so that I could rub at my mouth unobtrusively.

Maybe three minutes later, the door to the fish market opened and candlelight shone weakly out into the foul weather of the night. Nauja rose immediately and walked inside. There was a young man about her age waiting inside, wearing a heavy flannel robe. He had another one waiting, and wrapped it around her shoulders carefully before nodding to us and standing aside so that we could enter.

We went in, and the young man shut the door behind us. It took a couple of seconds for our eyes to adjust to the low candle-light, and then I saw why the Miksani were so upset.

They were in the middle of a funeral.

A dead man of middle years, resembling Nauja enough to be her father or uncle, lay on a table in the middle of the room. He was dressed in a mix of practical modern clothing and native garb, maybe sealskin, richly decorated in beads and ivory. His hands were folded on his chest, and a bone knife or spearhead of some kind lay beneath them. Nauja and her male counterpart took up positions on either side of a woman of middle age who stood beside the body, her expression drawn with grief. The three of them stared at me expectantly.

Carlos stepped close enough to me that he was almost touching. His hip bumped mine deliberately, and he looked up at the rafters of the little market building.

Dozens of bright eyes were staring down at us. I couldn't tell how many cormorants lurked in the rafters, but they were every-where, and waiting with the silent patience of predators.

I dragged my eyes from them back to the elder woman facing me. "I am Molly, the new Winter Lady," I said in what I hoped was a respectful, quiet tone. "I've come for the tribute."

"I am Aluki," said the woman in a quiet voice. She gestured toward the bier. "This is my husband, Tupiak. We sent to you for help years ago."

"I take it no help came," I said.

Aluki stared at me. Nauja looked like she wanted to fling herself on me and rip my eyes out.

"Well, the problem has been addressed, and now I'm here," I said. "Let's set things straight."

"What do you know of our troubles," Aluki said.

"I know they're on the *Betsy Lee*," I said.

Nauja's eyes suddenly became huge and black, and she all but quivered in place.

Carlos stepped between us and nodded respectfully. "Elder Aluki, I am Warden Ramirez of the White Council of Wizardry. We've been made aware of difficulties in this place. I'm here to help. If I can be of service in restoring balance to the Miksani, I will be glad to do so."

Aluki inclined her head to Carlos. "We are not a wealthy people, Warden. I cannot ask for your help."

Of course not. The Miksani were of Winter, and the Fae never gave or accepted gifts or services without equal recompense. The scales of obligation had to remain balanced at all times.

"You need not," Carlos responded. "I've come to a bargain with Lady Molly, who has already offered payment on your behalf."

Oh, that was an excellent gesture on Carlos's part. And it worked. Aluki gave me another glance, one more thoughtful, before she nodded.

"My predecessor," I said, "failed to make me aware of her obligations before she passed. Please tell me how Winter may assist you."

"No," Nauja hissed, surging toward me.

Aluki stopped the younger Miksani with a lifted hand, her eyes on me. Then she said, "Our enemy has arisen from the deeps and taken mortal shells. Each season, they take some of our number."

"Take?" Carlos asked. He nodded toward the dead Miksani. "Like that?"

Aluki shook her head and spoke in a level, weary tone. "The enemy has power. Our people survive by hiding among the mortals. Few of us are warriors. Only Tupiak, Nauja, and Kunik had the power to challenge the enemy. They tried to rescue those who had been taken. They failed. My husband was wounded and did not survive."

"Your enemy has captives?" I asked. "Right now?"

She nodded and said, "On the ship, belowdecks. While they are captive, there will be no tribute."

"Well, then," I said. I exchanged a glance with Carlos. He gave me a wolfish grin and nodded. I nodded back and said to Aluki, "The Warden and I are going to go get them out of there."

She lifted her chin. "You can do this?"

"I can," I said. "I will."

There was a low *thrum* in the air as I spoke the words, and I felt something go *click* somewhere in my head. I had just made a promise.

And Winter *kept* its promises.

Aluki stared at me for a moment, then sagged, bowed her head, and nodded. "Very well."

"Your people who were taken," I said, "how will I know them?"

Nauja bared her teeth and spoke with her jaw clenched. "They took our children."

><><

"God, I love hero work," Carlos said as we stepped back out into the storm. "No murky gray area, no anguished questions, no conflicting morality. Bad guys took some kids, and we're gonna go get 'em out."

"Right?" I asked him, and nodded. "This must be what my dad felt, all the time."

"Knights of the Cross never have any missions they question?" Carlos asked.

"I think they get a different kind of question," I said. "For Dad, it was always about saving everyone. Not just the victims. He had to try for the monsters, too."

"Weird," Carlos said.

"Not so weird," I said. "Maybe if someone had offered a hand to the monsters, they wouldn't have become monsters in the first place. You know?"

"I don't," Carlos said. "Maybe I've seen too many monsters." He settled his weapons belt a little more comfortably on his hips and wrapped himself up in his cloak again. "Or too many victims. I don't know."

Our steps crunched in the sleet, and between that and the rattle of more sleet and the crash of waves on the shore, I almost didn't hear his next words.

"About six months into the war," he said, "I was carrying pliers with me, so that I could take vampire teeth as trophies. That was how much I hated them."

I didn't say anything. Carlos, like a lot of the other young Wardens of the Council, had been baptized in fire. Harry had spoken of it once while doing his best to shield me from the war. He'd felt horrible leading a team of children, as he saw it, into a vicious conflict between the White Council and the Red Court:

I feel like I'm putting them through a meat grinder. Even if they come home in one piece.

"You hated them. And then they were gone," I said.

"Poof," Carlos said. "War over." He shook his head. "*Odium in-*

terruptus. And then it was supposed to be back to business as usual again. Just supposed to move on. Only I never quite figured out how. And half the bunks in the barracks were empty."

"Part of you misses it," I said.

His lips tightened, though it wasn't a smile. "I miss the certainty," he said. "I miss how tight I was with the squad. The rest I can mostly do without." He glanced at me and then away. "The Wardens' job isn't always simple. Or clean. I've done things I'm not proud of."

"Haven't we all?" I said.

We walked in silence for a few steps. Then he said, "Once we get these kids clear, I want to kiss you again."

My tummy did a little happy cartwheel, and my heart sped up to keep it company. "Oh yeah? What if I don't want to?"

He gave me a very direct, very intense look. His eyes were dark and hot and bold.

"You want to," he said.

He wasn't wrong.

>─<

We stole up to the *Betsy Lee* under my best veil, moving quick and quiet. We'd already worked out the plan. Carlos was going in first and was going to raise a hell of a racket and attract everyone's attention. My job was to stay veiled, grab the kids, and get them off the ship.

Then we'd kill things.

But halfway across the deck toward the door leading below, Carlos paused. He tilted his head to one side and narrowed his eyes. He glanced at me, lifting his brows in an unspoken question.

I paused, frowned at him, and then looked carefully around

the deck. It was empty. The boat rolled and pitched with the waves, but there was no other motion upon it. It was still and silent as a tomb. In fact . . .

It just *felt* empty, like an apartment with no furniture, like a school playground on the weekend.

Carlos suddenly moved faster, gliding to the stairs. He held up a hand, telling me to wait, and went down them in a rush. He reappeared within a minute.

"Empty," he reported. "There's no one down there."

"Dammit, something must have tipped them off," I said.

He nodded. "They've got eyes somewhere, all right."

I went back to the dock and then to where it met dry land. I couldn't see very well, but I murmured, "Akari," flicked my wrist, and created an orb of glacial green light in the air over my right shoulder. Green was a good color for this kind of work. The mortal eye can detect more shades of green than any other color on the spectrum.

I cast back and forth, but it took only a few seconds to find what I was after: a depression in the accumulating sleet, the marks of the passage of many feet. "Carlos," I said, and pointed at the ground. "Tracks."

He came over and squinted down. "Aren't these where they came back to the boat the first time?"

"Can't be," I said. "Our tracks from an hour ago are gone. These were made after we left."

He lifted his eyebrows. "Seriously, Aragorn? Where'd you learn this stuff?"

"Mom taught me. She was scoutmaster for my brothers."

"And to think I wasted my youth learning magic," Carlos said. "Can you tell if the kids were with them?"

"Dammit, man. I'm a Faerie Princess, not a forensic analyst." I jerked my head to tell him to follow me, and we set out after our quarry.

>—>—<—<

The trail ended at a church.

It was a Russian Orthodox church, complete with a couple of onion domes, and the sign out front read HOLY ASCENSION OF OUR LORD CATHEDRAL. It was also creepy and ominous as hell in the freezing night. Odd blue-green light glowed within the windows of the sanctuary. I thought I saw a shadow move past a window, sinuous and smooth, like a cruising shark.

"Oh," Carlos said, stopping short. I could see calculations and connections forming behind his eyes. "Uh-oh."

"What-oh?"

"This just got worse."

"Why?"

He licked his lips nervously. "Uh. How much Lovecraft have you read?"

"I haven't kept track," I said. "Somewhere between zero and none. Should I have?"

"Probably," he said. "It's always the last thing a formally trained apprentice learns about."

"I have a funny feeling my training wasn't formal," I said.

"Yeah. Neither was Harry's. Have you heard of the Old Ones?"

"I don't think it's a very kind nickname for the Rolling Stones. They still put on a great show."

He nodded and squinted at me. "I kind of need you to put on your serious face now."

"That bad?" I asked.

"Maybe," he said. "They're . . . kind of a collection of entities. Really old, really powerful entities."

"What, like gods?" I asked.

"Like the things gods have nightmares about," he said.

"Outsiders."

He nodded. "Only they aren't *outside*. They're here. Caged, bound, and sleeping, but they're here."

"That seems kind of dangerous."

"Yes and no," he said. "They feed on psychic energy. On fear. On the collective subconscious awareness of them that exists within humanity."

I squinted at him. "Meaning what?"

"The more people who know about them and fear them, the more awake and more powerful they become," he said. "That's why the people who know about them don't talk about them much."

"What's that got to do with the price of beer in Unalaska?"

"One of the Old Ones is known as the Sleeper. It's said his tomb is somewhere under the Pacific. And that goddamned moron Lovecraft published *stories* and *easy-to-remember rhymes* about the thing." He shook his head. "The signal boost gave the Sleeper enough power to influence the world. It has a number of cults. People get . . . infested, I guess. Slowly go insane. Lose their humanity. Turn into something else."

I remembered the captain's open mouth and writhing tentacles and shivered. "So you think that's what is happening here? A Sleeper cult?"

"It's the Holy Ascension of Our Lord Cathedral," he pointed out. "That means something way different to a Sleeper cultist than it does to most folks. They aren't exactly making it difficult to suss out."

"Okay. So, how does that change anything about what we have to do tonight?"

He nodded toward the cathedral. "You feel that?"

"It's capital-C creepy," I said, and nodded.

"It's worse than that," he said. "It's holy ground. Consecrated to the Sleeper. We go in there, we won't be dealing with a bunch of 'roided-up fishermen with tentacle mouth. They'll have power. It's a nest of sorcerers in there."

"Oh," I said. "Ouch." I thought about it for a moment. "So how does that change anything about what we have to do tonight?"

He bared his teeth. "Guess it doesn't."

"I guess it doesn't," I agreed.

"You know," he said, "I am pretty damned valorous."

"I know," I said.

"But I am not stupid. You're a Faerie Queen now, right?"

"Uh-huh, I guess," I said.

"Couldn't you whistle up a squad of ogres or something to help make this happen?"

I thought about it for a second and said, "Yeah, I could."

"Maybe something like that should happen?" he suggested.

I was quiet for a second before I said, "No."

"Uh-huh," he said, and nodded. "Why not?"

"In the first place, it would take time to get them here. In the second, this is Miksani territory, and the ogres would have to arrange payment for intruding and observe customs, and it would take even longer. And in the third place . . ."

I blinked. Oh. *That's* what Mab meant.

"What?" Carlos asked.

"This is my first showing. Everyone in Winter, every wicked and predatory thing in Faerie, is going to pay attention to it, and will interact with me based off what I do here. First impressions matter, and I'm not going to be a child who screams for help the first time she hits a bump in the road. I'm going to be the predator who freaking takes you apart if you cross her. I'm going to make sure I don't have to prove my strength to them over and over for the rest of this gig. So, you and I are going to go in there and handle it."

Carlos sniffed, then gave a short nod. "Right. Well. These people—they aren't human anymore. Something else moved into their bodies. There's nothing left to save. You get me?"

I got him. He meant that I could play hardball without fear of running afoul of the White Council. I squinted at the cathedral and said, "Okay. New plan."

>―<

Harry was a big believer in kicking in the teeth of whoever you planned to fight. Granted, those kinds of tactics played to his strengths, and it wasn't always smart or possible—but it *was* always a way to seize the initiative and control the opening seconds of a conflict.

Granted, Harry would have used fire. And I'm pretty sure he wouldn't have pulled out a wand and prepared the One-Woman Rave spell I'd developed. And I'm absolutely certain that he wouldn't have taken a moment to start up DJ Molly C's Boom Box spell, which would play C&C Music Factory's "Gonna Make You Sweat (Everybody Dance Now)" loud enough to be heard in Anchorage.

But I did. I wanted loud noise that was totally out of place and as weird as possible to whatever supernatural critters were riding around inside the fishermen—and the creatures of the supernatural world aren't exactly pop-culture mavens. Plus, it was dance music from the '90s. Nobody thinks that stuff is normal.

Heavy bass and lead power chords started thumping against the windows. I turned loose the One-Woman Rave, and the air around me filled with a light and pyrotechnics show that would make Burning Man look like *Mister Rogers' Neighborhood*. My heart started pounding in fear and excitement and something disturbingly like lust as I crossed the last few feet to the cathedral's entrance.

And then, just as the song screamed, "Everybody dance now!" I leaned back, drew the power of Winter into my body, and kicked the big double doors off their hinges as if they'd been made of balsa and Scotch tape.

At which point I learned the real reason Harry keeps doing that.

It. Is. Awesome.

"Give me the music!" I screamed with the song, and walked straight in. I might have had some hip and shoulder action going in time with the beat.

Look, I hadn't been out dancing in a while, okay?

I crossed the little vestibule in a couple of steps and passed into the sanctuary in a thundercloud of rave lights and showers of multicolored sparks, music shaking the air. I got a good look at the fishermen as I came in.

All twenty of them were there, scattered around the sanctuary, though three, including the captain, were up on the altar, along with half a dozen Miksani children, aged about four through ten. Their wrists were bound together with one long length of rope, which cut cruelly into their wrists.

Everyone in the cathedral lifted a hand to shield their eyes as I came in. The cultists' mouths gaped open and tendrils emerged to begin thrashing the air.

I felt the surge of power coming, an ugly, greasy pressure in the air, and as it gathered, physical darkness swirled and surged around the fishermen. And then, like a stream of fouled water, it surged from each of the cultists to the captain, where his tentacles gathered it, whipping and writhing, and sent the enormous collective surge of negative energy flying directly at me.

It came fast, too fast to dodge, too intense to be stopped by any magic I could manage, and struck my solar plexus like an enormous, deadly spear.

Or, at least, that's what it looked like, to them. I was actually about ten feet to the left, hidden behind my best veil while maintaining a glamour of my image. The bolt struck my little illusion, and the conflict of energies, combined with the difficulty of running the Rave and the Boom Box, made it too much to hold together. The image popped like a soap bubble, and the dark bolt tore through the flooring and foundation in the vestibule like a backhoe.

The captain froze for a second, unsure of what had just happened. I had no such moment of hesitation. I was already rushing down the leftmost aisle behind my veil, plastic-handled knife in hand. I reached the first of the tentacle-mouthed fishermen and, with a single flick, cut his throat.

I could barely hear the creature's sudden, high-pitched scream of pain over the thunder of the Boom Box, and I'd known it was coming. It didn't register on the other fishermen in the chaos, and I didn't slow down.

I killed three of them with my knife before one of the cultists saw what was happening and screamed, pointing.

Number four went down when he turned his head to look, but he writhed as he went down and I was splashed with blood.

Magically speaking, blood is significant in all kinds of ways. It carries a charge of magical energy inside it, for example, and can be used to direct a spell at a specific person from hundreds or thousands of miles away. This blood was stronger than mortal stuff and carried a heavier charge. The power in it flared into sparks as the blood hit my veil, and then it ripped a huge hole in it, and I was suddenly visible to the entire cult.

Another bolt of energy came my way, this one tossed by an individual cultist. It lacked the landscape-rearranging power of the first bolt, and I was lucky it did. I threw up a shield of enough strength to barely deflect it, and dove to the floor as others came winging my way, chewing chunks the size of my fist from the wall behind me.

From the floor I couldn't see much—but the cultists were howling and they had to be coming closer, sending their nearest members to rush me while the others kept me pinned down with their blasts of dark power. If I didn't move, and fast, I would be swarmed. Winter Queen or not, that wouldn't end well for me.

I let go of the remnants of the veil, crystallized a new spell in my mind, and gave it life. Then I hopped up and ran for the exit.

I also hopped up and ran down the nearest aisle of pews. I also hopped up and sprinted toward the altar. I also hopped up and started vaulting the pews diagonally, heading for the nearest fisherman. I also hopped up and backed up one step at a time, conjuring what looked like a heavy energy shield in front of me. I also hopped up and hurled a blast of deep blue energy at the captain. I also hopped up and . . .

Look, you get the idea: thirteen Mollies started running everywhere.

Blasts of dark power ripped apart pews and tore holes in the walls and shattered panes of stained glass. Some of them struck home, disintegrating the images, but the others continued to move and duck and evade.

Meanwhile, I stayed low and scramble-crawled twenty feet into the concealment of the confessional. I had done what I meant to do: entirely occupy the cult's attention.

Carlos made his entrance in perfect silence. The wall behind the altar was made of dark wood, but it just . . . fell apart into freaking grains of matter in an oval six feet high and three across, revealing the young Warden on the other side.

Without ceremony, Carlos pointed at a cultist, muttered a word, and a beam of pale green light struck it in the back. The man-creature simply *dissolved* into a slurry of water and what looked like powdered charcoal. The young Warden didn't miss a beat. Before the first cultist was done falling to the floor, he drew his sword and ran it smoothly into the nape of another cultist's neck. The creature arched for a second and then dropped like a stone, his mouth moving in frantic, silent screaming motions.

The captain whirled on Carlos and unleashed a wave of dark energy the size of a riding lawn mower. The Warden dropped his sword, slid his back foot along the floor, and dropped into a crouching stance. His arms swept up in smooth, graceful symmetry and intercepted the energy, gathering it like some kind of enormous soap bubble.

It was a water magic spell, Carlos's specialty. He rolled his arms in a wide circle, took a pair of pirouetting steps, and swept his arms out toward the captain, sending the dark spell roaring back at him. It hit the captain like a small truck, hurtling him off the stage and halfway down the sanctuary.

"Come on, kids," Carlos shouted. He recovered his sword and almost contemptuously deflected an incoming blast of cultist magic with it. "I'm taking you home!"

The little Miksani didn't have to be told twice. They got up, the larger children helping the smaller ones, and began hurrying awkwardly toward the escape route Carlos had created on the way in. He shielded them, backing step by deliberate step, calling up a shield of energy with his left hand, intercepting blasts of energy with it, or swatting them wide with his Warden's blade.

In a few seconds, he'd be out of the room, along with the Miksani children, leaving me with nothing but cultists. I tensed and began to gather my energy.

And then Clint's reddened, work-roughened, clammy-cold hand shot into the confessional and seized my throat. It caught me off guard, and the sudden pain as his fingers tightened and he shut off my air supply was indescribable. He lifted me and, without hesitating for a second, began to slam me left and right, against the walls of the confessional, each impact horribly heavy, with no more passion than a man beating the dust from a rug.

My head hit hardwood several times, stunning me. My knees went all loose and watery, and suddenly the Rave and the Boom Box were gone. The next thing I knew, I was being dragged by the neck toward the altar. Clint walked up onto it and threw me down on my back on the holy table. I blinked my eyes, trying to get them to focus, and realized that the cult was gathered all around me, a circle of tentacle-mouthed faces and dead eyes.

Carlos and the kids were gone.

Good.

"It isn't a mortal," Clint said, somehow speaking through the tentacles, albeit in a creepy, inhuman tone. "See? It's different. It doesn't belong here."

"Yes," the captain said.

"Kill it. It cost us our sacrifice."

"No," the captain said. "You are new to the mortal world. This creature's blood is more powerful than generations of the Miksani and their spawn." The tentacles thrashed more and more excitedly. "We can drain her and drain her. Blood more powerful than any we have spilled to pave the way for the Sleeper. Our Lord shall arise!" The captain's eyes met mine and there was nothing behind them, no soul, nothing even remotely human. "And he shall hunger. Perhaps . . ."

"Perhaps you should think about this," I said. I think my sibilants had gone slushy. "Walk right now. Leave this island and don't come back. It's the only chance you have to survive."

"What is survival next to the ascendance of our Lord?" the captain asked. "Bow to Him. Give yourself of your own will."

"You don't know who I am, do you, squid-for-brains?" I asked.

"Bow, child. For when He comes, His rage will be a perfect, hideous storm. He will drag you down to his prison and entomb you there. Forever silent. Forever in darkness. Forever in terrible cold."

"I am Lady Molly of Winter," I said in a silken voice.

The thrashing tentacles went abruptly still for a second. Then the captain started to shout something.

Before he could, I unleashed power from the heart of Winter into the cathedral, unrestrained, undirected, unshaped, and untamable. It rushed through me, flowed through me, both frozen agony and a pleasure more intense than any orgasm.

Ice exploded out from me in swords and spears, in scythes and daggers and pikes. In an instant, crystalline blades and points, a forest of them, slammed into being, expanding with blinding speed. Ice *filled* the cathedral, and whatever was in its way, living or otherwise, was pierced and slashed and shredded and then crushed against the sanctuary's stone walls with the force of a locomotive.

It was over in less than a second. Then there was only silence, broken here and there by the crackle and groan of perfectly clear ice. I could clearly see the cult through it. Broken, torn to pieces, crushed, their blood a brilliant scarlet as it melted whatever ice it touched—only to freeze into ruby crystals a moment later.

It took the captain, impaled against the cathedral ceiling, almost a minute to die.

And while he did, I lay on the holy table, laughing uncontrollably.

>—<

The ice parted for me, opening a corridor perhaps half an inch wider than my shoulders and the same distance higher than my head. I walked out slowly, dreamily, feeling deliciously detached from everything. I had to step over a hand on the way out. It twitched in flickering little autonomic spasms. I noted idly that it probably should have bothered me more than it did.

Outside, I found Carlos and the Miksani children. They were staring at me in silence. The sleet made the only sound. Few lights glowed in windows. Unalaska was battened down against the storm, and other than us, not a creature was stirring.

I closed my eyes, lifted my face to the storm, and murmured, "Burn it down."

Carlos stepped past me without a word. I felt the stirrings of power as he focused his will into fire so hot that the air hissed and sizzled and spat as he brought it forth. A moment later, warmth glowed behind me, and the crackle and mutter of rising flames began.

As we walked away, one wall was already covered in a five-foot curtain of flame. By the time we got the children back to the fish market, the cathedral was a beacon that spread an eerie glow through the sleet and spray. A few lights had come on, and I could see dark figures and a couple of emergency vehicles near the pyre, but there would be no saving the place. It was set a bit apart from the rest of Unalaska, in any case. It would burn alone.

Cormorants had begun to circle us, their cries odd and muted in the dark, and the children looked up with uncertain smiles. When we reached the market and went in, Aluki and Nauja were waiting for us. Nauja let out a cry and rushed forward to embrace the smallest girl, a child who cried out, "Mama!" and threw her arms around the Miksani woman's neck.

Cormorants winged in from out of the night through the open door, assuming human form with effortless grace as they landed. Glad voices were raised around the children, and more parents were reunited with their lost little ones. There were more hugs and laughter and happy tears.

That, I thought, should probably make me feel more than it does as well.

Carlos watched it with a big, warm grin on his face. He shook some hands and nodded pleasantly and was hugged and clapped on the shoulder. As I watched him, I felt something finally. I was admiring his scars, the memory of his skill, his courage, and I had an absolutely soul-deep need to run my fingers over him.

No one came within five feet of me—at least, not until Aluki crossed the room from the bier where her husband still lay, facing me.

"I assume you wish the tribute now," she said in a low voice.

I felt dark, bright eyes all over the room, focusing on me.

"I need rest and food," I said. "I will return when the storm breaks, if that is acceptable."

Aluki blinked and her head rocked back. "It . . . yes. Of course, Lady Molly. Thank you for that."

I gave her a nod and turned toward the door. Just before leaving, I looked over my shoulder and asked, "Carlos? Are you coming with?"

"Ah," he said, and his smile changed several shades. "Why— why yes, I am."

>―<

By the time we reached Carlos's hotel, the storm was raging.

And the weather had gotten worse, too.

Neither of us spoke as we reached his room, and he opened the door for me. It was a nice hotel, far nicer than I would have expected in such isolation. I walked in, dropping my coat to the floor behind me. It hit the ground with the squelching sound of wet cloth and crackles of thin ice breaking. Layers of shirts joined it as I kept walking into the room, until I was down to skin.

I felt his eyes on me the whole way. Then I turned slowly and smiled at him.

His expression was caught somewhere between awe and hunger. His dark eyes glittered brightly.

"You're soaked and frozen," I said quietly. "Get out of those clothes."

He nodded slowly and walked toward me. His cloak and coat and shirts joined mine. Carlos Ramirez had the muscles of a gymnast, and his body was marked here and there with scars. Strength. Prowess. I approved.

He stopped in front of me, down to his own jeans. Then he kept walking toward me until our bodies met, and he pressed me gently down to the bed behind us. My eyes closed as I let out a little groan when I felt the heat of his skin against my chest, and I flung myself into the kiss that came next like the world was about to vanish into a nuclear apocalypse.

The sudden explosion of desire that radiated out from him felt like sinking into a steaming-hot bath, and I reveled in it, my own ardor rising. My hands slid over his chest and shoulders, reached around to his back. He was all tight muscle, heat, and pure passion. His mouth wandered to my throat, then to my shoulders and breasts, and I let out groans of need, encouraging him.

Molly, said the voice of my better reason.

His mouth left me for a second as he pulled off my boots. I arched up to help him remove my jeans, and heard him kicking off his own. With an impatient growl, I sat up and ripped at his belt.

Molly, said reason again. *Hello?*

I flung the belt across the room, to tell reason to shut up, and tore at his jeans. I had never wanted anything so badly in my *life* as I wanted Carlos naked and pressed against me.

This isn't you, said reason.

I pushed his jeans down past his hips. God, he was beautiful. I took his hand and leaned back on the bed, drawing him with me. "Now," I said. My voice came out thick and husky. "No more waiting. Now."

He let out a groan as he kissed me again, and I *felt* him start to touch and then—

—and then I was sitting on the floor of the shower, shuddering, hot water pouring down around me.

Wait.

What?

What the hell?

I looked down at the water. The drain stopper was down, and it was seven or eight inches deep.

And pink.

Oh God.

I looked at my hands. My nails . . . my nails looked longer. Harder.

And there was red under them.

What had just *happened?*

I stood up and left the shower, dripping wet, not bothering to stop for a towel. I hurried back out of the bathroom and stopped in the doorway, shocked.

The room had been wrecked. The mattress was against the far wall—and the door. It had been torn in half. The lamps were out, and the slice of light from the bathroom lights provided the only illumination in a stark column. What I could see of the furniture had been trashed. Part of the bed frame was broken.

And Carlos . . .

He lay on the floor, covered in blood. One of his legs was broken, the pointy bits of his shattered shin thrusting out from the skin. His face was swelling up beneath the blood, his eyes puffed closed. He was covered in claw marks, rakes that oozed blood. He lay at a strange angle, twitching in pain, one hand clutching with blind instinct at his back.

His injured back. His weakness.

I stared down at my hands in utter horror, at the blood beneath my nails.

I had done this.

I had used his weakness against him.

"Mab," I breathed. I started choking and sobbing. "Mab! Mab!"

Mab can appear in a thunderclap if she wants to. This entrance was much less dramatic. A light in the far corner of the room clicked on and revealed the Queen of Winter, seated calmly in the chair in the corner. She regarded me with distant, opalescent eyes and lifted a single eyebrow.

"What happened?" I asked. "What happened?"

Mab regarded Carlos with a calm countenance. "What will happen every time you attempt to be with a man," she replied.

I stared at her. "What?"

"Three Queens of Summer; three Queens of Winter," she said, that alien gaze returning to me. "Maiden, mother, and crone. You are the maiden, Lady Molly. And for you to be otherwise, to become a mother, would be to destroy the mantle of power you wear. The mantle protected itself—as it must."

"*What?*"

She tilted her head and stared at me. "It is all within the law. I suggest you spend a few hours each day meditating on it in the future. In time you will gain an adequate understanding of your limits."

"How could you do this?" I demanded. The tears on my checks felt like streaks of hot wax. "How could you do this?"

"I did not," Mab said calmly. "You did."

"Dammit, you know what I mean!"

"You have been gifted with great and terrible power, young lady," Mab said in an arch tone. "Did you really think you could simply go about your life as if you were a mortal girl?"

"You could have warned me!"

"When I tried, you had no inclination to listen. Only to jest."

"You bitch," I said, shaking my head. "You could have told me. You horrible bitch." I turned to go back into the bathroom, to get towels and go to Carlos's aid.

When I turned, Mab was *right* behind me, and her nose all but pressed against mine. Her eyes were flickering through shades of color and bright with cold anger. Her voice came out in a velvet murmur more terrifying than any enraged shriek. "What did you say to me?"

I flinched back, suddenly filled with fear.

I couldn't meet her eyes.

I didn't speak.

After a moment, some of the tension went out of her. "Yes," she said, her voice calm again. "I could have told you. I elected to teach you. I trust this has made a significant first impression."

"I have to help him," I said. "Please step aside."

"That will not be necessary," Mab said. "He will not be in danger of dying for some hours. I have already dispatched word to the White Council. Their healers will arrive momentarily to care for him. You will leave at once."

"I can't just leave him like this," I said.

"That is exactly what you can do," Mab said. Her voice softened by a tiny fraction of a degree. "You are no longer what you were, child. You must adapt to your new world. If you do not, you will cause terrible suffering—not least of all to yourself." She tilted her head, as if listening, and said, "The storm is breaking. You have your duty."

I clenched my jaw and said, "I can't just leave him there alone."

Mab blinked once, as if digesting my words. "Why not?"

"Because . . . because it's not what decent people do."

"What has that to do with either of us?" she asked.

I shook my head. "No. I am *not* going to be like that."

Mab pursed her lips and exhaled slowly through her nose. "Stubborn. Like our Knight."

"Damned right I am," I said.

I'm not sure you can micro-roll your eyes. But Mab can. "Very well. I will sit with him until the wizards arrive."

I turned to regard Carlos's broken form lying on the floor. Then I hurried into enough clothes to be decent. I knelt over him and kissed his forehead. He made a soft moaning sound that tore something inside my chest.

"I'm sorry," I whispered. I kissed his head again. "I'm *so* sorry. I didn't know what would happen. I'm sorry."

"Time waits for no one, Lady Molly," Mab said. She had crossed the room to stand across from me over poor Carlos. "Not even the Queens of Faerie. Collect the tribute."

I gave him a last kiss on the forehead and rose to leave. But I paused at the door to consider, to consult Winter Law.

I had never really considered what the tribute *was*. But it was there in the law. I turned slowly and stared at Mab in horror.

"Their children," I whispered. "You want me to take their children."

"Yes."

"Their *children*," I said. "You can't."

"I won't. You will."

I shook my head. "But . . ."

"Lady Molly," Mab said gently. "Consider the Outer Gates."

I did.

Winter Law showed me a vivid image. An endless war fought at the far borders of reality. A war against the pitiless alien menace known simply as the Outsiders. A war fought by millions of Fae, to prevent the Outsiders from invading and destroying reality itself. A war so long and bitter that bones of the fallen were the topography of the landscape. It was why the Winter Court existed in the first place, why we were so aggressive, so savage, so filled with lust and the need to create more of our kind.

"You're filling me with a hunger I can never feed," I whispered.

"We cannot expect our people to bear a burden that we do not," Mab replied, her tone level, implacable. "You will learn to endure it."

"You want me to take *children*," I hissed.

"I am fighting a war," Mab said simply. "Fighting a war requires soldiers."

"But they're *children*. Children like my little brothers and sisters. And you want me to carry them *away*."

"Of course. It is the ideal time to learn, to be trained until they come into their strength and are ready to do battle," Mab said. "It is the only way to prepare them for what is to come. The only way to give them a chance to survive the duties I require of them."

"How long?" I asked through clenched teeth. "How long will they be gone?"

"Until they are no longer needed," Mab said.

"Until they're killed, you mean," I said. "They're never going back home."

"Your outrage is irrelevant," Mab said. Her voice was flat, calm, filled with undeniable logic. "I have condemned *millions* of the children of Winter to a life of violence and death in battle, because it *must* be done. If we fail in our duty, there will be no home to which they can return. There will be no mortal world, safe and whole for your brothers and sisters."

"But . . ." My protest trailed off weakly.

"If you have an alternative, I would be more than willing to consider it."

Silence stretched.

"I don't," I said quietly.

"Then do your duty," Mab said.

I opened the door and looked back at her. "I don't *yet*," I said, and I said it hard. "This isn't over."

Mab gave me the slow blink again. Then she inclined her head by a fraction of an inch, her expression pensive.

I turned and left the broken form of Carlos Ramirez behind me to steal away the Miksani's children.

And I couldn't stop crying.

SLEEPOVER

by Seanan McGuire

*"Love is love. Species, gender, how long ago they may
have died, none of that really matters. Love is love, and
without it, we might as well be howling into the void."*
—LAURA CAMPBELL

It was the last exhibition match of the season, and the Slasher
Chicks were attacking the track with such vicious precision that
they looked almost choreographed. Their captain, Elmira Street,
was organizing some of the most efficient blocking I had ever
seen, while their jammer—my cousin Antimony, skating under
the derby name Final Girl—was running rings around the oppos-
ing team. Literally. I watched her star-spangled helmet circle the
track, and I tried to find it in my heart to cheer.

Annie had worked hard all season, and she deserved the support of her family. Since her parents didn't give a crap about what
she did in her spare time and her siblings were both out of the

state, and *my* sibling refused to leave his basement fastness, that left her with a cheering section of one. Me, Elsinore Harrington, the girl with the broken heart.

The cause of that broken heart was behind Annie on the track, caught in the scrum with the rest of the Concussion Stand. Carlotta, better known as Pushy Galore when she was in the rink. Up until a week ago, the love of my summer, and now the latest in my long line of ex-girlfriends. Or, as my mother liked to call them, the "Gosh, Elsie, maybe if you knew how to commit to a relationship, I wouldn't have to keep picking up the pieces when you broke another one" girls.

My mother is not the nurturing type.

Anyway, what with Carly dumping me like last week's phone case—complete with "It's not you, it's me, I can't handle dating someone who isn't human, you understand, it's not a racist thing, I'm just not comfortable with this anymore"—I would have been completely within my rights to avoid the rink for the foreseeable future. Better yet, forever, since I kept falling for derby girls, dating them until they got tired of me, breaking up with them, and then having to deal with seeing them every time Annie had a practice or a game. It got old.

But Annie needed me, and not just for rides to the track. So here I was yet again, wearing my Slasher Chicks T-shirt, with a purse full of cookies and bacon wrapped in foil, waiting for my cousin to skate her way to glory.

Glory or a split lip, depending on whether or not she flubbed her next jump. Split lips were bloodier. I was hoping for glory, or at least for a lack of stitches.

The buzzer rang to signal the end of the game, and the Slasher Chicks took the bout by a respectable sixty-three points. Annie kept skating, thrusting her hands up in the air as if she had just been elected Queen Bad-Ass of Ass Mountain. The rest of her team swarmed around her, all of them clapping and hugging each other like a big family.

I was the one who'd brought her here, encouraging her to try out after she graduated from high school and had to stop being a cheerleader. This was where I used to go to blow off steam and pick up girls, not necessarily in that order. So why did I suddenly feel like the one on the outside?

"Which one's yours?" The voice was unfamiliar. Low alto, with a little bit of a Northern buzz to it, like the owner had grown up somewhere in Nova Scotia.

"The brunette with the pigtail braids," I said. Annie was following her team into the victory lap, shaking hands with every member of the Concussion Stand. I paused, reviewing the voice and the question it had asked, before adding hastily, "She's my cousin. I just come to support her."

"Oh," said the voice. "I see."

"I'm Elsie," I said, and finally turned to see whom I was talking to. I was promptly glad that I had gotten the pleasantries out of the way before I lost the capacity for rational speech. That, too, is me: Elsinore Harrington, the girl who sometimes gets slapped silent by beauty.

I am told that someday I will become smooth and easy with the ladies. I am pretty sure this is a lie.

The voice's owner was sitting next to me on the bench, looking at me with amusement. She looked about my age, mid-twenties, with long, wavy hair that might have been blond once but was now all the colors of cotton candy—pink and blue and purple and white. It matched her makeup, which was overdone in that awesome "my makeup isn't for *you*" way that always made me want to follow people back to their mirrors and learn all their secrets. She was wearing a Scream Queens league tank top and a black pleated skirt over striped tights, and as was all too often the case with me, I immediately wanted to know her better, even if that meant doing whatever she said.

"Hi," I said.

"Hello," she said, and smiled. "I'm Morgan. So, Final Girl's your cousin, huh? How does *that* feel?"

"Like I should buy stock in Band-Aids," I said. She laughed. It was a low, husky sound, sweet as the candy her hair resembled. I wanted to make her laugh again. I hadn't known her five minutes before, and now making her laugh felt like the most important thing I could possibly be doing with my time. "No, it's good. She really enjoys derby, and I enjoy watching my cousin kick the crap out of people twice her size."

"But you don't skate."

"I don't skate," I said, with a small shake of my head. "I'm a wuss." Well, that, and my blood was a natural narcotic that very few humans had any resistance to. Roller derby was a mostly safe place for me: more women than men, and little in the way of things that could stress me out and make me start sweating through my monster-strength antiperspirant. But being half succubus means never being able to say "oops" when you get a bloody nose. I'd be way too busy saying "No, no, please don't grab me, ow, that hurts, you don't really want to do that," and that was no fun for anybody.

Morgan rolled her eyes. It was a deeply sarcastic gesture, and it just made me appreciate her laughter even more. "Oh, please. They've been feeding you that party line about how 'pain is growth,' haven't they? Give me a nice, cushy seat in the stands and a box of popcorn any day."

"Besides, the view's good." I tried to make the statement sound casual, even as I was watching Morgan for her reaction. Most of the people who come to roller derby are laid-back enough not to respond to a gentle expression of interest with flung objects and pejoratives, but I've learned to be careful, especially when my heart has been recently broken.

Morgan responded by looking me slowly up and down, eyes lingering on the pink tips of my hair and the matching laces in my shoes. She smiled. It was the languid smile of a cat that had been locked in at the dairy and now had access to all the cream. "I think the view's just fine here in the stands."

My cheeks burned red. Well, that answered the question of whether or not she'd be okay with me flirting with her. "I, uh, like the view okay too."

"Looks like they're finishing up down there," said Morgan, with a nod toward the track. The Concussion Stand was taking their final trip around. They'd be loose in a few seconds, and I'd have to start playing everybody's least-favorite game, Will I See My Ex? No matter who won, I was going to lose. "Does your cousin need you, or can you run across to the food trucks with me? Maybe get something to drink, find another view to admire?"

She was going pretty fast, considering that we'd met only five minutes ago. But she was hot and I was lonely, and my head was still filled with all the hormones and heartbreak of my split with Carly. I looked at the track one more time.

Annie could get a ride home from Fern. It wouldn't be the first time I'd left in the middle of a bout, when I found something more interesting and less sweaty to do.

"Sure," I said, and slid off the bleachers and followed her to the door.

>—<

Let me just preface this by saying that I'm not a total pushover. I've taken self-defense classes with the best (in other words, my cousins), and I know how to handle myself in a crisis. Also, I always carry pepper spray in my vast monstrosity of a purse. Also-also, I am a strong, competent succubus in the modern age, and I don't need people to take care of me. I can take care of myself.

Also, she was really cute, and I think I should get some slack for that.

The evening air was cool and moist and tasted like roses—perfect Portland weather, in other words. The empty lot across from the warehouse had been converted into a temporary wonderland of assorted cuisines by the food trucks, which flocked all over the city during daylight hours and sought out events like roller derbies in the evening. Watch a couple girls eat track, and then stroll across the street for a grilled cheese sandwich made from all-local, all-organic ingredients. Or a hamburger made from ground-up pigeons and sold to you by a man named Doug. Whatever you wanted. We didn't judge.

Well, a lot of people would judge. Portland was full of people who liked to judge. But *I* wouldn't judge, and I was the one who mattered.

Morgan paced me step for step as we walked, slanting little smiles in my direction, toying with her hair, and asking all those meaningless, flirty questions that sounded sort of like an Internet quiz gone weird. What sort of desserts did I like? Did I have any pets? Was the blond part of my hair natural, or did I get it done when I had my tips dyed?

I answered her questions as honestly as I could, only dodging the ones that touched on my family. Mom and Dad were okay with me dating. They actually liked it when I got out of the house, since they thought that my social life might somehow inspire Artie to get one of his own. (As if. My baby brother got stronger pheromones from Dad than I did, and didn't get half the control. If he so much as sneezed in the presence of people he wasn't related to, he was going to be in a world of trouble.) But that didn't mean I was allowed to blow our cover, or to ever reveal more information than I absolutely had to.

"So, how did you find out about roller derby?" asked Morgan. She kept walking, passing a food truck that made excellent grilled-cheese sandwiches. My stomach grumbled.

Pretty girl, more important than food. "One of my ex-girlfriends was a skater. She used to encourage me to come and cheer for the team, and sometimes convinced me that I should work the merch table for her during halftime. She was pretty persuasive." And she'd kissed like it was her own invention, which helped a lot.

"Lost the girlfriend, kept the derby?"

"Something like that."

Morgan stopped in front of a food truck I'd never seen before. It was selling cupcakes. That wasn't unusual. You can't throw a rock in Portland without hitting half a dozen cupcake stands. "Just to be clear, you're Elsinore Harrington, age twenty-six, daughter of Theodore Harrington? Currently unemployed, no significant other?"

I gaped at her. "W-what?" I managed after a moment, recovering my senses enough to realize that something was extremely wrong.

"Good enough for me," said Morgan, and snapped her fingers.

The needle bit into the meaty part of my shoulder, deep enough that it felt almost like I was being stabbed. I jerked forward, trying to get it out of me before it could inject whatever payload it was carrying, and started to spin around to see my attacker. Only started: I might have unseated the needle, but I couldn't stop the injection, and as soon as it hit my bloodstream, everything began to spin without any help from me. My turn became a fumble, and then a collapse as my knees refused to support my weight any longer. I could still see, but I couldn't process what I was seeing. It was like my brain and my vision had become disconnected, turning everything into a soup of colors and shapes and jagged lines.

"I told you I could get her for you," said Morgan, her voice distant and distorted. "Now pay up."

"As agreed," said a male voice. I heard papers rustle, and then my face hit the food-court pavement and I stopped listening. It didn't seem important anymore.

>—<

Unlike my cousins, who seem to think that no day is complete unless they've knocked themselves unconscious on some obstacle or other, I have tried to maintain a life devoid of blackouts, concussions, and other forms of trauma. Maybe they're better at pulling themselves back out of oblivion than I am. I crawled back to myself one inch at a time, becoming slowly aware of the world around me, even though I couldn't force myself to move. It was like sleep paralysis, except for the part where I hadn't gone to sleep. Going to sleep would have been too easy.

The inside of my mouth tasted like a dentist's office crossed with a perfume counter. It was obvious what had happened. Dad's an incubus, which makes me a succubus. Half succubus, if you're splitting hairs. I got some of his powers—not all—and I got all of his weaknesses, which is entirely unfair if you ask me. Couldn't I have inherited some extra telepathy and skipped out on the violent allergy to aconite? The stuff's poisonous to humans, deadly to werewolves, and acts on Lilu as a combination sedative and mind-control drug. It's *awesome*.

(Incubi and succubi are both Lilu—just the male and female of the species. Ours is a complicated and inconvenient nomenclature.)

Whoever had grabbed me had shot me full of aconite, probably mixed with some more mundane sedative—or, hell, maybe it had just been mixed with saline. The end result would have been the same: one knocked-out succubus, no waiting, and no opportunity for me to get the hell out of Dodge.

This is why you don't follow pretty girls you've just met without telling someone where you're going, I thought sternly, and I accepted the chastisement as my due. This was all my own damn fault. I was the only one who was going to get me out of it.

Concentrating hard, I twitched my big toe. It moved sluggishly at first, and then more easily, like it was remembering what it meant to be connected to a body. I did it again and again, until it was moving as readily as it ever had. Good. My sleep paralysis was broken, and it was time to figure out what the hell was going on.

I opened my eyes.

I was sitting up: that much was evident from my perspective on the room, which was small and boxy and looked for all the world like it had started out as somebody's garage. My brother lives in a converted basement. Once you learn the tricks of repurposed architecture, they're difficult to overlook.

"She's awake," said a voice. I froze. It wasn't familiar, per se: I was pretty sure I'd never heard this *specific* voice before. But I knew it all the same. It was a male voice, late teens or early twenties, the sort of voice that I had heard in too many teen comedies and over too many live video game chat channels. I was a succubus tied to a chair, with a kid in the *Revenge of the Nerds/Weird Science* age bracket somewhere nearby.

This was not going to end well.

"She doesn't look like a demon," said another voice, slightly higher but otherwise interchangeable with the first.

"Succubi look like normal girls, only prettier," said a third. "Didn't you read my notes?"

"Her hair's pink," said a fourth voice. "I didn't expect a demon with pink hair."

It figures. My first kidnapping, and I get amateur hour. I yawned, trying to look as unconcerned by my situation as possible, before saying, "Anybody can have pink hair, if they understand the secret ways of Hot Topic and the local salon. Not that I use Manic Panic. You get what you pay for, right? Kool-Aid is cheaper and lasts about as long. Now, does this meeting of the Young Cryptologists Society want to come to order and untie me before I get mad?"

"You're trapped," said the first voice. He sounded like he was projecting bravado as hard as he could. "You have to do what we tell you to do."

"I'm not trapped, I'm tied up," I said. "There's a difference. It's a small one, granted, but it's big enough to matter. Now untie me, and I won't tell my parents about you." Dad would be annoyed. Mom would be *pissed*, and while she often tries to forget that she comes from a violent family full of violent people who solve their problems with, yes, violence, threatening her kids had always been an excellent way to jog her memory.

"The ropes are a precaution, not a prison," said the first voice. He seemed to be their spokesman. He was probably the one who had managed to track me down. I thought fondly of putting his head through the wall.

Property damage never makes friends. I looked down at the floor, finally realizing what they were implying. Sure enough, I was sitting smack in the middle of a Seal of Solomon. It had been painted on the concrete with the sort of precision that implied protractors and drafting tools had been involved, and I would have been very impressed if I hadn't been tied to a chair. That was taking up most of my capacity to care.

"Seriously?" I looked up again, scanning the walls for anything reflective that might show me my captors. They were somewhere behind me, probably out of a misguided belief that succubi shared certain attributes with gorgons. If looks could kill, I would have had a very different high school experience. "A Seal of Solomon? Where did you get your information—the D&D Monster Manual?"

Silence. Which was really an answer in and of itself.

"I am not bothered by the Seal of Solomon, because I am not A, a demon, or B, deceased," I said, speaking slowly and clearly. "I would have to be one of those two things before this would become a problem for me. Seriously, don't you know *anything*? You really shouldn't kidnap people if you don't know how to safely contain them. Actually, scratch that. You shouldn't kidnap people, period. Now come untie me, before I get pissed."

"You're right: she can't escape," said one of the boys. He sounded utterly amazed, like this was the culmination of all his birthday wishes. There was a rustling sound, and then he was stepping into view, staring at me in awe. That just made me more uncomfortable. It wasn't the sort of look you give another person. It was the sort of look you give a delicious cake, right after you've realized that it's all for you. "She's trapped."

My guess about their age was supported by his appearance. He was thin, in that not-finished-yet way that some people don't lose until they hit their thirties, with a scrubby brown mustache on his upper lip and hair that didn't appear to have encountered a brush in quite some time. He was wearing a T-shirt with a picture of a giant robot on it. Artie had the same one. In fact, just based on age and general scruffiness, this kid could have been my little brother, except for the part where my brother would never tie me to a chair, drop me in the middle of a Seal of Solomon, and invite all his friends over for a look.

Also, my brother didn't have that many friends.

"What are you, twelve?" I demanded. "This isn't how you meet girls. This is even worse than listening to pickup artists."

The kid blinked. "What?"

"Seriously, no woman is going to love you because you tell her she'd look good if she lost a few pounds. She's just going to punch you through the nearest salad bar. And no succubus is going to play the Jeannie to your Master just because you tie her to a chair."

He blinked at me again before turning an impressively bright shade of red. "That's not— I mean, we didn't— I mean, we would never do that. That's not okay."

I blinked. Apparently, I had been misreading the situation. That, or a hundred erotic fanfics had gotten it all wrong. "Then why am I here?"

"Because you're a demon," said a second boy, walking into my field of vision. He had short, curly black hair, dark skin, and a solemn expression. "We needed a demon, and when we asked around, you were the safest one we could find."

I wanted to tell him—again—that I wasn't a demon, but since it hadn't gotten through the first time, I wasn't sure what good it would do me. I settled for frowning at him sternly and asking, "Why did you need a demon? Demons don't grant wishes, you know. Mostly they play piñata with the people who mess with them. You're not full of candy. The average demon thinks entrails are just as nice."

"We needed a demon because a demon took my baby sister and I have to get her back," he said, and everything changed.

"Oh," I said softly.

Shit.

><-<

"Her name is Angie," he said. They still hadn't untied me, but all four of them were in front of me now. I was trying to see that as an improvement and not as a sign that they were planning to sacrifice me to something. "She's seven. She's the smartest kid you've ever met, but she's sort of dumb sometimes too, you know? Little kids don't always know that they shouldn't trust everyone they meet."

"Are you the one who hired Morgan to get me out of the derby game?" I asked. He looked away. "Thought so. Just as an FYI, sometimes adults don't recognize danger either. Everybody messes up sometimes."

"She followed this gray-skinned *thing* into the sewers," he shot back. "How is that messing up?"

A gray-skinned thing in the sewers was a lot more likely to be a bogeyman than it was to be a demon. I shook my head. "I still don't know what you want me to do. I'm a succubus. If you wanted someone persuaded to make out with you, I'd be your girl, except for the part where I don't do that sort of thing. It's shitty and date rape-y, and I refuse. But I can't find missing kids, and I can't reverse time to prevent bad decisions."

"You're a demon," said the kid with the scraggly mustache resolutely. Of the four, he was the least willing to budge from that point. "The person we hired to get you for us injected you with enough aconite to kill an elephant, and you're still alive. That means you can't be human, and you have to do what we say."

Anger suddenly swelled in my chest, hot and tight and unforgiving. "Wait, you mean you weren't *sure*?" I demanded. "You thought there was a chance I was human, and you had them pump me full of aconite anyway? Kid, you missed a murder charge by one mistaken identity. You get that, right? If your little honey trap had landed anyone else in that warehouse, you would have had a body on your hands."

"It didn't happen that way," said the first kid. "We hired professionals."

"Professional *what*?"

"Bigfoot hunters," said one of the other kids—one who hadn't been speaking much up to this point, apparently happy to let his friends dig their own graves while he stared, awestruck, at my breasts. "They came very highly recommended. And they had a money-back guarantee."

"Oh, that makes it all better," I said bitterly. There are two kinds of Bigfoot hunters in the world: the gently deluded ones who just want to meet something mysterious and who never manage to actually encounter a real Bigfoot, and the mercenary bastards who believe that everything in this world exists to be broken down for parts and sold on the alchemical, scientific, and pharmaceutical black markets. There are people who swear that powdered Bigfoot bones cure erectile dysfunction, or that the hair of a dragon princess will bring wealth. Bigfeet have been hunted to the verge of extinction by assholes looking to make a quick buck, which has forced their hunters to step up their game.

Catching me had probably netted them a few thousand bucks, enough to buy some better tracking gear and a bunch more guns. I supposed I should count myself lucky that there's not much of a market for succubus bits—we're not sex magnets like our male counterparts—but I couldn't help but feel like I had just dodged a bullet that should never have been pointed in my direction to begin with.

"It's not like you're a person," said the first kid, pulling my attention back to him. He quailed a bit under my glare, but rallied quickly. "Anyway, we didn't hurt you. We just needed you to listen. You have to get Angie back."

"Why would I do you any favors?" I asked.

"Because either you're a demon, and the Seal of Solomon means you *have* to do what we say, or you're a person who's also a succubus, and you can go where we can't. You can get Angie back."

His logic was sound, once you got past the part where it had started with a kidnapping. I looked at him flatly. "You're going to need to make me a promise and answer a question before I agree to help you. If you don't promise or you don't answer, then we're finished here. You can keep me tied up forever if you like. It won't get your sister back."

"But if we promise and answer, you'll do it?" he asked. The desperation in his voice was too raw to have been anything but real. He was at the end of his rope, and while I felt bad about that, I wasn't ready to forgive him for what he'd done to me.

"I'll consider it," I said.

"Anything," he said.

"First off, you have to promise me that you'll never do anything like this again, ever. No matter how important you think it is, no matter how much you want to go 'Well, it worked last time, we got a succubus and she fixed things for us,' you need to leave your friendly neighborhood inhumans alone. Got me? I am a person, I have a life, I do not need to get kidnapped by the Hardy Boys every time one of you has a hangnail. If I hear so much as a whisper of you doing this to somebody else, I will rain down fire and brimstone on your heads, and I will not be sorry. Got it?"

"Got it," said the boy with the missing sister. None of them had given me their names. It made sense. If they still thought I was a demon, they wouldn't want me to have that sort of power over them. "We promise."

"Good." I still didn't know whether it was safe to believe them, of course, but that would come later, after I had gotten out of this garage and told my family about the teenage demon stealers. These kids would learn the hard way not to mess with people if they ever tried anything like this again. "Now here's the question: How did you find out about me?"

One of the other kids, the one with the black hair and the uneasy eyes, told me.

"Oh," I said.

There was a momentary silence.

"Untie me," I said. "I need to go get your sister."

><<

Bogeymen have always been nocturnal. Long before humans were building cities with functional sewer systems, their close cousins were figuring out ways to get around without being seen, and coming up with excuses for why they never came out during the day. Lots of bogeymen got in trouble for being vampires during the Victorian era, or corpse eaters, or grave-robbers, even though they weren't any of those things. They were just polite, reclusive neighbors whose place on the hominid family tree wasn't quite so well lit.

Portland's bogeymen had a lot of light pollution and a high population of hipsters, Goths, and punks to contend with—all barriers to a comfortable nocturnal community. So they had done what any species that wanted to coexist with humans without actually talking to them would do: They had installed a bunch of lovely "sewer drains" that fed into a system of tunnels not found on any municipal map, connecting to basements all over the metro area. They could move from place to place without ever seeing the light of day, and they had entrances near several local grocery and big-box stores. Supplies weren't the problem.

Children, on the other hand . . . Children were always an issue. Because kids didn't understand why they couldn't make friends with the little boy down the block who just happened to have weirdly pink skin and fingers that were missing a joint or two. Kids wanted to play tag, and didn't understand fear of the unknown—not the way adults did. *Everything* was unknown to a child, and so they accepted what they didn't understand much more quickly, and embraced with much less restraint.

It didn't help that most bogeyman households had cable. Bogeyman children learned to see human children as friends they just hadn't met yet, which sometimes led to situations like this one.

I slid on the sides of my feet down the short embankment leading to the storm drain, all too aware of the four teenage boys who were on the sidewalk behind me, watching me go. I didn't look back. When I reached the flat ground at the bottom of the embankment, I stood up a little straighter and walked forward, into the open mouth of the tunnel.

The light cut off almost immediately. It was the middle of the night, after all, and the streetlights weren't designed to shine into the bowels of the Earth. Not for the first time, I wished my kidnappers had been willing to return my cell phone. Antimony had to be frantic by now . . . assuming she'd even noticed that I was gone. Her team had won, and I didn't always stick around for the after party, especially when I'd just gone through a painful breakup. She might think I was just fine.

"I need better cousins," I muttered, and walked onward into the dark.

Bogeymen like to live underground when they can. It affords them a lot of advantages. Humans tend toward claustrophobia, which makes them reluctant to follow shadowy figures into dark tunnels. Bogeymen, on the other hand, tend toward agoraphobia, and sometimes freak out if forced to stand in the middle of a grassy field. It's a perfect balance. But living underground doesn't mean living in squalor. Anyone with a nose would have known that this wasn't really a storm drain. It smelled of damp metal and clean dirt and nothing worse—no mold or decay or waste products. The local human homeless probably slept down here occasionally and found themselves gently encouraged to seek shelter elsewhere, before the signs of their presence were scrubbed away.

I walked deeper, and smiled as the urge to turn back began to bubble in the recesses of my mind. This was careful, meticulous work, doing its best to convince me that this whole enterprise had been a terrible mistake. Succubus work, in other words, probably performed in concert with one of the local hidebehinds. Nobody binds a simple illusion or telepathic command to a static charm like a hidebehind. Which would be a terrible slogan for a business, all things considered.

The feeling that I wasn't supposed to be here just kept getting stronger as I kept pushing onward, until I reached a dead end, my fingers brushing against hard-packed earth in front of me. "Nice," I murmured, and closed my eyes and walked into the wall—

—only to slam face-first into the same thing my hand had encountered. The dead end was not an illusion. I stepped backward, rubbing my nose, and tripped over a bump in the tunnel floor. I spun to my right, reaching out to catch myself—

—and fell as the tunnel wall proved to be an illusion. "Oh, come *on!*" I protested. I had been dumped into a second, wider tunnel, lit by dimly glowing bulbs that hung like party lights from hooks on the ceiling. It was a little bit like stepping onto a circus midway after the show had closed, all soft illumination and the faint, sweet smell of sawdust.

If anyone heard my exclamation, they didn't come to see what I was doing there. I picked myself up, dusted the tunnel dirt and sawdust off my knees, and started walking away from the false wall.

Little by little, the sounds of life drifted out to meet me. Voices raised in greeting or argument; laughter; a brief, sharp burst of an argument. By the time the voices began to form actual words, I was moving with quick assurance.

That assurance died when I came around a corner and found myself facing what looked like an underground parking garage crossed with a flea market, and packed with bogeymen, almost all of whom had turned to wait for my arrival. They were tall, oddly jointed people with grayish skin and pale eyes. That was where their uniformity ended. Some were fat and some were thin; most had dark hair, but a few were blond, and one had shockingly red curls that held their color even in the dim light that the community favored. Most were wearing human-style clothing. Add a hoodie, and they could pass unnoticed among the population of Portland. That was the point.

"Uh, hi," I said. I knew bogeymen in passing, but I didn't know any well enough that I could really call them my friends. More like "acquaintances in shared persecution." I cleared my throat and continued anyway. "My name's Elsie Harrington? I'm Ted Harrington's daughter? I was wondering if I could speak to somebody in charge?"

"If you're Ted's daughter, that means you're also Jane Price's daughter," called a voice from the back of the crowd. "How do we know this isn't a trap?"

"Um, well, I'm not armed, for a start, which is basically proof that I'm not here as a Price," I said. "Also, I'm alone. Also, I'm a succubus, so if the Prices had gone back to being killers instead of conservationists, I'd be seeking sanctuary right about now. I'm here because Angie's brother is worried about her. He asked me to come find her." The part about him kidnapping me seemed like it was better left unsaid, at least for right now. I had already come into these people's home without permission. I didn't need to kick the beehive.

"Angie?" One of the bogeymen stepped forward. She was wearing a red dress in a traditional bogeyman cut, tight around the collarbone and flowing otherwise, allowing her hyperflexible limbs the space to move. Her hair, the color of dust over granite, was looped into an ornate braid atop her head. She must have been one of their leaders. Only the people in charge of a community held to the old fashions, because only the people in charge were never required to go among humans and try to pass. "There's no one here by that name, Lilu. You have come to the wrong place."

"Maybe there's no one who's *supposed* to be here, but she's here," I said, trying not to flinch at her use of the proper name for my species. Male Lilu are incubi and female Lilu are succubi, and it's an insult to call any individual by the singular species name. I don't know why. It's just the way things have always been. "Her brother saw her go into the storm drain with one of your children, and he sent me to get her back. He's worried about her."

The bogeyman leader bristled. "Are you calling us child thieves?" she demanded.

"No, I'm saying that one of yours decided to invite a friend over for dinner but forgot to get permission from her parents first," I said. "Look. Right now, it's one teenage boy who saw his sister go underground with a stranger, and one succubus in your living room asking for that sister back. If I don't succeed, who knows what that kid is going to send down here next?" Belatedly, it occurred to me that if the boys had known how to find monster hunters, they could have cut out the middleman and sent them down here directly, instead of messing around with me. I wondered whether it was the teenage tendency toward baroque planning, or whether they had understood that sending a bunch of professional killers into a bogeyman community would have been like killing a spider with a machine gun: unfair in the extreme.

The bogeyman leader narrowed her eyes. "You're threatening us?"

"Uh, not so much, if you actually listen to the words I'm saying and not to the script you think I should be following. I am saying that I am the easy option. Give me the little girl, and I'll walk away from here, and you can have a nice, long chat about stranger danger and why we don't invite humans over for slumber parties, okay?" I held out my hands, showing that they were empty. "It's after midnight. Humans aren't nocturnal. Come on, just give the kid back, and we'll call it good."

"I didn't mean to." This voice was soft, and sweet, and distinctly prepubescent. The adult bogeymen shuffled to the sides, turning toward the speaker: a little bogeyman girl, her curly black hair in pigtails, her grayish skin made up with human cosmetics in that garish way that only appeals to little girls playing dress-up. She looked miserable. "Angie and me were playing, is all. And then her parents said it was time for her to go to bed, but they hadn't seen me, and I said that it wasn't bedtime where I lived, and she said, 'Okay, let's go,' and I'm sorry, I didn't think anybody would notice that she wasn't there anymore. . . ."

Fat tears were starting to slide down the little girl's cheeks, cutting paths through the dime-store blush she had slathered on. It made me want to hug her and teach her about doing her colors, all at the same time. I cleared my throat, forcing both urges down.

"So, see, she *is* here," I said. "Where's Angie, honey?"

The little girl sniffled and said, "She fell asleep. I guess maybe it was her bedtime after all."

I looked at the bogeyman who seemed to be in charge, raising an eyebrow and waiting for her to say something. She looked at me, and her face was a sea of rage, sorrow, and simple, mundane regret. She didn't like that this had happened on her watch; she liked even less that I was right.

"I'll bring you the girl," she said finally. "I'm going to tell your father you came down here."

"To retrieve a human child who had been kidnapped, even if it was by accident, so that you wouldn't get into trouble with your neighbors? Yeah, he'll be real pissed at me. Be sure to tell him how you called me 'Lilu,' okay? Because, hell, maybe he'll buy me a new car." I folded my arms. "The girl?"

"Wait here," said the bogeyman leader. She turned away, and the little girl in the wrong shade of blush followed her.

I felt no triumph, no rush of victory.

There was no victory here.

>—<

Angie's brother and his friends had been waiting for me when I emerged from the storm drain, a sleeping little girl in a sundress and a feather boa cradled in my arms. The relief on their faces had been palpable—as had the calculation.

"No," I had said, holding Angie close, refusing to give her up until they understood. "You made me a promise, remember? You're going to keep it."

"Or what?" asked one of them.

"You don't want to know," I'd replied. "Now somebody get my purse from wherever you stashed it. I need to call a cab."

The last I'd seen of them, they had been retreating into the house, a sleepy Angie walking between them. I felt a little bad for her. She had made a friend, and she was never going to see that friend again. The bogeymen were already sealing off the entrance I'd used to get to them; they wouldn't move their community, but they'd make damn sure they stayed secret.

But that was for later, when there was time to regret. I had taken the cab back to the warehouse, where my car was still parked at the back of the lot. A half dozen messages from Antimony blinked on my cell phone, waiting to be answered or acknowledged. It was late enough that the after parties had all broken up or moved on, and I hadn't seen a single living soul as I drove the familiar route across town.

Raising my hand, I hammered on the closed apartment door until my knuckles ached, and then I hammered some more, just to get my point across. Someone shouted from inside. I knocked harder.

The door was wrenched open, and there was Carlotta—lovely Carlotta, with the lips I had kissed so many times—snarling, "It's three in the fucking morning, you—"

She stopped herself when she saw me, going pale. I looked at her wearily.

"You dumped me because I'm not human," I said, no preamble, no softening the blow. "Did you really have to tell your sister about me? You promised me you wouldn't."

"Elsie . . ." she began, and stopped, clearly unsure how to continue.

"She told her kid, Carly. She told her kid, and he told his friends, and they hired some mercenary assholes to shoot me full of aconite because they needed a demon. I know we're not dating anymore, but *damn*."

"I didn't think she'd talk about it," said Carlotta weakly. "This is a lot to put on my shoulders, Elsie."

"You mean my survival? Yeah, it is." I stepped closer, seeing the way she flinched when I entered her personal space and hating it. Still, I forced my voice to stay level and cold as I said, "My life is more important than your bigotry, Carlotta. You want to talk about what a shit girlfriend I was? Fine. But you gave me your word you'd keep our secrets, and you're going to do it. If you don't, I am not going to make any promises about your safety. Do you understand?"

To my surprise, she laughed. "This is why we had to break up," she said bitterly. "Because my safety matters more to me than your secrets."

"Keep my secrets, and you'll have nothing to worry about," I shot back. "You get one shitty ex moment. This was yours. Now prove that I was right to love you." I turned on my heel and stalked away before she could say anything else.

I made it back to my car before I started to cry. I buckled myself in and kept crying, until the tears ran out. And then I checked my mascara—waterproof for the win—started the engine, and drove myself home. I would answer Antimony's texts later. Right now, I wanted a gallon of ice cream, my own bed, and late-night cartoons on Adult Swim.

Sometimes all we can do is have a sleepover with ourselves.

IF WISHES WERE

by Tanya Huff

Vicki had always hated the smell of hospitals—the smell of cleansers so overpowering that the trained police officer part of her wondered what they were hiding, while the antisocial, easily annoyed part wondered why they couldn't use scent-free products. Nor was she fond of fluorescent lighting, the horrible pale green paint they clearly bought in bulk, and the staff cutbacks that meant nurses were working their asses off to cover the basics and, as a result, were barely maintaining a white-knuckled grip on civility.

Bottom line: she hated hospitals for the same reason everyone else did. If she was in a hospital, it meant one of two things. She'd been hurt. Or someone she loved had been hurt.

She didn't get hurt anymore. Not in ways modern medicine would understand. Not since she'd had to choose between changing and death. Not since she'd lost everything in her old life but Mike.

She listened to his heartbeat and told herself he'd be fine.

"It's creepy when you hang around and watch me sleep."

"Tough." There was enough light for her to see him and not nearly enough for him to see her, but he always knew when she was there. Moving out of the shadows to the side of Mike's bed, she wrapped her fingers gently around his right hand, careful not to disturb the cannula. Most of the damage was on the left—arm broken in two places, collarbone broken in one, three cracked ribs, multiple cuts from broken glass, and impressive bruising for those impressed by that sort of thing. "Besides, it's not like you're providing anything else to watch."

"Excuse me for being boring." He cleared his throat, and she offered him a drink; laid the straw against his bottom lip and studied him while he swallowed. He had a purpling bruise on his cheek, but his body had absorbed enough of the impact that by the time his head had hit, he'd gotten away with only a concussion. "How are you feeling?"

Pushing the straw away with his tongue, he snorted. "Like I went out a second-floor window and hit a Buick."

"You hit a Toyota."

"Buick's funnier."

The plastic cup shattered in her hand.

"Not ready to joke about it?" he asked as she knelt to wipe up the water with a handful of tissues.

Not ever. The aluminum bar running along the lower edge of the bed buckled in her grip. "Do you remember anything?" she asked as she stood.

"No more than I did yesterday."

"So SFA." The wet tissues hit the garbage with a dismissive splat.

"Pretty much."

The doctors called it retrograde post-traumatic amnesia. Pointed out that it was relatively common in cases of moderate to severe concussion. Offered a not even remotely reassuring number of recovery statistics involving hockey players.

He remembered going to Scarborough to question a witness. After a non-illuminating interview, he and Dave Graham, his partner, had gone into a Second Cup for a coffee, where Dave had run into one of his exes. As Dave and Cynthia caught up, Mike had taken his coffee outside to enjoy the spring sun. Someone had screamed. Mike had yelled at Dave to call it in, and he'd run toward the sound. The next thing he remembered was waking up in hospital.

Dave remembered Mike flying out the second-floor window in a shower of glass, clearing the sidewalk, and landing on the roof of a parked sedan. Police found the apartment empty of both the tenant, Amy Shaw, and of anyone who could toss a six-foot-three, heavily muscled police detective out a window. Shaw, at five-two and barely a hundred pounds, according to the neighbors, was considered more a witness than a suspect.

"You going to whammy me?"

Vicki raised a brow at Mike's question. "Whammy?"

"The vampire mind-meld."

"You're on the good drugs, aren't you?"

He ignored her. "I know—you promised to never whammy me, but, as I want the name of the jackass who threw me out a window, I'm asking."

"You have a concussion. I'm not playing with your brain while it's bruised."

"Vicki . . ."

"No." She slid back into the shadows as a nurse came into the room, and returned to Mike's side after the woman left. "You should listen to the scary lady, Detective Celluci, and get some sleep. I'm going to go have a look at the apartment."

"Be nice when you whammy the uniforms," he murmured, eyes closing.

She bent forward, pushed a strand of hair off his forehead, and tried not to notice how much of it was gray. Kissed the damp, exposed skin, nose wrinkling at the scents of so many other people. "I always am."

><><

The apartment looked more like a junk shop than a residence. Every horizontal surface was piled high with old dishes and magazines and, occasionally, a second horizontal surface, also piled high. Vicki spotted six old rotary phones, a Commodore 64, three waffle makers, and two nearly complete sets of thirty-year-old grocery-store encyclopedias. Lamps, electric and oil; velvet paintings, Elvis and otherwise; and a stack of soup tureens—identified with the help of *Downton Abbey*. Stepping around a disemboweled vacuum cleaner, she found herself reluctantly impressed that when Mike had been thrown out the window, half the contents of the apartment hadn't gone with him.

The refrigerator held a liter of milk and an assortment of aging condiments.

In the bedroom, a twin bed had been shoved into a corner; the rest of the floor space was taken up by a maze of bookcases. The contents were eclectic at best.

Vicki could smell dust, a variety of molds, and the fear stink of a human female, recently but not currently present. Her clothes were in the closet. Her toothbrush and medications were in the bathroom. The stack of mail on top of a box labeled CAT TOYS held bills and beg letters and a flyer for a chain hardware store. Vicki took photos of the bills. She found no computer, but a laptop and a phone charger filled some of the limited space on the kitchen counter.

Amy Shaw would be back.

And she'd walk right into the waiting arms of the law—who got enthusiastic about making an arrest when one of their own was attacked.

Vicki wanted a crack at her first. For exponentially the same reason.

She *acquired* a copy of Amy's picture from the uniform in the stairwell: slender, mid-thirties, white female, short green hair, dark rectangular glasses, and an apparent fondness for liquid eyeliner. Amy clearly didn't cook and, without a car, it was unlikely she traveled far to eat. Unfortunately, sunset had been at 8:01. Vicki hadn't gotten to the hospital until after ten, and there wasn't a restaurant in the area that stayed open after eleven on a Tuesday. She might be the only person in Toronto who missed January and darkness by five.

For all that she'd bitched about Mike using her as a hunting dog, she couldn't track the scent of a single woman she didn't know through Scarborough when that scent was nearly ten hours old. The trail led down the stairs, out the back door, into an alley, along the alley to the sidewalk, and then disappeared under half a hundred footprints. A stranger in the midst of strangers.

With Mike in the hospital, she saw no point in returning to the house they shared in Downsview and drove instead to her office. She caught a familiar scent on the west wind as she got out of the car. A familiar fear. When she was three meters from the entrance to the building, the slender, green-haired woman sitting on the step raised a trembling hand.

"Don't come any closer."

Vicki stopped. "Amy Shaw?"

"That depends."

Sometimes it did. Appearances could be deceiving. Arbitrary identities were far from the strangest things Vicki dealt with.

"Are you Vicki Nelson?"

"I am."

Amy's arms tightened around the bundle in her lap. "I need your help."

>—<

Getting both of them inside while maintaining the two-meter distance Amy swore was necessary had been an inconvenience, given the double doors and keyed locks. Fortunately, the building's other tenants had learned to ignore Vicki and her clients, although most of them weren't sure why.

"The detective came too close. I warned him, but he didn't listen." Leaning against the inside of the office door, Amy gently rocked a roll of purple fabric back and forth. "I don't like being touched, right? So that's what I asked for, to make it so no one touches me."

Vicki perched on the edge of her desk and shoved her office chair across the room. "Sit. And asked who?"

Amy unrolled the fabric—it turned out to be a Ryerson University hoodie—and held up . . .

"A brass gravy boat?"

"It's a magic lamp. With a genie inside." Amy frowned, pulled the chair closer, and sat down. "They told me you dealt with the weird stuff."

"I do," Vicki sighed. "But hope springs eternal." With luck, the smell of scorched metal was coming from the lamp and not the building's wiring. Again. "So, let me see if I understand the situation. You found the lamp."

"I bought it at a charity yard sale with a handheld vacuum and an old Underwood typewriter. I know a place I can get ribbons. For the typewriter," she added, when Vicki frowned.

"Okay, sure. When you got it home, you rubbed the lamp."

"It was really tarnished."

"Then the genie appeared."

"Not what I expected." Amy shook her head. "I mean, even if I'd been expecting a genie—and I wasn't, right?—I wouldn't have expected that."

"What?"

"Fire that didn't burn." Her heartbeat sped up. Her breathing grew shallower and faster. "A voice I could hear"—trembling fingers touched her forehead—"in my head not my ears. It said it was a genie and, as I was the owner of the lamp, it would grant me three wishes."

Fire that didn't burn would make a fairly persuasive case, Vicki acknowledged. "So, you wanted to not be touched, and the genie interpreted that as 'Toss anyone who comes within two meters out a window'?"

"Only people intending to touch me!" Amy protested. "Not random people in a crowd."

She was so defensive, Vicki frowned and wondered if she'd been at Victoria Park station yesterday morning. Two teenage boys had gone off the platform and were nearly killed by the next train. Police had assumed they'd shoved each other. Maybe not.

Amy pushed at her glasses. "I don't want anyone to get hurt." *Arm broken in two places, collarbone broken in one, three cracked ribs, multiple cuts from broken glass, and impressive bruising . . .*

"You sure about that? I doubt Detective Celluci intended to touch you."

"He wanted me to calm down."

Which might not have put touching entirely off the table. And then Vicki remembered why Mike had been in Amy's apartment. "You screamed. Why? Was it the genie?"

"It was my second wish." Her shoulders rose protectively and she curled around the lamp. "I wanted to find something that would make me special."

Given the state of her apartment, it wasn't hard to work out what *something* meant. A lost da Vinci. The Arkenstone. Metal arm with a star on the shoulder. "And did you? What was it?" she asked when Amy nodded. Mike wouldn't have responded to happy screams.

Instead of answering, Amy set the sweater and the lamp on the floor and stood. She unzipped her oversized Windbreaker and let it slide off her shoulders. She was naked to the waist, but, in the grand scheme of things, bare breasts weren't particularly notable next to a second and third set of arms. . . .

Not arms—tentacles, Vicki corrected.

. . . which unwrapped from around Amy's waist and stretched out to either side, bifurcated tips spreading. "I *found* them"—all four tentacles twitched when she sketched quotes around the word *found*—"when I took my sweater off. Special."

Vicki wasn't sure if *special* emerged on a laugh or a sob. "Can you control them?"

"What difference does it make? I'm not keeping them!" She grabbed her jacket off the chair and shoved her arms back into it. The tentacles writhed, apparently unhappy about being hidden away again. "You need to fix this!"

"What was your third wish?"

"I only made two." Elbows clamped against her sides, she struggled with the zipper. "What does my third wish have to do with—"

"Use the third wish to fix it yourself," Vicki snapped. It wasn't that she was unsympathetic; she thought of Mike lying in a hospital bed. Actually, she was entirely unsympathetic.

"No. I'm using the third wish to . . ." Amy pressed her lips tightly together into a thin, pale line.

After a moment, when Vicki was sure she wasn't going to be

told about the potential third wish, she sighed. "You've got tentacles. I'm not sure what you think I can do. I'm a private investigator, and there's nothing about that to investigate." She allowed her voice to pick up an edge. "You've also acquired a potentially deadly *don't touch me* zone, and that's reason enough to take you down." For those two boys. For Mike.

"Take me down?"

"You're a danger the police can't handle. Dealing with that's my job."

"You're supposed to help me!"

"How?"

Amy opened her mouth. Closed it. The sides of her Windbreaker billowed.

"You've got the means to help yourself, Ms. Shaw."

"I don't."

"Use the third wish." If Vicki's eyes silvered and her voice dropped past command into coercion, she figured an Amy Shaw without tentacles would thank her.

Amy's shoulders slumped. She dropped back onto the chair and picked up the lamp. "Do it now?" she asked in a voice that suggested she'd finally realized this was something she'd done to herself.

"Yes." Given time to think things over, Vicki doubted she'd go through with it.

"Here?"

"Yes. Here and now."

"I didn't intend to hurt anyone."

"I admit that's a nice change." Most of the people Vicki dealt with fully intended to cause as much damage as possible.

Lamp cradled against her body with her left hand, Amy began rubbing it with her right. From the way the Windbreaker rippled, it seemed the tentacles had joined in.

Vicki hadn't expected *I Dream of Jeannie*—in her experience, reality seldom made an accurate crossover to pop culture—but neither had she expected a trickle of flame to become a column of fire that lapped against the ceiling and threw no heat. If the genie spoke, she couldn't hear it, but she could sense an ancient, barely restrained malevolence, and her reaction was instinctive. Her eyes silvered again, her lips drew back from her teeth, and she snarled.

It had been paying attention to Amy, much the way a child with a magnifying glass pays attention to an ant, but now it turned to her.

Vicki snarled again.

"Nightwalker?" Beyond the flames, Amy's voice trembled on the edge of panic. "Undead and undying. Death in the darkness. What are you talk— Blood drinker. Oh." And it dove off the edge. "Vampire! She's a vampire!"

"Amy!" It seemed Amy's accepting attitude toward genies didn't extend to others in the metaphysical community. "Amy! I won't hurt you!"

Amy ignored her, the power in a name not enough to break the power of the genie over the one who held its lamp. "Of course I know what vampires are! No, I don't want to die! I don't . . . Do you promise? You won't let her kill me? I know. I can say that. I can. I wish—"

"Amy!" Vicki charged forward, hit the two-meter mark, and slammed against the far wall under the loft. She bounced up onto her feet, her bones too dense to break but bruises already rising.

"I wish for the genie kept captive in this lamp to be free!"

The flame roared.

Vicki leapt onto her desk and flung herself up into the loft she used as shelter from the day, slamming the steel door behind her. She could smell paint blistering. Wood scorching.

Smoke.

Pork.

The inside of the door grew hot under the pads of her fingers.

She'd had the loft built to withstand fire. If the building went up, she wouldn't be comfortable, but she'd survive. Although explanations, she acknowledged silently, would be a bitch.

The fire alarms in the studio should have gone off, setting off the building's alarms. They hadn't.

At nine minutes, the inside of the door felt cooler.

At ten, Vicki opened it.

Her office was empty. She took a quick look under the loft. Completely empty. Except for puddles of melted metal and glass and a pile of ash and bone residue by the door that looked like it had been tipped out of a cremation urn. Crematoriums burned between 1,400 and 1,800 degrees Fahrenheit. Wood and fabric burned at a significantly lower temperature than flesh, which explained why her furniture appeared to have been vaporized. The walls, ceiling, and floor looked scorched, but she saw no structural damage. The fire alarm and the brass lamp were the only untouched items in the room. Although the bathroom door was closed, so it was possible the plumbing had survived.

"Genie redecorating. I suspect I won't be collecting on my insurance," she muttered, dropping down from the loft. Her phone and keys were in her pocket, but everything else had been lost with her purse. "I'm half inclined to hunt you down for that alone, you inconsiderate shit." Squatting beside Amy's remains, she poked at the lamp. "Okay, protecting the fire alarm was you being funny—I get that. And you definitely had a few anger issues when the leash came off. But if the lamp is your prison, why not take it with you rather than risk someone using it again?"

It was obviously still magical, or it would have been destroyed like everything else.

She poked it again. It slid about six centimeters across the floor. Smart money said genies couldn't handle their own lamps. "At the risk of stating the obvious, Ms. Shaw, it looks like you solved your problem."

>—<

She watched Mike sleep. Listened to him breathe. The person who'd put him in hospital had been dealt with, and four and a half hours remained until dawn. Vicki stood in the shadows and pretended it was these most recent injuries that had aged him.

He'd be sixty in a couple of years.

She'd always be thirty-four.

>—<

". . . say there is no way all twenty-five hundred ounces of gold could have been removed from the fourteen thousand windows of the Royal Bank Plaza."

Vicki stopped drying her hair and started paying more attention to the television.

"Except that all twenty-five hundred ounces are gone from both the south and the north towers," Ian Hanomansing of CBC News pointed out.

A muscle jumped in the jaw of the middle-aged white man with the two-hundred-dollar haircut and the three-thousand-dollar suit. "Until our investigations are complete, we're assuming it's a trick of the light."

"Because otherwise it would have to be"—Hanomansing raised an eyebrow—"magic?"

The muscle jumped again. "And we all know there's no such thing."

"Damn, genie," Vicki snickered, "pretty ballsy way of restoring your finances." Given that bankers weren't known for thinking outside the box, the odds were extremely low they'd ask her to track the perpetrator down, so she allowed herself to enjoy the spectacle. Sure, at almost fifteen hundred dollars an ounce, it was a sizable theft, but, as evildoing went, it didn't even register on the measure she used these days. No harm, no foul.

"As the gold was a microcoating to reduce heat, how could its removal have weakened the glass?"

"As I said, we're not certain the gold has been removed."

"The police say that the piece that killed Kai Johnston had been stripped of gold."

"That may have happened after it fell."

Harm.

And foul.

With her laptop slagged and her phone in the charger, she wrapped the towel around her waist and settled in front of Mike's computer.

The Royal Bank could deny all it wanted, but the gold was missing and Kai Johnston, a fifty-three-year-old Hawaiian-Canadian, was dead. The triangular piece of gold-free glass that had killed him at 2:34 in the afternoon had fallen from a shattered section covering fifteen square meters of floors thirty-one and thirty-two on the east side of the South Building. Two other people had been injured, but given the amount of glass that had fallen and the number of pedestrians often around the plaza, it was a miracle no one else had died.

The gold had been gone when the sun came up. The weakened glass had taken eight hours to fall. If it had fallen at either the beginning or the end of the workday or when the sidewalks were crowded during lunch . . . The removal of the gold couldn't have weakened the glass, yet something had. That was the problem with magic: all bets were off.

An Internet search on genies was not particularly helpful.

"Supernatural creatures from Islamic and pre-Islamic Arabian mythology. Come from another world beyond the known world. Well, that depends on whose known world you're referencing, doesn't it?" Her known world was larger than it had been. "Can take different forms. Have free will, can be good or evil." Vicki considered Amy's remains, scooped into a plastic bag and currently sitting on the corner of Mike's desk. "What do you think?" she asked, poking the bag. "Good genie having a bad day, or psycho nutbag? What's that? Yeah, I'm going with psycho nutbag too. It's not all Disney out there, Ms. Shaw."

Searching *how to defeat genies* pulled up a list of gaming forums too specific to be helpful.

"Once again, people are your best resource."

Vicki had been changed for only nineteen years and, not surprisingly, most of the resources she'd nurtured during her years on the police force were seldom helpful in her weird new world. But Henry Fitzroy, the vampire who'd changed her, had been around for more than four hundred years—the tomb of the bastard son of Henry VIII at Richmond empty for all that time. He'd gathered an impressive Scooby Gang over the years, some of whom she'd inherited when he left Toronto. If Dr. Sagara didn't have the information Vicki needed, she'd know where to find it.

>×<

"So, Dr. Sargara says you need information about the jinn." Dr. Hariri stared up at her, eyes narrowed. "For work. What exactly do you do?"

Vicki handed him her card. "I'm a private investigator."

"Vicki Nelson. Otherworldly crimes a specialty? You believe a jinn has committed a crime?"

She shrugged. "Client confidentiality, Dr. Hariri. I don't judge." She could get the information and leave him unaware they'd ever spoken, but she'd rather add a new member to her HR team.

"I see." He tapped his upper lip with a finger, then shrugged. "What exactly do you need to know?"

She pulled the lamp out of an old backpack and set it on Dr. Hariri's desk. "How to get one back into one of these."

"That's not . . ." As his fingers touched the handle, he froze and leaned forward, expression shifting from dismissive to awe. "Where did you get this?"

"My client found it at a charity yard sale."

"The inscription isn't Arabic. It's Aramaic. The lamp itself looks Assyrian, so that would put it post–Babylonian conquest, sometime between 605 and 612 B.C., which, if I'm right—and I may not be, of course; we'd have to do testing—this could be among the oldest Aramaic inscriptions ever found. Do you have any idea how incredible this is?"

She thought of her empty office. Of Amy in her plastic bag. Of a triangular piece of glass. "*Incredible* is one word for it. Can you translate the inscription?"

"Probably, but not off the top of my head. You'd need to leave it with me." Attention locked on the lamp, he slid it across his desk. "Something like this will take time. I'll have to consult—"

"Dr. Hariri."

He met her gaze. Wet his lips. His breath slipped in and out, fast and shallow.

"Get it translated as soon as possible." Without breaking eye contact, she tapped the card on his desk as she stood. "Call me the moment you have a result."

>−<

A new club out in Parkdale meant new business opportunities, so Vicki headed west for a bite to eat. Club drugs were mostly Ecstasy, meth, and LSD, but she found an entrepreneur also selling

Rohypnol and led him into the dark corner between the back of a public parking lot and the rear wall of the club.

Nostrils flared, she leaned in closer to the pulse in his throat as he pulled a leather card case out of his pocket. Few dealers used. He smelled clean.

He barely bothered to fake a smile. "So, just the candy, or can I interest you in something else?"

Her smile was completely sincere.

The smell of fresh urine overwhelmed the stale residue at the base of the wall.

She left him propped against the fender of a Buick—Mike was right; *Buick* was funnier than *Toyota*—missing his drugs, his cash, and any desire to continue in the same business. He'd probably shake the compulsion in a day or two, but he'd see her in his nightmares for a while, and that might be enough.

In turn, she'd have to deal with the addicting taste of his terror. Make sure it was entirely out of her system before she fed like this again. Giving in to that darkness would lead to loss of self and eventually torches and stakes, and she wouldn't do that to Mike.

When he di—

When she los—

Later, she'd have to fight to stay on this side of the light.

>—<

"You okay?"

"Shouldn't I be asking you that?" When Mike's brows rose, she smiled the most human smile she had left, the one she saved for him. "Don't worry; I ate emergency rations."

"Dave says Amy Shaw hasn't been home."

"Smooth segue." He understood he couldn't supply all her needs, but he didn't want to hear the details. Which was fortunate, as she had no intention of telling him. "Do you remember anything yet?"

"Not a damned thing. Doc says I might never get the memories back." His grip on her hand tightened. "You looking into that fatality downtown with the windows and the missing gold?"

"Yes."

"Is it connected to what happened to me?"

In the old days, Vicki had been a terrible liar. That had changed when her humanity became a lie. She thought about lying to him now, but there were too many external factors she couldn't control to get away with it. "Yes, it is."

"You dealing with it?"

"Yes, I am."

"Good." He shifted carefully, favoring his left side. "Unless I start pissing blood, they're sending me home tomorrow."

No. Stay here. Where you're safe.

One corner of his mouth curled up. "I told them I had someone who could watch me at night."

"I thought you didn't like it when I did that?"

He waggled his eyebrows lecherously. "I like it fine when you're watching up close and personal."

I don't want to watch you die.

She blinked the thought away before he could read it off her face and bent to kiss him good-bye.

"You don't taste like drug dealer," he murmured against her mouth.

"I brushed my teeth."

She dropped Amy's remains into the medical incinerator on her way out of the building.

><-<

"Well, if it isn't Victory Nelson. You never text; you never call. Was it something I said?" Mama Sweet's arms weren't as strong as they'd once been, but even at seventy-seven, her mind was as sharp as ever. She held Vicki out at arm's length and frowned. "And this isn't a social call, is it? Even though you promised me three months ago that you'd stop by for drinks."

"I know. I'm sorry." Mama Sweet didn't accept excuses, so Vicki didn't make any. "I'm looking for someone. I thought you might be able to help me find him."

"Might be able to?" The older woman snorted and sat back down at the table, waving the three heavily muscled young men away. "Go play Pokémon or whatever it is you kids do these days. I'm safer with Victory than I am with the three of you."

"Pokémon?" Vicki asked when they were alone.

"Pissing off the young is one of the greatest pleasures I have left." She folded her hands, the knuckles swollen and painful-looking. "What do you want?"

"Person I'm looking for needs to convert a lot of gold." The genie had been locked away for a while, and gold wasn't a viable currency anymore.

"Two downtown towers of it?" When Vicki said nothing, Mama Sweet rolled her eyes. "Fine, don't tell me. And in return?"

Vicki slid a piece of paper across the table. No one came to see Mama Sweet empty-handed. She'd started out in Toronto's Jamaican gangs in the sixties and objected to the lack of opportunities for women, and when she got out of prison—the objection had involved the application of a baseball bat—she'd worked her ass off to become the best fixer in the city. Back when she'd been on the force, Vicki had arrested her twice. She'd gotten off both times and insisted Vicki stay in touch. Which had been weird enough, but Vicki had. Over the years, Vicki'd watched Mama Sweet age, and if Mama Sweet had, in turn, noticed Vicki wasn't aging, she hadn't said anything. Yet.

Mama Sweet frowned at the description on the paper. "Who's this, then?"

"That's the man who dumped the body of one of your people in the Don last week."

"And you didn't take it to the police because?"

"Because the police wouldn't consider my witness credible." *Because the police don't believe a troll lives under the Bloor Viaduct.*

"But you do."

It wasn't a question, so Vicki didn't answer it.

Paper refolded and slid into the pocket of the man's dress shirt she wore, Mama Sweet nodded toward the door. "Wait on the porch. I'll make a few quick calls."

>—<

Vicki perched on the porch rail and watched traffic go up Ossington. And down Ossington. And listened to a passing gaggle of teenagers argue in two languages. One of them might have been Farsi; she had no idea what the other was. The topic seemed obvious, given the way they were waving their phones around.

She turned when the door opened.

One of the muscular young men handed her a piece of paper and said, "Mama says a not-very-big guy beat the shit out of Two Ton until he gave up Marie Bilodeau who, in turn, gave up Eddie Ease. Mama also says come by next Tuesday evening." He frowned. "Bring pie."

>—<

Eddie Ease owned a condo in a building across from St. Lawrence Market. An upper-middle-class building beginning to show its age;

the lobby looked as though it had been renovated recently to make room for a concierge. Vicki flashed her fake badge through the glass and, once the door opened, walked straight to the desk and the middle-aged white man behind it. Probably downsized recently from a better job, he clearly thought being a middle-aged white man was protection enough. *Idiot.*

Vicki smiled and let him fall into the silver in her eyes. "I was never here. When I leave, you won't see me."

"You weren't. I won't!" He licked his lips, his knuckles white where he gripped the edge of the desk. "I'm sorry. Please, I . . . I have a family."

Not as much of an idiot as she'd thought. Or a more perceptive one, at least. "Good for you. Next time, check ID and ask questions when someone flashes a badge. Don't just open the door; these things aren't hard to come by."

"I will. Thank you. I'm sorry."

She could feel the pull of his fear all the way to the stairs and felt it fade the moment she stepped out of sight and literally out of mind. The temptation to step back was strong. Hunger fighting control, she gritted her teeth and climbed to the sixth floor, moving too fast to register on the security cameras. Eddie Ease had a corner unit at the far end of the brightly lit, freshly painted hall. Odds were very good he kept his business away from his home.

As she walked, she sifted through the surrounding lives. Hearts beating; blood flowing, slowed in sleep.

Power.

The hair lifted off the back of her neck and continued to lift as she approached Eddie's door. She remembered fire, and the Hunter broke loose as instinct took over from rational thought. She raised a hand to force the door. It opened just before her palm made contact.

"I didn't hear anyone knock," Eddie said over his shoulder, and turned to look at her and moaned. His heart sped up. Visible skin gleamed with sweat. Blood pounded through wrists and temples and throat. Vicki snarled before she could stop herself. Eddie staggered back until he hit a wall; then he slid to the floor, eyes rolling up, consciousness surrendering to terror.

"A little extreme, don't you think, Nightwalker?"

The genie was . . . five-seven. Six-two. Dark. Fair. A slender Asian. A burly redhead. Female. Male. Both. Neither. No heartbeat. No blood moving temptingly under white, black, brown skin. Nails cutting half circles into her palms, Vicki pulled herself back from a darkness she didn't own and said, "At least he wasn't a screamer."

"Oh, well done. You know what I am and still manage a jest." It rose out of the leather club chair and became a pillar of smokeless fire. "You have found me. What do you want, Nightwalker? Have you come to pay homage?"

"Not even close."

"Then why are you here?"

She frowned, suddenly realizing she had no idea of what to do now. For fifteen years, she'd been the fastest, strongest, darkest. She'd come up with a way to find the genie, found it, and faced a pillar of fire. How did she defeat a pillar of fire? She didn't even have the lamp.

"Ah, hubris." Vicki could hear the amusement in the fire's voice. "I stand between the gods and humanity, little blood drinker. When I last walked this world, taking who and what I desired, there were heroes and sages and mighty wizards fit to challenge me. Now your wizards are children, your sages are unable to see the truth, and the only hero I have to face is you. A hero out of the darkness for a time without light. I tremble. I shake. I . . ."

"Am a genie. *You're* a genie," she clarified.

"Jinn."

"Right. Jinn. Given you're a jinn, why do you need Eddie to

change your gold to currency? You took the gold off a skyscraper. Can't you change it yourself?"

"I did." It moved aside, and Vicki saw coins spilling out of a basket on the floor next to the chrome-and-glass coffee table. "But the daric is no longer in use, and I am unfamiliar with its modern replacement."

Makes sense, Vicki acknowledged silently. There were more than a few Canadians still having trouble with the new plastic bills, and they hadn't spent centuries locked in a magic lamp. And it clearly couldn't just create what it wanted, or it wouldn't have taken the gold. "You plan on staying around?"

"The way to my home has long been closed."

A troll lived under the Bloor Viaduct. Surely the city had room for a displaced jinn?

"All right." Her city. Her rules. "Amy held your prison; you get a pass for frying her. Kai Johnston could be considered an accident. Don't have any more. Humans aren't toys; don't play with them. If you stay, no more of them die at your hand."

To her surprise, the fire began to laugh. In her own defense, even given her life, laughing fire was still way out past the borders. "Oh, I have missed the ridiculous arrogance of your kind. For such enjoyment, you may live a while longer."

One moment, she was enclosed in flame.

The next, she stood in her empty office.

>—<

"What part of *it's creepy when you watch me sleep* do you not understand?"

Now that he was awake, Vicki settled on the side of Mike's bed, pressed against his hip, enjoying the warmth she could feel through the thin hospital blanket. "The part where I care about being creepy."

"Yeah, I guess you're a few pints past that." He took her hand, wrapped it in his, and pressed it to his chest over his heart. "What happened? You look thrown. And not through-a-window thrown either. Find something new in the woodpile?" When she hesitated, he tightened his grip. "Talk to me."

"Not here." She saw a flicker of red in the corner of her eye, turned, and realized it had to have been an LED on the machine shoved into the corner of the room. Had to have been, because there was nothing else in the room. "There's too many vulnerable people here. I need a favor," she added, before he could respond. "I'm waiting for a call from a Dr. Hariri. If it doesn't come in before dawn, I want to forward it to your phone. Tell him I've been detained, that he should get some rest, and I'll see him in his office at nine tomorrow—" It was five thirteen. "Tonight."

"You want to use my phone *and* you want me to pass on a message?" The creases around Mike's eyes deepened when he smiled. "What did your last slave die of?"

She could hear the nurses talking down the hall. Room 417 was terminal.

"Vicki?"

"Don't die."

"Hey . . ."

"Just don't."

He studied her expression for a long moment, then kissed her knuckles. "I wasn't planning on it. Not until I'm old and wizened and people give me shit about robbing the cradle."

He pulled her head down onto the right side of his chest, the side not arguing his mortality with cracked ribs, and she listened to his heartbeat and thought, *Not then either.*

>—<

". . . police were already on their way, called in to assist a member of the staff having trouble with a customer. The assumption is that the two incidents aren't connected, as a preliminary investigation by the fire marshal suggests the cause of the fire that destroyed the restaurant was most likely an exploding gas range. The customer is assumed to be among the nine dead. The fire marshal had no comment on why the fire seemed to be contained within the restaurant, not spreading to the surrounding buildings or the apartment upstairs."

Vicki gently leaned the bathroom door against the slightly scorched wall of her still-empty office and released the crushed handle. She had a comment. She had a few comments. Most of them involved profanity.

>—<

"The words engraved on the lamp appear to be the spell that contained the jinn. It seems the"—Dr. Hariri paused, rubbed tired eyes, and sighed—"*wizard* who imprisoned it wanted to ensure the jinn could be reimprisoned, should it escape."

"Just what I wanted to hear." Vicki patted the lamp. "How does it work?"

"The words are inscribed in a circle"—he moved a book from the closest tottering pile on his desk and flipped it open to a tabbed page—"sorry, *carved* in a circle. The lamp is placed in the center of the circle. The jinn is summoned. That's another spell. . . . Wait." He yanked at a piece of paper protruding from the bottom book.

Vicki caught the top three books as they fell.

"I had to call in a few favors." The notes had been written in two different colors of ink. "Fortunately, I have a colleague at Istanbul University cataloging its ancient literature collection. Took her about four hours, but she was able to put her hand on what I needed. I was fairly certain I'd read a reference to it in a 1930s dissertation, but eighty years later, there's no telling where the manuscript might have gotten to. It was written by . . ."

"Dr. Hariri."

He blinked.

"The spell?"

"Right. We had to fill in a few words with frog DNA. . . . That's a *Jurassic Park* joke."

"I know."

"It's just you're a little young for . . . Never mind. The spell. Problem is, it won't work."

"Because of the frog DNA?"

"No, that should hold. It was synonyms mostly. It's because"—he pulled on a pair of white cotton gloves and opened a book even Vicki could tell was ancient—"you don't have an angel."

"I'm sorry?"

"In the Koran, jinn, humans, and angels make up the three known sapient creations of God. As jinn predate the Koran, I suspect the word *angel* actually refers to one of the lesser gods who helped humanity lock away certain trouble-making jinn."

"Okay. How do we summon this lesser god?"

"We don't. We can't. Mythology is not reality, Ms. Nelson. It doesn't matter anyway, because the *angel*"—Dr. Hariri touched the text with a white cotton finger—"approached the wizard."

"Wonderful." She swept her gaze around the room—at the books, at the papers, at the lamp. "All right. Back to square one. What does the lamp actually say?"

"'Place me in the center of words carved round'—I won't read the words you're to carve." He traced the etched lettering. "And after, 'Summon the jinn to be sealed with immortal blood.'"

"Say again."

"'Summon—'"

"After that."

"'Sealed with immortal blood'?"

"Thank you, Dr. Hariri. You've been a great help." She picked up the lamp and the summoning spell and frowned down at the paper. "Could you write this out phonetically?"

>—<—<

"He's buying one of the last of the old warehouses on the waterfront." Eddie Ease twitched in Vicki's grip. "Said he needed room to build a palace. He doesn't want to deal with the city, so I'm acting as his agent."

"He's not a he," Vicki growled.

"Yeah, well, that's his choice, isn't it?"

To be fair, Vicki acknowledged, it was.

>—<—<

Vicki was impressed the jinn had found real estate in the Lower Don Lands that hadn't already been gentrified. But then, *jinn*. It could be convincing in ways other buyers couldn't.

The bulk of the warehouse had been given over to storage—a huge, two-story space with high windows and a stained concrete floor. The security lights provided an artificial dusk; plenty of light for Vicki to carve the words on the lamp into the enormous circle she'd drawn on the floor with a tire iron, a rope, and a piece of sidewalk chalk. Not her first rodeo—*approximately* a circle wouldn't do. Retrieving the tire iron and setting the lamp in its place, she began gouging out the words of the spell as quickly as accuracy allowed, the concrete rolling up like lines of chunky orange peel. It was almost eleven. She didn't have all night.

At two forty-three, she straightened, cracked her back, and moved to stand beside the lamp, paper in one hand, knife in the other, prepared to read the summoning.

"As if I wouldn't know you were here." The pillar of fire moved around the outside of the circle. "As if I wouldn't feel words of binding in a space I'd claimed as my own."

Probably for the best. Her French accent sucked; her phonetic Aramaic could only be worse.

"Do you assume you're safe from me, Nightwalker, there inside the words you carved?"

"Talking pillar of fire," Vicki pointed out. "I'm not assuming anything."

"Clever meat sack." It advanced toward her, crossing the spell.

Sealed with immortal blood was a little unspecific regarding the necessary volume. Figuring too much beat too little, she drew the blade of the knife across her left forearm, then her right. She hissed at the pain, and, about to be engulfed by fire, took the fight to the jinn, throwing her arms around the flames.

It screamed.

And it burned.

Vicki screamed and hung on.

The flames became a lion, fetid breath in her face as teeth tore at her shoulder.

The lion became a snake, length looped around her, her ribs cracking.

Through the pain, she wondered if she'd wandered into the wrong story. Or if the sidhe were jinn seen through a different geography and culture.

The snake became a fucking enormous crow with a beak like a pickax.

Tentacles . . .

Then a man. Broad shouldered, dark eyed, skin slippery with her blood. "I can give his youth back to you, Nightwalker." It smiled knowingly. "I can give you two or three times the years you have remaining. Delay the time you'll spend in darkness without him."

What would she give to delay Mike's death? To delay watching him die?

If she changed him, she'd lose him the way Henry had lost her. Vampires were apex predators and they did not, could not, share a territory. Not that it mattered; Mike would never agree to the change. He'd made that profanely clear on more than one occasion.

If the jinn changed him, made him young again . . .

. . . She would lose him the moment he realized she'd made the decision for him. It might be worth the risk with someone else. His youth restored, she could wait a year or two while he dealt with the betrayal of his trust. But that wasn't something Mike would, or could, forgive.

She knew what the future held. He'd lose his strength. Muscles would weaken. Bones would grow fragile. Hands that now touched her with passion would turn to swollen joints and tremors. If he were lucky, his heart would fail before the rest of his body wore out a piece at a time. She would watch, forever thirty-four, as he diminished.

Died.

Rotted.

The last anchor to her humanity gone. No one left who'd known her before. No one left to say *Enough*.

Did it matter if he never forgave her, as long as he had a few more years before death claimed him?

Yes.

Because it wasn't about Mike. It was about her. Always had been.

Mike would live the life he chose, and she would love him for however long that lasted. When he died—at the end of a mortal span, or next Thursday while trying to bring in a couple of Scarborough gang-bangers—she would mourn him. She would weep and she would rail and she would paint herself with the blood of the undeserving. Of the dark dregs of society who dared to live while he was dead.

And then she'd stop, because she was Vicki fucking Nelson, and if she was strong enough to watch the man she loved wither, if she was strong enough to watch him go into the ground because that was what he wanted, she was strong enough to do what she had to.

"Make a wish, Nightwalker."

Her lips drew back. "You have nothing I want," she snarled, and slammed her forehead into his nose.

He swore as he jerked back, eyes wide, nose bleeding.

Tossed his head, became fire again as a drop of blood fell . . .

. . . and hit the lamp.

Vicki stumbled, arms empty, a little faint from pain and blood loss.

Sealed with immortal blood.

"Points for originality," she muttered, and touched the growing lump on her forehead. "Also, ow."

Licking her own arms, as undignified as it felt, put the coagulant in her saliva to work, and by the time she'd eradicated the spell—not the sort of thing she wanted left lying around; that never ended well—the bleeding had stopped. A spray bottle of bleach took care of the DNA evidence—splatters of blood on a torn-up floor would be investigated sooner or later. Probably later, given the backlog in the labs Mike kept complaining about, but, still, no point in being careless.

The lamp . . . Three wishes and, after, the jinn would still be confined.

Glass falling.

Mike thrown through a window.

And the sort of metaphysical SOB who thought nothing of lives lost.

She picked up the lamp, holding it carefully so as to keep from even suggesting the faintest possibility of a rub. The brass felt warm, satin smooth, and smelled alive. She touched it to her cheek, bit through her lip, and wrapped the sneaky SOB carefully in three layers of green plastic garbage bag.

><><

It was 5:37. Sunrise was at 7:25. She should wake Mike so they could spend at least part of that two hours together, both of them conscious. She'd fed on the way home—another packet of drug money donated anonymously to Covenant House. The edge taken off before Mike insisted on their reaffirming he was alive. For however much longer he had.

He threw an arm up over his head and the sheet slipped down around his waist. The gray threaded through the thick mat of his chest hair turned silver in the predawn light.

Maybe watching him sleep *was* a little creepy.

Vicki slipped out of her clothes and slid into bed on his right side, tucking her face into the curve of neck and shoulder, listening to his heartbeat, lips against his pulse.

The lamp was downstairs in her basement crypt, safely hidden.

Not the least bit tempting . . .

SOLUS

by Anton Strout

"Pixies!"

The word echoed across the elevator on tiny wings of hope. *Something* had to kill the awkward silence between me and the man assigned the Herculean task of keeping me alive these days.

Connor Christos's attention shifted from counting the passing floors. He gave me a sidelong glance meant to shut me down.

"No," he said.

Short. Curt. The pit of my stomach sank, and it wasn't because of the motion of the rising elevator car. Breaking through to him was quickly becoming my personal pastime, my quest, the windmill-giant task to my question-jousting Don Quixote, but I fought to shake off my mounting failure.

"Gnomes?" I tried next, undeterred. These damned Department of Extraordinary Affairs stuffed shirts *would* like me, dammit.

Connor's eyes went back to the numbers on the wall, the display rolling through the seventies. "Uh-uh."

"Beholders?"

My mentor paused for a moment before he answered and scratched his head, which only mussed the lone gray streak that ran through his otherwise sandy sea of hair.

"Not even sure what that is," he said. "But probably not."

"It's from the Monster Manual," I offered.

He shrugged, the shoulders of his tan trench coat rustling in the silence of the elevator. "If that's a new training pamphlet going around the office, I must have missed it."

I shook my head. "Not quite," I said. "It's from D and D." Then, catching his blank stare in the mirrors of the door, "Dungeons and Dragons?"

"Ahh," he said, his eyes lighting with recognition. "Well, don't believe everything you read, kid."

His eyes shifted back to the ever-fascinating crawl of numbers as silence once more fell between us.

I took it as a small victory, if not a bitter one. I had hoped to impress. One of the perks of being a psychometrist was absorbing knowledge that I would have normally written off as useless. When I came across a used Dungeons & Dragons book a few weeks back, it gave me a chance to show Connor I had at least taken an interest in versing myself on a whole paranormal world I was unfamiliar with. As a new recruit in Manhattan's Department of Extraordinary Affairs, I thought my initiative might earn me a pat on the back, but apparently not.

Frustration filled me right down to my nerves. How else was I supposed to learn the truth from pure fantasy out there on the supernatural streets of New York City anyway? So far in these first few days of partnership with Connor, the only thing I had learned was how to brood. If the Department quizzed me on how to be barely tolerated by a mentor, I'd easily have an A++.

I bit my tongue for the next several floors. It was clear Christos came predisposed to hating on me for reasons I could not fathom, and given my fruitlessness at finding out why, I instead took a moment to regain my composure before going back to my previous line of questioning.

"Mermaids?" I asked, pressing my luck.

He sighed, turning to face me for the first time during our entire ride. Although his face didn't look much older than my twenty-three years, his deep-set eyes held a lifetime of otherworldly horrors in them that aged him considerably when he met mine.

"Unconfirmed, at least not since early sailor records we keep down in the archives," he said. "Most agents write them off as the delusions of old-timey hard-core drinkers, victims of long-seabound scurvy, or possibly those stricken with a bit of syphilitic madness from their adventures when in port. If I were you, Mr. Canderous, I wouldn't worry about those fishy ladies of the sea. You're better off, though, assuming all fantasy creatures are real."

"I am?" The idea that I'd need to memorize the totalities of the Monster Manual drove a mind-numbing spike straight down into the center of my brain.

Connor nodded. "One of the prime tenets of working for the Department of Extraordinary Affairs is *Believing is seeing*. Don't rule anything out, because that'll be right about the time that ruled-out monster eats your disbelieving face right off. Trust me on this."

"Okay," I said, paling at the thought, wanting to move the conversation on. "How about zombies, then?"

"Also real," Connor said with a shudder. "You haven't taken Shufflers and Shamblers yet?"

I shook my head. "The department isn't offering it until next month," I said. "Although I suppose I'm encouraged that they think I'll survive on the streets until then."

"Typical Department of Extraordinary Affairs," Connor said, shaking his head. "Where keeping agents alive is job two. Or three."

"On-time training alone would cut the Incident Reports paperwork in half," I said.

Connor glanced over at me, annoyed again. "Are you trying to apply logic to our line of work, kid?"

Kid. Did being twenty-three technically count as being a kid? *Hell to the no,* I thought, especially when coming from someone I guessed was in his mid-thirties. Before I could cut into him, my stomach lurched as the elevator slowed to a halt and its doors opened.

Wind. Strange that I could feel it as we stepped out, but it became clear immediately: we were on the very roof of the building itself. A set cobblestone path lay at my feet, and as odd and out of place as the stonework looked, it was nothing compared to the multispired stronghold that stood off across the vastness of the roof. If I were looking at a photo in front of me, I would have laughed at the cut-and-paste job of slapping an entire medieval structure onto the top of a modern Manhattan skyscraper, but seeing it there for myself struck me with awe instead.

"We have castles?" I asked, trying to keep cool and mask the sheer wonder in my voice.

Connor nodded. "Where there's money, there's eccentricity . . . and castles."

My position as part of Other Division presented challenges every damned day, but processing an elaborate Disney-style castle jarred me in a way that the rooftops of Manhattan usually didn't. Standing upon them often brought a strange comfort to my soul, or at least to the soul of my criminal past, anyway: casing joints, finding convenient escape routes . . .

Black, tarred weather sealant or concrete ruled the usual

places I frequented. Stately sights such as this one rarely entered the picture.

"How do you even know about places like this?" I asked, trying not to lick my lips at the promised opulence of it all. The criminal opportunist might be suppressed these days, but he definitely wasn't dead.

"We're the Department of *Extraordinary* Affairs, Simon," he said. "Dealing with places like this is the new norm. *Extraordinary* is right there in our name, and I think you'll agree this fits the bill, no?"

I nodded, a wicked grin spreading across my face. "I can't believe this is my job."

"Technically, it isn't," Connor said as he started walking away. "We're off the clock on this one."

"We are?" A tension released in me that I didn't realize I had been holding in, and my shoulders relaxed. Trying to impress my partner/boss-of-me on the job was one thing, but knowing this wasn't actually work helped take a real load off me. "Then why *are* we here?"

"This?" Connor said, stopping to point at the castle. "This is just a spot of fun. A bit of paying it forward, if you will. Consider it field training. Plus, if you screw up, we won't end up generating an avalanche of paperwork back at the office."

"Such a vote of confidence," I said. "I'm touched. Really. So, again, why exactly *are* we here?"

"You'll see," Connor said, and continued off in the direction of the castle once more. "For now, just keep quiet."

I was all for paying it forward. Lord knows I had been selfish enough with my psychometric powers over the years—to the point of near jail time. Doing good for goodness' sake felt like a calming bath meant to wash away the sins of my past, and my step lightened as the two of us crossed the roof.

The scale of the castle against the New York skyline made it seem deceptively close, but getting to it felt like forever. Only when we were near the stone steps leading up to an enormous set of dark wooden doors did I spy any signs of life nearby. A lone woman in a houndstooth suit sat next to a row of tree-lined planters at the top of the stairs, and only when our footsteps were in earshot did she look up from a laptop precariously balanced on her knees. The ponytail of her severely pulled-back black hair bobbed nervously as she fumbled to close her computer, shoving it into a hideous gigantic handbag sitting at her side.

She stood as we ascended the stairs, meeting us by the doors as she pulled her suit coat and trim of her skirt into a less wrinkled state and gave a nervous smile to Connor.

"Thank you for coming so quickly, Mr. Christos," she said, almost at a whisper, her voice tinged with a little Brooklyn or Long Island.

"Of course, Bev," Connor said. He rapped his knuckles against the solid stone archway of the door. "Time is of the essence and all that. I know how precious your commission is to you."

"Hey!" she said, with a little mock offense to it. "That hurts."

"The truth usually does," Connor said as he looked up at the building. "I can only imagine what state the place must be in for you to have called."

The woman nodded. "The Sedgwick Estate is a landmark catch for any Realtor, carefully brought here by the family nearly a century ago from England and painstakingly reconstructed. There is little like it in all of New York, I assure you. The estate sale of one Agatha Sedgwick was going well until . . ."

The Realtor stopped herself as words failed to form on her lips and her eyes drifted from the doors to the ground. Just what the hell had happened here?

After a moment, she regained her composure and smoothed down the lapels of her suit coat once more. "Still, there's enough damage already to bring the value down considerably. As it stands, the repairs will be astronomical. I mean, you can't just look up *castle construction* with the District Council of Carpenters."

"So this is actually a real castle?" I blurted out. "Does it come complete with a dungeon?"

The woman's face screwed up, and she looked over to me for the first time.

Connor's gaze shot daggers, killing any further questions. I reminded myself to listen next time when my mentor told me to stay quiet.

"Sorry about my partner," he said, his face softening as he turned back to the woman. "Beverly Rodell, this is my new partner, Simon Canderous."

She narrowed her eyes at him. "Ms. Svenson is retired, then?"

Connor's face went blank, a familiar coldness in it. "Something like that."

Had this Ms. Svenson been his previous partner? Getting anything personal out of him had so far proven harder than finding a cab at one minute past five, and it seemed Beverly Rodell's mention of the woman caused him to shut down the way he often did with me. The same sort of silence I had experienced alone with him in the elevator fell over the three of us. I needed to break its spell.

"So, is this place a real castle, and *does* it have a dungeon?" I repeated.

"Yes, it's real," the woman said, looking relieved that we were back on track with solving whatever her problem was. "And yes, there's a dungeon. Racks and all. The Sedgwicks may have been eccentrics, but they were detail-oriented ones at that. A prominent

New England family. Some of the New York–based clan took their pride more seriously than others, it seems, and moved their ancestral estate from England to here, stone by stone."

I couldn't help but smile at that, which only drew another look of disdain from Connor.

"Forgive Simon," he said. "He's a bit excitable . . . in a new-puppy-about-to-pee-on-the-floor kind of way."

"I'm mostly house-trained," I countered, unable to stop myself.

Connor turned with the same glare on his face, but the woman touched his arm, drawing his attention back to her.

"He can be whatever he likes to be, as long as you can take care of," Beverly said, gesturing to the Sedgwick estate, "*all this*."

Connor waved her toward the door. "Then by all means, lead on."

The woman shook her head, her face going a sickly shade of green usually reserved for cartoon witches. "I'd rather *not*. I barely believe in this hoodoo of yours in the first place, but I don't think my heart could bear to watch this place destroyed any further. I was nearly beaten to death in the main library by a flurry of books flying from the shelves. Thankfully, I didn't escape through the kitchen. The scullery would have left me in bloody pieces on the floor."

"We'll keep damage to a minimum," Connor assured her, then glanced over at me. "Well, at least one of us will, anyway."

I fought the urge to protest, and instead pulled my jacket closed over the retractable bat that hung from my belt within. I had no plan to draw it unless absolutely necessary.

"See that you do," the Realtor said, and headed down the steps toward the elevator off on the far side of the roof. "I'll be at the bar across the street, awaiting the damage report. It is highly unlikely that I will be sober."

The sound of Beverly's heels rang out as she carefully descended the castle stairs, but once on the open roof, her feet quickened to the point that I thought she might break out in a full-on high-heeled sprint for the elevator leading back down to street level.

Once the Realtor was gone, I turned to Connor, suddenly unable to control a burst of anger I found welling up inside of me.

"An estate sale?" I spat out while also breaking into a sweat. "You brought *me*, of all people, to an estate sale?"

Connor stared, nonplussed, his eyes burning through my head. "Is that problematic?"

I nodded so hard I feared my head would fall off. I imagined it rolling across the roof, bouncing over the edge, and falling down into the streets of Manhattan. "This entire place is going to be brimming with psychometrically charged material. Estate sales always are, more so, I imagine, in a friggin' castle!"

"So?"

"Not sure I can handle going into such a place," I admitted, though it pained me to do so. I was pretty sure telling your superior that you couldn't quite hack it in the paranormal-investigation business was the opposite of impressing him. In fact, it felt a hell of a lot like failure in my ongoing struggle to fit in with the department's Other Division. Maybe if I could make him understand . . .

"Old landmarkish places like this are *always* filled with a psychometric energy that matches their rich history," I explained. I wiped the sweat of my trepidation from my brow. "A place like this is the atomic bomb of power drains. Sorry."

Connor's eyes fell upon me, and much like Frodo under the gaze of Sauron, the judgment and disappointment in them was almost too much to bear. To my surprise, however, he gave a skeptical half smile. "Were you ever a Boy Scout?"

"What?" I asked, thrown. "What does that have to do with anything?"

"Plenty," he said. "You could learn a lot from them, you know."

"Aren't I Boy Scout enough, just being part of the Department of Extraordinary Affairs?"

"Fine, then," Connor said, holding up one finger. "What's the Scout motto?"

I stopped and searched my mind with the random turn the conversation had just taken, struggling for a moment until it came to me. "Be prepared?"

"Be prepared," Connor said with a nod. "Well, are you?"

"For *what*?" I asked with building frustration. "I didn't even know where we were going!"

"That shouldn't matter," he said, adopting a bit of the training tone his voice took when he attempted to drill something into my brain. "This is New York City. It's an old town, relatively speaking. Everything here is potentially charged with rich history, right? So I can assume you've loaded up on Life Savers to keep your sugar up, yes?"

"To a point," I said, my nerves creeping into my voice. "But come on! You brought me to a *castle*. You think I'm prepared for *that* level of potential power use? Maybe if I stuffed my pockets full of Life Savers—hell, even wore bandoliers of them—"

"You still think you'd probably drop from the blood-sugar drain of your psychometry going out of control in there? Really?"

I sighed as I thought out how to best explain it to someone who hadn't had to live with my power. "Half the reason I joined the Department of Extraordinary Affairs was to *avoid* situations like this, Connor. I can't always tell when or if a psychometric vision will kick in when I touch an object, and when it does, the preternatural price my body pays to do so is high. It's not a hypoglycemia-inducing condition I can really talk to a normal doctor about, you know? How the hell do you expect me to keep it in check in this place? I'll lose control."

Connor shrugged, turning to take in the massive doors in front of us, silent sentinels guarding the mysteries within.

"Then don't lose control," he said with a tight-lipped smile. "Simple."

I sighed, a sharp, staccato exhale. "You're supposed to help me, you know," I reminded him, "not kill me."

"Think of it as tough love," he said. He examined the iron rings that hung from the doors themselves.

I shook my head. "Worst. Teacher. Ever."

"That's Other Division for you," he said. "Trial by fire."

My mentor pulled the iron ring, and the door gave a long, slow creak as it cracked open. He let go of the ring and headed in.

"*Other Division*," I grumbled as I watched him disappear into the darkness within. I resisted my knee-jerk urge to tell Connor in a swear-laden fashion what I really thought of being assigned to the office equivalent of the Island of Misfit Toys.

I followed my mentor/partner into what looked like the King's Landing feast hall set from *Game of Thrones*. By Manhattan standards, its area certainly beat most loft spaces and one-bedrooms easily, by a factor of at least a thousand. Spacious to the nth degree, fit for either a festive dinner or competitive jousting.

Tapestries depicting unicorns in all manner of poses covered almost every inch of the walls. Medieval weapons of every size and shape hung alongside. Suits of armor—some mounted troops, even—sat displayed around the vast open space. Our footsteps echoed throughout the great hall, as if in a museum.

"Quick follow-up from the elevator," I said when I could finally take my eyes from the mythological-beast tapestries. "Unicorns. Real?"

Connor held out his hand and waggled it back and forth in a gesture of uncertainty. "Not officially," he said. "Not on the books, anyway. The archives have been trying to reclassify the existence of creatures documented *before* the past century. Might be a while before they confirm their existence. You know how much paperwork the DEA generates, so who knows?"

I took in the grandeur of the room, struck with an awe and reverence for the lives of all those who had passed through here over the centuries, long before this structure had been transported to Manhattan.

"So what the hell are we actually looking for?" I asked.

"You tell me, kid. Why do *you* think we came here?"

I shrugged, my eyes drifting back up to the tapestries all around us. "I dunno," I said. "Zombies? Ghouls? Taking down a unicorn fight club, maybe?"

Connor's face went stern, his brow furrowed, and then he pointed at his forehead in what I thought was a gesture for me to use my brain, but I discarded that notion when my eyes fell on the gray streak in Connor's sandy brown hair.

"Ghosts," I said, acknowledging the sure sign of his having been touched by one previously. "We've got a ghost sitch here, don't we?"

Connor touched the gray streak itself, acknowledging with the gesture that I was indeed right. "There's hope for you yet, kid."

"Not for getting a streak of gray all my own, I hope." It had been an adjustment learning how to handle the types of spirits Connor took in stride as his area of expertise. Years of training had built a callus over him, one that made him impervious to the plights, pains, and restlessness of these earthbound souls, but for me it was hard to ignore. Maybe it was years of psychometrically exposing the intimate details of other's lives—experiencing them firsthand—that left my empathy dialed up to eleven, but there was little I could do to change that about myself. The knob on my emotional amplifier had snapped off years ago, stuck there. Instead, I worried about the things that I could hopefully control, and ran my fingers though my jet-black hair as I wondered how it would look with a ghost stripe like Connor's.

"Just don't let any of the deceased clan Sedgwick pass through you," he said as if reading my mind. He moved into the great hall to scope it out. "Remember your training. If a ghost passes through you, it's going to feel like your entire body is being pressed through a sieve, leaving you unconscious after you scream in pain and pass out. Who knows what'll happen once they have you down?"

"Are you *sure* I don't get to punch the time clock on this?" I asked, fanning off to the far side of the hall. I couldn't hide the nerves in my voice. There was so much stuff here in the way of antiques, so much potential for my powers to go into overdrive.

"Relax, kid," Connor's voice echoed out. "This should be good for you, especially with your particular skills."

"It's easy for *you* to relax," I said. "You touch something in here and you won't end up flopping on the floor like a goddamned fish gasping for breath."

"You've got your gloves on," Connor said, pointing to my hands. "So I stick with my initial statement: relax. Besides, you might score something."

I stopped and cocked my head at him, unable to ignore the hint of disdain in his last sentence.

"Excuse me," I called out after him, "but what the hell was *that* about?"

Connor stopped and looked over at me, his face a blank mask. "What?"

"I might *score something*?" I said, repeating back to him as I locked eyes and refused to look away.

Connor broke eye contact first. "Just don't touch anything—okay, kid?"

I stopped, holding up my right hand. I waggled the black leather fingers of my glove at him. "Yes, sir. I didn't realize we had a problem. Sir."

"Just keep your hands to yourself," he repeated, this time with open toxicity in it.

I couldn't hold back. "What's this all about, Connor? What's your problem with me?"

"The Inspectre told me all about you and your past," he said.

My stomach clenched. "He did?"

"You think I'm going to partner up with someone new without knowing the score?" he asked with a laugh. "A former art thief is still an art thief in my book, kid."

"So that's what this is all about," I said. "My criminal past. First of all, it was more of a personal hobby than a career path, really. . . ."

"Hobby, eh? Just a patron of the arts, then? How noble!"

I felt the blush of red rising in my cheeks, and hated how I felt I needed to justify my past to him. The lack of trust and compassion knotted my stomach, a sensation I was more than familiar with after years of social awkwardness while sorting out how to control my power.

"Listen," I said. "You don't grow up with a power like mine and not fall in love with arts and antiques, okay? Especially in New York City. And I admit that knowing the secret histories of their creation is a delicious drug all its own."

"I'll bet," Connor said, disapproval thick in those two words. "A city like this? A veritable gold mine when it comes to them, right? Entirely understandable."

I wanted to shake the condescension out of him. "I'm no saint," I admitted. "Sure, I may have occasionally helped myself to a nugget or two, but I wouldn't call that being a habitual recidivist. People can change. Show some compassion."

"Right," he said, drawing the word out, but there was no conviction in it. "Look. I need to know I can trust you, especially while we're trying to hash out what is happening here that's got Bev so spooked. For now, just keep your hands to yourself."

"You do know what the word *former* in *former art thief* means, right?"

I locked eyes with him, then slowly stuck out my hand in defiance and rapped my knuckles hard on one of the nearby suits of armor.

Connor started for me in a straight line across the room. "You do know what the words *don't touch anything* mean, right?"

"I am former," I shouted at him as he got closer. "Criminal-wise, short of using my power to nail some choice antiques for my apartment. One too many brushes with the law and working with other, unreliable, bat-shit-crazy thieves will do that to a guy, you know?"

Apparently, he *didn't* know, and kept charging me. I refused to back down.

His hand clamped over mine as he pulled me away from the armor. Even as covered up as I was by my leather jacket and gloves, the gesture exposed my wrist, and the electric crackle of my power kicking in slammed hard into my mind's eye before I could stop it.

Psychometric flashes from an inert object were one thing, but direct contact with a living person was another, the pained mental equivalent of forcing a bowling ball through the pinhole of my mind. My eyes and brain felt physically sucked out of my body and slammed into those of my partner; flashes and glimpses of his past flickered in bursts among my own thoughts. Driven by the

124 | ANTON STROUT

agitation and trust issues he clearly had with me, I bent my focus toward anything connected to his own personal issues.

The narrow halls of a dark, abandoned school filled my mind's eye, all of it through Connor's perception, as if I were piloting him. While he had often refused to even mention his previous partner in Other Division, the woman in her late forties or early fifties who stood at Connor's side amid a sea of what looked like the living dead was no doubt her. Because I *was* Connor, her name came to me. Evelyn Svenson.

Her wild mane of graying hair swung around as if in its own personal hurricane while she fought off a horde of zombies at his side in the close quarters of the school halls. Connor was holding his own, using a child's tiny school chair to stave off the attacks, but it was clear the numbers were against the two of them.

Evelyn sensed their looming doom, as well. As the vision's time rolled into slow motion, she slid her leg behind Connor's, forcing him to the ground as she stepped past him and ran down the still-clear hallway behind them.

"Sorry," she said with a grim smile. "Svenson's rule thirty-four of the zombie apocalypse: I don't have to be the fastest runner to survive. I only have to be faster than you." She turned and, without a second look, left Connor to the zombie horde descending upon him.

My mind's eye flickered as the undead closed in, reality forcing its way back in through the vision. Given my usual difficulty in pulling myself out of such visions, it surprised me, but what I found even more surprising as the real world took hold of me once again was the violence with which I was being slapped around.

"Snap out of it, kid," Connor called out, his open hand connecting with a sharp sting on the side of my face.

"We're in a slap fight, are we?" I said, weak from the short but intense psychometric burst.

"I'm not fighting you," he insisted, grabbing me by the lapels of my jacket. "We've got bigger fish to fry."

"Fish?" I mumbled, still in a haze. I reached for the Life Savers in my pocket to reduce my vision-induced blood-sugar loss.

The vision. I shuddered, recalling with perfect, horrifying clarity Connor's betrayal by his old partner.

"I'm sorry about using my power on you," I said, apology thick in my voice. "I didn't mean to. How did you escape those zombie hordes?"

Connor's face went awash with shock, either from the toll my vision had taken on him or from having his past poked and prodded straight out of his private thoughts.

"You can thank New York's shitty building codes for that," he said. "Condemned building, that many bodies converging in on one section of the hallway . . . The floor gave out. I barely got out of there alive. My partner, not so much. Her treachery and escape didn't go *quite* as planned."

"No?"

Connor shook his head. "She didn't make it out of the building," he said. "Next time I saw her, two floors down, I had to chop off her head when she tried to tear my throat out."

I paused, fighting to find words of apology but unable to. For invading his mind, for my behavior in the face of his trust issues.

"I'm sorry," I finally managed to get out, but Connor was already backing away from me across the width of the great hall.

"Save it for later," he said. "Let's just see how you fare keeping us alive. Hopefully a lot better than my previous partner, anyway."

"Huh?" I asked, shaking the last of the cobwebs of fuzziness off my brain.

A cacophony rose from somewhere in the great hall, but at the moment, all I could barely manage to focus on was Connor.

He spread his arms, indicating the rest of the hall, and I managed to finally shift my attention to it.

All around us the room had sprung to life. Or, rather, all the inanimate objects had. Suits of armor shook and clanked on their pedestals. The tapestries all around the hall fluttered with the wind of an unseen force, the weapons on display twisting and swirling around on their wall mounts.

I shook my head at the spectacle of it all. "Effing ghosts," I muttered.

"Effing ghosts is right," Connor said. "Probably a whole lineage of familial haunts or else disquiet victims of the owners of this damned castle—I'd bet my reputation on it." Connor looked out into the center of the chaos, cleared his throat, and addressed no one thing in particular.

"Attention," he shouted. "I'm Connor Christos, a registered member of Other Division of New York City's Department of Extraordinary Affairs. I'm ordering you to cease and desist with any and all supernatural operations that may endanger myself or my partner, one Simon Canderous."

When the crazy around us faltered and died down, relief filled my heart, but only for a second.

Much to my great personal dismay, the cacophony rose again, redoubling as the agitation in the room became more and more palpable. At the far end of the great hall, the terrifying whinny of a horse echoed. My eyes darted in its direction just in time to catch sight of the disembodied armor of a grand steed rearing up on its hind legs, a mounted knight astride it with lance raised to the heavens. The steed's invisible hooves came down with a thunderous crack on the stone floor of the room, followed by a shuffling canter in a half circle as it decided which of us to charge, which didn't take long.

Me.

Of course.

"Thanks for pointing me out to the dead guy on the horse, Connor," I called out. "You're a real pal."

"Think nothing of it," Connor said, stepping further back from me. "Just trying to vest you with the authority of your station. Try not to die. Think of the paperwork it would cause me."

Whether he was kidding or not, I welcomed the distraction of his banter in the heat of the battle. A little levity went a long way in our line of work, if only for sanity's sake.

"I know death is always an option," I said, not sure which way I should dodge, "but I never considered jousting as the way I go out."

The armored steed trotted in place for a moment, invisible legs working behind the armor strapped to them. The knight upon it spurred his mount forward with the metallic clank of his heels. Like a terrifying medieval tank, it charged forward at a breakneck pace. Sheer fright overtook me, but luckily the first rule drilled into me during Other Division training kicked in.

When in doubt, run.

I turned and my legs pistoned into action, carrying me down the length of the hall, the space so massive that I could really give it my all as I tore off. Faster and faster I pushed myself, legs burning, but with every step the sound of the charge grew ever closer. I didn't dare chance a look back. All I could hope for was to keep going to the end of the hall. By then it would be too late for my foe to course correct, overcommitting the horse's hefty weight to forward momentum.

I threw myself against the wall in front of me, spinning around at the last second so my back took the blow, pain exploding across my shoulders.

The knight loomed even closer than I had imagined, leaving me little time to react. My pulse rose in my throat as if my heart were trying to escape. With few options in mind or at hand, I gave a quick, desperate roll to my right, crouching myself as tightly as I could in the corner of the room.

The point of the lance pierced the wall where I had stood nanoseconds ago, sticking there like a giant dart as the horse and knight plowed hopelessly into the wall itself. The suit of armor remained intact, collapsing to the floor like a rag doll, but the components of the steed's armor did not, and flew off in every direction like so much shrapnel from a war movie. With barely time to take the scene in, I raised my arms just as a large piece of the barding slammed into me, and I tumbled back onto the pile of disassembled horse armor behind me.

"You okay, kid?" Connor called out from the far side of the room.

"Think so," I said as I tried to right myself, and checked for damage while stumbling my way noisily out of the piled pieces. "Nothing *feels* broken, if we're talking bones. Only thing really hurt is maybe my pride. That was a bit less than graceful."

"Grace is overrated," Connor said, walking over and offering a hand to help me out of the armor at my feet. "You're alive. I'd call that a win."

Clanking arose behind me, the sound like that of a car crashing. Pieces of the now-lifeless horse armor were being shoved aside from beneath as the dismounted knight rose from the pile. A weary sigh escaped my lips and I turned back to Connor, looking for some guidance.

"Hey, mentor," I said. "Start menting!"

"That's not a word," he said, and reached into his trench coat, searching within. His hand emerged a moment later with a stoppered vial in it. Pulling out its top, he wound up like a pitcher on the mound and aimed directly where I stood.

"Get down!" he shouted.

Even though it meant throwing myself back onto the pile of armor, I did as Connor instructed. As the vial lobbed overhead and hit its target, the smell of patchouli filled my nostrils, gagging me as a noxious brown cloud spread out and swirled up around the figure of the knight. Once enveloped, the creature struggled against the invisible confines of the containment cloud, but his efforts were in vain.

Connor gestured toward the containment cloud. "Care to do the honors?"

"Batter up," I said with a nod, and stood, pulling the retractable bat from my belt. I keyed my password sequence into its button pad and it *snickted* to extension, assuming the size and shape of a full-sized bat. I cocked it back into a stance Babe Ruth would have been proud of, and swung for the fences at our captured foe. The bat hit with a clatter, then went through the figure. The knight came apart on impact, his helm rolling across the great hall like a disturbing runaway gutter ball at a bowling alley.

"Huh!" I said, and gestured at his scattered but clearly empty pieces. "Nobody home."

"Don't be too sure," Connor said, pointing past me.

I turned, hoping the armor wasn't reassembling itself, which, to my relief, it wasn't. In fact, everything looked normal behind me, much of the earlier chaos having died down.

That was, until I noticed the walls. Subtle at first, they shivered with movement as the weapons along them shook and clanged, struggling to break free from their mountings. Pops and snaps of metal tearing free from the stone echoed throughout the great hall, drifts of powdered castle walls wafting down onto the floor.

"I suggest we find less dangerous quarters," Connor said as he took off, but not before grabbing my arm and dragging me along behind him.

Blades and blunt instruments tore free and shot after us. I pulled free from my mentor's grip, fell in step next to him, and bolted past. *Score one for youth!*

Scanning the great hall, I changed my course. Most of the doorways leading out were arched, but only one housed heavy wooden doors, and that was now my new target. Connor followed as I ran for it, ducking and lurching out of harm's way as various weapons flew through the air after us.

Once through the open doors, it took all my strength of will to *not* slam them shut before Connor caught up, even more so with the variety of deadly projectiles chasing after him. I stood at the ready, watching as Connor—trench coat flapping out behind him like a superhero's cape—ran, dove, and slid into the room. Several of the pursuant weapons shot overhead, thunking into the heavy doors as I slammed them shut.

I turned and threw my weight against it to hold them closed, while Connor scrambled to his feet.

"Might want to rethink that, kid," he said.

The doors were thick, but *how* thick I hadn't been sure, and, as if to prove Connor's point, a dull pain pushed against my back at a singular point. Pulling away, I spun, craning my neck to see the leather of my jacket torn where it had acted as armor, stopping a blade tip that now poked through the door.

I spread my arms wide and pressed my hands against the door, cautious of any other blades that might work their way through.

Connor joined me, taking over one of the doors.

"We need answers," he said. "Now! Trying to contain one of those spirits didn't lessen our problem."

The sounds of attack on the door increased, as if a thousand hands were pounding away at it.

"The Sedgwick family is *pissed*," he continued. "And if we can't wrap our minds around the why of it, we stand little chance of releasing them. So, gloves off, Simon."

In my haste to exit the great hall, I hadn't taken in my new surroundings. As I turned, brightness blinded me. The noonday sun and the New York skyline greeted me through great glass walls that made up a sizable open atrium. Glass shelves lined every wall all the way to the highest heights of the ceiling. On every last one of them were hundreds of tiny glass animals of every size and color.

A single animal, I realized.

Unicorns.

Connor whistled, taking in the collection from where he held the door shut. "Jesus. This isn't just the last unicorn; this is *all* the unicorns. Creepy."

"No," I said, something familiar sparking inside of me that I couldn't quite place. "This is an obsession. A true collection."

I needed to know more, and before I had completed the thought, my gloves were off. Every piece had a distinct look, an odd charm all its own, but it took no time to spot the most prized item. A raised pedestal at the center of the atrium held a piece that clearly occupied a place of honor. I approached it, my hand not even touching it yet, and I could already feel the crackle of psychometric power radiating from it.

I scooped it up. Rearing up in motionless beauty, the carved glass figure, its mane and tail awhirl in flowing waves, was coursing with exquisite action.

I focused on the unicorn in my hand, and the world around me fell away as my mind's eye flooded once again with the images of another.

I expected to see the family Sedgwick, but instead flashes of a lonely blond girl filled my brain, a mix of shyness with the childish enthusiasm of a ten-year-old. Books of fantasy lined the shelves of a vast library I had yet to see inside this castle, all of them lovingly pored over through the years by this girl. The exuberance of her love for the fantastical shone out into every aspect of her life—images of her costumed as elves, knights, and wizards flew through my mind's eye, the girl taking on all the roles from those fantastical tales.

The vision shifted into a fast-forward of the young woman's life. She aged from a girl into a teenager, but this love of hers never waned, not even when trying to socialize herself into a public-school setting. Instead, her fixation only drew stares and whispered insults that snaked their way into her ears.

Hagetha, they called the young Agatha Sedgwick, a name not welcomed, a dark spike in an otherwise beautiful, fragile heart.

A blackness filled her, a slow and silent rage wormed its way into her, her family choosing to educate her at home away from the taunts and jeers, making this only child more and more the shut-in, her only lonely solace taking form in her collection of glass, one of the few things she allowed herself to find joy in. Here, in her menagerie of unicorns, there was a comfort, and as I watched through the vision as she aged into an old woman, her collection grew, but so too did her loneliness.

The bittersweet sorrow of her soul filled my own heart with a great and swelling pain.

As the psychometric vision died, the profound pain didn't, and I awoke experiencing what riding a mechanical bull must feel like—or a real bull, for that matter. My very being seemed stuck in my own personal earthquake as I struggled to shake off my postvision haze, unable to fathom just what the hell was going on around me.

It was possible—as my mind cleared a bit—that it might have something to do with the long glass spear sticking out of my chest.

My heart raced as I feared being run clean through, but the very fact that my heart could race was proof positive that I probably hadn't been.

I had been impaled, though, but only through the soft area of my jacket, in the space between my torso and underarm.

><<

I pulled it out and slumped to the floor. Already I was fishing for the Life Savers in my pockets, cramming half a roll in my mouth at a time to counter my shaking dizziness.

Somewhere off behind me the crash of breaking glass filled my ears over and over while I waited for my sugar to rise. I managed to roll myself over like an infant, only to discover Connor holding my bat at the ready and going toe to hoof with what had impaled me.

Most of the shelves in the atrium were now bare, their contents joined together in one multicolored, one-horned creature that was larger than life.

"Great," I managed to croak out. "No one told me we'd be dealing with enchanted battle unicorns."

"Unicorns aren't so cute now, are they?" Connor called out, bringing my bat down on it. A section of the creature's neck tore off, its component pieces flying away. Even as they hit the floor, the unicorn's neck started to re-form, many of the damaged pieces flowing back to rejoin the creature.

"Stop hitting it!" I shouted after a quick assessment. "You're only giving it more broken and jagged pieces to jab at us with."

"So, what?" Connor asked, annoyed. "We just let family Sedgwick run us through with their pet?"

Focusing on what I had psychometrically seen and all I had felt from the vision, I tried to piece together the puzzle of Agatha Sedgwick from what I knew.

"It's not the whole family," I said. "It's just one person, and I don't think she's trying to kill us."

Connor backed away from the glass creature and handed my bat back to me as he helped me up off the floor, jabbing a finger at the torn hole in my jacket.

"You sure about that, kid?"

He let go and started off across the atrium, giving the glass monstrosity more than a single target to choose from.

I nodded. "I think so," I said. "I think we're dealing only with the most recently deceased, Agatha Sedgwick. Killing us is just sort of an inadvertent by-product of her intent."

Connor looked back to me with both eyebrows raised. "Meaning?"

"I think she's throwing a tantrum. It's just a mix of the rage, frustration, and confusion she felt from her life."

"That might make some sort of sense," Connor said. The unicorn turned its newly re-formed horn in his direction. "Lingering feelings from the living can get a bit amplified after death. Ghosts have a tendency to go over the top. The question is, What's she so angry about?"

The horn jabbed at Connor. He shrugged his trench coat off his shoulders and brandished it at the unicorn like some sort of urban matador.

"Whatever its motivation," he continued, "it's too pissed off for me to contain it or ghost-whisper it out of crazy time."

Legs still shaking, I moved toward the creature. Fighting every instinct I had to flee, I tapped my bat on the tiled floor.

"Hey!" I shouted, hoping to draw the creature's attention. When it didn't respond, I chose a different tack. "Hey, *Hagetha*."

It whirled around so hard that pieces flew from its formidable form. The cold, dead eyes of the creature found me as it briskly stomped its way across the room toward me. I raised my bat, simply to have something between the two of us to calm my nerves.

"That's what they called you, isn't it?" I asked. "Those who mocked you."

The creature stopped, hesitating as it shuffled in place with a great grinding of glass.

"That was *life*, Agatha," I said. "And that time is over. No one can hurt you now."

The glass unicorn cocked its head at me and, lowering its horn in my direction, the tip catching the very end of my extended bat, slowly circled the whole of it as if we were fencing and she were doing an envelopment.

"I understand you," I said. "I really do. I get it."

I raced the words out as fast as I could. Hopefully, I could finish before the creature changed its mind and decided to ram its stabby end through me.

"I get you," I said to her. "Because I'm your kind. I've spent my life alone, always on the outside." I held my hand out to the creature. Moving with care, it inched closer to my touch, and just as the crackle of my power began to kick in, I pulled my hand back. "I've seen your life, Agatha. I know your loneliness. This 'gift' of mine has been more a curse than a blessing. It's who I am, and I can barely control it. It's done nothing but ruin every relationship I've ever tried to have. Every person I've ever tried to get close to has had their secret histories revealed to me almost against my will. I *know* awkward. If my life's been anything, it has been nothing but."

I slid my gloves back on and stepped toward the massive glass animal.

"They called you Hagetha," I said, running my gloved hand down the creature's neck. It pressed back against me gently. "Just like they called me a criminal. But I'm more than a word. One word does not define me, nor does it define you. Let your spirit rest, Agatha. Let yourself go. There will be a better place, where you'll be among your kind. Whatever there is out there, I *have* to believe it is a better world than this, one filled with like-minded souls who love what you love, with just as much passion and with the openness that you craved in life. Me? I've found my tribe." I looked to Connor, who watched me in stunned silence. "My partner here and the people we work for are the kind who can help me. You can be with yours too."

Connor turned away. Maybe he felt a little bad about browbeating me as a criminal earlier, but I wasn't worried about what he thought at the moment. This was about Agatha.

I dropped my hand from the unicorn's neck and picked up the original unicorn I had scooped up earlier. I hesitated as I watched the light of day shine through it. It would be easy enough to simply slip it into my pocket—a memento of this kindred spirit's soul—but after lingering a moment longer on it, I strode across the atrium and returned it to the pedestal at the center of the room.

"Go," I said again. "It will be better. It *has* to be."

The piecemeal creature stood to its fullest height, an impressive display of pride. Sunlight shone through it like a prism, filling the room with a thousand shafts of multicolored light going off in every direction. Then, one by one, the menagerie came apart, its pieces falling to the ground.

Glass tinkled like chimes on the wind, a euphoric sound, but as the last of them joined the rest in the pile on the floor, a bittersweet ache filled my heart.

I stood in silence before Connor edged toward the pile, gently prodding it with the tip of his shoe.

"This house is clean," Connor said, in one the worst little-old-lady-from-*Poltergeist* impressions I had ever heard. "Good job, kid. You reminded me that this isn't just about busting ghosts. Didn't know you felt so strongly about a heaven."

I shrugged. "I don't know if I do," I said, "but I know there has to be somewhere better to go for a spirit like her."

Connor nodded, then gestured toward the doors, pulling one of them open to reveal swords, spears, and knives sticking out of it like pins from a cushion.

"Let's hope so, kid," he said.

I gave the broken menagerie one last, lingering look, tried to settle my soul, and headed out the doors. "So where *do* they go?"

Connor shrugged as he stepped into the quiet of the great hall. "We're bound to find out," he said. "And being Other Division, probably sooner rather than later."

"At least we won't die from paperwork on this one," I said, trying to shake off my melancholy mood.

I knew there was clear proof of hope for me and my powers, a chance to fit, to redeem myself, to be less of an outsider. But what the hell did I know of the afterlife I had promised Agatha?

"Score one for freelancing," Connor said.

I stopped in the middle of the great hall. "But seriously . . . Where do we go?"

"The poet Robert Louis Stevenson once said 'To travel hopefully is a better thing than to arrive,'" Connor said, leaving me behind as he headed toward the doors leading out. "The version of the great ever-after you sold Agatha on sounded nice to me. What's wrong with that one?"

"But what's the *real* answer?"

"Does it matter?" He turned back, some of that old, familiar annoyance on his face again. "Like I said, we'll find out soon enough. The lifes pan of the average Department of Extraordinary Affairs agent is at least seven years shorter than that of the average New Yorker."

He turned and walked off. I sighed, starting after him, hoping I'd fare better than the average agent, if only to prove to him that, like Agatha, I was not defined by one word, that there was a chance for me to find peace among my own.

Although looking at the rampant destruction of art, armor, and tapestries all around me, I wanted to cry.

"Sometimes I miss my life of crime," I muttered to myself, and headed off after Connor.

I guess the things we were—the things we *are*—never truly die. I had to believe it, and I held to the tiny winged hope that I had sent the last occupant of this castle to a place where it was true. If not for her sake, then at least for mine.

PEACOCK IN HELL

by Kat Richardson

They'd fled into a cul-de-sac where a wall built of eternally tormented bodies of the damned moaned and writhed on three sides, rising toward the billowing fire of the sky for at least thirty meters. Peacock turned back with her knives at the ready, but the only thing still behind her was Lennie Redmayne. He was as dark skinned and blood covered as any hellhound, but he was the spoils, not the spoiler. She flicked smoking ichor off her bane-forged blades, and they gave off an eerie green glow before she sheathed them. Then she pushed against the wall to test its stability.

The wall shrieked from all its mouths as she touched it. Redmayne jumped and spun in panic, his thin dreadlocks swinging and spattering gore against the rampart and Peacock. "The bloody hell is *that*?" he croaked. His voice hadn't recovered much yet—years of screaming in agony weren't repaired in an hour.

"Lost souls," Peacock replied. "Just the garden variety—nothing fancy like you. Pile up like garbage here." She ignored the blood now streaking her messily cropped blond hair and disappearing into the surface of her red leather garments as she studied the barrier for a moment. "We'll have to climb."

Redmayne goggled at her. "Climb . . . that? It's undead bodies as far as the eye can see!"

Peacock shrugged. "It'll be a little slippery, but there're plenty of handholds. Not too bad, unless you put your hands or feet in their mouths—that could get messy."

"Fucking hell," Redmayne muttered.

"Where else did you think you were?"

"Smartarse." He was healing quickly—his voice more South London gutter and less advanced case of throat cancer now.

Peacock grinned. "Sometimes. Up you go," she added, and crouched, offering Redmayne a leg up. He was a few years older and nearly a head taller, but he was thin and couldn't weigh much in his current condition, though physics didn't always function normally here.

He glanced between her and the wall with his singed eyebrows raised in horrified bemusement. "Me?"

"Unless you'd rather be tail-end Charlie. We stay down here, those hellspawn *will* find us. I don't see any other way out that doesn't put us back where we came from. Frankly, I prefer the climb."

"Bugger," Redmayne grumbled, and put his bare foot into her open hands.

His naked and savaged groin was uncomfortably close. Peacock closed her eyes and turned her head aside. "Don't get any idea that I'm enjoying this," she said as she hefted him upward with a mild grunt. "The view's not spectacular."

"Sod off." He sank his hands and off-side foot into the wall's bleeding flesh. "It in't you who's had his skin peeled off in strips every day for eternity."

"Don't be melodramatic. It's only been eight years."

"I'd tell you to go to hell, but as we're already here . . ."

She chuckled as she pulled the crimson hood over her light-colored hair and then scrambled up below him. "Think brutal thoughts, Redmayne—it keeps *me* going."

"I am. I'm just thinking 'em out loud."

Peacock rolled her eyes.

The damned shifted and howled as Peacock and Redmayne hauled themselves upward until the noise became background. They climbed for unmarked hours wrapped in the stink of blood and bones and brimstone. Their motions became mechanical—tug from one hand- or foothold, sink into the next, and on and up, on and up. . . .

Teeth bit into Peacock's foot, and she jerked free to drive her boot heel into the dead thing's head. As she glanced down, Redmayne's foot flailed past her face. She jammed her toe into the wall, anchored herself deep in unseen flesh and bones with one hand, and looked up. "Careful," she said while grabbing his loose heel with her free hand. "You don't want to fall now." She pulled in tight against the grotesque wall to keep her hold and didn't flinch as teeth gnawed at her leathers.

"What? You think it would hurt? I'm fucking dead, mate."

She held steady until he got his foot planted in the grim cliff again; then she pulled loose from the hungry dead and continued upward. "You know that there's worse can happen. Only hellspawn and lords can die here—for fairly weird definitions of 'die,' that is."

"And you know this how, Miss Peacock?"

"I've been here before."

"You're dead?"

"At least mostly dead—pretty much the only way to get here."

She remembered falling. She even remembered hitting the ground, though some other details were fuzzy now.

Run . . . Just run like hell. *She'd bolted across the rooftop, vaulting the vents and dodging behind any available cover.* They're back there and gaining.

She'd glanced over her shoulder as she'd run and spotted the men behind her. Holy shit . . . That can't be. . . . *Her recollection was foggy, but the roof's edge had been coming up and she'd burst desperately for it. She'd dug her toes into the graveled surface and pushed off. . . .*

But she'd stumbled, or the parapet was slippery and she'd launched wrong. She'd flailed and smashed against the next building with her full force. Pain bloomed in her chest and back. Then she'd slid down. . . .

The giant terra-cotta faces around the upper story had projected her out into empty air, and she'd tumbled down without control. Only three stories, but enough to smash her like a ripe plum.

"Answers how you got here, but not why."

Peacock shook off her memory. "What?" she asked.

Redmayne kept climbing, but called down, "I'm asking why *you*, in particular, are pulling *my* raggedy arse out of Hell."

"Because Peter Fiore *wanted* you filched out of Hell, which would take the best thief in the business. And that's me."

"You? Work for that bastard?"

"Whether I like it or not."

"He heads up the Directorate of Occult Incursion Control now, yeah?"

"Thaumaturge in Chief," Peacock replied. "But that begs the question: What does *he* want with *you*?"

Redmayne scoffed. "Couldn't just call him Lord High Inquisitor, could they? Right. So . . . I'm an artificer—was at any rate. Worked with him at DOIC back in the day."

"Jesus . . ."

"Watch it."

"Things must be worse than I thought if he's fishing guys like you up from the pit."

"*Guy* like me—singular. No more left, living or dead. That's my 'get out of Hell free' card."

"Free I can't manage—Fiore owns me," she added, bitterly. "I'm taking you straight to him as soon as we're on the other side."

"Well, that's proper fucked, in't it?"

"Proper as it comes."

They climbed in silence a while.

"Hey, you got any other name?"

"Peacock."

"A first name, wisearse."

"Why do you want to know?" she asked.

"As you're half-dead and I'm all dead, and we've both worked with Peter Fiore, I was thinking we might have a few other things in common. I'll trade you a bit of magical blackmail for it."

"I already know your first name, so that's not gonna wash."

"Nah, this is better—secret about me no one but me mum knows. C'mon . . . it's worth it. I promise."

Peacock considered the offer for a couple of meters. "You ever call me by it, I'll shove you back down this cliff and let you make your own way up."

"Deal."

"It's Emily Anne."

"Peacock suits you better. I'm Lennie."

"Yeah, I know."

>─<

"Lennie Redmayne must be retrieved. I can't send an army into the Nether to get him, so it'll have to be done by stealth. Which is exactly the sort of job I hired you for."

"One of which got me killed." Peacock looked at him askance. "Thanks for the reminder."

Peter Fiore was a big guy, bald and white-bearded, and he was good at intimidation, but Peacock wasn't having any. Once you've been dead, your shit-taking limit drops way down, even with master mages.

Fiore narrowed his cold gray eyes at her. "Don't blame me for your mistakes. I had to scrape you off a sidewalk, Peacock, so I don't see where you have much cause to complain. I gave you that power—"

"I already had the veil talent. That's why I'm the best thief in the country."

"Best in the *worlds*, now," Fiore added. "And that you *do* owe to me. Along with the fact that you're up and breathing."

Peacock snorted. "Breathing . . . in a manner of speaking."

Fiore shook his head. "Don't get bitter, Emily. Would you rather I'd abandoned your broken body in that alley? I don't leave my assets behind—even if I have to raise them from the dead."

"Asset." *You smug bastard.* Time to change the subject, before she gave into her continual urge to throat-punch him. "This Redmayne—he's one of yours?"

"One of *us*," Fiore corrected, and glanced away. He wasn't capable of embarrassment, so it *might* have been remorse. "And yes, he was."

"I notice you didn't raise *him* from the dead, O mighty necromancer."

He cast a glare back at her. "I didn't have that option."

"What's so important about him that I have to go to Hell to get him back?"

"That's not something I can tell you. You know how this works.

Just remember: There's a reason he is where he is and you can't trust what the damned tell you."

Peacock rolled her eyes. *Like we aren't* all *damned.* Fiore was laying it on thick, but she couldn't refuse; he was the only person who had the literal power of life and death over her and, bitching aside, she'd rather have the former than the latter, even if it required putting up with Fiore.

"All right, I'll go get him. Where am I gonna find your tortured soul? Hell's a big place."

"Are you familiar with Dante?"

"Not really."

"Good, because he only got close."

>—×—<

"Is this secret what got you sent down here?" Peacock asked.

"No, I— Oi! I think we made it!" Redmayne kicked and disappeared over the cliff top, as if he were swimming away into the cinder and flame of Hell's sky. Then he choked back a scream.

Something nasty up there . . . Peacock hauled herself over the last of the damned and onto the upper surface. Her left palm sizzled on something hot, but there was no place else to put her hands. She sucked her breath through her teeth and endured the searing until she'd cleared the drop-off. Then she got to her feet and searched for Redmayne.

Beyond the crumbling edge, the land was as black and gritty as an ancient stovetop. Intense heat and the reek of burning iron rose from it. Peacock spotted Redmayne a few meters away. He whimpered in pain as he stumbled toward a line of low gray mounds and scattered rubble nearby, leaving burned footprints on the dark surface. Peacock's leathers and boots smoked as she jogged forward and grabbed him. She wasn't strong enough to carry him, but she could tug one of his arms over her shoulders and get him to cooler ground quicker.

She dumped him on rotting stone in the shadowed slope of a chalky mound. Then she crouched near him and studied the area.

Redmayne crawled away from the heat of the iron ground and huddled on his backside, watching her. "Your cheek's burnt," he said.

Peacock held up her palms without turning her attention. "Yeah. These, too," she said. "But not as bad as you. I think we've got a little breathing room now, so long as nothing flies by and spots us before we're healed up enough to move."

Satisfied with what she saw, Peacock sat back against the stones and turned to Redmayne. "How are you doing on that score?"

He glanced down at himself. "Major bits are coming along, but the surface is still a bit tatty. Burns didn't help."

Peacock just nodded.

"You think we're safe? I mean . . . don't you think that outfit stands out a bit?"

"Have you noticed the color scheme around here? We blend right in. And red's a short wavelength. The hellspawn don't see in color, so it just looks gray to them—same as most of this place. You're dark to begin with, and with those wounds you look like any other forsaken soul out here. Now, if a lord passes by, that could be a problem, but only for as long as it takes me to kill it." She paused, thinking. "Actually, that might be a good thing. Since lords aren't he or she, they just wear armor and draped cloth. You could wear the cloth like a toga or something."

Redmayne lay back against the dusty scree and closed his eyes. "Well, there's a silver lining to everything, in't there?"

Peacock chuckled.

"Glad someone's finding humor in this," Redmayne grumbled.

"So far, you're the most amusing thing I've ever stolen. And you owe me a secret."

"Yeah, I do. First I gotta ask, you work for Fiore voluntarily?"

"No. It was supposed to be one contract. It turned into . . . something else."

Redmayne looked her over and tugged thoughtfully on one of his locs. "So, the thing is . . . I got this funny talent—"

"Artificer."

"Not *just* that one," he said, and held up two fingers.

"You're bi-talented? Well, that's not so rare that I'd call it 'funny. . . .'" She trailed off as he shook his head.

"I'm a mimic," he said. "It's not something I want most people to know about. Jealous bunch, Talents. Don't like other people borrowing their stuff."

"How does it work? Clearly you don't just touch somebody and get their powers."

"Yeah, it's not that simple. There's got to be blood contact, see, and I only get a copy of the other person's magic for a little while. But it's still like having it full power, so I get the downsides just as hard. Magical Engineering doesn't play well with some talents—'specially not death and destruction. It's like coupling matter to antimatter."

"That would suck. But you haven't picked up mine, and we've certainly passed blood contact by now."

"It don't work here. No one changes in Hell—trust me, I tried. You can cast an illusion—"

"But they don't work on 'spawn or lords."

"So, you have talents."

"Just the one—I can veil—but mostly I rely on my regular skills. Best in the business."

Redmayne sat up and studied her. "A true veil, not just a light-bend?"

Peacock shrugged. "Sure. I can look like someone else or I can look like nothing at all, but it'd be a waste of energy here."

"You act like it's nothing," he said, looking astonished. "Veil's rare and can't be duplicated in any sort of artifact."

Just like an engineer—always thinking about the toys. She rolled her eyes, then glanced around and shifted her weight onto her feet again. "We'd better get moving. It's a long way to the exit."

"Something wrong?"

"Nothing specific, but you talk too much, and we've had too much grace."

"Expecting the next shoe to drop, yeah?"

Peacock nodded. "Uh-huh." She picked up a handful of incinerated stone and crumbled it. The dust stuck to her burned skin.

Redmayne winced at the sight as he crawled to his feet. "Whyn't you wear gloves or something?"

"Can't feel through gloves. Besides, all damage heals here. That's how eternal torment works—you grow back together so they can take you apart over and over."

"Yeah, I noticed."

Peacock started forward without further comment.

After a few steps, Redmayne said, "With your talent, you could lose me anytime you like."

She sighed. "Why would I come down here and pull you out of a pile of flesh-tearing hellhounds just to dump you?"

Redmayne offered a bitter smile. "It's all about the torture, in't it? And what's worse than hope?"

That was almost amusing, and she let go of half a smile. "'Spawn can't anchor a talent, so . . . what?" She drew the mental veil over herself, formless and reflective, and flickered out of view. He gaped, and she chuckled from within her illusion. "You think I'm a hell lord in disguise?"

A shadow moved over them with a thunderclap. Peacock let her talent fall away, and they both dove for cover as a lord descended. It was three or four meters tall, human in form, but winged and monstrous. The crown of Peacock's head would have barely come to its sternum if they stood toe-to-toe. The lord's incomplete black armor didn't reflect the fiery sky, and its crimson drapery flowed in the air like blood in water.

"Fucking hell," Redmayne cursed.

"Secondus," Peacock said, and drew her baneforged knives. "Could be worse. Run diagonally from its line of attack and stay out of the way."

She stood tall and faced the lord with both the eerie green blades held low. She wasn't an assassin, but she'd picked up a few tricks.

"Fugitive souls," the hell lord rumbled. It wheeled and folded its wings, rushing forward with the momentum of its fall.

Redmayne fled toward a nearby pile of rock.

Peacock ran toward the lord and ducked. She swept the blades outward as it passed over her. The knives jerked in her hands, and she dug in against the backward drag as blades cut moving flesh.

The hell lord roared and flipped a wingtip, pivoting to keep Peacock in sight as it landed. Ichor sprayed from its wounded backward knees, and it staggered left, its foot twisting a little. *Got you!* Peacock danced aside. The lord swiped at her, and she slashed. The creature jerked back a hair too late. A talon as long as her hand clattered to the iron ground and slid toward Redmayne. *Not so fucking invincible against these, are you?* The lord raised its sliced hand in surprise.

Peacock leapt at its weak side. She planted one foot hard on its injured knee and vaulted upward. She reversed the near blade and shoved it toward the lord's armpit with a downward swing. The creature twisted and swept its elbow down, knocking Peacock aside.

She rolled across the searing ground as the hell lord screamed; then she flipped to her feet and faced it. Her blade stuck out below the mark, sunk only half its length into the lord's side. Smoking ichor poured from the wound, but the monster was still on its feet.

Peacock's cheek was blistered from the heat, and her remaining blade steamed with gore. She spotted Redmayne scuttling onto the burned earth to snatch up the severed claw. "Leave it, you idiot!" she yelled. *Gonna be the hard way, I guess.* "Back me!"

The lord turned toward Redmayne, and Peacock threw herself forward. The creature whirled around, snapping out a wing with taloned tips that raked across her chest and throat.

The blow spun Peacock into the air, and blood fanned from the slash across her neck. She hit the ground and sprawled onto her back in a twisted heap, carmine blood running across the black plain in wide swaths. The wounded hell lord bounded toward her. Redmayne started after it with the dismembered claw clutched in his hands.

Her memory was much more clear now: She had glanced over her shoulder as the roof edge loomed, and maybe it was the action or maybe it was the sight of familiar faces that had made her miscalculate the leap. . . .

But Peacock figured it was the bullet that had been shot into her back.

The lord bent unsteadily over Peacock, laughing in spite of its running wounds. It drew back its uninjured hand to strike.

Redmayne leapt onto its back and stabbed it with its own severed claw. The talon didn't sink in deep, but it did pierce the lord's armor, and a narrow stream of ichor squirted into the air. The lord shrieked and shook out its wings to dislodge Redmayne, sending a gust of hot air booming forth.

Peacock spasmed, her head lolling and wobbling as the wound in her throat began to close. She rolled to her knees and flipped her blade upward, then lunged, shoving it hilt-deep into the hell lord's gut below the edge of its breastplate. She pushed with both hands until the pommel rang against the metal, then ripped sideways and down with the weight of her own falling body. The blade tore through the hell lord's hide to the scarlet sash that wrapped the mailed kilt around its hips. The infernal creature collapsed as its guts spilled out onto the smoking field.

Peacock lay trapped under the dead hell lord, gasping and blinking. *Damn, but it stinks.*

Redmayne danced from one burning foot to the other as he shoved the creature aside. "I'm sorry, I'm sorry," he said as Peacock wriggled free.

Her exposed skin was crisply blackened by the time she reached the nearest rocky ridge, and her leathers were badly singed. She flopped into the crumbling stone and coughed on pain and dust as her wounds closed and her skin resolved from ash to flesh. Redmayne hunched nearby with the hell lord's claw in his hand. When she caught her breath, Peacock beckoned him to her.

Redmayne crept close and bent down, and Peacock punched him in the face. "You set me up."

He landed on his back. "No!"

Peacock knelt over him. "Bullshit! You're an artificer. You knew my drawing the veil would send out a ripple. A hell lord won't attack another of its own kind without provocation. You really thought I was one of them! You figured that one would fly on by—"

"That's a bloody-minded assumption you're making, sunshine."

"It was a lousy trick to pull on me, *sunshine*," Peacock spat back. "I ought to leave you here to scream your guts out for the rest of eternity!"

Redmayne scowled. "Fiore wouldn't like that."

"Don't you lecture *me* on what that scheming bastard would or wouldn't— Oh . . . damn it all," she added, winding down in disgust. "I need to get you out of here, or I'll never get a shot at him." She rested on her heels.

Redmayne struggled to sit up. "Who? Fiore? He's betrayed you, hasn't he? Bloody good at that, he is."

She peered at him. "He screwed you over, too."

Redmayne avoided her gaze. "Let's say we didn't part friends."

She studied at him a minute or so longer and then sat down, crushing handfuls of fragile, baked stone and rubbing the dust into her oozing skin.

"Why d'you do that?" Redmayne asked as he watched her intently. He was less eviscerated, but still a bit flayed and gnawed.

"I don't like to drip. And, crazy as it sounds, it seems to speed up healing. You could use a little yourself."

"Should take some out of here with us, then," he said, but he didn't follow her example.

"It's tricky getting native things out of Hell. You're going to have to leave that." She pointed at the claw.

"Hah! You barmy? This, my stealthy friend, is pure artifact gold and worth what it took to get it." He waved the talon. "I'd rather stay here and dodge hellspawn than leave it behind."

"Seriously?"

"I'd take my chances," he replied, his expression grim.

"Why?"

He gave her an odd smile. "You ever seen one of these things in the breathing world?"

"No."

"Useful, these are—at least if you're someone like me. Almost indestructible out in the world, and, since it's hellbound, it has a positive yen to return from whence it came, or send other things in its place."

"Literally?" she asked. Redmayne nodded. Peacock glanced at the gutted hell lord and shuddered. "Good thing it's dead."

"Who says they stay dead?" Redmayne asked.

"I jammed a foot of baneforged steel into its guts. I've never seen anything get up from that."

"How many lords have you killed?"

"That makes two—but I admit I didn't stick around the last time."

Redmayne's smile was sly.

Peacock scowled at him and growled, "There goes my exit plan."

"You really had one?"

"Of course. I never go in without having at least two exits. But neither of my escape routes accounted for bringing anything along besides you and me. Even my blades were gonna stay behind."

"There's other doors between the worlds, *if* we can find one down here."

"It'll have to be a wide one, which means the hellborn probably already know about it. I'll have to check the map," Peacock said, and dug into a pocket hidden under one of her scabbards. She drew out a wisp of gauze that gleamed with tiny points of colored light.

Redmayne gaped at her. "You have the Liminal Map?"

"I have *part* of the map. I stole it."

"You're a fly one."

"I'm a thief."

"Where'd you enter?"

"New Straitsville, Ohio. There's a coal mine that's been burning there for more than a hundred years. Closest superposition to where I found you. Easy in, but it's a flesh lock on the way out. Now shut up and let me look—this thing's hard to see."

Redmayne put out his hand. "Let me."

Peacock wasn't sure she could trust him, but he couldn't get far without her—and the hell lord's clothes—so she handed over the bit of ethereal fabric.

"This looks familiar." He glanced down at his still-ragged body. "That'll do." He laid the map against a strip of raw flesh on his chest. The map dissolved, and Redmayne sucked his breath through clenched teeth.

"What the—" Peacock started.

"Hang on," he gasped. "It's coming. . . ."

The map gleamed into sight as a tattoo of living silver sparked with tiny gems. It was as clear as printing, and when Redmayne moved, it adjusted its north by his position.

"Well, fuck me," Peacock murmured.

"Likes a bit of flesh and blood, this thing."

She grinned. "How'd you know?"

Redmayne cocked a sarcastic eyebrow. "Artificer. How'd you think?"

"You made this map?"

He scoffed. "Nah. Nobody *made* it. Compiled over centuries. Happens, though, that I did work on this bit right here," he said, and poked one glittering portal marker. "Never used it, but should be a good door—unless a lot more has changed than I imagined."

><-<

The broad portal was closer than Peacock had feared and less protected. The Netherworld was riddled with caves here, and she crouched with Redmayne in the mouth of one while studying the landscape.

"You sure this is right?" she asked.

"Course it's right. The map can't lie, and we're"—he pushed aside the tunic they'd made from the dead lord's blood-red draperies and pointed at the bright star that seemed to shine on his chest—"right here. Practically on top of it."

Redmayne had bound his feet with more cloth and made a sort of pack from armor parts; he'd filled it with the lord's claw and other things he deemed useful. While he'd never pass as a lord on visual inspection, he certainly smelled like Hell.

Peacock shook her head. "There's no sign of a guard, aside from a couple of wandering 'spawn, or that the portal's in use at all. I can't even see it."

"It's there. Trust me." He squinted in pain. "This little bugger burns."

"It's just . . . something's funny. You're certain?"

Redmayne heaved an exasperated sigh. "Look, mate, I want out of Hell as much as you do. I count m'self bloody lucky it's you got sent to retrieve me, and I'm not gonna ditch you. I used to be on the side of the angels, and Fiore always thought whatever he did was justified if it kept the darkness back, but it's not. Some things are evil, simple as that. It's no accident I'm down here—I damned m'self. I did things and knew I'd end right here—"

Peacock raised a hand. "Hush! There, by that steam fissure in the hillside, there's a gleam," she whispered. "See where that 'spawn's digging?"

"Yeah. That's the liminal point. It's a transverse."

"A what?"

"Passes through Limbo and changes orientation. Nasty trip, but it'll get us out in one piece, and the lower orders of hellborn can't follow. Must be a bit of odd there."

"Probably why that 'spawn's so interested. Have to get rid of it before it attracts attention." She checked position of all the 'spawn in view. "All right. You need to be close, so follow me until I turn, then wait."

"Wait—" he started.

She ignored him and slipped out into the shadow.

She tucked tight and ran along the wall's base. She avoided the hellspawn's sight until she reached its blind spot. Then she turned sharply, keeping directly behind the creature, and dashed across the open space toward it and the crevice. She spotted a few more 'spawn wandering farther out on the plain where it flattened to hot iron. They might not see her, but they could hear and smell better than any dog. They'd come running if the hellspawn by the portal howled.

Peacock timed her leap and came down on the hellspawn's back with one blade out, sweeping forward and under its elongated jaw. She sliced through its throat before it could make a sound and fell on top of it.

She breathed a long sigh of relief and glanced back. Redmayne was right where she'd told him to be. She waved him forward and turned her attention to the other 'spawn. They hadn't turned toward the rock face. At least not yet.

Redmayne tiptoed a path to her side and crouched. She reached for the portal's gleam, and he snatched her hand away. "No. We're not done here."

Peacock growled at him.

He released her hand. "Tried to tell you earlier. Soon's we're through that door, things change. You have to cut this bit of the map out of me chest first. It'll want to stay there ever after otherwise, and I'd not like that."

She was appalled. "You're kidding."

"Wish I were. Now, quick, before that lot takes note of us."

"Have you got anything sharp and stabbity in that pack?" she asked.

"Whyn't you use your knife?"

"Baneforged. Wounds don't heal."

"Right. Bugger."

Redmayne unslung the pack and rummaged through it until he found a sharp bit of armor scale. He handed it over to Peacock and cast a nervous glance toward the hellspawn. "Just nick the edge and tear it out. That'll have to do."

Peacock winced. "That's gonna hurt."

"No doubt."

She'd been able to hear him from a long distance before she'd found him. "We'd better be ready to jump," she said.

"Put your back to the cleft—that'll be easiest."

She turned, and the portal leaked a cold wind along her shoulders. Redmayne gripped his pack with both hands, squeezed his eyes shut, and grimaced in anticipation. He was silent as she sliced the edge of the Liminal Map free and caught it in her fingers. She yanked.

Redmayne shrieked, arching in agony.

The hellspawn turned as a body and raced toward them, raising a clatter on the iron ground like a hailstorm. Something roared and Peacock shot a glance toward it. Clouds seemed to boil both overhead and across the searing plain. Monstrous faces resolved from the fiery sky and rushed into shape as they fell upon the two fugitives. Lords and hellspawn by the hundreds.

She threw herself back against the portal.

It resisted.

"Shit. Redmayne—"

He lurched forward, the pack falling into her lap as he bowed over her and thrust his hands into the rift. Blood spattered and ran onto her face. Amid the howls of incoming hellborn, she could barely hear him spit out a word that shook the rock face behind her.

They fell though the portal and the screams of Hell's fury cut short in suffocating silence. Redmayne twisted and caught one hand in the closing portal.

><—<

Limbo was a luminous gray nothingness. Two streaks of light— one red, one gold—showed in Peacock's vision as she glanced side to side.

"D'you hear that?" Redmayne asked.

"I don't hear anything."

Redmayne flickered as he crouched beside the thin red line. "Bloody hell. Fiore, you bastard," he whispered. His voice was hoarse and trembling.

"Holy crap, Redmayne," Peacock muttered. "What are you doing?"

"Bleeding and holding on."

She reached for the infernal rocks in Redmayne's pack. "You're not gonna heal like you do in Hell."

"Don't!" He slapped her hand aside. "We've only got minutes before we're back in the lion's den. Could you put a finger here? Any one will do perfectly fine."

Peacock flipped him the bird, and he shoved her hand into the fiery light. It burned against her flesh and seemed to gnaw on her digit.

"For the love of everything, don't move," Redmayne said. "Open your suit and give me one of your blades."

"Over your dead body."

Redmayne snorted. "Later, mate. Look, I know these are the worst of circumstances, but you have got to trust me. Fiore's a right bastard, and he doesn't mean either of us any good. You don't imagine he's dragging me back to play tiddlywinks, do you?"

"No."

"Then listen. Back in the day, I didn't just work with Fiore; I was his boss. The ambitious little prick didn't like that, and had plans to put me under his boot same as you are. We needed a necromancer and I couldn't get rid of him, so I damned m'self, and took a hard way down so he couldn't drag me back by blood and fire. With my funny talent, you can imagine how that would have gone. Fiore wants to make this homecoming hurt, and I've a mind to deny him that pleasure, but Limbo's the only place my plan can work. Straight truth: I need you or we're neither one of us coming up for air. So, what's it gonna be? Time's almost up."

She grinned, and Redmayne shivered at the sight. "Oh, I'm in."

><><

The carmine light whirled away and she tumbled through the nothing. They were torn apart, tossed, and spat out.

Peacock lurched into a smoking cavern and sprawled on the floor. Both her knives, the map, and the pack's contents were scattered around her, but Redmayne was gone. She yanked up her suit zipper and gathered the junk Redmayne had collected. She didn't even consider running—there was nowhere to go that Fiore couldn't follow, except Hell itself, and she wasn't ready to return to that venue just yet. She had other things to do.

She hiked out and found a retrieval team waiting for her in the fuming bowl of a West Virginia hillside—another unending coalmine fire. And there was Redmayne, held by two goons, bound in silver and still wounded. Pallor turned his dark skin gray where it wasn't abraded or lacerated scarlet, and he was so gaunt he looked ready to shatter. But he snarled and fought every attempt to stanch his wounds until his captors gave up and left him to bleed.

"Hurt much?" she muttered, keeping clear of him.

"Like hell."

They were delivered to Fiore's office. Their escort had already patted her down and confiscated her knives as well as the pack. *At least he didn't make me undress, the creep.* He marched them to the desk where Fiore stood, handed over the pack, and left. The soundproof door shushed closed behind him.

Fiore smiled. "Nice job, Em—bit slow, but no harm done." He turned his attention to Redmayne. "Welcome back, Lennie."

"Fiore, you blackhearted, murdering sod." He didn't even sound angry.

"Oh, come on, Redmayne. You were never really director material, talent or not. And it was so good of you to—"

Peacock stepped between them. "You shot me, you son of a bitch." She whipped one hand out for his throat.

Fiore grabbed her wrist and wrenched her hand aside. "I always knew you'd get wise." Fiore glanced at Redmayne. "Did *you* tell her?"

Redmayne scoffed weakly. The wound on his chest was still

oozing blood. "After my time, mate. Think she couldn't figure it out herself, you silly, fat bastard?"

Peacock jerked her arm against Fiore's hold and he yanked her farther sideways with a snarl. She propelled herself into the motion, jumping and sliding onto the desktop to ram her near foot into Fiore's gut. He dropped his grip, and she rolled off with a gratuitous kick toward his face as she passed. Fiore reeled back and shook his head clear.

The pack fell and spilled rocks and bits of black armor across the rug. Peacock dove and snatched the sharp bit of scale she'd used on Redmayne.

Fiore took a step and kicked her in the side, rolling her hard against the wall.

Peacock flipped and used her legs to thrust herself upright. Fiore closed the distance, and she slashed at him, back to the wall.

He snatched for her hand and caught her forearm, crushing his weight against her. He rammed her into the plaster. "Temper, temper, Emily," Fiore murmured. "I figured I'd have to scrub you soon, but with Lennie back, I won't miss you that much."

He started muttering under his breath. She felt like she was unraveling around the edges, but the necromancer would have to cut her throat to finish it, and right now his hands were busy. She rammed a knee upward. It was feeble, but enough to cut off his breath for a moment. *C'mon, Redmayne. . . .*

"You set this up from the beginning, you rat bastard," she snapped. "Hired me, killed me, drew me back up so you could run me. You sent me to Hell for your own amusement—"

From his knees, Redmayne heaved his bound weight upward against the desk, and it rocked into Fiore's back.

Fiore twisted a furious glare over his shoulder as Redmayne

staggered. Peacock seized the opening and slashed Fiore with the sharp bit of armor. It grazed his ear. Fiore whipped around, snapping Peacock's wrist with the motion. The blade dragged down her cheek as he flung her toward Redmayne.

Peacock ducked into a ball, and her cut cheek slapped hard into the bleeding wound on Redmayne's chest.

Redmayne vanished and Peacock collapsed to the floor in his place.

Fiore strode over and dragged Peacock to her feet. He held her by the throat and shook her as she hung stiffly from his hands.

"Lennie!" Fiore shouted. He glared around the room. "Come out! You know how I'll kill her, and you don't want to watch that."

There was a rough hiss near Fiore's back, and Peacock choked in his grip. She muttered, "You can fucking try, mate, but it'll be a bloody good trick when she's behind you."

Peacock's appearance melted away and revealed Redmayne snarling in Fiore's grip.

Less than a foot from Fiore's spine, Peacock herself, her leathers unzipped to the waist, yanked a long needle of the hell lord's claw from a slit in the skin below her breast. She jabbed it an inch into her boss's back.

Fiore twitched and dropped Redmayne. A black cloud erupted from the floor beneath Fiore and engulfed him. The dark smoke swirled and writhed to his screams, binding him within its coil, then flowed away again like ink down a drain and dragged the necromancer with it. Only an echo and the stink of hot iron lingered to mark their passage.

The air was thick and still with anticipation. Then the desk groaned and toppled. Peacock jumped back from it with a startled hiss.

Then she laughed and flopped down next to Redmayne in the soundproof silence. Fiore's guys knew better than to interrupt while he was working, so she could afford a moment to catch her breath. She picked up a hell-baked stone and crushed it in her grip so she could rub the dust into her broken wrist and scatter the rest onto Redmayne's chest. Blood ran down her cheek from the cut she'd put there, but she ignored it. "Well. I wasn't sure about that hell lord's claw, but it seemed to work. Where do you suppose it sent Fiore?"

"You can't guess from the reek? I'd lay odds he's having a natter with the original owner about now."

"Aww . . . and I didn't even get to say good-bye."

Her wrist straightened with a sound like popcorn exploding. "Ow," she yelped. She shook out her hand and wiggled her fingers, then zipped her suit closed, and helped Redmayne into a sitting position. "I have never been so glad for stupid men. The guy who frisked me was too busy copping a feel to notice that damned needle."

"To be fair, it was rather small, and you've got some nasty scars to hide it under," Redmayne replied, and squirmed. "Could you get these shackles off me? Right irritating, they are."

Peacock pulled a couple of picks from the seams of her leathers and started on the lock.

Redmayne watched her work. "I'd not count him out entirely yet. Necromancers don't just walk back out of Hell, but he's still alive down there until something kills him, and he'll be looking for a way out."

"Like you did?" she said, opening up the restraints.

"Ta," he said, rubbing at his arms and wrists. "Nah. I started by looking for a way *in*, but I'd never been to Hell and I had to guess a lot and go on theory. Then I had to find the right liminal point and make sure I had someone I could trust to get rid of my remains. Had to figure out exactly how black and which shade of damnation my soul had to wear to land in exactly the right place. Had to leave bits of intrigue behind that only I could solve for him. I knew he'd have to send someone for me eventually. Bit of luck it was you."

"Luck?"

Redmayne nodded self-consciously. "Yeah. I didn't have much of a plan for when I got out. It was chatting you up made it come together, but Fiore laid the ground himself. If he hadn't bent you over, you'd have had no cause to throw in with me."

Peacock gave him a cynical look. "You had no plan at all? You didn't know I was coming, didn't trick me into attracting that lord's attention so you could get its claw?"

"Maybe the claw, I did. The rest was mostly the happenstance of you being you and saving my arse. I'm not so bleeding clever, or I'd have come up with some way to avoid the whole thing. At the time, we couldn't run the Directory without a necromancer, and Thaumaturge in Chief didn't have the kind of power that Fiore's built up since then. And I'm not good at killing people—all that—"

"All that blood," Peacock finished. "You're a twisty bit of work, Redmayne. I'm still wondering what happens to *me* now that Fiore's gone. I'm surprised I haven't dropped dead already. And how much better off are *you*? I mean, technically you're—what?—some kind of hellspawn now?"

Redmayne shrugged and grimaced. "Well, hell*born*, yeah—bit of an affinity after walking out. This body *looks* the same as what Fiore murdered—or it will when I'm not portal-sick—but I'm not sure yet on the functional details of living in this world in flesh created in Hell."

"I guess we'll find out."

"I guess." Redmayne gave her a crooked smile. "Think I can get me old job back?"

Peacock started scavenging in the wreckage for weapons. "I'm willing to help you try."

EYE OF NEWT

A Dan Shamble, Zombie P.I., Adventure

Kevin J. Anderson

I

The afternoon got a lot more interesting when the one-eyed lizard guy stumbled into our offices, begging for protection.

At Chambeaux & Deyer Investigations, even on quiet days, there's always paperwork to do, files to close out, dead cases to resurrect or just bury for good. I'm a detective—a zombie detective. I can throw a mean punch and stand up to the ugliest, foulest-smelling demon, but paperwork has never been my forte. That's why I have an office assistant, Sheyenne. She's a ghost, and she's also my girlfriend. It doesn't matter that we intermingle our work lives and our personal lives, since neither of us is alive anyway.

Sheyenne had been realphabetizing files while I looked over cases I had recently wrapped up, some in more dramatic fashion than others, a few even verging on "end of the world" dramatic, so it's a good thing I'm skilled at my job. In studying the files, I wasn't looking for mistakes; just reviewing my greatest hits and wishing we had another case to work on at the moment.

My lawyer partner, Robin Deyer, was in court, prosecuting a case of cemeterial fraud and incompetence—an underclass-action suit against a tombstone engraver who had committed far too many misspellings. Now that zombies were rising frequently from the grave, the formerly silent customers noticed the typos on their headstones, and a group had hired Robin to sue for damages on their behalf.

That left just Sheyenne and me in the offices. We had a dinner date planned for that evening, but we hadn't settled on a restaurant yet. It was mainly an excuse for us to be together, all form and no sustenance, since I rarely ate anyway and a ghost didn't eat at all.

In the meantime, as she flitted from one file cabinet to another, Sheyenne watched a small TV tuned to a local cable channel that covered the Stone-Cold Monster Cook-off, which was taking place downtown in the Unnatural Quarter. A variety of skilled chefs competed in the daylong event; the crowds were getting larger now that the cook-off was down to three finalists. Sheyenne watched the unnatural chefs go about their extravagant preparations with enough pots, pans, and utensils to equip an inhuman army. She jotted down a recipe suggested by the loud, green-skinned Ragin' Cajun Mage, just in case she ever got around to cooking.

Then the office door crashed open, which was all the more remarkable because the creature that barged in was barely three feet tall. A scrawny lizard man with speckled brown skin, one yellow eye, and gauze and surgical tape covering where the other eye should have been.

"I need your help!" he said, in a phlegmy, hissy voice. "Are you Dan Shamble? You've got to help me!"

"It's *Chambeaux*," I corrected him as I came out of my office to greet him. I moved stiffly on joints that were still recovering from rigor mortis.

Sheyenne is usually very professional, but she cried out in delight when she saw him. "Oh, aren't you cute! Look, Beaux—he's from the car-insurance commercials."

After stumbling inside, the lizard man slammed the door behind him with surprising strength. "That's a gecko," he snapped. His long tongue flicked in and out. "I'm a *newt*. There's a difference."

"Sorry if I offended you." She drifted forward to meet him. "Come in, sir. You're safe here."

I made sure my .38 was in its hip holster, just in case the lizard man was being imminently pursued, but when no slavering, eye-stealing monsters charged after him, I figured we had enough time for a normal client-intake meeting. "Tell me what's going on, Mr., uh, Newt."

"My name is Geck." That must have been embarrassing for a guy who was too often confused for a humorous gecko insurance spokesman. "There's a hit out on me, and I was attacked last night."

"Who, exactly, is out to get you?"

He shook his head. "I don't know! I didn't think I had any enemies. I mean, I'm a warm and fuzzy guy . . . as far as an amphibian can be."

In the conference room, I had to bring him a booster chair so he could see over the edge of the table. If Robin were here, she would have been taking copious notes on a yellow legal pad, but I just sat and listened. The one-eyed newt didn't seem at all bothered by the bullet hole in the center of my forehead or my gray pallor. "Tell us your story, Geck."

He licked his lips. "I'm walking home, minding my own business, whistling to myself, and then . . ." He shuddered. "Suddenly, I get accosted by two big thugs: a rock monster and a clay golem.

'Get him! He's the one we've got a contract out on,' says the rock monster. And the golem says, 'Don't end a sentence with a preposition.'

"And they grab me. Because it's a cool night, I'm a little lethargic. If I'd been sunning myself on a hot rock, I could've scurried out of their grasp, but I was too slow. They grab me, slam me up against the brick wall of an alley, then . . . they take out a long spoon." He shuddered again, sobbed. "They scoop out my eye, quick as you please, and pop it in a glass bottle. The golem holds me while the rock monster just laughs! 'We'd get twice as much if we took your other eye, too,' he says. 'You better watch yourself.' Then the golem says, 'He won't be watching much of anything now. Come on, we got what we need.'"

The newt self-consciously touched the wadded bandages on his face. "Then they went away and left me there. The golem seemed guilty, even sorry, but the rock monster was just mean."

"I'm not surprised," I said. "Rock monsters tend to be hard and grumbly, while golems are made of clay, so they are softer in general."

"What am I going to do?" Geck wailed. "If there's still a hit out on me, someone might try to take my other eye. I'm not safe."

I knew I could take him down to the precinct and ask for protective custody from my BHF, my best human friend, Officer Toby McGoohan, but that would be only a temporary solution, and this needed more direct intervention.

"We have to find out who took out a contract on you," I said. "Learn what you did and try to make amends. Do you have *any idea* who it was? Who's got a grudge against you? Do you owe money?"

"Any idea at all?" Sheyenne pressed, hovering close to him.

Geck hung his head. He looked ill, although I knew the greenish brown tinge to his hide was probably natural. "Only the library comes to mind. I think I've seen the rock monster and the golem there—they sometimes work as security guards. And I do have an overdue book and a fine." He blinked his remaining eye. "You don't think . . . ?"

Even Sheyenne paled, and I steeled myself. "You don't mess with the Spider Lady of the Unnatural Quarter Public Library. Everyone knows that." This was going to be a more dangerous case than I had expected. "We'd better go face her—in person, you and me—and see if we can resolve this. You won't be safe until you're off her hit list."

II

Geck and I headed through town toward the Unnatural Quarter Public Library main branch and the Vault of Secrets. We made a side trip to his dank lair, a communal subbasement where other newts shared the rent, with mud and moss for carpeting and a steady drip through the ceiling for running water. Not a good place to keep an overdue library book, I thought. At least he had it on a high shelf, away from the drip. Geck hauled over a stepstool so he could retrieve it.

"So, tell me about this book you checked out," I said. "How long is it overdue, and why is it so important?"

"A month overdue. I kept putting it off, Mr. Shamble. And then it got worse and the fines built up." He held the thick volume close.

"How much?"

"Ten bucks."

"Better take twenty. We may need to pay off the Spider Lady, but we'll get you back on the straight and narrow."

He looked down at the heavy volume that seemed too big for him to carry. For the sake of efficiency, I took it from him and we set off, while two other newts were waiting to stand under the ceiling drip for a shower.

"Never even finished it." Geck sounded guilty. "I went to the library for something to read in a puddle on a sunny day. I really enjoyed all the Harry Potter books, and I heard that the Harry Dresden novels by Jim Butcher were excellent, but they were all checked out.

"Then somebody said Shakespeare in the same sentence with Butcher, so I decided to look into that Shakespeare guy as my second choice. The only copy available was a rare special edition, *The Complete Pre-Humous Writings of William Shakespeare*. It was even autographed."

I frowned, knowing that someone who purported to be Shakespeare's ghost had been publishing new posthumously written plays and sonnets, but his claim had been debunked. He was, in fact, just another aspiring ghostwriter with a good costume and literary airs, but apparently the library hadn't caught up yet.

"I tried to read the Shakespeare stuff, but I couldn't get into it," the newt said. "It wasn't like Harry Potter at all. It was boring. But I kept trying. And then the book was late and I felt guilty, so I kept trying to read it. The fines piled up, and then I started getting threatening letters, so I was afraid to come to the library. And then . . ." He self-consciously touched the bandages covering his right eye.

"You need to bring the book back, and you'll have to make amends to the librarian," I said. "That may be the only way we can keep you intact, more or less. When we get to the library, let me do the talking. And bring your twenty bucks."

On our way across the Quarter, we passed vampires sitting outside under sun umbrellas at a blood bar. Two werewolf women offered discounts on "full claw treatment" pedicures. A mummy rode by on a bicycle, wobbling and unbalanced; he was taken completely off guard when one of his unraveled bandages caught in the chain, and he and the bicycle tumbled into the gutter.

We passed Ghoul's Diner, where I often liked to sit at the counter with an abysmally bad cup of coffee and a disgusting miasma of a daily special. The diner and its unfortunate food were upstaged now, however, as the entire block had been barricaded for the final rounds of the Stone-Cold Monster Cook-off. A grandstand had been set up for the culinary acrobatics, and spectators gathered around, hoping for—or dreading—free samples.

I assumed the diner's business had suffered due to the event, but the ghoul proprietor never seemed to pay much attention to the outside world or his customers. It was business as usual.

In fact, everyone in the Unnatural Quarter—monsters and humans—got along about as well as anybody got along in the rest of the world. Ever since the Big Uneasy more than a decade ago, the world had been settling down from the change. The event had been caused by a strange alignment of planets and a completely coincidental spilling of virgin's blood on an original copy of the *Necronomicon*, which resulted in cosmic upheavals, rifts in the universal continuum, and a shift in reality.

But after all that was over, naturals and unnaturals had to learn how to coexist, and everyday life returned with surprising stability. It could have been a real zombie apocalypse, but it wasn't so much an apocalypse as an awkward reunion.

Back then, I was a private investigator who hadn't seen much success in the real world, but I found a whole new clientele among the unnaturals. My business partner, Robin, joined me because she insisted that downtrodden unnaturals needed legal representation, too. Everything had been going fine—until one of my cases went south and I ended up being shot in the back of the head.

These days, that isn't quite as final as it might sound. I rose from the grave and got right back on the case, eventually solving my own murder, then moving on.

It goes to show how much the world has settled into a new normal if a crowd of naturals and unnaturals can get excited about a cook-off.

Up onstage, after a round of digestive elimination, the Stone-Cold culinary marathon had settled on its three finalists. On the left side of the grandstand was Leatherneck, a burly man in a leather apron, leather mask, and upright shocks of greasy hair. He used a rusty shovel to scoop mangled animal remains into the hopper of a meat grinder that was about the size of a wood chipper.

"To make Texas chain-saw chili," he said, "any sort of roadkill will do—as long as it's been seasoned with hot sun and asphalt for at least four days."

The meat grinder whirred and spat out a brownish red paste flecked with hair and fur that glopped into an already bubbling cauldron. The big chef added a pinch of salt, bent over to sniff the pot, then held up a gigantic razor-edged butcher knife. He raised his left forearm, which was a network of white scars. Without flinching, Leatherneck drew the blade down his forearm, opening up a wide gash that bled profusely into the pot. He held his arm over the chili as red dripped into the sauce, then with bright eyes behind his leather mask, he said, "And now for the special ingredient." The crowd fell into a hush, and the big man lifted a jar of green spices with his nonbleeding arm. *"Oregano!"* He sprinkled a third of the jar into his pot.

The vampires in the audience had become extremely attentive when they watched him shed blood for his chili, but the oregano left them with sour frowns.

Next up was a heavyset, matronly woman whose beehive hair had a white lightning stripe, like the Bride of Frankenstein. Her skin was chalky and pale but her eyes were fiery red. Sheyenne sometimes watched her TV show, *Kitchen Litch*, and she complained that the Kitchen Litch considered herself superior to her viewers. "The sort of person who would say 'tomaaahto coulis' instead of ketchup," Sheyenne had described her.

The Kitchen Litch held a large sauté pan over a gas burner. "Every ingredient must be frrrresh," she said with an exaggerated roll of her r's. "First, we start with clarified butter." She ladled a greasy yellow pool into the pan, then reached inside a wicker basket and rummaged around. "And the frrreshest of frrresh is an ingredient that is . . . *alive!*"

She pulled out a black beetle as large as her hand. It squirmed and thrashed, but she threw it onto the sizzling pan. "And I always keep a special container of fresh bloodsucking gnats for garnish, but that will be for the finish." She reached into the basket to grab another beetle, while the first beetle flopped and hopped, dancing on the hot pan surface. Its black carapace cracked open, and it buzzed its wings to fly away.

"No, no!" The Kitchen Litch swatted with a spatula as the second skittering beetle also tried to take flight. She smashed that one into a pulp, and it sizzled in a little beetle patty in the frying pan. The first beetle, though, got away, winging up from the stage. Three more beetles escaped from the still-open wicker basket, and the flustered Kitchen Litch slammed the lid back down. Trying to recover her composure, she said to the audience, "Of course, frrresh ingredients also pose certain challenges." She busied herself nursing the beetle patty with her spatula.

The third chef, a loud green-skinned man, the Ragin' Cajun Mage, cooked flamboyantly beside two large glass aquariums filled with thrashing ingredients. He looked at the Kitchen Litch with scorn. "I agree with my incompetent rival: fresh ingredients are key, but so are *secret* ingredients, and I have about a dozen secret ingredients."

The Cajun Mage rapped his knuckles against the aquariums filled with silty gray-brown water. Swarms of thrashing tentacles writhed at him like a wrestling match between a squid and an octopus. Armored claws clacked in another aquarium. "We have a live mutant-crawdad tank and a live assorted-tentacles tank. They'll wait, though, until my nightmare étouffée is ready. It takes half a day to simmer properly. First, we make a nice roux, starting with some perfect sassafras filé." He dumped a gray-green powder into the bottom of his stockpot. "Then some toadstool filé."

His eyes twinkled as he lifted a crystalline vial. "And for the perfect seasoning, the tears of heartbroken girls. Two tablespoons will do." He poured the vial into the pot, then whisked it around as he increased the heat.

Geck and I had paused to watch the show. The smells wafting around the grandstand were an odd mix of appetizing and disgusting. My client glanced around the crowd, fidgeting and nervous, as if afraid someone might attack him right there out in the open, but I was sure he would be safe here. The Spider Lady from the library would not make a move on him at the Monster Cookoff. She had already delivered her ominous message.

One of the escaped black beetles buzzed through the air toward us, wobbling like a drunken bumblebee. Geck's yellow eye brightened, and he swiveled his salamander-like head, poised, tense. . . . Then he lashed out with his tongue. But he missed the beetle entirely, which buzzed away unaffected.

Geck groaned. "Bloody depth perception! I'm going to starve!"

As the green-skinned Cajun Mage moved to the next stage of his highly complex recipe, I nudged the newt along. "Come on, then. It's off to the library. This is a matter of life or death."

III

The Unnatural Quarter Public Library and Vault of Secrets was not meant to be a terrifying place, but Geck looked as if he would rather have been going to the dentist—and I didn't even know if newts had teeth.

The large stone building was impressive in one sense, looming in another sense. A poster in one of the dust-specked windows said "Come for fun in the library!" in dripping-blood letters. Because the stone steps were so widely spaced, I had to help Geck up each one.

As we climbed to the pillared entrance, he seemed more and more nervous. "You have to face this," I said. "If we can resolve your overdue library book, the Spider Lady will take you off her hit list. Then you won't have to worry anymore." The newt swallowed and moved on.

At the top of the broad steps, two fierce-looking stone lions crouched on pedestals. Just as we reached the top of the platform, a nervous-looking vampire scuttled out of the library entrance with a book hidden under his arm, and the two stone lions woke up. The ferocious living statues snorted, snarled, and rose on their heavy paws.

The nervous vampire clutched his book and scuttled backward, looking from side to side, trapped. One lion bounded off its pedestal and pinned him to the ground. He flailed and screamed. "I'll check out the book, I promise. I'll check it out!"

The vampire had been trying to smuggle out a hardcover copy of *Twilight*.

With a snort, the stone lion smacked the vampire and sent him careening back into the library. Though uninjured, he was extremely embarrassed to have his reading material revealed.

The incident did little to calm Geck's nerves. I tried to reassure him. "I'm here to protect you and negotiate on your behalf." I did not point out that even the most highly skilled zombie P.I. could do little to protect against giant stone lions or demonic head librarians.

The main library smelled of books, that weighty, dusty aroma that always brings back nostalgic memories. The patrons included humans, particularly college students doing reports on the social changes brought on by the Big Uneasy. Mummy scholars worked with large stacks of papyrus, jotting down notes in hieroglyphics. Vampires developed family trees, while full-furred werewolves stood muttering together in the pets section.

On the high shelves, accessible only by rickety ladders that looked more dangerous than the evil-spell books themselves, a cleaning crew of goblins skittered about, stringing cobwebs. In the middle of the floor, two large spinner racks held paperback bestsellers.

Geck looked around nervously, scanning the library. He whispered, "I don't see the rock monster or the golem. They're usually guarding the doors. Maybe they're off stealing someone else's eye."

"Or maybe it's their day off," I said.

"Or maybe they're waiting to pounce on me again! Keep your eyes open, Mr. Shamble. You have more of them than I do."

At the main reference desk sat a withered, prim old woman who looked as if she suffered from chronic hemorrhoids. Her hair was pulled back into a bun so tight she didn't need a face-lift, and she wore cat's-eye glasses that were large enough to be used as a weapon. She scanned the library like a high-tech targeting system, and when a young college couple began talking too loud, she suddenly reached out with a freakishly long, multijointed arm that held a ruler. Even though they were twenty feet away, she rapped on the table in front of them. "Quiet, please, in the library!" The old woman folded her extra arm back down under the desk.

Her nameplate said, "Hi, I'm Frieda. I'm here to help."

I nudged Geck, and we walked up to the desk. The newt was far too short, and I had to lift him up so he could meet the cat's-eye glasses with his remaining eye.

I looked behind the counter and saw that Frieda the Spider Lady had a nest of additional multijointed limbs all curled up beneath her flower-print dress. One set of hands was typing, while another paged through a printed book; behind her, two more limbs reached out to pluck volumes off a shelving cart. She gave us part of her attention. "How may I help you?"

"I'm Dan Chambeaux, private investigator, ma'am, and this newt is my client, Geck. I'm afraid there's been some misunderstanding, and I'm here to help resolve it."

The librarian frowned. "Misunderstanding? If words and sentences were stated clearly, there would be no misunderstandings."

"My library book is late," Geck blurted out, sounding ashamed.

The Spider Lady practically recoiled, as if he had hurled a terrible insult at her. "That changes things. Substantially."

I interjected, holding up the Shakespeare *Pre-Humous Writings* volume I had carried from his dank quarters. "My client has incurred library fines, which he is willing to pay, so long as he stops receiving threatening letters from the library. As you can see, he has already suffered a great deal of physical harm." I used my "be reasonable" voice, which rarely worked against villains; even so, the detective-training handbook suggested being reasonable as a first step.

Frieda's voice was filled with venom. "And what is this book? How valuable is it?" Beneath the counter, her hidden limbs twitched. Many of them ended in claws. "And how despicable are you?"

Geck stammered and held out a rumpled receipt, while I slid over the book. The Spider Lady nudged her cat's-eye glasses, and her face seemed to wither even more. "This was part of our special Shakespeare collection—do you have any idea what sort of damage you've done? How many college treatises have been delayed because the authors had no access to this wonderful tome?"

"I . . . I'm sorry."

"And it's autographed, too!" said Freda, as if that were the last nail in the coffin.

"You do realize that the autograph is fake, ma'am?" I pointed out, hoping that might mitigate her ire. "The author of the posthumous works is not the real Shakespeare's ghost."

The librarian sniffed. "It's still of historical and popular interest." She shuffled papers and withdrew a formal parchment document that looked like a death-sentence decree. A dozen names were written on it, seven of which had been crossed off, as if terminated.

Geck the Newt was on the list, third from the bottom. "I'm sorry, I'm sorry!" he blubbered, then quickly slapped a moist and rumpled twenty on the counter next to her nameplate. "I'll pay the fine—I'll pay double!—just please don't send your goons after me. Don't take my other eye!"

Now it was the Spider Lady's turn to look off balance. "Take your other eye? Why on earth would I wish to do that? My sole reason for existence is to *encourage reading*. If I took your other eye, that would be against my principles, although the library does have a large selection of unabridged audiobooks."

I stood up for Geck. "My client was recently accosted in an alley by a rock monster and a golem, both of whom are known to work here in the library. If you didn't send them to steal his eye, then who did?"

The Spider Lady seemed flustered. "You must mean Rocky and Ned. They're just part-time contract security guards. It's so hard to find good security guards in the Unnatural Quarter—they tend to suffer unfortunate ends. But I had to let Rocky and Ned go. I caught them eating in the library, which is inexcusable."

She snatched the bill and used one folded arm to squirrel it away in a small cash box, while another arm took the book and stacked it on the shelving cart behind her. With a third hand, she stamped PAID on her hit list next to Geck's name.

She reached out with another one of her long arms and slapped a zombie reader who had unconsciously folded down the corner of a page in order to mark his place. "Damage to library property! I *will* write you up."

I got her attention again. "If you didn't put out a contract to take my client's eye, then who did?"

"How should I know that?"

I indicated the sign on the desk. "It says you're a reference librarian."

"I'm afraid you'll have to do your own research, Mr. Shamble.

You might begin by asking whether this action was a punitive measure against Geck specifically, or if someone actually needed the eye for some other purpose."

IV

I knew we could get worthwhile advice from the Unorthodox Lab Equipment and Organ Boutique, a small specialty business that catered to a broad clientele ranging from hobbyist mad scientists to evil corporate research centers with underground monster-development programs.

An imp named Gunther managed the place and kept all his wares in total disorganization on the shelves, like a secret code that only he knew how to interpret. His business had picked up dramatically after the demise of Tony Cralo's Body Parts Emporium, a giant organ superstore run by an obese zombie mobster. After I had exposed Cralo to justice, his business completely collapsed. Score one for the good guys. That annoyed many of the Quarter's mad scientists, however, because they could no longer do one-stop shopping.

The little imp was climbing a set of shelves and stacking glass jars filled with specimens preserved in formaldehyde. The jars themselves were as big as the diminutive imp, but he was strong. Gunther nearly lost his grip on a jar filled with intestines labeled with a sticker that said "Great for decorating!"

Seeing us, he swung down with simian agility and dropped with flat feet on the countertop. His gaze turned immediately toward the newt, and he focused on the bandages. "Looks like somebody's in the market for a new eye! I have a wide selection." He clucked his pointed tongue. "I'll have to take socket measurements, though. Would you like to match the original color, or should we try something more fashionable?"

Geck said, "I'd rather have my own eye back—and I want to keep the one I still have."

When I explained how my client had been attacked, the imp proprietor seemed very disturbed. "The Unnatural Quarter is going down the tubes. Sure, people used to get roofies and wake up in hotel bathtubs, missing a kidney or two, but that was just an expected part of the business. Taking an eye out right on the streets?" The imp shook his head in disgust.

"Have you had any customers asking for an eye of newt?" I asked.

"Not in particular. Yes, newt eyes are rare, but I have a selection of perfectly adequate toad eyes and salamander eyes. They'll do in a pinch." He clucked his pointed tongue again, and touched Geck's bandages. "I could make do, find something that'll fit you, though it might look a little odd. Any decent scientist could install one, so long as it's in good condition."

"But is there a reason why someone would particularly want Geck's eye?" I asked. "What are newt eyes used for?"

"I used mine for seeing," Geck snapped.

"I meant, what would someone else use it for?"

The imp pondered. "Various organs have potent sorcerous aspects, particularly the organs of magical creatures. Livers, spleens, pituitary glands, testicles, and the like. Rare, ancient magic books listed eye of newt as a vital ingredient for every sorcerer to have in the pantry, but it was never used to work magic. Those tomes weren't spell books." Gunther gave an impish grin. "They were recipes, you see."

"Recipes?" Wheels began to turn in my mind.

"Yes," said the imp. "Eye of newt is primarily used in cooking."

>––<

With a sinking feeling in the pit of my stomach, like the after-effects of a bad pepperoni pizza, I hurried with the newt back to the Unnatural Quarter's Stone-Cold Monster Cook-off.

We bumped into Officer Toby McGoohan, who was walking the beat and presumably maintaining order. The only orders, though, were being taken by shuffling zombie waitresses at the outside tables of Ghoul's Diner.

"Hey, Shamble!" McGoo tipped his blue patrolman's cap. "Just another day on the job. There've been reports of culinary unrest." He nodded toward the grandstand, where the three finalist chefs were finishing their hours-long preparations for their masterpiece dishes. Runners dispersed small samples among the spectators, who would then vote on the winner. No doubt there was illicit gambling, with bookies taking bets as well as exchanging family recipes.

"If the wrong person wins, McGoo, there'll be some digestive upset among the crowd."

I noticed he was eating something wrapped in dripping paper, a meal from one of the food carts that catered to the human audience members: a hot dog wrapped in bacon and stuffed inside a glazed jelly doughnut. McGoo took a bite, then frowned at the show onstage. "I don't know how anybody can eat that stuff." He wiped the congealing mess from his lips.

"We already have enough to make our stomachs queasy, Mc-Goo. A couple of thugs roughed up my client, Mr. Geck. They took his eye last night. At first we thought it was payback for an overdue library book, a contract taken out on him by the Spider Lady herself."

McGoo paled, which made the freckles on his cheeks seem more prominent. "The Spider Lady?"

I held up a hand. "But it wasn't that. We think these thugs *stole* Geck's eye . . . for some nefarious purpose."

"There's always some nefarious purpose. Did you get a description of the perps?"

"Just general details. One's a rock monster; the other's a golem. Names are Ned and Rocky."

"That's enough to go on." McGoo pursed his lips. "I've been patrolling the crowd here. Lots of spectators, but I think I noticed that rock monster. Now that you mention it, he was with a golem. They were sitting at one of the outdoor tables at Ghoul's Diner. I only noticed them because the rock monster was eating a bagel— a *toasted onion* bagel, but with *strawberry* cream cheese on it." He frowned. "That's the sort of thing an attentive cop will notice."

To the roar of the crowd, Leatherneck ladled out samples of his Texas chain-saw chili and passed small cups around the crowd. He had reopened the big gash on his forearm so he could spruce up each bowl with a splash of blood. The vampire spectators crowded forward, eager to get their sample, even with the addition of oregano to the pot. The persistent Kitchen Litch had managed to fricassee enough of the large beetles that she was prepared to serve, though she had not yet garnished the meal with her blood-sucking gnats.

The three of us hurried off to the diner at the edge of the cook-off crowd. Albert Gould had set up rickety card tables and temporary benches to take advantage of the additional customers, even though they were all watching the cook-off. McGoo pointed. "There's the bagel!"

I did see the onion bagel covered with strawberry cream cheese—which was certainly out of the ordinary—being held by a lumpy rock monster, a creature composed of assembled stones and a large yawning mouth just made to pulverize bagels. Next to him sat a gray clay golem sipping a tiny cup of espresso. I was shocked because I hadn't known Ghoul's Diner served espresso.

Geck hopped up and down, trying to see. "That's them!"

On the stage, with his big booming laugh, the green-skinned Ragin' Cajun Mage stirred his cauldron of nightmare étouffée. "Almost finished! Enjoy those other morsels while you can—and be prepared to surrender your taste buds to the Mage."

McGoo and I stepped up to the table, interrupting the rock monster and the golem. I tried to be as tough and determined as a zombie detective can be. "Are you Rocky? We'd like to have a word with you."

The rock monster turned its blocky head so I could see blazing red eyes deep within cavelike sockets. "I'm *Ned*. He's Rocky." He gestured to the golem, then took another big, grinding bite of his bagel.

"We need to talk with both of you," I said.

McGoo puffed up his chest. "We've heard reports that you assaulted a citizen of the Quarter."

"Me, me!" said Geck, bouncing up and down. The newt was so short, he didn't come up to the edge of the table, and the two thugs hadn't noticed him. I gave him a hand, lifting him up so the two could see him. "You stole my eye!"

"You got proof of that?" grumbled the rock monster. "It was dark in that alley. How can you be sure it was us?"

"So, you admit you were there," McGoo said.

Rocky the golem said, "Considering this person's condition, he's unreliable as an *eye*witness."

Ned the rock monster snickered.

"It was them!" Geck said. "I'd point them out in a lineup any day of the week."

The rock monster rose to his feet, towering over us. "We took a job; we got paid. We're just blue-collar workers."

Rocky stood up to join him. "A golem is required to follow whatever commands a master issues, even a temporary master. There's been a legal precedent. We're not responsible for whatever we allegedly did or didn't do."

Ned added, "Besides, five bucks is five bucks."

"And assault on a newt is still considered assault," said McGoo. "I'm going to have to—"

Geck suddenly cried out as he jumped onto the table, disturbing the tiny cup of espresso and knocking the half-eaten bagel to the ground. "Look, look! That's my eye!"

Onstage, the Ragin' Cajun Mage stood over his noisome vat of nightmare étouffée. He tried to impart a sense of awe on the spectators. "And the last, the rarest, the most special secret ingredient— not available at stores!—we add for the finish: *eye of newt!*"

The crowd gasped.

Geck shrieked.

The green-skinned Cajun chef dangled the vial containing the stolen amphibian eye and let the silence hang for a long and dangerous moment. Even the large aquariums of live mutated crawdads and live assorted tentacles thrashed and churned, either applauding or dreading the imminent moment when they would become part of the cooking performance.

"That's my eye!" Geck yelled again, and bounded toward the stage.

The crowd stopped munching on their fricasseed beetle

samples or Texas chain-saw chili. Many dropped their cups on the ground.

McGoo withdrew his service revolver and pointed it at the Ragin' Cajun Mage. "Stop right there! That eyeball is private property. Everyone else, stay calm."

Of course the spectators panicked.

Knowing the crowd could turn ugly—well, the crowd was already ugly, but it could get worse—I pointed at the golem and the rock monster. They were both mercenaries to the core. "Five bucks if you help us resolve this," I offered.

"Each?" asked Ned.

I hesitated only a second and considered it a worthwhile investment. "Each."

The two large gray forms lumbered into the crowd.

The newt dashed up onto the stage with the speed of a sun-warmed lizard. Geck threw himself with full fury at the Cajun Mage, attempting to tackle him and seize his eye before it fell into the cauldron of étouffée. Alas, unaccustomed to his lack of depth perception, Geck missed. He only brushed against the green-skinned cook and instead careened into the live aquariums, which the mage chef had opened, preparatory to serving. Both glass cases toppled over, dumping out a menagerie of edible horrors. Hundreds of mutated crawdads and assorted live tentacles went thrashing into the crowd. People began screaming.

McGoo yelled, "Watch out! The ingredients are loose."

Tentacles flung themselves on fleeing mummies. Crawfish clipped their pincers on the spiky fur of a punk-rocker werewolf, who clawed his own cheeks in an attempt to get them off.

The Kitchen Litch quickly evacuated from the grandstand, taking the last samples of fricasseed beetles with her, but in her alarm, she bumped the sealed container of frrresh, live bloodsucking gnats that she had reserved for garnish, and the swarm of black biting things flew up, indiscriminately buzzing around everyone on the stage.

Next to the cauldron, the Cajun Mage flailed, trying to beat back the frenzied one-eyed newt.

Rocky and Ned cleared a way through the crowd with all the finesse of two bulldozers, knocking people aside on their way to the stage. I followed them.

Ned bellowed at the chef in his cavernous voice, "We're going to need that eye back!"

"*I'm* going to need it!" Geck jumped up and down, grabbing for the vial clenched in the Mage's green hand.

More large black beetles had escaped from the Kitchen Litch's wicker basket, and Leatherneck, seemingly unfazed by the chaos, reached out with his big strangler's hands and grabbed them to add to his pot of chain-saw chili.

McGoo stomped on the assorted tentacles and kicked away crawdads that nipped at his ankles. "Keep calm!" he yelled.

The golem and the rock monster got themselves so entangled in the rebellious ingredients that I made it to the stage first. The cloud of bloodsucking gnats swarmed around me, but the biting creatures went away disappointed, with no taste for embalming fluid.

The Cajun Mage looked indignantly into his étouffée. "But this would have been the perfect batch. You've ruined everything!" He dodged the newt and opened the glass vial. "Without the secret ingredient, it might as well just be a casserole. I must finish for the sake of the culinary arts!" He upended the vial over the cauldron.

As if in slow motion, Geck groaned, "Nooooo!"

But I got there just in time, lashing out with my outstretched hand. I caught the detached eye of newt in my palm and it plopped there, sitting moist and squishy, unpleasant to the touch, but safe.

Rocky and Ned reached the stage just as I backed away cradling Geck's eye. The golem and the rock monster grabbed the Cajun Mage, lifted him up, and dumped him into the large pot of nightmare étouffée, where he stirred and whisked himself helplessly.

Geck hurried over to me, trembling. "You saved my eye! Do you think it can be reattached?"

"There's a good chance. We have the best mad scientists in the Quarter," I said. "Though from now on, you may need reading glasses."

Rocky the golem loomed over me. "That'll be five bucks."

"Each," said Ned.

I carefully handed the jiggly eye over to Geck's loving care, then dug in my wallet. By now most of the crowd had run screaming and the loose ingredients had dispersed.

The Kitchen Litch had run away, plagued by vengeful beetles, and the only one remaining on the stand was burly Leatherneck, who calmly ate his chili straight from the ladle. "Last chef standing. I guess that means I win."

McGoo handcuffed the thoroughly étoufféed Cajun chef, who was still trapped inside his cauldron, although out of courtesy he turned the heat down to a slow simmer. The Ragin' Cajun Mage struggled to lift a goopy finger to his lips and tasted it. "After all that, it still could use salt."

I called Sheyenne back at the office and asked her to look up the best eyeball replacers in the Quarter. I suggested that Gunther the imp might be able to give a recommendation.

Out in the wreckage in front of the grandstand, I saw Albert and two of his waitresses running around with shovels and five-gallon buckets, scooping up the dropped samples of Texas chainsaw chili and fricasseed beetles. I could guess what might be on tomorrow's special board for Ghoul's Diner.

Leaving McGoo to take care of the arrested chef, I led Geck back toward my office. I recalled that I had promised to take Sheyenne out for a dinner date, but I realized I didn't have much appetite.

Maybe we would go dancing instead.

WHAT DWELLS WITHIN

by Lucy A. Snyder

We should not be out right now. The telepathic voice of my ferret familiar, Pal, was strained with anxiety. He peered out our borrowed Toyota's passenger-side window, whiskers twitching. Scanning the late-afternoon clouds for signs of the Virtus Regnum, no doubt.

I couldn't blame him. If my protective spell failed, the Regnum's huge enforcer spirits would tear the Ohio sky open and burn us to ashes. And they wouldn't care too much about who else got expunged in the process. Humans were little more than vermin to them at the best of times. Whatever greater power in the universe had put them in charge of protecting the Earth from all the eldritch horrors out there must have done it to punish their species. On the bright side, their distaste for humanity left them totally unimpressed by any bribes that even powerful wizards could think up. So most of the time you could count on them to treat everyone the same: with near-complete contempt. But at least we were all equal in their law-abiding eyes.

Except me, Jessie Shimmer. I'd slain one of their kind. Entirely in self-defense, mind you, but that detail didn't matter to them. I'd done something no human was supposed to be able to do, and so I was a threat to be dealt with. Public enemy number one. Dead woman walking.

"It'll be fine," I said aloud as I turned south on High Street, passing Graeter's Ice Cream and a couple of upscale wine and candle shops in trendy brick storefronts.

I could have answered him telepathically. But that required a bit more concentration, so I saved it for when we were around other people. A seemingly one-sided conversation with a ferret tends to make folks think you've had a psychotic break, and then everything gets awkward.

Vague premonition itched like hives in the back of my mind, worse now than it had when I woke from a nightmare at five a.m. I couldn't remember the alarming dream, not even one detail, so I'd tried to ignore the whole thing. But the psychic irritation just kept building until I wanted to slam my head through a wall. *Something* was up, but neither meditation nor the couple of divination spells I'd tried gave me any clarity. My boyfriend, Cooper, was off with his little brothers and I didn't want to interrupt family time with something I figured I could handle fine by myself. Eventually.

Sometimes having Talent sucks. Magic is seldom straightforward when you need it to be. So I gave Mother Karen—thank God she'd been willing to give us a place to stay—a bullshit story about wanting to take a jog around Antrim Park, and borrowed her Corolla to see if being out and about on a mild Sunday evening would give me any relief or get me any answers. Karen's a sharp witch and normally she'd twig to my lie right quick, but a couple of her foster kids were having a fight over the TV and she was so preoccupied with them that she just handed me the keys.

I'd put my shotgun in the trunk, just in case, but it wouldn't do any good if the Regnum paid us a visit.

We should be staying put until the meeting with the Governing Circle, Pal fussed.

"I know." He wasn't wrong; if Circle leader Riviera Jordan were willing to offer us safe haven, we'd be relatively okay staying in the city. Relatively. Riviera seemed like a fair lady, and she knew I'd gotten a raw deal. But she hadn't made her decision yet, and going against the Regnum was an awfully big one. If I landed us in some kind of mess before the meeting and pissed off anyone else in the Circle, she would almost certainly wash her hands and tell us to get the hell out of Columbus.

This is really quite dangerous, Pal said. *And if you wanted to go to the park, we should have gone north.*

"I know. We're not going to the park." The buzz of premonition had moved from the back of my head into my chrysoberyl eye, and the scars around it were starting to itch a little. A flashback memory of fiery demon's blood spraying across the left side of my face made me wince. My enchanted stone ocularis was damned handy for seeing all manner of things that normal humans couldn't spy, but getting my eye melted out of my head was a memory I wished I could purge.

My left hand and forearm were getting a pins-and-needles feeling, too. The same demon had bitten that arm off just below the elbow, and one thing led to another, and that arm became a torch of hellfire for a while. No more fire—thank God; constantly setting off smoke detectors is *not* a good way to keep a low profile—but now I had an eerie white replica of my lower arm that I couldn't definitely say was flesh. I'd undergone an hours-long healing and exorcism ritual in Switzerland, and the ceremony was supposed to regrow my arm and restore it to normal, but the magic just couldn't quite get there. Too much demonic residue in my system.

Eerie or not, I wasn't about to complain about getting a working limb back. Sure, it was cold as a refrigerated corpse and glowed faintly blue in the dark, but I could feel through it just fine. I kept telling myself that functionality was what mattered. Most days I told myself I still wore my magically flameproof gray opera glove just in case it flared up again, but, frankly, seeing that creepy white thing at the end of my arm made my skin crawl.

Besides, if I touched anyone with the glove off and I wasn't paying attention, there was a chance I might drag the both of us into my personal hell dimension. Awkward. Very awkward.

Where are we going, then? Pal asked.

"Trust me—I'll let you know as soon as I figure that one out."

He made an exasperated squeak and curled up on the gray passenger's seat in a tight, frustrated ball, his nose buried under his fluffy sable tail. He looked completely adorable, but now was not the time to tell him that. Probably he was wishing he were in his grizzly bear form so he could wrestle me for the wheel and get us turned around. But then he'd be far too big to fit in the compact car, and, besides, he needed a strong electrical jolt to trigger his shape-shift. We kept a stun gun around for that, and it wasn't pleasant. I'd recently worked out an electroshock spell, but that wasn't any nicer than the zapper.

I'd have hated to be in his position. He was my first and only familiar, and when I got him, I didn't realize that intelligent familiars are all indentured souls trapped in animal bodies. It's kind of a horrifying system if you learn much about it, but familiars are so handy that nobody wants to know that part. Pal would have gotten freed eventually, once he'd served a fairly long sentence for a mistake he'd made when he was young, but I'd screwed that up by getting on the Regnum's shit list. We were both outlaws now. Sticking by me meant his life was always going to be in danger. And in many ways he *had* to stick by me. We were still magically linked as master and familiar, and nobody but I could hear his telepathic speech. The magic binding familiars is powerful, and I didn't know how to fix things so he'd be entirely free. And I couldn't ever pay him back for everything he'd already done for me. If I thought about it too hard, I had Beck's "Loser" playing as the soundtrack inside my head, and that wouldn't do either of us any good, so I just tried to not think about it.

"I'm not crazy," I told him. "Well, okay, I *am* sort of having the crazies today, but this is me trying to fix that. I'm having a premonition I can't figure out, and I'm hoping something jumps out at me."

Why didn't you just say so? He sounded cross.

"Because I figured it would sound dumb when I said it out loud."

When has that ever stopped you before?

"Oh, bite me," I said affectionately. If he was snarking at me, that meant he couldn't be *too* angry.

I followed my itchy instincts and turned left onto North Broadway. Soon we were approaching the bridge over I-71.

Wait. There was something on the overpass fence. But I caught a glimpse of it only through my ocularis; my flesh eye hadn't seen a thing. I clicked on my hazards and pulled over to the side of the road, annoying the driver of a little yellow Volkswagen Beetle behind me. He honked indignantly and zoomed around me. Nobody else was coming from either direction.

I stared at the spot; through my ocularis it was an indistinct blur slowly moving up the fence. Man-sized, maybe? I started blinking through other enchanted views through the stone. Blur . . . blur . . . darker blur . . . bright blur . . . And suddenly I saw a thin, shirtless white guy with brown dreadlocks and blue basketball shorts struggling to climb the chain-link fence, his flip-flops giving him little purchase on the galvanized wire.

"Holy shit, that's Kai," I told Pal.

Where? my familiar peered around, confused.

"On the fence. Someone turned him invisible. *Mostly* invisible. Come on."

Pal hopped onto my shoulder as I killed the engine. I hadn't seen Kai in months; I'd sublet a room in his run-down Victorian rental for a few days while I was recuperating after the demon fight. I was seriously messed up in pretty much every way you can imagine, but he had a little crush on me anyhow, and he'd really been a huge help when I'd sorely needed it. Bit of a stoner, but a good guy. A little naive, but he was still a teenager after all. As far as I knew, he didn't hang out with anyone else who knew magic. Who could have turned him invisible?

"Hey, Kai!" I stepped out of the car, pocketed the keys, and shut the door. "What are you doing out here?"

"He said . . . He said . . ." Kai muttered. His voice was slurred, like he was drunk. Or under a magical compulsion.

I waited for a silver Honda Odyssey minivan to pass and then jogged across the street. Kai still seemed determined to get up the fence. "What did he say?"

"He said jump off a bridge. . . . He said jump off a bridge. . . ."

"Whoa, no!" I reached up and grabbed his hairy leg. "Come on down from there. Let's go get some coffee."

Well, I can see him now, Pal remarked inside my mind. *The spell fails at close range. Whoever cast that didn't do much of a job.*

Fast and sloppy, I thought back. *But it had to work only well enough to keep anyone from seeing him until he'd thrown himself over into traffic.*

It would be a quick death, maybe, but I cringed to imagine the massive freeway pileup that would follow. What if he splattered across the windshield of a car full of little kids? Jesus. Even if they survived the wreck, they'd never get over seeing something like that. Whoever did this definitely wanted Kai gone, but they were both too lazy to do it themselves *and* perverse enough to want his death to cause mayhem. That was a kind of twisted you didn't see every day. I liked Kai and owed him a solid. But even if I'd hated his guts, I wanted to get to the bottom of all this, because whoever would cast a spell like this deserved to get their ass kicked. A *lot*.

"He said jump off a bridge," Kai insisted, clinging to the fence with white knuckles, trying to pull his leg from my grasp.

I had to do something to break the enchantment and free him. But I didn't have any spell ingredients on me. What could I use? I scanned the ground and spied a brown sparrow's feather sticking out of a wind-drifted pile of dead grass and dust in the gutter.

"Bingo." I released his leg, plucked the feather, and stepped back to concentrate on the chant.

Ubiquemancy is the art of finding and using magic in everyday objects. It's just a *little* tricky. And I hate performing it out in the open, where random people can see. It isn't just that public displays of magic are of those universally verboten things. It's that ubiquemancy looks hella goofy. It's the magical equivalent of speaking in tongues, and once I start a chant, for all I know I could end up barking like a dog or clucking like a chicken. I don't have an overabundance of dignity, but some things you just feel better about doing in private.

I took a deep breath and let it out slowly, trying to center myself.

"Don't you dare start laughing at me if this falls flat," I muttered to Pal.

Perish the thought. He was gazing at Kai struggling up the wire.

At least the kid wasn't making fast progress, so we had a bit of time. *Serious situation is serious.*

I closed my eyes, focused on the feather in my cupped hands, took another deep breath, and started speaking words for freedom and release. The magic kicked in smoothly, and ancient, lost words started spilling from my lips. I could feel the little feather heating on my palm, smell it starting to burn. My chant grew louder, stronger, and I could feel the magic it carried pushing against the spell binding Kai. Tension rose, higher and higher, as the invisible forces torqued against each other.

Suddenly the feather exploded with a *pop!* and Kai gave a startled yelp.

"Whoa! What the hell?" His eyes were huge and panicked. It looked like I'd managed to nix both the compulsion and the lazy invisibility.

"Where am I?" he asked.

"You're on the North Broadway overpass," I told him, trying to sound soothing. "Just come down from there, but go easy. Your body might not do what you want it to for a little while."

I helped him down off the fence, and he stood there, gasping, on shaky legs, looking gray faced and frail. Like a confused old man. For the first time, I noticed that his right eye was purpled and swollen, like he'd taken a solid punch in the face sometime in the past few hours.

"What happened?" I asked him. "Who did this to you?"

"I . . . I don't . . ." He shook his head, but then his eyes seemed to focus and I could practically see the memories swarming back into his mind. "Oh, shit. Oh shit, shit, *shit*."

"Dude, stop panicking!" I put a comforting hand on his shoulder. "Deep breaths. Tell me what happened."

"They took Alice! Oh, Jesus, we gotta find her, Jessie. They're gonna do something terrible to her!"

"Slow down, bro. Who's Alice? Who took her?"

"She . . . I met her a few weeks ago. She's like you; she knows magic. I figured from the start she knew some dangerous dudes, but . . . Well, we got this jeweled statue of Santa Muerte that we were trying to sell off. I mean, the thing creeped me out and I wanted to just leave it in an alley someplace, but she was all, 'We can get good coin for this,' so—"

"Wait." There were some perfectly nice people in the world who prayed to lovely Saint Death, but most of the ones I'd met personally were either necromancers or hired guns working for the narco cartels. And *nice* wasn't part of their job descriptions. "What were you doing with a statue of Santa Muerte?"

"Uh." He scratched his scalp nervously. "After you left, I rented your room to this guy named Halulu, and he came up with the idea to do a deal with some gangbangers to make some cash for the rent. I thought it was just going to be weed, but it was meth, and the whole thing went sideways."

Oh, Mensa is bereft of this lad, and its members weep, Pal intoned from my shoulder.

"A drug deal?" I said. "For God's sake. Really?"

"Yeah, okay, I know. Okay?" Kai looked embarrassed. "Halulu had this way of making it seem totally reasonable, but I know it wasn't. I'm not *stupid.*"

He rubbed his arms as if he were remembering something terrifying. "Some really freaky shit went down. One of the gang dudes got shot; I spoke to his ghost, and there was this *thing* in the room with us. . . ."

He trailed off, looking horrified, but shook himself and continued.

"Alice sort of took charge afterward and helped us get out of the mess. We were able to pay back the guys in Detroit, and it was all good. I mean, except for the dead guy. But all we had left over from the deal was the statue, and we still needed to pay the rent. So Alice started checking around—friends of friends, you know? And someone was interested in the statue. And they came to the house this afternoon and . . . Oh, god."

He went pale, his lips a clamped line.

"Could they have been friends of the dead guy?" I prompted.

Kai shook his head, his dreadlocks brushing his shoulders. "He was a murderer—his ghost told me so—but he was regular, you know? Maybe a sociopath or whatever, but he was just a guy. But the ones who showed up . . . I don't think they were even human. They were just trying to look like people. They wanted the statue, but they also wanted Alice, and when I tried to stop them, the boss guy backhanded me across the room like I was nothing and told me to jump off a bridge. And . . . I don't know much after that."

I paused. Kai didn't know *any* Talents before me. He hadn't been mixed up in anything more dangerous or illegal than a pair of sad marijuana plants he and his roommates were growing in the basement. Could my brief stay at his house have made him vulnerable to darker forces and set all this in motion? I didn't voice my concern to Pal; he'd tell me that I couldn't think that way or else I'd drive myself crazy and blah, blah, blah. But I *was* thinking that way, and consequently I felt even worse for Kai. Even if he *had* been a dumbass.

"I guess Alice means a whole lot to you?"

"Hell, yeah." He had a dreamy look in his brown eyes that made me certain he was hard in love with her. "She's great. You'd like her, Jessie."

"I'm sure." If she was as much of a loose cannon as I suspected she was, we'd either get on like a house on fire or want to stab each other in the face. "Let's go back to your place, and we can start tracking her down."

>——<

Kai's rental on East Avenue was a huge old Victorian single in desperate need of a fresh paint job; the glow of the setting sun didn't make it look any better. The broad front porch had surely been stately a hundred years before. Now the floorboards were warped and the railings were as broken and gray as a meth addict's teeth. Ragged lawn chairs surrounded a squat red plastic table covered in crumpled Pabst Blue Ribbon cans. Cigarette butts spilled from an old brown glass ashtray.

Ah, hovel, sweet hovel. Pal's telepathic voice dripped with sarcasm.

"Your roommates around?" I asked Kai.

"Nah, Mikey and Patrick went down to Athens for a house party. They'll probably roll in late tonight."

"Just as well," I replied. "They probably couldn't have stopped the guys who took Alice, either."

Assuming that they'd even try, Pal grumped to me. *Neither of those two seemed to have an overabundance of bravery.*

Shush, I thought back.

"Ah, shit, the door's open." Kai ran up onto the porch and pushed into the house. "Dammit!"

"What?" I called.

"Someone stole our shit!" He pulled at his dreadlocks, looking like he was going to cry. "The flat-screen and our game stuff are gone! Today is just fuckin' *fired.*"

No surprise that someone had seized the opportunity to loot the house. You could leave your door unlocked in some neighborhoods, but north campus was not one of them. "Deep breaths. I can help you with that, too, but let's worry about Alice first, okay?"

"Yeah." He rubbed his eyes with the heels of his hands. "It's just stuff, right? I should be glad to be alive right now."

"But speaking of stuff, do you have any of Alice's I could use to try to track her?" I asked. "Like a brush with her hair, or some piece of clothing she's worn?"

"Sure, yeah. Come on in."

I followed him into the living room. His battered thrift-store entertainment center was empty and toppled in the thieves' haste to leave, as were the makeshift bricks-and-boards shelves that had held his movie and game collection. The rest of the room looked okay, or at least okay by college-bro standards. In some guys' places, you'd be hard-pressed to know if they had been ransacked or not.

But a red gleam on the floor by the bricked-up fireplace caught my attention. I stepped closer and saw a glittering ruby surrounded by dark, faceted onyx on a shattered fragment of bronze. It was maybe as big as the lid of an Altoids tin and looked to be part of Santa Muerte's dress. And it was lying in a puddle of dark ooze.

"Did anyone throw or drop the statue over here?" I asked Kai.

He shook his head. "Sorry, I don't remember."

I grabbed a ballpoint pen from off the cluttered coffee table and used it to flip over the fragment. The edges of the metal looked pale and twisted, as though something had wrenched the bronze apart. On the floor where it had lain, I saw a shred of gray-ish, leathery membrane, and I caught a strong whiff of amniotic brine and brimstone from the ooze.

Well, this is unexpected, Pal whispered.

"There was an egg inside the statue," I said to Kai. "And whatever hatched was strong enough to tear the metal apart."

"Whoa," he replied. "So *that's* what was making that scratching noise we were hearing. We thought we had a mouse someplace."

What could have been hiding in there? I thought to Pal. *My knowledge of Mexican magical lore is pretty rusty, but I don't remember anything about Santa Muerte's figures containing any icky little piñata surprises like this.*

My guess is it's some kind of devil larvae that survives through spiritual parasitism, he said inside my mind. *It can slowly grow inside the statue, feeding off the prayer energy directed toward it by worshippers.*

That's pretty sneaky, I thought back. *Even for a devil.*

The question I'm most concerned with is, Where did it go after it hatched? Pal said.

Yeah. We don't want whatever was in that statue running around loose, I replied to Pal before speaking to Kai. "Maybe the guys who grabbed Alice took the hatchling with them, but maybe they didn't. Let me try using some of the fragments to track it. . . ."

Kai lent me a pair of pliers to pick up the gooey bit of membrane. I'm not squeamish, but you just don't want to touch fluids from any diabolic creature unless you know for sure what it can do. I'd been possessed before and it's not fun.

I closed my eyes, focused on the membrane, and started chanting old words for *find*. I'd done tracking spells before to find devils; generally all my trouble came after I found them. As the words spilled from my lips, I started to get a hazy image of a two-story house—

Wham!

The blocking magic felt like an armored fist smashing into my forehead, and for a moment my vision went entirely white. I came awake sprawled on my back on the dirty wooden floor. Pal had leaped off my shoulder when I fell and was safe on the nearby ottoman.

What happened? my familiar asked.

"Junior's protected," I croaked, hoping the room would stop spinning sometime soon. "We gotta try for Alice."

Kai peered down at me, looking worried. "Can I get you anything?"

"A Coke or Pepsi would be great," I replied. "And some of Alice's hair if you have it. *Head* hair, please and thank you."

Kai jogged into the kitchen and brought back a cold can of Faygo cola. "It's all we got, sorry."

"Thanks." I sat up and took the drink, hoping he wasn't secretly a Juggalo. Drug dealing and dark magic I could handle, but terrible taste in music might make me question our friendship.

Are you okay? Pal asked me, as Kai went upstairs to look for Alice's hairbrush. *You're quite pale and rather sweaty.*

"I'm fine. Just feeling kinda shaky from the spell block. Sugar and caffeine should fix me up, though." I took a long swig from the can, then let out the inevitable belch.

Kai soon returned with a foofy ball of ash-blond hair. "Will this work?"

"It should." I cupped the blond wad in my hands and began the chant. Soon, that same mundane-looking two-story house came into my mind, sharpened. I saw a street sign: Kilmuir Drive. I knew the area; it was in the Hilliard suburb a mile or so to the south of Tuttle Mall. A far nicer neighborhood than the one Kai lived in, the kind of 'burb young professionals with kids settled in because of the modest home prices, nice parks and good school system.

The kind of place an unleashed devil could do a whole lot of damage in a hurry if it had the chance.

I looked at Kai. "You wouldn't happen to have a gun around here, would you?"

He nodded. "Yeah, I got a nine under my bed. Ammo, too."

"Go get it. And put a shirt and some real shoes on." I pulled out my phone and started texting Mother Karen and Cooper to let them know where I was going. "Better get some food if you haven't eaten, because this could be a long night. . . ."

>>><<<

We got to Kilmuir Drive well after sundown. I slowed the car, scanning the houses, looking for the one from my vision. And there it was, sitting innocently in the middle of the block. Developers probably built it sometime in the late eighties; it was the kind of two-story, two-car-garage place you could find in most any suburb in America. White aluminum siding. Picket fence. Red decorative shutters. Manicured lawn with a freshly mulched flower bed of chrysanthemums (white or yellow; I couldn't tell in the near darkness). The porch light was on, and a fluorescent glow from the kitchen illuminated the first-floor windows. Everything else was dark.

The more I stared at the entirely pleasant-looking place, the more dread I felt. Something was desperately wrong, but there was no physical sign of it. I blinked through to the ocularis view that would show me hidden magic and enchantments.

Wham!

"Shit!" The kick was to my eye socket this time, and I quickly blinked to a more mundane view.

"What's the matter?" Kai and Pal asked, nearly simultaneously.

"That's a heavy block. No tracking, no viewing. For all I know, we'll get fried the moment we set foot on the porch." I pulled out my cell phone and dialed Riviera Jordan's number. It was only for emergencies, but this was starting to feel like one. Or it would be an emergency once we got inside.

The call went to her voice mail. I left her a quick message explaining the situation, and gave her the street address.

"Feel free to drop on by. Probably we'll need help. Thanks, and good-bye." I ended the call and shut off my ringer.

I've never known you to willingly call for Circle assistance, Pal remarked. *Are you sure you're feeling all right?*

I'm pretty sure I don't feel like having my arm bitten off again, or getting my other eye burned out of my head, I thought back, irritated. *Besides, if something happens and she finds out I could have warned her but didn't, what do you think the odds are that she'll kick us out of Columbus?*

Rather high, Pal admitted.

"Okay, so let's do this," I told Kai. "*Quietly.* Follow my lead. Keep your gun holstered until I tell you different."

He nodded, white faced. "You're the boss."

Kai shouldered a black nylon backpack laden with rope, flashlights, kerosene, a first-aid kit and sundry tools. I retrieved my twelve-gauge Mossberg 590 shotgun from the backseat. It was fully loaded with cartridges that contained eighteen pellets of mixed silver and iron buckshot: a little something for any sort of hostile creature I might encounter, magical or mundane. Ubiquemancy wasn't ideal for rapid attacks. I had done a few offensive spells often enough that I could get them to work with a fast phrase—*trip* and *shove* were good quickies, and I was still tweaking *zap* to change Pal—but killing words were considered one of the worst kinds of necromancy by pretty much everyone. As much trouble as I was in with the Regnum, I didn't want to make my situation any worse with serious dark-side stuff.

We shut the Toyota's doors as quietly as possible and crept toward the front door, hoping none of the neighbors would see and call the cops. There were very few magical combat situations that mundane police forces couldn't make two hundred percent worse.

Should we wait for Riviera to show up? I thought to Pal as we reached the cover of the front porch.

I am quite concerned about this newfound prudence of yours, he replied.

No, seriously. Should we wait? Or will waiting get Kai's girl killed?

"Do we go in?" Kai whispered, his voice shaking.

There's no guarantee that Riviera checks her voice mail promptly, Pal thought to me, *and I doubt any of her people are as effective at killing devils as you are. Our lack of apparent support may lull our opponent into a false sense of complacency.*

He paused. *Or it could get us killed. One or the other.*

Wow, you're a help, I thought to him.

I knew he meant his words to be encouraging, but they made me feel a little sick. Because, if I was honest with myself, I knew he was right. I was very, very good at killing devils. And I might have felt okay if my destructive talents had stopped there. But it seemed I was pretty good at killing damn near anything. Way better than I was at keeping people alive. My avoiding murder words had nothing to do with the Regnum's rules. It was because I really didn't need them.

I hated being good at something so fundamentally rotten. And I hated that I lived in a world where those particular skills came in so very handy. I wanted to be a good person, and I wasn't sure that was really possible once I got enough blood on my hands. Even if most of it was ichor. But I didn't feel right walking away from people in trouble, either, and I wasn't about to back down from a fight someone else started.

"Yes, we're going in," I replied, voice low. I leaned my shotgun against the white vinyl porch railing and pulled off my opera glove. Shoved it in the pocket of my jeans. I stared at the doorknob. "Odds are the house has some kind of protection, but maybe not. Pal, go to Kai, just in case."

He hopped over onto Kai's shoulder. I took a deep breath and gently touched the front doorknob with my flesh hand.

A hot blue bolt of magical electricity arced through me. My muscles spasmed painfully, and I peed myself a little. And then I dropped like a sack of potatoes onto the Astroturfed porch boards.

Kai knelt beside me. "Are you okay?"

"Crap on a cracker, that hurt." I sat up, trying to shake the buzzing numbness out of my fingers. I didn't see any new lights coming on in the houses around, and nobody seemed to be peeking through blinds. "No surprise, though."

"What do we do?"

"Get insulated." I looked around. "You got a candy wrapper? Something made of plastic or wax paper?"

"Lemme check." He dug through his pockets and found a wadded-up cough-drop wrapper. "Will this work?"

"It should. I need it to work for only a minute or two." Heck, I *wanted* it to work for only a minute or two. I held it in my hands and began my chant, as quietly as I could, and as the old words began to summon magical forces, I felt a plasticky film start to shroud my skin.

Still chanting, I got to my feet, motioned for Kai to follow, and grabbed the doorknob. Locked. I switched up my chant and spoke an ancient word for *rust*. The metal crumbled when I gave it a third hard twist.

And then we were standing in the dimness of the living room.

"Stay behind me," I whispered to Kai. Already I could feel the filminess disappearing. "I can see in the dark; try to leave your flashlight off."

Adrenaline surged in my bloodstream. Being pretty good at killing didn't mean I wouldn't get killed myself. I took a deep breath, blinked through to the night-vision view and stepped into the living room. My flesh eye showed me only the rough details of the dim room, but through my ocularis I saw a drip of blood spotting the pale carpet. The dark trail led to a door beneath the stairs.

You see that? I thought to Pal.

The basement, he replied. *Of course it's in the basement.*

We did a quick sweep of the first floor and upper floor, stepping as gently as possible to avoid squeaking the floorboards. Kai followed close behind me, quiet as a ghost. The rooms were mostly empty; what furniture was there seemed like the kind of stuff Realtors placed to stage houses for sale. There were few signs that anybody was actually living there.

I went back to the basement door and tried the knob. No jolt. Not locked. I pushed, and it swung inward with a creak that seemed far too loud. Immediately, the stench of decaying flesh made my eyes water. The bloody drip continued down the carpeted stairs; it and the stairs ended at another door. I held my breath, listening. Nothing.

"What now?" Kai whispered, barely audible.

"We go down," I whispered back. "Get your nine out. Don't shoot me in the back."

His "Okay" was an anxious exhalation, syllables swallowed by dread.

We descended.

At every careful step, I wondered if I should ease the basement door open or kick the thing in. If they didn't know we were there and weren't watching the door, a stealthy opening would give us an advantage. But if they knew we were coming, kicking it open might work better. Assuming the slam didn't startle someone into firing a weapon. Assuming they wouldn't just start firing at us whether they were startled or not. *Shit.* I hated this part.

Instinct took over when my hand was on the knob. I swung it open, fast and hard enough to bash anyone lurking on the other side. Nobody was.

I took in the whole scene in just two heartbeats. The basement was unfinished and had no furniture or appliances besides the furnace unit in the corner. Someone had smeared a yards-wide, complex necromancy diagram in the middle of the concrete floor with blood. It looked to be the kind of thing you made to open an extradimensional portal. To either side stood a pair of gangly figures in dark clothes; their faces had a shiny, unformed fetal look, and their arms and legs seemed just a bit too long for normal human proportions. A hairy, naked middle-aged guy, blindfolded and ball-gagged, lay crucified in the middle of the diagram, his hands and feet staked to holes in the floor with rebar. I couldn't tell if he was still alive or not.

Above the crucified man stood a pretty blond girl, maybe eighteen or nineteen, also naked. . . . And her eyes were the inflamed purple of the recently possessed. Alice, but not really. Not anymore.

And all around us were a dozen reanimated dead guys. The source of the terrible stench. Some of them were maybe just days dead, bloated and crawling with maggots, but others had been gone a long time, their desiccated flesh stretched and ragged over dry bones.

Not-Alice hissed and made a "Get them!" motion. The zombies lunged toward us with surprising speed; I had to admire the necromancy. The gangly figures pulled pistols from their waistbands but hung back, waiting.

Take 'em! I tossed Pal up in the air and spoke an ancient word to trigger my electroshock spell.

A tiny, bright bolt of lightning sprang from my fingertip and hit him in the flank as he approached the apex of my throw. His fur went *poof!*—I'd worked the spell to steal the required energy from his hair. His tiny naked legs and tail windmilled in the air for the briefest moment. In the space between two of my own jackhammering heartbeats, his tail shrank, his legs and body lengthened and thickened faster than gravity and a new, thick pelt of heavy brown fur sprouted on his expanding hide.

His entire transformation took less than a second. When his paws landed on the concrete floor, he was no longer a slinky little ferret but a grizzly bear. Eight hundred pounds of muscle and bone and righteous fury. He reared back, thunderously roared and took the head off the nearest rotter with a single paw swipe.

I started blasting the zombies with my shotgun. Aimed for the neck and not the head. Decapitation's what stops zombies if the brains are already rotted away. The boom of my weapon made my ears ache. The air filled with a choking haze of smoke and stinking rot.

In seconds, my shotgun was empty. Kai had drawn his 9 mm and was plugging away at the zombies still standing. Pal swiped the head off another of the creeps.

In the back, the ganglers were taking aim with their pistols. I dropped my spent shotgun and shouted an ancient word for *shove* as I pushed into the empty air. I felt the slam in my arms as my spell connected and they stumbled backward, their gun arms shoved to their sides.

This was my chance. I sprinted forward, sprang over the crucified guy and slapped not-Alice on her shoulder with my cold white hand. And dragged us both into my personal hell.

This was what remained of the nightmarish world my boyfriend Cooper had been enslaved in when he fell into a trap laid by a powerful, pain-consuming devil called a Goad. It was a pocket dimension, an extradimensional space whose reality I controlled completely ever since I'd killed the Goad that had created it and rescued Cooper. The hellement became a permanent part of my magical landscape.

I'd tried to mask the evil of the place by turning it into a perfect replica of my childhood bedroom. Perpetual late-afternoon sunlight streamed in through the mini blinds, my stuffed animals lined up at attention on the dresser, my Buzz Lightyear comforter draped the bed. Beneath the pink dust ruffle, a thousand horrifying memories from the Goad's many victims slept in glass jars.

"What have you done? What is this place?" growled not-Alice, looking furious but a little uncertain. I'd managed to throw the creature for a loop. She appeared as a strange double image now, the possessive devil visible as a kind of dark twin right behind her.

"You're in *my* house now." I reached under the bed, pulled out my longsword and pointed it at her. "Talk. What are you doing in Alice's body?"

"Useful. It has magic," the devil replied.

"For what?"

"To bring Mother here."

"And why does your mother want to be here?"

"Souls," the devil hissed wistfully. "So many delicious souls."

I sighed. That's all devils ever seemed to want. Human souls were apparently the popcorn shrimp of the spiritual world. I kept hoping a devil would tell me it was here for gambling, or to drink all the whiskey and download a bunch of porn, or steal the secret recipe for Coca-Cola. No such luck. It was all souls, all the time.

"Let Alice go and I'll be as nice as I possibly can," I said.

The devil shrieked and lunged at me. I spun aside like a matador and grabbed the darkness clinging to Alice with my left hand. She/it fought me, clawing at my arms, but I held on, wrestled them both down to the floor.

Ignoring the stinging blows she was landing on my face, I tightened my grip and yanked as hard as I could. The darkness ripped clean away from her with a scream that could have shattered glass. Alice tumbled forward, jerking in the throes of a seizure. I was left gripping a dark, squirming mass that reminded me of an enormous liver fluke.

"I get it. You're still just a baby and you don't understand," I told it as it struggled to break free. It was clammy, frigid through and through. Devils tend to be creatures of heat or cold. I was glad that this one was cold, because I worked better with fire.

"This is *my* place." I stared at the wall and willed a blast furnace into existence. Mount Doom didn't burn half as hot. "I don't *need* to do magic here. This *is* my magic."

I flung the boneless devil into the boiling metal. The thing writhed, shrieking and jerking and steaming. It tried to haul itself out of the inferno, but I slammed the grate on it. The furnace shook as it struggled, but I held fast. Through the bars I watched it burn. Watched it die. When I was satisfied it was nothing but ash, I erased the furnace and knelt beside Alice to see how she was doing.

She was pale, breathing shallowly. Clearly suffering from shock. Exorcisms take time for a reason. It's a trauma to your system to have another entity take over your mind and body, but it's even worse to have that control suddenly torn away.

"You're lucky you didn't stroke out and die." I brushed a sweaty strand of hair out of one of her wide-staring blue eyes. She really was lovely; I could see why Kai had fallen for her. A tiny little thing, thin and pale and maybe just over five feet tall. So vulnerable, especially here in my hell. I could do whatever I wanted in here. I could tie her down and slowly pull her guts out and listen to her scream. . . .

"Jesus!" I jerked back, suddenly aware of how hideous my thoughts had turned.

Not my thoughts. Those can't be my thoughts. I stared around at the room; suddenly all the replicas of my toys seemed to be silently mocking me.

Magic always had a cost. And the cost to me in this place was my humanity and sanity. I couldn't stay, or I'd become just like the devils I'd killed.

I quickly gathered up Alice, carried her to the big red portal door in the corner and took us back to the real world.

When we rematerialized in the basement, I saw that Pal in his grizzly form had decapitated the remaining zombies and mauled the ganglers. The uncanny pair lay in pieces scattered across the concrete, molasses-thick ichor pooling around their torn limbs. Definitely not human.

"What are they?" I asked Pal.

Some kind of sidhe, I think. Hired minions, regardless.

Kai hurried over, sweaty and spattered with blood and ichor. "Oh, god. Is she okay?"

At the sound of his voice, Alice's eyes fluttered, and she began coughing and gagging. I quickly set her down on the concrete and turned her head to the side. She started vomiting up the dead hatchling. It looked much as it had in my hell, though thankfully it was much smaller.

"Oh, god!" Kai looked like he might start puking himself.

"She needs a healer," I told him. "But at least she's alive."

"So does this fellow." Pal was peering down at the crucified man. "I think he's one of the Governing Circle agents. I think I remember seeing him at the meeting we had with Riviera."

"He's still alive? Wow." I pulled out my cell phone. No service.

"Guys, I'm going upstairs to call Mother Karen," I told them. "She'll know what to do."

I ran up the stairs, out of the house and onto the front lawn and had just lifted my phone to my ear when the wind kicked up and I heard an ominous rumbling.

Oh, shit.

The sky opened, a bright lightning gash in the black firmament, and a creature that looked like an enormous crystalline replica of some alien solar system cruised through. A vast cloud of fiery plasma in which a dozen jewel organs circled a glowing magma heart. A Virtus, one of the prime enforcer spirits of the Virtus Regnum.

I stood there very still, feeling like an inchworm seeing the sole of a giant boot coming down. At first I felt nothing but gut-churning terror: I was so, *so* dead. So incredibly dead. And so were my friends, if the Virtus spotted them. I prayed Kai would stay put in the basement.

But then I felt hope: maybe if I did some first-class fast talking, it would leave Kai and Pal and Alice alone? Then came a squelch of despair: mercy was not part of the Regnum's program, and I damn well knew that. I was the worst kind of idiot to think for even a moment that it might care the teensiest, most minuscule bit that I'd just stopped an invasion of soul-devouring devils. This creature respected only the letter of the law, and the rule book wasn't on my side.

And that's when frustration and anger started skipping in circles through my mind. *Goddammit, I was* so close *to making things right here.* Why did the Virtus have to show up and screw up everything? *Dammit. Dammit, dammit,* dammit!

I mightily resisted the urge to scream and flip double birds at the spirit in the sky. And that moment of self-restraint was a mistake. I'd let my adrenaline ebb just a little, and suddenly complete exhaustion flooded through me, suffocating my rage and will to fight and everything else. My bones suddenly felt like they'd turned to concrete. I was completely beat. And probably the Virtus knew it.

Its icy diamond eyes fixed on me, beholding me like an exterminator sizing up a fire-ant nest. It had probably been shadowing me for a long time. Probably it had hoped that the devil would do its job for it and it wouldn't have to bother with killing me itself.

"You have disobeyed the law," it boomed. The ground shook. "You have violated the prohibition against grand necromancy. You have murdered. You shall be destroyed."

I'd heard it all before, but this time I didn't have the power to defend myself. When I killed my first Virtus, I was flush with the magical energy of a very powerful devil. And, frankly, I'd had more than my share of blind shithouse luck that day. I couldn't jump up and drag this new Virtus into my hell, and even if I did, I wasn't sure the power I wielded there would be enough. And I couldn't run back into the house; the Virtus would just burn it all to ashes and consider it a job cleanly done.

So I did the only thing that seemed reasonable to my exhausted self: I fell to my knees on the grass, shut my eyes and waited to die.

"Stop!" I heard a woman shout.

I opened my eyes. Riviera Jordan stood by the curb, looking fashionably stern in a dark designer suit a lawyer might wear to some big trial, backlit in the headlights of a big gray SUV, her short silver hair a bright halo around her face.

"I have authority here!" She held up an ivory tablet inscribed with some kind of ancient runes. "You may not harm Miss Shimmer. She's under my protection. Leave now!"

The Virtus glared at Riviera. "If you deny me my duty, we will not return to Columbus. Your city will be without the protection of the Virtus Regnum. Do you truly want that?"

"I think we need her more than we need you," Riviera drawled in her upper-crust Southern accent. "And you lot weren't doing much to protect us anyhow."

"Insolence," the Virtus grumbled, but it disappeared back into the night sky, the lightning gash sealing behind it, leaving behind only the smell of ozone and a faintly glowing ring of smoke in the air.

I slowly climbed to my feet. "Two people in the basement need a healer. One is your guy. They were gonna use him as a sacrifice in a portal-opening ritual. He's in bad shape."

"Devil or necromancer?" Riviera asked.

"Devil." I stretched, and my spine popped.

"You kill it?" She pulled a pack of Marlboros from her suit jacket and tapped out a cigarette.

"Yes, ma'am!"

"Good girl."

Riviera turned her head to call over her shoulder: "Rafé, Loretta, grab your kits and head down to the basement!"

Two Circle agents in dark suits with armbands bearing red crosses and white canvas shoulder bags piled out of the back of the SUV and hurried into the house.

"Thank you," I said to Riviera. "I guess this means Pal and I get to stay in Columbus."

She smiled and lit her cigarette. "Just don't make me regret this."

HUNTER, HEALER

by Jim C. Hines

Julia Chapel woke to the sound of cursing from the next room of her apartment. She checked the alarm clock and groaned. Not yet midnight. Hob had roused her early. It must be an emergency. "How bad is it?"

"Get yer cross-eyed tits out here and see for yourself." Hob was a hearth fairy, and considered himself a poet of profanity. "And stop yelling. I'm trying to check this corpse-fucker's vitals!"

Julia grabbed a worn terry-cloth robe from the floor. For almost two decades, she had lived in this crumbling building, healing anyone and anything that came to her door. Most patients arrived during the night, preferring to avoid notice. Recession had reduced Detroit's human population in recent years, and other things had moved in to fill the void, meaning such interruptions to her sleep were more and more frequent.

Her second soul groaned, just as weary as Julia herself, but less reticent about complaining. "I know," Julia said sympathetically. "But something needs our help."

She donned a pair of old slippers and hurried into the living room. After so many years, few things could crack Julia's composure, but the sight of a harvester bleeding over her carpet gave her pause. She shouldn't even have been able to see the harvester so clearly. The mystical scavengers usually drifted in limbo, materializing only to feed on lingering magic from the dead. Who the hell had power enough to burn away the thing's cloak of shadow and carve the lifeless flesh beneath?

"Temp's thirty-four," said Hob. "Cold as Jack Frost's cerulean scrotum. You want the holy water?"

"Not for this. Get the rubbing alcohol." She wasn't certain what holy water would do to a harvester, but the alcohol shouldn't be a problem for its undead nerves and tissues, and it would protect the dead flesh from infection.

She reached without looking to take the plastic bottle that had appeared in Hob's outstretched hand, and squirted the contents onto the worst of the wounds, a deep puncture in the stomach.

Where the harvester was a mummified nightmare, Hob was anything but threatening: barely taller than a child, with sticklike limbs and an ill-fitting white fedora. A thick beard emphasized his jutting chin and oversized teeth. His left ear was missing, making his hat sit crookedly on his head. Julia had saved his life years ago, but the ear had been lost down the gullet of a hellhound.

"This is the creepiest uncle-fucker you've had in here since that soul-leech thing in 'oh-nine."

"It doesn't matter." Every supernatural creature in the city knew her name and her rules. Julia Chapel would treat anyone and anything as long as they left their wars outside. Blood drinkers and demons, sewer witches and hunters—all were welcome unless they violated the peace of her home.

No healer for a thousand miles could match her power, and no one knew when they would next need her aid. Whatever fights raged across the city, they stopped at her doorway.

She had hoped this peace, this life, would also help her to heal herself. Her selves, rather.

It's time, she commanded silently, dragging her second soul from its stubborn sleep.

A pair of flickering, spectral arms peeled away from Julia's body to tug the shadows away from the harvester and give her a better look at the thing's withered gray chest.

Her hands—her real hands—began to shake. She clasped them together and closed her eyes until she regained her calm. The harvester needed her help.

She cleansed the rest of the injuries as the spirit hands pulled threads of gold light through the gouge in the stomach. Most of the cuts were shallow. Tentative. And the pattern was familiar. . . .

She seized the harvester's left hand. The gash across the palm was just as she remembered from that day more than two decades before. "Who did this to you?"

The harvester couldn't answer, but Julia didn't need it to. She clenched her hands together and waited for her second soul to finish its work. Once they were done, Julia inspected the stitches and fed the harvester just enough of her own magic to sustain it before drawing the cloak back into place.

It left without a word. Julia pulled her spirit limbs back into her body and approached the sliding-glass door on the far side of the living room. She pulled the curtains aside, opened the door, and stepped out onto the small balcony. A single plastic chair sat to one side. A half-dead spider plant hung from a hooked nail she'd pounded into the underside of her upstairs neighbors' balcony. She gripped the rusting iron rail with both hands and searched the parking lot until she found the man she'd known would be lingering in the darkness, waiting for her to respond to his message.

"I'm going out, Hob."

Hob stared out through the bars of the railing. "Fuck a Smurf and call him Gimpy, is that who I think it is?"

"Yes."

"Want me to come with you? I'll fuck him up, down, and inside out. He'll be pissing through his nose and shitting his own dick by the time I'm done with him."

At any other time, the fairy's bravado would have drawn a smile. "He's a hunter. If he thinks you're a threat, he won't hesitate to put you down."

"What about you?"

"He won't kill me." What he wanted from Julia was far worse.

><

No one would have recognized Terrence Chapel as Julia's father. For one thing, he was white. He also looked forty years her senior, thanks to her unnaturally extended lifespan. Age had turned his close-cropped hair cotton white and added to the wrinkles rippling from his crooked nose, but his eyes were the same narrow brown pits of anger, determination, and disappointment she remembered from her youth.

His worn pea jacket was open, revealing a holstered automatic on his right hip and a double-edged dagger on the left. Doubtless the same knife he had used to stab and torture the harvester. The nearby streetlamp had burned out—probably his doing, to conceal them from passing traffic and curious neighbors.

"Good to see you both." His lip was swollen. Black-edged blisters covered the right side of his face. The harvester had fought back, drying the life from his flesh. The dead skin cracked with every movement, but no pain made it into his voice or expression. "You know, if you hadn't warded me out, I could've just knocked or texted you or something instead of going to all that trouble."

"What do you want?"

He scratched the side of his jaw. "Truth is, I need your help."

"No. Is there anything else?"

Her cell phone buzzed. She split her attention between Terrence and the new text message. *Tell him he's a cum-bloated, devil-buggered tick from an elephant's moldy pubes!*

Not for the first time, she wondered why she'd let Hob talk her into getting him a smartphone.

"I've missed that coldhearted attitude of yours," he said. "Look. I've left you alone like you wanted. I've let you play doctor in peace while I was—"

"In *peace*?" Silver light flashed from Julia's mouth as she spoke. "You attacked a harvester and sent its broken body staggering to my doorstep."

"Didn't kill it, though." He paced along the edge of the parking lot. "You did a good job on these wards. I don't suppose you'd show me how you got them to block not only me, but any attempt to get a message to you?"

When she didn't respond, he shrugged. "You forced my hand. Nothing can stop a harvester. It's in their nature, their role in the world. It's the only way I could get your attention."

Her fists tightened until the nails threatened to pierce flesh. "How long did it take you to match every cut?"

"Couple of hours. The real trick was catching the thing in the first place."

"You should go. While you still can."

He had sense enough to step back. "The man I'm hunting is like you. You and your sister."

She stopped breathing.

"I can't kill him alone. I need—"

"I know what you need," she whispered. "I won't do it. *We* won't do it."

"Then a lot of people are going to die, Jules."

"Don't call me that."

"He calls himself Shard. He's a nasty piece of work. Kills for pleasure. Started with ordinary humans, but then he discovered new prey. His being double-souled means he's too strong for me to take down."

"I know what it means." Better than he ever would. "Why are you the one hunting him?"

His silence was answer enough.

"You hunted together, didn't you? You found another double-soul, and you had to have him, no matter how twisted he was."

"He wanted to kill, and there are things in this world in need of killing. We did a lot of good, before—"

Her second soul seized him in a grip of light and magic and rage. Julia regained control an instant later, but in that time, her sister's spirit threw Terrence to the ground hard enough to kill an ordinary man. He coughed blood.

"Clean up your own mess," she snapped.

"It's been twenty years. You can't save her." Terrence spat and wiped his chin. "Once Shard learns the truth about you and your sister, he'll know you're a threat. Not to mention a challenge, a trophy. He won't stop until he's standing over your bloody corpse. Either I can help you, or you can fight him alone."

"And you'll make sure he learns about us, won't you?" One way or another, he would maneuver her into the hunt again. Force her—force *them*—to fight the way they used to.

He jerked his chin toward the apartment. "I lost your sister. I don't want to have to bury you, too."

"Maybe we'll both get lucky." Julia backed away, watching for any twitch that could telegraph an attack, but he didn't move. "Maybe Shard will kill you first."

>—◄—

There was no trace of the harvester's blood when she returned to her apartment, and the used equipment had all been returned to its proper place. Any medical waste was bagged for disposal at a nearby incinerator. There were advantages to having a hearth fairy as an assistant.

"Your father is a cheese-rectumed pustule of a man," Hob said, once Julia shut the door. "May he be blown by a thousand diseased piranha."

"Don't call him that. My father, I mean."

Hob adjusted his hat. "What'd he want?"

"Me." That was a lie. It wasn't just Julia he wanted. She had never told Hob the truth about her sister, but if Terrence had loosed a murderous hunter on her, it endangered him, too. "And the second soul I carry."

"Well, smoke my dick. I've wondered, but I thought double-souls were a myth. Is it true you've got twice the power of that shit smear out there?"

"More than that."

"Then why don't you just kill the hemorrhoid-sucking ass-breather and be done with it?"

"Because of Jessica." She sat down in the lone recliner and slowed her breathing until her second soul grew calm. "She was—is—my twin sister. Terrence adopted us from South Korea when we were fourteen months old and brought us to America. He sensed the power and potential in us both. He raised us to be hunters. Growing up, I thought our lives were normal. Moving from city to city, killing monsters and protecting humanity. We learned about demons and darkness with our letters. A is for *antichrist*, B is for *Bhūta* . . ."

"C is for *cock-zombie*."

"Jessica was stronger than me. Or that's what we both believed." Jessica's spirit was still restless after their encounter in the parking lot. Most of the time, Jessica was unaware of what happened around them. She slept and she dreamed, but she could feel Julia's anxiety, and violence turned those dreams to nightmares. "This is what he really wanted. This is why he searched the world for twins with strong magic. He meant to create a double-souled hunter, to trap us in one body, make us powerful enough to fight the darkest threats."

Julia walked to the bedroom to change. "You should leave. It's not safe here anymore."

"Did you shove a lemon-scented dildo through your frontal lobe? I stay with you."

There would be no changing his mind. A fairy's sense of debt was unbreakable. "Then let's go."

"Where to?"

Hob wasn't the only one who owed Julia a debt. Julia rarely left her apartment, but there were others who knew everything that happened on the streets of Detroit. "To find out if Terrence was telling the truth."

>——<

By the time they reached Birch Street, a mile and a half from her apartment, six stray dogs had begun to follow them. They herded her and Hob to a bridge by the freeway on-ramp. The sloped concrete underneath was covered in mounds of fur and garbage, the majority of which was alive. One of the larger mounds turned to ask, "What brings you here, Doc?"

"A hunter called Shard." She had to raise her voice to make herself heard above the rush of vehicles overhead.

The Dog King of Detroit was a peculiar figure. He wasn't human, not exactly, but Julia had never figured out just what he was. He dressed in layers of ratty coats and torn blankets. His head was a mane of matted hair and beard, which masked his sunken eyes. Layers of scars thickened his hands and fingers. Every dog here—at least forty—had tasted the Dog King's blood, and in the process had become members of his pack. Julia didn't understand exactly how his power worked, but he was connected to just about every stray and feral mutt in Detroit.

If he had a human name, Julia had never learned it. But she'd healed both him and his dogs many times over the years.

"Yeah, I know him. Killed a skinwalker by the river two nights ago."

Julia flinched. There was only one skinwalker in Detroit, a harmless old Chippewa woman named Sandra Pego who'd moved here decades before. Julia had treated her twice, once after she'd had a run-in with a pair of blood-drinkers, and once for the symptoms of menopause.

"Hunters aren't going to be able to bring this one down," the Dog King said. "You, on the other hand . . . I can smell the power inside of you. You might have a chance."

She closed her eyes and forced herself to relax until Jessica settled back down. "I don't do that anymore. I heal. That's all."

"This fellow doesn't leave anything for you to heal. Angels and demons, spirits and mortals, he kills 'em all. He enjoys it."

A dog barked a block away, a deep, angry sound that cut off abruptly. The Dog King pulled an old revolver from somewhere on his person and whistled. The pack scattered, all but a handful of the largest and strongest animals. The rest disappeared into the shadows, through doorways unknown to mortals.

"You should leave, too." She wondered briefly how Terrence had led Shard to her so quickly. He must have tracked her once she left the protections of her apartment. "I'm the one he's after."

"This is my kingdom."

Hob spat. "This is a septic cave of piss, shit, and fur, you flea-fellated son of a bitch."

"My mother was human, thank you very much. My father, well, he's another matter."

"I say we kick this guy's double-souled ass so hard, he shits through his skull," said Hob.

"You'll have a better chance of surviving with my help." Terrence Chapel strode toward them, gun in one hand, dagger in the other.

Julia could feel her sister slipping into the madness of battle and death. Sweat trickled down Julia's chest, and felt like blood. "Survival isn't everything."

"You can't help anyone by dying," said the Dog King.

Julia wasn't so sure, but she pushed that thought aside. To Terrence, she said, "You followed me. Led him to us."

"Why prolong the inevitable? This way we control the site of battle, and you have allies to fight by your side."

All true, but it was also true that by luring Shard here, Terrence had forced her hand, robbing her of the time she needed to come up with an alternative.

"Be ready," whispered the Dog King, searching the shadows.

Before she could answer, Jessica's spirit flared to life, leaping out to intercept an assault Julia hadn't even seen coming. Shard's second soul was a feral thing of silver light and sparks that ripped and clawed at Jessica, seeking to get through her to the fragile human body beyond.

Julia clamped down hard, spreading her shared power into a shield while she assessed their prey— *No, dammit. Not our prey.* That was Jessica's thought, her fragmented memories fighting to the surface.

A trail of silver light and sparks connected their attacker to a mortal body standing on the edge of the road. Shard was younger than she'd expected, with a smooth face and blond ponytail and perfect teeth. Old enough to drive, but not to drink. He wore camouflage fatigues and heavy boots. His eyes stared into the darkness, empty like those of a blind man.

The Dog King's revolver thundered, the sound amplified by the bridge. Shard's second soul flickered around to deflect the bullet. Terrence circled, trying to catch Shard in the cross fire.

A black-and-white dog lunged, jaws snapping. Shard's spirit arm reached through the animal's body, yanking the life from the flesh before Julia could cry a warning.

In that moment of chaos and grief, Jessica came fully awake. She lashed out at Shard and Terrence both, knocking them to the ground. It was like standing in the middle of a lightning storm, energy crackling out blindly.

Terrence dropped his weapons and pulled a charm made of knotted silver chain from his jacket. Keeping one arm over his face to protect himself, he hurled the charm at Shard. Shard's second soul curled inward like paper blackened by flame. "This is your chance, Julia! Finish it now!"

Even after more than a decade apart, that commanding tone triggered instinctive fear and obedience. She seized her sister's soul, shaped it into a weapon, and lunged. . . .

Her souls pierced Shard's. Just as had happened with Jessica years ago, she fell into Shard's memories. She saw his life, saw everything that had shaped him.

Shard screamed and stumbled back.

"Julia!" Terrence moved closer, but Shard was flailing too wildly, like spiritual power lines whipping about in a storm.

She blinked to clear the tears from her eyes. "You bastard."

Cars honked and screeched to a halt as the bridge began to crumble from Shard's onslaught. Chunks of concrete slammed onto the road. Steel warped and twisted.

Hob tugged her arm. He and the Dog King pulled her toward a hole in the earth, a hole that hadn't been there moments before, and then they were falling into the darkness.

>—<

Julia had killed her sister half a lifetime ago. Despite everything Julia had done since, Jessica remained trapped in that moment, unable to leave the pain and betrayal behind, reliving her death again and again.

Through Jessica's eyes, Julia saw herself at age fourteen, crying as she drove the knife into Jessica's stomach. She felt the punch of impact, the explosion of breath from her lungs. She heard herself sobbing "I'm sorry," over and over.

Even with a blade in her gut, Jessica was a dangerous fighter. She punched Julia in the eye, nose, and throat within the span of a single heartbeat. Julia yanked the knife free, making her sister scream in pain. Jessica warded off the next strike with her left palm and kicked Julia hard enough to crack ribs. Julia fell back, and Jessica produced a gun from a holster strapped to her back. One hand clutched her bleeding gut, while the other lined up a killing shot.

Their father had spent years building Jessica into a warrior. Julia's training had been focused on healing and on manipulating the soul.

Jessica's body was dying. Julia seized her sister's soul and pulled.

In that moment, she and her twin became one. She saw the truth in Jessica's memories. How their father had tormented Jessica for every mistake. How he punished her for any trace of mercy or compassion. He forged her into a murderer, rewarded her for every kill, encouraged her to take pleasure in suffering and death.

He'd wanted Jessica to become a monster. He'd come to Julia, his voice hoarse as he described how her sister had tortured innocent people, how she'd fallen to the darkness. How it was Julia's responsibility to put an end to her sister's crimes.

He'd known Julia would have to use soul magic. Just as he'd known two souls that once shared the same womb could share a body again. Everything he'd done was to lead them to this moment, to create a double-souled hunter, exponentially stronger than either had been before. Becoming another weapon in his arsenal.

>—<

They emerged into a junkyard, a maze of crushed automobiles fenced in by ten-foot chain link and barbed wire. Dogs pressed past her, tails between their legs as they sought comfort and safety from their king.

"We should be safe for the moment." The Dog King sounded exhausted.

"Great," snapped Hob. "We get a few more minutes of life before that double-ended dildo of death kills us all."

"If Shard could have followed us through the Dog King's tunnels, he'd be here already." Julia collapsed on the ground, her back to the hard, crumpled steel of an old truck. "We're miles away. We have time to plan."

A long-haired mutt put his head in her lap and whined. She stroked the dog's fur, instinctively calling on Jessica to reach inside and heal the animal's broken leg.

The power wouldn't come.

Jessica . . . Her sister's energy was a knot of pain and confusion, snarled with Shard's attack and the memory of her own death. Julia tried to calm herself, to spread that calm through them both, but her own thoughts were too chaotic.

"You hesitated." Terrence's power charged the air like static, making her want to vomit. "You had him."

Julia didn't bother to turn around. "I thought you'd found another double-soul, but it was worse than that. You didn't find Shard. You made him. Just like you did me."

"What choice did I have? If you'd stayed with me, I never would've needed Shard."

"His name was Anthony." How could she calm Jessica when all she wanted was to burn this man to ash? "His brother was Darren. I saw what you did to him, just like I saw what you did to Jessica. How long did you search after I left before you found Anthony and his brother? You spent years fanning his bloodlust and hatred. You pushed him deeper and deeper into the darkness, and when he fell, you brought Darren to murder his brother."

Hob turned on Terrence. "I oughta fuck yer teeth with a rusty cheese grater."

"Only it didn't go as you'd hoped, did it?" Julia continued. "Darren wasn't as strong. Or else you hadn't prepared him well enough. I watched him try to control Anthony's corrupted soul. I watched him fail."

He didn't deny it. "Anthony and me, we hunted a hundred threats, saved thousands of lives. Don't blame me if Darren wasn't strong enough to—"

"You told me Jessica was beyond redemption. I believed you. Right until the moment I killed her. I saw her then. I saw what you'd twisted her into, but I also saw the part that remembered joy, the part that hated what she'd become and wanted so desperately to be free. I took that hope away from her."

"None of that matters now," he said. "Shard isn't like you or your sister. You bloodied him pretty good back there. He'll be more determined than ever to track you down. And if he kills you, he kills what's left of Jessie, too."

The Dog King licked his lips. "He has a point."

"Aye," said Hob. "Butt-munching dick cancer that he is."

"You don't know what that fight with Shard did to her." Julia blinked hard, trying to separate herself from her sister's turmoil as Jessica screamed and cursed, unable to move beyond her own murder. "It's the only reason I haven't killed *you*."

"Now you're starting to sound like Jessie." Terrence grinned crookedly.

"Don't call her that." She folded her arms and let a hint of her power light the air between them. "It's time for you to leave."

"You think you can stop him without me?"

"I won't let you hurt her again." She pushed herself to her feet and stepped toward him.

He scowled but didn't argue. Within moments, he had disappeared into the shadows.

It was too easy. "He thinks he's won."

The Dog King cocked his head to one side. "How so?"

"Because he expects me to fight, with or without him. That's all he wants. He believes I'll do anything to protect Jessica, and that means he can still use me as a weapon. All he has to do is steer his prey toward me. Threaten my friends and my sister. And once he knows he can control me again, he'll never stop."

"What a grade-A, purebred ass-weasel," said Hob. "So what's the plan?"

She turned to the Dog King. "Take your pack and go. You've already lost too many."

He didn't move. "All due respect, but kings don't take orders."

"Kings don't abandon their subjects, either." She looked pointedly at the injured dog by her feet.

"That's why we fight," he said. "To protect them."

She crouched and tried again to heal the dog's leg. This time, with Terrence no longer looming over them, she was able to mend the broken bone. "Please."

He sighed, then enveloped her in a firm, musty-smelling hug. "Nothing I say is gonna change your mind, is it?"

"No." She waited for him to go, then turned to Hob. "You should leave, too."

"And you should go fuck a cactus. Now where are we going?"

"Home."

>-><-<

"Some shit can't be healed." Hob sat on the edge of her counter, scarfing down a bowl of leftover chili. He had needed almost no time at all to prepare her apartment for what was to come. "I don't know about your sister, but some souls aren't wounded or misunderstood. Some souls are just fucking evil."

Julia looked around at the sedatives and anesthetics Hob had laid out along the counter, each one in a drawn, uncapped syringe. None of them worked instantly, and there was a good chance Shard would kill her before she got close enough to administer them, but it was the only option that gave her any hope of escaping her father's trap.

A dog barked in the distance. Her shoulders tightened, and Jessica's anxiety sharpened in response. It could have been nothing, but her old hunting instincts knew better. "Mask, please."

Hob handed her a surgical mask, despite the fact that his hands had been occupied with his meal a second before. Julia tightened the mask over her nose and mouth, then opened a pouch of brown powder.

Shard had enough of a connection to Terrence Chapel to trigger Julia's wards. She felt them surge to life, felt him rip them into dust. Moments later, glass shattered from the building's main entrance. That would be Shard forcing his way inside. Julia's skin began to glow. "Stay with me, Jessie," she whispered. "I'll keep you safe." *One way or another.*

Her door splintered inward. Julia swung her open pouch, spreading a brown cloud through the air. Light spun from her hands, turning the cloud into a vortex and funneling it at Shard's face.

He had been prepared for an attack, but not like this. Cinnamon swirled into his mouth and lungs. He doubled over, coughing uncontrollably. Julia snatched a syringe and jumped forward. One dose of Etorphine, and he would be out within seconds.

Shard's second soul smashed the syringe from her hand. The assault that followed was like nothing Julia had ever felt. There was no subtlety, no technique, nothing but hammer blows smashing at her and Jessica both.

She recognized her mistake as she rolled across the floor, trying to evade the worst of the attack. Unlike her and Jessica, Shard's physical body—Darren's body—was little more than a vessel. It was Anthony who was in control. Anything short of killing the host body would have little effect.

Hob swung a lamp at Shard's head. "Fight this, ye rotted sack of sheep balls!"

A glowing arm destroyed the lamp and tossed Hob against the wall.

Jessica shielded Julia from the next blow. The attack's power cracked the floorboards below. Someone screamed from another apartment, but Julia couldn't spare any worry for the neighbors.

Jessica struggled to break free, to fight and kill. Sparks spat from their hands. Jessica's madness dragged at them both like an undertow.

Julia picked up a thicker syringe, one she had hoped not to need. There was one other way to deliver a drug to Shard. Flesh and spirit were bound together, and her souls had touched Shard's once before. If she injected herself while they were entangled the way they'd been at the bridge, the drug should affect them both.

"I'm sorry, sister," she whispered. Death would be quick and relatively painless. Jessica would be at peace, and they would be free of Terrence Chapel's control. She readied the syringe. They weren't likely to get a clear shot at Shard, but she could achieve the same thing by lowering Jessica's guard long enough for his soul to strike through their heart.

A Doberman snarled and jumped through her doorway, lunging for Shard's leg. The Dog King followed, leaping like a madman onto Shard's back. Both were thrown aside with hardly an effort.

"Stay out!" Julia shouted.

Instead, more dogs rushed into her apartment. Nor were they alone. A harvester wrapped its dark arms around Shard, who screamed in pain. A fey creature called a moonblood scampered upside down across the ceiling and dropped onto Shard's head, all teeth and claws and snarls. More beings from Detroit's supernatural underworld crowded into her apartment, adding their strength to the battle.

Julia smelled burning flesh. Shard looked to be on fire, so hard was his second soul fighting. The harvester stumbled back, its dark cloak smoking. Two dogs fell and didn't move. A hunchbacked woman cried out as energy blackened her chest.

Stay with me, Jessica. Julia tossed the syringe aside and extended her spirit arms into the melee. She gripped Shard's legs and reached deeper.

Shard was double-souled, and that meant something of Darren still survived, trapped within his own body. She called silently, searching for that second life. He had to be here, beneath the hate and the rage.

Shard's hands wrapped around her neck and began to burn. Shadows crept through her eyes. She continued to search, lending her strength—*their* strength. *We don't have to kill him. Help me save them. Help me heal what our father did to them.*

Slowly, Jessica stopped fighting and added her strength to Julia's.

Shard tried to pull back. He hadn't been expecting a battle from within. His grip around her throat loosened, but Julia only held tighter.

I've got him, said Jessica.

Together they gathered what was left of Darren, a snarled knot of guilt and pain, helpless to stop his brother's rampage. They shared their strength and pulled at Anthony's soul, dragging him back. Shard screamed and raged and fought, but he couldn't overpower three of them together. Shard collapsed to the floor, and Julia pulled herself free.

"It's all right," she shouted. "It's over. Let him go."

The others backed away, wary and ready to resume the attack at the slightest provocation. But there was no need.

Shard lay in a trembling ball. Julia could see multiple bruises and bite marks, a dislocated shoulder, and a badly broken ankle. "Darren?"

He opened his eyes and tried to speak, but he was shaking too hard. He managed a small nod.

"Hob, he's injured. I need my things."

He raised a stubby middle finger in her direction, but limped away to gather her supplies.

Julia looked around in confusion. Never had her apartment been so full. "I don't understand. How . . . Where did you all come from?"

"My pack has been busy." The Dog King sounded smug. Or as smug as one could sound with a black eye and several missing teeth. "This place, the things you do, they matter to a lot of people, Julia. We thought it was worth protecting."

Holy men and creatures of darkness, blood magic and angels, all together in her home. Now that the immediate danger had passed, they were eyeing one another with wariness and, in some cases, outright hatred, but they respected her truce. It occurred to her that this might be the first time so many enemies had come together in . . . not peace, exactly, but a common cause.

"Thank you." Looking them over more carefully, she called out, "Hob, I'll also need holy water, fresh clay, a pint of pig's blood, and a lot more bandages."

"Yeah, yeah. Hold yer ass."

"What of Terrence Chapel?" asked the Dog King.

"He thought he could turn me into a killer." Her lips quirked slightly. "He failed. Twice now." She touched Shard—Darren—and tried to calm him the way she did her sister. "He invested years of his life in us, and years more in Shard. Maybe he'll be wise enough not to waste a third attempt."

"Yeah, right," Hob shouted. "And maybe my dick will turn all it fucks to gold!"

Julia shrugged. "If he creates another double-souled hunter, we'll try to heal that one, too."

Is he all right? Jessica said. *Did we save him?*

Tears filled Julia's eyes. In all the years since she'd driven the knife into Jessica's stomach, all the years she'd spent trying to reach her and help her heal, tonight was the first time she'd heard her sister's voice. The first time she'd felt the company of her sister instead of the hunter. The first time both of them had truly been at peace.

Yes. I think we did.

BAGGAGE

by Erik Scott de Bie

Thump. Thump, thump, *wham*.

The heavy bag jangled on its chain, swinging back and forth with the force of that last kick. I danced back and shook out my hands and legs. My right shin burned a little, but in a good way. I threw in a few more for good measure, making the bag shake as I kicked it over and over: one, two, three, four. My body was a tight, cycling machine.

My one and only friend, Andre—head bartender at my bar and a great guy whose heart I'd have broken by now if he weren't gay— had been badgering me for weeks to join a gym. "I'm worried about you, V," he'd said. "You've been low. Lower than usual."

"So cardio's the answer?" I asked between shots of whiskey. "Free weights? Maybe you want me to try CrossFit."

He made a face, then extended a laminated membership card across the bar. Puget Sound Body. "It's a fight gym—just around the block," he said. "I signed you up for a month."

"Aw, you shouldn't have," I said. "*Really.*"

But I went anyway, because I'm not an asshole. And just then, after kicking the bag ten times in a row, the gym seemed like not such a bad idea after all.

Also, with my water bottle full of whiskey, I felt really loose and comfy.

I should back up. I'm Vivienne Cain, aka Lady Vengeance (fear powers—it's a whole thing), former demon-possessed supervillain turned edgy it-girl superhero turned fugitive from vigilante justice. It's not a part of my life I talk about much, partly because so many people are trying to find me and kill me, and partly because, well . . . I kicked the bag an eleventh time, savoring the crunch my shin made against the leather.

The late hours worked particularly well for high-functioning alcoholic night owls like myself. Stuck on the cusp between being a legit fight gym and a gym meant to cater to a twenty-four/seven fitness crowd, Puget Sound Body couldn't decide exactly which way to go, so it tried to be everything to everyone. It had lots of bags and lots of hours, a bunch of shiny new weight machines, and not many customers. Practically no one showed up at PSB at night. At most I could expect the occasional drunk frat boy posse (probably coming from my bar, no less) or the same homeless guy looking for a bathroom a couple of times a week.

I shared the lonely stretch between one and three a.m. with the girl up at the front desk, a twenty-something plugged into earbuds and reading. Nicole, I think her name was. We had exchanged maybe a dozen words over the past week, and she seemed nice enough. I didn't mind her aura, either: a lot of people that age give off a cloying optimism, a sour narcissism, or a dull indifference to the world. Nicole, on the other hand, seemed positive but not deluded, tough but not hardened. Ambitious but grounded. Good kid.

There was darkness in her, too, but hey—join the club.

I focused on my combinations, launching a series of jabs punctuated with crosses and hooks. As I fought, I felt violent power resonating in the walls, and I went with the flow.

As a fight gym, PSB felt light and fierce, its younger clientele gradually adding to an undercurrent of angry passion that fueled a heady, powerful rush. Like a ring on fight night just before the audience gets there, the gym crackled at night with anticipation of glorious violence. PSB hadn't been open long enough for all that hope and power to crumble into desperation for results and despair when they didn't materialize. Older gyms become sweaty dens of regret, the walls constantly saturated with years' worth of tears of frustration and pain.

For an empathic projector like me, such places hold deep wells of power I can tap into. I metabolize all sorts of emotions: anger, lust, fear—*especially* fear. With my powers, I could beat the snot out of Rocky Balboa in any practice ring, let alone surrounded by thousands of screaming fans. I mean, assuming he was real and I wasn't stone drunk basically all the time. The booze keeps my powers from functioning out of control.

It was exactly that—my constant inebriation buffer—that blinded me to the demon at first. Somewhere after my legs started to burn from all the kicking, I recognized a note of deeper darkness among the ambient gym rage. Not something a human could produce, and I'd known some pretty dark motherfuckers in my day. Been one, in fact. The demon hadn't attacked, but I could feel it watching. Waiting.

"Oh, you wanna play, huh?" I asked in a whisper. "I'm game."

I felt the guy before I saw him. Even before the door opened, I heard the discordant cymbal of hungry lust among the relentless thundering drumroll of the gym. The answering spike of anxiety from Nicole is what got my attention, though. We can suppress our fear—convince ourselves to ignore it—but it doesn't go away. Was the demon in him? Maybe. I shed my black bag gloves down to my purple wraps, took a hit off my whiskey bottle, and headed over, unwrapping as I went.

There he was: muscle-headed type, leaning on the desk, biceps flexed, greasy smile on his thick face. He was that guy, the one who made sure to work out next to women in the gym to show off his muscles, who talked too long to any female staffer at the front desk, or lurked outside yoga classes, doing curls. You know that guy.

"No classes after six p.m., Steve," Nicole said as I approached. She knew him and liked him about as much as I did. "We have classes tomorrow, though. Like, boxing? Kickboxing?"

"How 'bout your Zumba class?" Steve asked. "You know I like watching your moves."

Definitely that guy.

Nicole's anger spiked, and I felt more than saw her getting ready to punch the asshole.

Time to intervene.

A little flicker of power and the room darkened. The gym felt colder, like the heater cut out, and the lights dimmed a couple of notches. The fluorescent light overhead buzzed and died with a disconsolate sigh, then winked back on, flickering. It cast strange shadows across Steve's suddenly pale face. Nicole's wide eyes looked around for the source of the disturbance.

"Hey," I said as I unwound the wrap around my right hand. "This guy bothering you?"

They both stared, momentarily at a loss. I'm not all that intimidating on my own—just a former goth girl, twenty years past the makeup—but with a little bit of fear channeled into the right theatrics, I can give trained killers pause. I could handle one maybe-possessed douche-bag bodybuilder. I couldn't tell, so I had to poke him. See if the demon came out.

"This . . ." Steve shrugged off the glamour. Good for him. His eyes narrowed, and I could see him thinking up an appropriate insult. "This doesn't concern you, bitch. Step off."

Charming. Couldn't identify my ethnicity, so the prick went with the one-slur-fits-all.

I started uncoiling the second wrap, not being as delicate about it as the first. The wraps served two purposes: one, purple is my favorite color that isn't black, and two, since that was the only spot of color on me—black clothes, black hair, et cetera—it kept his focus on my hands.

"She said no, dude," I said. "Walk away."

I realized I wanted him to make a move. Stupid, but the booze had kicked in, and I was a damn romantic at heart. Damsel in distress and all that shit. Plus, y'know, possible demon.

Steve stepped up, towering a foot over my less-than-commanding five-six. Mistake one.

"Or what?" he asked. "You gonna make me?"

He met my merlot red eyes like I was a little puppy he could stare down. Strike two.

"Maybe," I said. "You gonna *make me* make you?"

He grabbed my bare upper arm with his grubby fingers, clenching tight. Three.

My power boiled up all on its own—no will, no direction, no objection—and coursed up his arm to hit him right between the eyes. Steve drew up to his full height, as though stabbed with a cattle prod. His pupils went huge and I saw white all the way around the thin rings of iris. His hands shook and his breath came in rapid spurts.

Fear powers are a bitch.

He threw a lazy right hook—more to drive me away than hurt me—but it still counted. I ducked under his arm, caught him around the torso, and pulled him over me and to the floor. Hard. I felt as much as heard ribs crack in his thick chest and kept thinking, Shoulda done more core. At least there was a mat. Unfortunately, that also meant Steve was just a human: no demon involved.

I stood up shakily. Nicole stared at me like I'd lost my mind, and maybe I had. Shit. Normal people aren't just supposed to judo-throw each other. Another night, another fuckup.

Without a word, I left Steve mewling on the floor and walked out. Only when I got to my bike did I realize I hadn't grabbed my gloves, bottle, or duffel—which had the keys in it.

"Screwed that pooch, V," I said to myself. "Good for fucking *you*."

And just like that, I was no longer alone.

Oh, right. *Demon.*

There's nothing magical about intuition. Your body picks up on something that your mind can't quite process. It might be a particular observation you don't consciously see, a faint smell, or a subtle change in air pressure. When your body reacts to something, it's almost always right. Getting your mind involved is bad, because it gives you a chance to talk yourself out of it. The trick is to trust your instincts, particularly when you've honed them over more than twenty years of fighting superheroes and/or supervillains.

(I'm complicated.)

My body knew there was something behind me, and I went with it. The alley gave me some advantages: enclosed space, privacy, and a moderate level of fear energy. We invest alleys with anxiety and uneasiness, as though violence is more likely there than in our own homes. I powered up and turned, arms wide in challenge.

"Come at me, demon," I said.

Something skittered in the darkness on more legs than any animal, and I tried to get a sense of its aura. It felt dark and numb, the way demons always do. They don't have the same emotions humans do, making them hard to read or digest. Good thing I had years of practice. I could taste its tinny desire and the spicy ambition that drove it. It was a social and political climber looking to make a name out of Lady Vengeance, Lord Azazel's favorite mortal.

"I know you're there," I said, breathing through the swirling murk of its resonance. "I know you're watching. Just show yourself already."

The darkness stirred, and I sensed a cold, precise focus, almost like determination.

The back door to the gym banged open and I whirled, ready for a fight. Then I felt the bright stab of worry and caution from the newcomer and eased back.

"Hey!" Nicole saw me standing next to my bike, ready for a fight, and tensed herself. She had my duffel in one hand, and she held it ready to swing. "Are you okay?"

Damn. I would have preferred a pissed-off Steve. Him, at least, I could maul without feeling bad about it.

"Fine," I said, relaxing my stance. I couldn't sense the demon anymore. "Don't worry—that won't happen again. I'm dropping my membership."

"Are you kidding?" Nicole crossed her arms. "That was badass. Like, the attitude more than the throw. Your technique could use some work."

"Some work, huh?" My world-class martial-artist sensei wouldn't have liked that feedback at all, but skills get rusty with disuse. "Who's gonna teach me? You?"

"Yes." She handed over my duffel. "I'm a purple belt in BJJ."

"What's that?" I rummaged in my bag for my keys. "Sounds like a sex thing."

That made her smile. "Brazilian jujitsu," she said. "I've also got like a four-oh amateur record. I'm training to go pro. Nicole Vergaro. Look me up."

"Nice." I'd fought superstrong bruisers, apocalypse robots, and, like, a thousand ninja. But she was gorgeous. "Sure you wanna train me? I did just put another member in the hospital."

"You mean Steve? He's my ex, not a member." Nicole shrugged. "Also? Fuck that guy."

Gorgeous and awesome and straight. Oh, well.

"Thanks, but no, thanks." I fit the key into the ignition and turned the engine over. "I'm not great at taking direction and I don't play well with others. Laters—"

She stepped in front of my bike. "Hire me as your trainer," Nicole said. "We'll fix that throw and work on your punches."

"Really?"

Nicole put her hand over mine on the throttle. *Really.*

She was a hard woman to turn down. And it'd be a chance to watch for that demon.

"Vivienne Cain," I said, knowing I would regret this. "Call me V."

>—×—<

A week later, as a fist connected with my face, I realized I loved the *shit* out of this.

"Keep your hands up," Nicole reminded me for the twentieth time. She'd started giving me a reminder tap after the eighth slipup, so I'd grown accustomed to the routine by now. Not that it made the little pats sting less.

"Show me that combination. Launch from the face and pull right back to defend."

I nodded, too low on breath to verbalize. My booze-heavy diet didn't exactly make for much stamina. I hit her with a flurry that ended with left hook off the jab, a sucker punch that had taken down many an unsuspecting boxer. She blocked it easily and nodded.

"Good," she said. "Again."

On this, our third session, we'd skipped bag work and gone straight to sparring in the half-open ring. My fundamentals had deteriorated over the past ten years, but I'd always been a quick study. We squared off, and I focused on her white gloves with the red wraps beneath.

I'd felt the demon's presence off and on during the week, but it hadn't yet shown itself. Sure I was here to confront it, but increasingly I had to admit I really liked Nicole beating me up.

She hit me on the cheek again. "Come on, hands up."

I held up my hands like claws, and she nodded in approval. That first day, she'd called my striking stance Muay Thai, which meant nothing to me but seemed to be a compliment.

"You need to start eating right," she said. "Lots of veggies. Avoid meat and dairy."

"What are you, vegan?" I went at her gloves.

"As a matter of fact"—she deflected my combination—"I am."

"How do you get your protein?"

She rolled her eyes. Like she'd never heard that one before.

We fell into the rhythm of the fight. I'd launch a combination, slapping her training pads hard enough to bruise, staying on the balls of my feet and hitting with the hips rather than the arms. My sensei had always told me that if I could hit with my butt, no one stood a chance. I got in a few good ones, and the thick shin pads made reassuring crunches against Nicole's legs.

As I hit her, I remembered sparring with Tony, under the watchful eye of his stepfather, Hugo, the second Raven. We were kids again, flirting as much as punching, and his burning eyes promised me this wouldn't end on the mat. I hadn't thought about that moment for ten years: not since New York, with Supergroup Tower shaking around us, when Tony put on his mentor's armor to fight me and I tore his eye out for his trouble. And now he wanted to kill me.

Antonio DeSantes. *Damn.*

"Your striking is decent," Nicole said. "Let's see what you've got for grappling."

I shivered and pushed the memory away. "No problem."

Next thing I knew, I hit the mat with a sound like a gunshot.

"Your judo is insufficient." Nicole clapped her gloves together. "On your feet."

I climbed back up and glanced around woozily. Pretty much everyone in the gym had stopped what they were doing to watch the girl fight. Not that I blamed them: I was having a pretty good time watching Nicole pound the snot out of me, too.

"You've gotta relax," Nicole said, a refrain that she'd repeated a dozen times since day one. "You know, loosen up your shoulders. You're gonna hurt yourself."

"Hard night." Partly true, but not the reason I was tense. The flashback wasn't doing me any favors, and the perky high coming off Nicole exacerbated the crushing hangover. I didn't want a repeat rib-breaking incident, so I didn't drink before our sessions, making the world raw and jumpy. Shoulda known better than to fight (mostly) sober. Shoulda, coulda, woulda.

"Stop dancing around and come at me," Nicole said. "I won't hurt you. Much."

"*That's* reassuring."

We'd drawn a pretty big crowd at this point, blurry in my peripheral vision and thunderous to my empathic sense. Being sober, I got dizzy from the collective emotional swarm of that many people gathered in one place. I tasted excitement and more than a little unrequited lust. And I won't say we didn't deserve it—at least Nicole. She was in her element, a warrior woman as much as any I've ever met. And I've met a *lot* of warrior women.

I went for her legs, and she snaked around with incredible grace to cling to my back. Her legs wrapped around my waist and her ankles locked in front of my stomach.

"Now you're in a pretty tight situation here," she said, calm while I grunted and cursed. "You've got to get around to a guard. Do your best."

On my hands and knees, I gave her a piggyback ride around the ring, trying to twist out of the hold, but every time she corrected me with a tap on the ear. Finally, I shoved her back against the cage, which gave me leverage to twist around, putting us front to front. I lay back as she straddled me, arms crossed over her chest. She carried herself gracefully, as if we were dancing rather than wrestling. It was beautiful and more than a little bit sexy.

God, V, I thought. *Grow the fuck up and stop crushing on your trainer.*

"Seriously?" Calmly, Nicole swatted me on the side of the head, and I snapped out of it. Tony had never done anything like that. "Hands up."

I put my hands up to ward off more blows and frowned sourly. "What now?"

"Now you turn things around," she said. "Try one of the techniques I showed you. The goal is to get out—so you can go back to striking—or get me in a lock." Her eyes sparkled with challenge. "Make me submit."

Shit.

It had been too long since I'd done anything like this. I got her leg once and tried to pull it, but she slipped out and left me flat on my stomach, panting, while she held on to my back.

"You weren't kidding about being bad at this," she said. "Here. Let's switch up, and I'll show you some things to try." She lay down on her back. "Put your legs around me."

I didn't need to be told twice. We got into the same straddling position as before, only this time *she* was on guard, and I was holding on to her.

"If your guard is good, you've got the advantage." She held up her arms to demonstrate proper form. She grabbed my wrists and locked my arms. "Okay, what would you do from here?"

"Head butt," I said.

She smiled. "I'm serious."

"So am I. You'd be surprised how effective a good head butt can be."

"Launch some punches at me," Nicole said. "Watch what I do."

I did, and she fended them off with shoulders, arms, and gloves. Then she caught my arm, and before I knew what had happened, she had my wrist in one hand, wrenched my leg under her body, and held it at the edge of breaking.

I flashed back again. Tony was screaming, crushing me under him, drizzling blood onto my face from his gaping eye socket. I shook, unable to breathe.

"Okay!" I gasped. "I give up."

I tapped my hand on the mat, and Nicole let go. "Are you okay?" she asked, concerned.

"Yeah." That was a big, fat lie. "What the shit did you do?"

"Leg lock," she said. "Did you see how I got there?"

"No," I said, trying to get a hold of myself. "Show me again."

We walked through the moves step by step, and I watched Nicole make the transitions with fluid grace. She showed me leg locks and arm bars and even a choke or two. I'd never had quite as good a time having my limbs almost broken. We switched back and forth, and she showed me a number of holds, and I didn't do too badly. The swell of emotion from our audience made me feel dizzy and light-headed, drunk on their enthusiasm.

It was inappropriate, I know. She was my trainer, she was fifteen years younger than me at least, and she was straight. But *damn*.

This. *This* is why I started drinking.

Well, this and the nightmares. And the demons.

Nicole had just put me in a right-arm bar when I saw him: a tall, good-looking man standing toward the back of the group. Where the others moved around a bit, staying limber or angling for a better look at Nicole's technique, this guy stood very straight and still. With his strong features and dark complexion, he looked— Holy *shit*, he looked like Tony. The fucking one-eyed *Raven*. Then I saw his liquid black eyes with no whites—both of them. I hadn't felt him before, but now that I focused on him, I could tell he wasn't secreting any human emotions. He felt dull, his resonance flat, like stagnant water that had collected a fine layer of dust on top.

"Hey," I said, looking right at him. "Hey!"

The man stared right at me and opened his mouth slightly. His tongue was a licking orange flame. There was a fire inside him, and that meant he was no man at all. He turned to go.

Nicole hadn't noticed my distress, so when I pulled away, she clung tighter by reflex. Trained fighters know to stop when someone submits to them or—if they're the ones doing the locking—they hang on until someone stops the fight. Unfortunately, it wasn't until my arm cracked that I remembered to tap out. Nicole let go immediately, looking at first surprised, then horrified. "What the fuck, V?" she asked.

I didn't have time to explain. I staggered up, ignoring the liquid fire that kept pumping up my right arm. Wincing, I held it braced against my side as I scrambled to the edge of the ring and slipped through the open part. Purple fire accumulated in the palm of my injured arm without my conscious command. Using the powers in front of so many people was a big no-no in the "don't get caught" playbook for ex-supervillains, but maybe they'd think it was a trick of the light combined with my purple wraps.

I stumbled out the door into the street, where I had to shield my eyes from the bright sun. Trust this to be the one week a year that Seattle has glorious weather. Cars zoomed past entirely too quickly for a residential neighborhood. I saw only one other person on the sidewalk: a hefty lady holding a cat and glaring at me. Weird and a little unsettling, but definitely human. I couldn't feel the demon anymore. A curious pigeon cocked its head and looked up at me.

"Yeah," I said. "Fucking brilliant."

I fell to one knee and clenched my arm, which had started sending shocks of pain through my shoulder and clicked when I moved it. I flexed my fingers. It hurt, but that was better than numbness. A massive bruise was already starting to form around my elbow.

"Holy shit!" Nicole appeared. "That's not— I'm so sorry. I didn't mean—"

"I know, it's my fault." I winced and cradled my arm. "I'm a spaz sometimes."

"You were chasing someone," Nicole said. "Who?"

"*My* ex. Sort of." Shakily, I stood without her proffered aid and immediately regretted it. She helped me to a green-painted bench.

"Really?" Nicole wore a perplexed expression. "I thought you liked, you know, *women.*"

"That obvious, huh?" I sighed. "Both, unfortunately. So I'm fucked either way."

Nicole stared at me, trying really hard to suppress a smile. It took me a second to realize what I'd said, and then I smiled. She laughed; I laughed. We laughed. Together.

Fuck.

>—<

Spraining my arm put me out of training for at least a week, and I thought that would be the last I saw of Nicole for a while.

Wrong.

The following Friday night, she came into my bar while I was in the back, mixing drinks one-handed. It was trivia night, so the place was packed with mostly twenty- and thirtysomethings exerting their impressive grasp of useless information. I'd waited on a few of my regulars, as well as a tableful of college kids celebrating a twenty-first, currently too drunk to protest the trivia kicking off. No one really interested me until Nicole strolled up in a classy black blouse, jeans that showed off her muscular lower half, and a pair of boots I would have robbed an armored truck to get on my feet. I'd never seen her in normal clothes, and, by the looks of things, that had been a damn shame.

"Madonna," she said, answering one of the trivia questions. It was currently a music round, but she might as well have been talking about me.

"Holy shit," I said.

"Found you," she said as she leaned against the bar. "So, this is your place, huh?"

"Yep." I looked around the room. The number of wide-eyed gawkers convinced me Nicole was really here. "What can I get you? Vodka and Red Bull?"

"Ugh." She made a face. "How about a White Russian?"

I hesitated. I hadn't expected her to order that. Then I got out the vodka and a carton of coconut milk. "You want a menu? I guarantee you we serve nothing you can eat."

"What makes you say that?"

I looked her over. "What are you, twelve percent body fat? Fourteen?"

She looked amused. "Thirteen."

I nodded. "I stand by my statement."

"I'll have a Caesar salad anyway. We can skip the cheese, if it makes you feel better." She slid onto one of the bar stools. "You thirsty?"

"Yes." I cleared my throat. "Yes, I am."

I poured her a coconut White Russian, plus a double Johnnie Walker neat for me. I'd been drinking steadily since three p.m., so I put in food orders for both of us.

"That looks gnarly." She pointed at my arm and smiled. "How'd you do that?"

The doctor had put me in a sling but no cast, but the questions had come anyway. I played along. "Depends," I said. "Truth, or one of the thirty stories I've made up so far today?"

She laughed. "I really am sorry, you know," she said.

"Not your fault. I did it to myself."

"Well, I wasn't going to say it." She sipped her drink. "Where are you from, anyway? You look so—"

"Boston."

She frowned, then flushed in the cheeks. "Sorry, I thought you were Middle Eastern," she said. "Was that racist of me?"

"Seattle racist, maybe," I said. "Anyway, you're half-right. My mom was Irish Catholic, and my dad was from Iran. I got the looks, but not a lot else." I nursed my drink—I was already about twelve ahead. "And where are you from? Colombia? Nicaragua?"

"San Rafael," she said. "It's beautiful this time of year."

"Cheers to that."

We drank. We chatted. We murmured answers over the loudspeaker to the trivia questions. I poured a few more drinks for other patrons. Our food came—her Caesar, no cheese, my big basket of Tater Tots drowned in melted cheese, jalapeños, olives, and green onions.

Nicole took one look at the mound and cleared her throat, impressed. "What is *that*?"

"Irish tatchos," I said. "Like nachos, only tots—"

"Talk about Seattle racist," she said. "And you gave *me* a bad time about my fat percentage."

"I'm not training to go pro."

I took a fork to the mound of carbalicious goodness, but not before Nicole had snuck a taste herself. Now, *that*—that took me off guard. Seeing her eat some of that delicious sinfulness. She looked at me with just the right mix of capricious innocence.

"So," she said. "Are you gonna tell me?"

She may have been a presumptuous kid, but Nicole's resonance said she really did want to help me. I didn't deserve a friend like her—or a friend at all.

I opened my mouth, but something in her face made me choke up. My eyes welled.

"Whoa," Nicole said. "It was just a Tater Tot."

"It's not—" I grabbed a napkin to dab at my eyes. "It's fucking embarrassing."

Nicole's eyes widened a little. "Is this about what happened in the gym? And don't try to deny it. Most people don't almost tear their own arm apart willingly."

"Like I'm gonna dump all my emotional shit on you."

"It's okay. Really." She touched my hand on the bar. Her skin felt cool and soothing against mine. "You can talk to me."

We didn't know each other that well. Hell, we'd met only a week before. But the way she said it and the earnestness in her eyes made me believe it. Goddammit.

I gave Andre a nod, and he covered for me at the bar. Great guy, Andre. He'd walk through fire for me. He has, on numerous occasions, even without powers to protect him.

I led Nicole over to a booth in the back, close to a group of thirtysomethings earnestly engaged in some deep philosophical discussion. They wouldn't notice us. Nicole sat quietly, waiting with her hands folded on the table. Her eyes reflected the dim light of the bar, making her look both sad and fascinated. I could tell she wanted to hear my story.

And like the drunk, fucking idiot I was, I told her.

I told her how I'd first been possessed by a demon at age fifteen, and how it had used my powers—oh, by the way, new friend, I have fucking *fear* powers—to hold an entire city hostage. How the team of capes unoriginally called Supergroup had defeated the demon and rescued me, and I'd joined as their newest member. Lady Vengeance, they called me: little miss bad-behavior tabloid princess who partied with rock stars, never went to rehab, and did anything but respect herself. The dark, edgy, unpredictable one on the team who could never be fully trusted, 'cuz once a villain, *always* a villain. They made goddamn comic books about me, and though my depicted outfit was trashier than the real thing, it wasn't by much. Right-wing media hated me, the counterculture fucking *loved* me, and I drank and drugged it all away in a perpetual haze.

"It's all online. There're records," I said. "Of course, the Net won't tell you how it *feels*. How the demons never go away. How every person who looks at you wrong could be a demon or could just be one of the *everyone* who doesn't trust you."

I didn't tell her all about my powers, only the basics: absorbing emotional energy, particularly fear, using it to make myself stronger, faster, more durable. Creating things. Et cetera.

I didn't tell her the really fucked-up part. About how when Azazel had first taken control of my powers, I'd been awake. Aware. And though I'm not sure if I could have stopped him on my own, I didn't try. Not because I was afraid, but because I *wanted* what he offered.

Some nights, I still do, and I drink until that impulse blurs away.

At the end of the story, she looked at me solemnly. She'd believed the whole story. It must have sounded vaguely correct to her, like something you lived through as a kid but only occasionally heard about when you grew up. Before her time, I guess. God, she was too young for me. "So, you're, like, a superhero?"

"Like one, yeah," I said. "I'm retired. Ten years now. I've . . . been in hiding."

"In hiding?" Nicole frowned. "Why? If I could do what you do, I wouldn't hide it."

"You—" I paused. I thought about her—about this girl I'd just met—who'd managed to get me to tell her things I hadn't told anyone. Ever. And it wasn't the booze, and it wasn't an accident. It felt *purposeful*. It must have been the booze. That's why I didn't notice it before.

My intuition flared, and suddenly everything seemed different. Well, shit.

I had to be sure, so I took her deeper.

"You remember those friends I mentioned? Supergroup?" I looked down at my clenched hands on the tabletop. "Something happened to them."

"I don't understand what you mean. Something happened to them? Something like—"

She stopped short and her face went pale. I nodded gravely.

I tried to give the short version. "Their rogues' gallery—sorry, that's powered lingo for a bunch of our frequent bad guys. The kind we fight often, put in jail; then they break out and we fight 'em again." She nodded, vaguely understanding. "A bunch of them got together and attacked while we were having a reunion sort of thing. We all hated each other by the point, and hadn't been together for years, but we still met. My sister—it was her idea."

I had a sudden memory of my half sister's bronze face contorted in pain and rage as blood gushed from her mouth. The look in her eyes . . . I took a long drink to steady myself.

"So, they— What? Attacked you and your friends? Killed some of you?"

"All of us," I said. "*Almost* all of us. I made it out, and so did Tony, my ex." Tony was roaring at me, and I could see the gooey flesh inside his half-empty eye socket. Attacking me. Punishing me for what he thought I had done.

"The guy you saw at the gym?" Nicole asked.

"Sort of," I said, pouring another. I was glad I had the bottle.

"I'm sorry you went through that," Nicole said. "That—that's a goddamn tragedy. But that doesn't have to define you." She touched my hand on the table. "I've watched you. I see you fighting it. You can put it behind you."

I closed my fingers so tight around the glass, I almost broke it. "Thanks for the pop psychology," I said. "But it's not that easy."

"Why not?" Nicole's eyes were burning at me now, full of youthful fire and optimism. I felt it coming off her like heat from a radiator. She probably thought herself wise beyond her years. At least she meant well. "It wasn't your fault. You survived. They didn't. Sucks to be them, but they would want you to move on with your life. To be happy."

"What do *you* fucking know?" I slammed the glass down on the table, startling Nicole. "My friends were total assholes. They hated me. They would not want me to be *happy*."

"Okay, fine." Nicole leaned back and crossed her arms. "So fuck what they would want. You're alive. You're here. What do *you* want?"

If I still thought of her as just a bright kid, that would have sounded goddamned supportive. Trouble was, I knew the truth. Shit.

I waved to Andre at the bar, but when he started over, I gave him a curt, cutting-off gesture. The signal. His face lost some of its luster. Quietly, he started approaching the various tables to encourage them to leave. The regulars caught on quick, though some of the drunker barflies made unsatisfied noises I hoped Nicole wouldn't notice.

"Hey." Nicole leaned across the table and put her hand on my arm. "You survived. It's totally okay to feel guilty about that. Totally normal. A lot of people in your situation would."

"Would they?" I poured my fourth drink of this conversation.

"I'm sure you did everything you could," she said. "It's not like *you* killed them."

Silence.

She stared at me for a long time, her eyes growing progressively wider. "You— You didn't have anything to do with it, did you?" she asked. "Vivienne?"

I looked at the tumbler of whiskey in my hand.

"I don't know," I said. "I don't *remember.*"

We sat in silence, listening as trivia night progressed. They were on the final round, which commenced with a mashup of dramatic music from various movies. At first I thought it was the theme from some spaghetti Western, but an electric guitar intruded. We didn't compare answers this time; only stared at each other. I kept her attention. I didn't let her notice the people quietly leaving the bar. Andre had kept the music playing in part to cover up the exodus.

"You wanna get out of here?" I asked. "I know the boss, and she'd totally let me bail."

Her face lit up, surprised and pleased. "Yes." She smiled weakly. "God, yes."

The plan was simple: get her out to the parking lot, onto the bike, and out of here. Maybe head down into SoDo or to one of the city's many construction sites—anywhere away from people. Then we could have a conversation.

At the door, Nicole stepped close enough to me to hold. She felt hot as a furnace against the chilly night air from the parking lot. "Are you sober enough to drive?" she asked.

Damn. Hadn't thought of that. Typical—the drunk is undone by a dumbass-drunk thing. "I'll have you know that I'm a high-functioning alcoholic," I said. A pretty good try, I think.

Crap. Nicole was looking around the emptying bar. Her notice fell on a twentysomething couple that was arguing with Andre about their check. It must have seemed obvious he was trying to get them to leave. Suspicious as fuck.

"I see." Nicole drew me back into the bar—entirely the wrong direction. "You know what? I think we should stay here." She clung close to me. "I like it here."

"Maybe this was a mistake," I said. "It's getting pretty late." I checked my watch: 11:54.

"What time is it?" she asked, her breath warm against my ear.

Time was up.

"Time for you to get out of that poor girl, I guess."

Nicole pulled away, looking at first hurt and confused. Then her expression hardened. "How did you know?"

"Other than me dumping the insanity of the century on you, and you don't bat an eye?"

"Other than that." She tried to pull away, but I held her hand. She stared at me. Hard.

"I didn't—not for sure," I said. "But I think you've been influencing Nicole since that first night."

"Oh?" Her voice dropped half an octave. "How so?"

"Little things never really added up with Nicole. Call it intuition." I ticked off the reasons on my fingers. "One: a young woman running the gym alone after dark? Maybe, but there's gotta be a rule about having at least two people at the gym at all times." I raised a second finger. "Two: the fake Raven to distract me. What else was the point of that?" Three fingers. "The flirting. I mean, sure, but Nicole just screams alpha straight girl. And you were really goddamn pushy. And then at the bar." I held up four fingers. "When you ordered a White Russian and a Caesar salad, and then you ate some of my tatchos. Nicole's a vegan."

She smiled wryly, mockingly. "Maybe I'm just a naughty one."

"Maybe." I shook my head. "Or maybe *fuck you demon—get out of my friend.*"

The demon narrowed Nicole's eyes. "Good thought, trying to lure me away." The voice was Nicole's but very low—threatening. "Wouldn't want to mess up the place."

"Or kill innocent bystanders, but whatever."

The kids fighting about the bill had stopped arguing with Andre and were now staring at us like frightened deer on a country road. A man sat at the bar, all but passed out from booze, oblivious to the world around him. Andre had pulled out his favorite Louisville Slugger, for all the good it would do against a demon.

Nicole chuckled deep in her throat and stepped toward the bar, but I held her hand tight. "This thing is between you and me," I said. "Leave the others out of it."

"They're already in this." The demon's voice rolled like thunder, as tremulous as boulders cracking under their own weight. "You really think you scare me, little girl?"

"Oh, nice try," I said. "I can tell you're not Azazel. That fucker knows better than to try to intimidate me." I folded my arms. "So, whose little bitch ass do I get to fuck up today?"

She waded in with a series of jabs that I deflected mostly by keeping my head down and my hands up. Her bare knuckles hurt, but I prepared for that by channeling some of my fear energy into sheaths of purple armor that rippled along my arms and shoulders. Nicole retreated, wincing and shaking out her arms. I drew fear into my hands, encasing them in glowing purple gauntlets of energy. I was drawing more emotional resonance from the people in the bar, and the more scared they became, the more power I could draw. Game over, demon.

"You're a real loser—you know that?" I asked. "You couldn't get me to let you in by pretending to be a human, so now you're going to break me open? You've already lost."

Nicole wrapped her arms around my waist and put me on the floor like it was nothing. A table exploded under us, and the air left my body in a rush. I landed on my sprained right arm and momentarily blacked out from the pain. Nicole leered over me, straddling my waist and in complete control.

"You want her?" the demon said over me. "You'll have to beat me out of her."

I caught her hands to hold them away from my face. Saliva ran down her chin from where her lips drew unnaturally far back from her teeth.

"Nicole," I said. "If you can hear me, I don't want to hurt you."

"Don't worry." The demon squeezed tighter. "You won't."

Grappling negated all my advantages. Nicole was accustomed to fighting stronger opponents, and my armor did nothing against her holds. My right arm was useless. I did better than I had in class, but she twisted onto my back and I was huffing sawdust, beer foam, and grime off the floorboards in seconds. Should really do a better job cleaning up around here.

"Should have paid more attention to my moves than my body," the demon said. "Then you'd know what to do when I've got your back."

"Fuck face," I said. "I absolutely know what to do."

I channeled the last of the fear into one hot point in the center of my hand, strained to reach up, and touched Nicole's cheek. Power flared.

Her body went instantly rigid, as though I'd blasted her with a stun gun. Her control fell apart, and she looked at me, dizzy and confused. I head-butted her, and she fell off me entirely.

As blood ran down from her nose, I grinned. "Told you."

"What—?" Nicole staggered back into one of the booths and

upended the table there with a flick of her wrist. Her head shook and her eyes rolled. "What have you done to me?"

"Not to *you*—to *her*." I raised my glowing purple hand. "I conjured up her worst, paralyzing fear and hit her between the eyes with it. You're hard to scare, but Nicole? She's only human, and we're all afraid of something."

Nicole turned away and vomited. At first I worried I'd given her a brain-injuring concussion with that hit, but then I saw the disgusting sludge pumping out her mouth. Those weren't her guts she was puking out, but something far darker and worse for both of us.

"Go!" I hissed at Andre. "Get out of here!"

He didn't need to be told twice. He slid something across the bar in my direction: a black leather satchel marked "For Emergencies." Like a first-aid kit, only better. Then he ushered the last patrons out into the rainy night, leaving me alone with Nicole and her demon. I made a mental note to give him a raise after this.

Unfortunately, the black mess was between me and the claw. As I started to creep around, I felt an influx of power that made me stagger. The room abruptly dropped ten or twenty degrees, and I could see my breath. Here it came.

The lights dimmed, fizzling and crackling to usher in madness. The demon rose from the pool like a patch of liquid night, muscular arms stretched wide as though to soak up the power of the place. Its darkness had no firm lines but instead shifted among half a dozen shapes, from something like a man to a flow of spiders and maggots to a thing mortal minds were never meant to process. Then it took the shape of the Raven sans eye, because that terrified me most.

A shadow demon. Of course. Tricky, vicious, massive inferiority complex. *Dangerous.*

Empty and caught in her fear, Nicole lay senseless, leaving just the demon and me.

I started to speak, but the demon pounced on me and knocked the air out of my lungs. It raked icy claws of darkness across my body, ripping through my jacket and jeans like wet paper, then hurled me into the bar with enough force to crack it. The creature leaped on me, but I pulled fear energy into my legs and kicked it off. It flowed to the center of the room, hovering and dangerous. I blinked away the pain and climbed limply out of the crater I'd left in the bar.

"I thought you'd put up more fight," the demon said in a thousand jabbering voices. Its amorphous body made it hard to see, and my wounds didn't help either. At least its touch was numbingly cold—like being stabbed to death by syringes full of morphine. "The great Lady Vengeance, mortal consort of Azazel the Many-Eyed, hated and feared and loved throughout the bowels of eternity."

"Ew." As I got to my feet, I reached over and claimed the emergency kit on the bar. I took out a weapon I hadn't worn for a long time: a silver gauntlet with sharpened claws for fingers. Even with my movements made awkward thanks to my injured right arm and the adrenaline, I fit it on my left hand with practiced efficiency. "You never told me your name, demon. After I humiliate you, I want to be able to tell the story accurately."

"You'll not trick me, woman." It smiled and nodded toward the bar. "I'm going to kill you, then everyone you've ever loved—"

Nicole's flying knee came out of the dim, flickering light and smashed into the demon's back. She had launched herself with the force of a charging bull, and it knocked the demon staggering toward the bar and me. I met it with a rising slash of the silver claw, and the demon shrieked as the talons tore through its shadowy flesh. I might not be a saint, empowered to smite demons with my bare hands, but blessed silver works regardless of your personal moral standing.

Roaring, Nicole launched a blistering combination of punches, kicks, and elbows that made *my* face ache. I felt no more fear in her, just pure, righteous anger. I approved.

We stood in the ruined bar, arranged in a kind of fighting triangle. I panted and bled, but my powers kept me standing. Nicole looked pale but royally pissed off, hands and arms shaking with white-hot rage that tasted exhilarating. The demon cursed in its profane language, looking for an opening but finding none. Demons may not have the same emotional range as humans, but one we definitely have in common is fear, and its terror tasted like fine fifty-year-old scotch.

"You're outmatched, demon," I said. "I'll give you one chance to—"

The creature roared, boiled away into smog, and flowed through the open back door with a sound like wind droning through grass. Through my powers, I felt the instant the demon left: all that delicious fear gone. What a shame.

"Huh," I said. "I was sure he'd stay for a good monologue. . . ."

Words slid apart and seemed too much hassle. The ground shivered under my feet. Maybe just a little nap. That would be nice. . . .

Nicole caught me as I slumped down, blood flowing and the fear that bolstered me abating. She had her mobile pressed to her ear.

"Don't worry, V," she said. "I called nine-one-one. An ambulance is on its way."

"Great." I coughed, which hurt. A lot. I heard voices outside the bar: people drawn back to the noise. Andre tried to stop them from coming inside. Good man. "Because bleeding to death in my own bar would be a *lame* death."

Nicole put pressure on, which made it better. "Is it gone?"

I nodded. "It's gone."

Nicole sniffed. "Really?"

"Really."

A relieved shiver passed through her. "I'm so sorry," she said. "I didn't know what was going on. I could control myself at first, but then *it* took over and I was just watching. I—"

"Not your fault," I said. "I'm the one who should apologize. You didn't ask for this shit."

"But I got it anyway."

"Yeah." Her fear for me bolstered me physically and psychologically. That's what it was, I realized. Her worst fear was hurting her friends. "I've got a lot to tell you."

"Later." Nicole smiled. "We've got time."

The silence stretched between us, long and soft and easy. Despite the lingering gloom, I felt warm.

SALES. FORCE.

by Kristine Kathryn Rusch

He said: *Our love is deep and powerful, epic.*

He said: *It will last for all time.*

He said: *Forever.*

He died on a Thursday afternoon in midwinter, in Kaylee's arms, in a stupid hospital room with stupid white walls and a stupid brown blanket covering half of him, on a stupid hospital bed with stupid rails that dug into her back, and stupid machines that beep-beep-beeped, then beepbeepbeepbeeped before the stupid alarm sounded and the stupid doctors and nurses ran into the room with the stupid crash cart that did absolutely nothing.

Because, she knew, long before the doctors and nurses arrived, he had taken his last breath.

Never even opened his eyes, not after the damn car accident. Never smiled at her again, never said *I love you* one last time.

There was nothing pretty about the death, nothing pretty about him at the end.

Just her. Standing in the corner of the stupid hospital room, watching the pathetic doctors and nurses with their pathetic crash cart do everything they could to resuscitate a corpse.

>──<

"Fine," she'd say angrily to anyone who asked. "I'm *fine*."

But of course she wasn't fine. She'd never be fine again.

She told everyone she moved out of the apartment because she couldn't live there anymore without him, and everyone took that to mean the memories were too much for her, when really it meant she had to move, as in legally.

She had to do a bunch of things that she didn't want to do because, as she learned the hard way, there was a difference between planning to get married and actually *being* married.

People even looked at her grief differently. *At least,* they'd say, *you still have a future.*

And she'd glare at them angrily, because what could she say, really? *It's a future I don't want?* Or, *Do you really know what the hell you're talking about?* Or, *Do you think about the words that come out of your mouth, or do you just let fly with whatever comes to mind?*

Yeah, she was angry, and yeah, she knew anger was step one of the grief wheel or whatever they called the dumb thing, but she also knew that she'd always been just a little angry. She suspected she'd been born angry, coming out of the womb with tiny fists clenched, spoiling for a fight.

Dex had loved that about her. He'd said he loved everything about her.

He'd said he would never leave her.

She should have known better than to believe him.

Hell, she should have thought it through:

Every relationship ended. Sometimes it ended voluntarily with a break-up or an affair. Sometimes it ended with death.

Only the lucky ones died together.

Everyone else had to suffer through being a *survivor*.

And she hated that term most of all.

>―<―

She went back to work after a week. Her boss, Nia, maybe the only person who understood how much Kaylee had loved Dex, told her to take more time.

But she didn't want more time. She'd moved back to the scruffy one-bedroom she'd had before Dex, which the landlord said he'd been holding for her, but they both knew the place was too tiny and too dark to rent to anyone else.

Her stuff fit in it just like it used to—the battered table, the mattress on the floor, the thrift-shop dishes. The only things she'd taken from Dex's place—and yes, *taken* was the right word, since she had no legal right to anything—were his books. She left a few—the ones she'd read—but his family wouldn't know what he'd had and what he didn't have, and they weren't readers, so they wouldn't miss the books.

She'd slunk away, feeling like she was being evicted from the only home she'd ever had, and after she left, after she'd locked the keys inside, she regretted not taking at least one of his shirts or his blanket or something, something that smelled like him.

Then she squared her shoulders and vowed to move forward. Memories of him would hold her back, not that she could get rid of them.

Not that she wanted to, deep down.

But the memories that kept coming up were the memories of his promises: *We're forever, blondie, just you and me. Forever.*

Forever was awfully damn short, and love was grand for an afternoon, and she was right back where she started, in a tiny little apartment with a great kitchen and no real light, and nothing to do but count the stains on the wall.

So why wouldn't she go back to work?

Work, at least, got rid of the aggression. Work gave her a purpose, made her feel alive. Okay, that last wasn't true. Work didn't make her feel alive.

It justified her numbness.

Because, really, who could kill something day in and day out and remain one hundred percent in touch with her feelings?

Maybe, she thought as she drove to the dying wharf where the office was this week, *it's good Dex is gone.*

He'd been making her too sensitive, too touchy-feely.

Hell, the reason she hadn't married him yet was because she hadn't been able to figure out how to tell him what, exactly, she did for a living.

You see, Dex, there are magic creatures in the world, and most of them are pretty damn evil, just like in those books you read, and all of them—all of them—want a piece of someone's soul, so it takes someone without much of a soul to make them really and truly dead.

I'm the person without much of a soul. So don't love me, Dex. Don't love me, don't marry me, don't stay with me.

She'd never said those words to him, but apparently he'd heard them. He hadn't married her.

And he sure as hell hadn't stayed.

><×<

The office, in a dilapidated building near a rotting pier, was warded. It also smelled strongly of fish.

Kaylee made a face as she stepped inside. Nia stood near a long folding table that tilted to the left.

Nia was tiny, and would've been called cute by folks who

weren't paying attention, the folks who didn't see the daggers in her chocolate brown eyes. Nia kept her black hair shaved close, she said, to control the curls, but Kaylee knew it was to make the work easier. Work took too much think time, time that shouldn't be wasted on hair care or product or even a shampoo.

Maybe Kaylee would go for the shaved look too, although her skull wasn't as symmetrical as Nia's. Nor was Kaylee little or cute.

Kaylee had never been little or cute. Always big, always a bit of a bruiser, and, over the years, she'd developed muscles on her muscles, as Dex used to say with admiration.

Nia held a clipboard. A dozen others hung on the wall from nails newly placed in the peeling paint. An ancient filing cabinet stood near a door that led to a small bathroom. The bathroom looked even more disreputable than the office did.

There was no computer equipment because Nia didn't play well with computers. Besides, computers left an electronic trail, and Nia didn't like leaving trails. Not for this business.

She had a pencil behind her ear and a black pen in her hand.

"Last chance," she said by way of hello. "I'd beg off if I were you. Don't want be at home? Take a vacation, see the sites, find a grief-counseling group, volunteer at a charity or something."

"Can you see me doing any of that?" Kaylee was a little offended that Nia had suggested it.

"I don't care what you do," Nia said. "I'm just warning you. You're perfect for this job, and that's a bad thing."

Kaylee stared at her. Nia was tough. She had a heart, although most people never saw it. Kaylee had. When Kaylee fell for Dex, Nia tried to talk Kaylee into leaving the business altogether.

Love and magic don't mix, Nia had said. *Pick one, K.*

Apparently, Kaylee had picked one. She had picked magic.

"Who'm I supposed to kill?" she asked, keeping her voice level.

She used to debate even asking that question, because often what she was sent to kill wasn't a *who*. It was a *what*. And *kill* might be a relative term. Sometimes *destroy* was better.

"You're not killing this time," Nia said.

"Just because I had to deal with Dex's death—"

"No," Nia said. "That's not why. You're investigating this time."

Kaylee let out a sigh. She hated investigating. She had given it up long ago. Others went into various parts of the city, investigated reports of dark magic or evil intent, and then reported back to Nia. Nia would assign someone to destroy the magic or the mage or both.

Kaylee had an affinity for destruction. She did not investigate well. Investigations required subtlety, and she was anything but subtle.

"I don't investigate," Kaylee said.

"You're the only one we got," Nia said.

"I'm not in the mood to investigate," Kaylee said.

"Tough shit," Nia said. "You stayed. You begged for work. You're doing this."

"I'm leaving," Kaylee said, feeling at loose ends. She had wanted the work, but not finesse work. She needed to crack some heads.

She went to the door, but it glowed red.

"You said I could choose," she said, without turning around.

"And then you asked who you were supposed to kill," Nia said. "That activated the wards. You're in now."

Kaylee felt a flash of irritation. It held back full-blown anger. But she knew, she *knew*, Nia was right. Once the agreement to take a job was made, it was binding.

Kaylee just couldn't believe Nia would give her the wrong kind of work.

Kaylee took a deep breath before turning around. Nia hadn't moved. Her pen remained poised over the clipboard.

"So what's the job?" Kaylee asked, letting her irritation flow through her voice.

"You're going in as a client."

"In where?"

"Armand's Potions on Fifth."

Kaylee sighed, pushing back even more irritation. "You investigated Armand's when it opened, or don't you remember? Legit white magic, no whiff of black—at least in the magical potions. Most everything else has too much alcohol and will simply make the client feel good."

"Yeah, I know," Nia said. "We're not investigating Armand. He's doing a potion sharing."

Kaylee felt her lips tighten. She hated potion sharings. They were the wine tastings of the magical world.

"Why would he do that?" she asked.

"Because I asked him to." Nia opened the clip on the clipboard and removed a piece of paper. It was a flyer advertising a love potion. The flyer smelled like perfume and made Kaylee a bit light-headed just being near it.

Nia smiled.

"Thought so," she said. "You're perfect."

"What does that mean?"

"Some of our regulars have been asked to invest in the love potion," Nia said.

"And you want to know if it's a scam," Kaylee said. "Send one of them in. Remove the spell if the potion works."

"Read the damn flyer," Nia said.

Kaylee didn't want to touch it. It glowed pink and made her feel happier than she wanted to feel.

The flyer claimed the potion didn't make someone fall in love. It took someone who had given up on love or who had lost too much in their life to ever try to love, and repaired their belief in love.

Kaylee had a slight headache now. "I'm perfect?" she asked.

"Yeah," Nia said, and let the word hang. The reason she was sending Kaylee in was obvious to both of them.

"What's the catch?" Kaylee asked.

"That's what you're going to find out," Nia said.

><><

The potion sharing wasn't being held at Armand's. Instead, it was in the back room of one of the swankiest restaurants in the city. Even the back room was swanky. Done in black and white with soft yellow lighting falling on the potion bottles scattered on various tables, the room looked elegant.

The clientele for this thing would be upscale, and even that made Kaylee nervous. She wasn't upscale. But Nia had dressed her that way. Kaylee had even had to go to a fitting. She wore some slinky, glittery black thing that covered her muscular arms in soft material and made her look fat, not buff.

She liked buff. Buff made her intimidating. Buff got her in a room. Fat reminded her of high school, before she discovered her singular talents, back when she'd walk in a room and everyone would snicker.

At least cargo boots with dresses were in style, protecting her from having to wear heels.

Nia wouldn't magic her either, no protect spells, nothing. If Kaylee got hit with the wrong potion, well, then the magical medics on hand would have to handle it, and if somehow that goddamn love potion actually worked, Nia promised she'd unspell Kaylee and the victim of her love/lust.

Kaylee hoped that would happen before there was any damage.

Armand stood near the door. He was short, black-haired, and spray-tanned. He took her hand in his as she greeted him. Then he leaned forward and kissed her on each cheek, enveloping her in some kind of sandalwood cologne.

"We shall do this together, *oui?*" he said in her ear.

"If you say so, bub," she said, pulling back. Then she grinned at him so that her words didn't seem so harsh.

His eyes twinkled for just a moment, and her heart fluttered. He was aware of the game they were playing. She hadn't forgotten that, but she hadn't realized he would be so deeply involved.

"I was so sorry to hear about your fiancé." He spoke louder and his accent was softer, weirdly enough. "When the heart hurts . . ."

He slipped her hand through his arm. Then he nodded at her courteously.

"For such hurt," he said, leading her toward one of the nearest tables. "We have remedies."

She looked at the bottles scattered along it. Genie bottles, Dex had called them once when he visited the office in its temporary digs on 42nd Street. She had laughed and told him, *Yes, genie bottles. Don't touch.*

"For the pain," Armand said now.

Others stood near the table, some holding drinks, the bottom of their glasses wrapped in paper napkins. Waiters mingled with the guests, carrying silver trays with crudités. Kaylee wondered briefly if anyone had vetted the food: it wouldn't do to have a guest turn into a frog because they had a potion mixed with wine mixed with the wrong kind of pâté.

She had to bring herself back to the role. She wasn't watching the people; she was looking at the potions. She touched the descriptive cards on three bottles. Two cards remained unchanged, but the third released white smoke, which then wrapped around her hand.

The smoke whispered, *I will help you forget.*

She drew back as if it had bitten her, and looked at Armand in very real alarm.

"I don't want to forget him," she said before she could think.

This, *this*, was why Nia said she was perfect. The pain, the grief, the loss, it took away a cautious part of her brain. It made her vulnerable to these very spells, the kind that preyed upon the weak.

"Forgive me, *mademoiselle*," Armand said. "Perhaps something a bit less . . . intrusive?"

She swallowed, wishing she hadn't accepted this assignment. Beneath the playacting, the anger was rising. She wanted to kill them all just for having a good time.

She blinked, took a deep breath, said, "I just want a new future."

"*Mais oui, mademoiselle*, don't we all." Armand smiled at her and squeezed her hand against his side. Weirdly, the movement was comforting.

She didn't want to be comforted. She wanted to hang on to the anger.

"Maybe this will help you," he said, and led her to a table farther back. "A warning: It is expensive."

"Money is no object," she murmured, wishing that were true. But she wasn't buying. The company wasn't buying. They were *sampling*.

The table stood by itself. Extra lights poured down on it, soft lighting, the kind that theaters used on starlets, bathed a single bottle in warmth. The bottle, shaped like a flower about to bloom, glowed pink.

"Ah, it recognizes you, *mademoiselle*," he said. "It will work with you."

He snapped his fingers, and a young man stepped out of the shadows. His features blurred. She wasn't sure if that was deliberate or if he wasn't really human.

It was not her job to find out. She was to taste the potion, and see if it was real.

The young man took a flower-shaped glass from a tray she hadn't seen, and poured just a bit of potion. A pink glow swirled out of it. She had a quick, panicky feeling that she shouldn't do this, that this was wrong, that she was betraying Dex, and then the glow swirled into her face, going up her nose.

She felt it, like an ice-cream headache, then it flowed into her, and she, and she—

Burst into tears.

Somewhere, in the back of her brain, her real self crossed its arms, and judged. She did not cry. Crying was weak. Crying was an indulgence. Crying was something no one should ever ever do.

Armand patted her back, clearly alarmed, and the young man— she had been wrong, he had sculptured features, almost vulpine, and dark intense eyes—enveloped her in his arms, comforting, holding, and she let him, dear God, she let him hold her because it felt right.

Not that she had fallen in love with him, or even that she was attracted to him. She had just needed someone to hold her since that car slammed into Dex, right in front of her, before she could even stop it, while she screamed for help, and then crouching with his broken body, wishing she had healing magic, not violent magic, although some of that leaked out too, because the car careened into a group of parked cars, and the damn driver died, just like he should have, careless son of a fucking bitch—

"Here, here," the young man said, handing her a tissue. She took it, but it was useless. He dabbed at her face, then wiped her tears with his thumbs, and she worried about him capturing her essence, even though he had tears on his jacket and she would have to report that to Nia, she would have to report it all—

Kaylee took a deep breath. And just that quickly, the tears were gone. But so was the ache she had felt since that goddamn hospital bed, on that bleak afternoon.

"What was that?" she asked, surprised that her voice did not shake.

"We call it a love potion," the young man said. "But that isn't quite true. It restores the heart, makes love possible again. You'll see."

"I didn't drink it," she said.

"No," he said. "You must buy the bottle to drink. And it is not a onetime potion. It is a treatment, really. It gets you past your grief and into your future. Isn't that what you wanted?"

Had he overheard her conversation with Armand? Or was this part of the sales pitch?

"So, it won't make me fall in love?" she asked.

"It will *allow* you to love again," he said. "It is very delicate and very powerful."

"And very expensive, I'll bet." She sounded more like herself again, even though the anger had gone. She felt hollow without it. Hollow and a bit giddy, as if she were real-people drunk instead of Kaylee-drunk. Kaylee-drunk was usually bar-fight furious, and had gotten her arrested more than once.

"Ten thousand a bottle," he said. "But considering that it restores your heart, opening it to love, the price is low."

"How many bottles does it take to 'cure' someone?" she asked.

"Only one," he said. "We are not in the business of addicting someone. Only helping people."

It sounded so right, so smooth, so perfect. The real Kaylee, tucked in the back of her brain, arms crossed, knew that was a warning sign, but this Kaylee, still under the spell, nodded.

"I don't have ten thousand tonight," she said. "Can I get this at Armand's?"

"Only if you do so within the week," the young man said. "This batch, which seems to have an affinity for you, is nearly gone. If we do not sell the remaining ten bottles this evening, the rest will go to Armand's. But I must warn you, we do raise the price when there are fewer than five."

She nodded, almost without thinking. She wanted the bottle right now. Thank heavens Nia did not give her money. She would have spent it.

"I'll tell Armand to save me one," she said. Another tear leaked out of her eye. *Dammit.* She dabbed at it. "Thank you."

Then she staggered away from the young man. He had her tears, but she had some of his skin collected on the edges of her glittering dress. An even trade, or so her real self said. Her real self, which was still observing.

She passed Armand, and waved a hand at her eyes.

"I need to fix my face," she said.

"Yes," he said. Then, softer, *"Merci."*

She almost asked *For what?* then remembered. Investigation, mission.

She staggered out of the back room into the restaurant and toward the ladies' room, which was near the back door. She pushed it open, and stepped into the alley.

The cool night air did not clear her head, although it made her chapped cheeks sting. She pivoted, almost went back inside—*She could find ten thousand dollars. If a whiff of the potion made her feel like this, imagine what the entire bottle would do*—but she managed to follow the plan.

She walked down the alley and turned left on the side street where Nia had parked her battered van. Kaylee climbed inside.

Her real self wanted to say, *Get it out of me. You don't know what it's doing to me,* but the rest of her looked at Nia, realized just how cute she was, wondered why they hadn't been closer friends—

"Tilt your head back," Nia said. "You drank, right?"

Kaylee shook her head. "Breathed it," she managed.

"Oh, sneaky," Nia said. She took a pipette, lit a match at the bottom of it, and then tapped the side, muttering a spell that Kaylee didn't recognize.

Pink glow streamed out of her nose and mouth, into the pipette. More hovered. Nia took another pipette, and then another, capping them as she trapped the glow inside.

In the end, six pipettes with vibrating, glowing pink smoke stood in a little case, like an evil drug.

Nia continued the spell with four more pipettes, then did some kind of heal or reverse. Kaylee didn't know.

She was exhausted, battered, and empty.

And then, deep down, she realized with bitter amusement, she finally felt angry.

><><

She slept for almost two days, in a bed in the tiny back room of the wharf office, with someone watching her twenty-four/seven. By the time she woke up—really woke up, not stirred enough to eat, roll over, and head back to dreamland—they'd finished testing the spell.

Nia accompanied Kaylee to her ratty apartment for a change of clothing, a shower, and a surprise pizza (paid for—even bigger surprise—by Nia). As they bonded over pepperoni and sausage in that kitchen too nice to fit into the rest of the apartment (and clean, because Kaylee had hardly been there since she moved back in), Nia proclaimed the spell elegant and powerful.

Kaylee knew about the powerful. The entire thing had left her shaken, and midway through her marathon sleep session, she had demanded that Nia check to make certain no trace of the spell remained inside Kaylee.

It hadn't. The sleep, Nia had said, was probably overdue.

And now that Kaylee was awake, she figured Nia was right: Kaylee hadn't slept well since Dex died, and the exhaustion from the spell probably carried into the exhaustion from her grief.

What she didn't tell Nia was that the grief wasn't there anymore, not like it had been. Not overwhelming and ever present. Kaylee didn't dare confess that it had altered, because, in part, she was afraid she altered it.

She was a woman without much of a soul. Maybe she could only mourn so long. Maybe she could only love so deep. Maybe—hell, not maybe, actually—she wasn't like other people, and that probably extended to the way she grieved as well.

At least the pizza tasted good. Nia had also brought a six-pack of her favorite microbrew, and the dark beer seemed appropriate, both to the pizza and Kaylee's mood.

"So," she said, after three pieces. "The spell's legit. Expensive, but legit. What's wrong with that?"

"Nothing," Nia said. "Armand was happy. He makes a healthy commission off the sales."

"We weren't doing this for Armand, were we?" Kaylee tried to keep the question casual, but she didn't want to think she had (possibly) sacrificed her grief for Armand. She liked him, but she didn't like him that much.

"No," Nia said. "It's the investment angle. It still bothers me."

Kaylee had forgotten about the investments. They were what had interested Nia in the first place.

"It's an expensive commodity," Kaylee said. "There's clearly money to be made."

"Yeah." Nia took another piece of pizza. The cheese, still warm, clung to the rest of the pizza. She snapped the piece off with the edges of her fingers. "It's the method that bothers me. They're going for small investors. People who can put in a few thousand dollars and get some kind of stock. When you're selling a bottle for ten thousand dollars, that seems like tiny money."

Kaylee didn't pretend to understand investments. She barely had enough coin for this ratty apartment. She never asked for a raise because money hadn't meant much. Still didn't. What did she need besides food, a warm place to lay her head, and something to do every day?

"Maybe they're going to expand," she said.

Nia raised her head, frowning. "You said the potion was a one-time dose."

"That's not what he told me," Kaylee said. "You took it a bit at a time until you finished the bottle."

"And then, didn't he tell you, no more bottles?"

"Yes," Kaylee said.

"Onetime use." Nia said that almost to herself. "So they're constantly in need of new customers. *That's* the flaw in the spell."

She got up from the table, leaving half of the last piece she had taken uneaten.

"You," she said to Kaylee, "are brilliant."

"Sometimes," Kaylee said. "Apparently."

Nia grinned at her and then gathered her things. "I'll be in touch."

"I'll be here," Kaylee said, but she spoke to an empty room. Nia hadn't even used the door. She had simply disappeared.

Kaylee hated wasting magic like that. She only used her magic for big things. Well, the big things *she* could do. She couldn't make crash carts work or doctors arrive on time or men crushed by the front bumper of a car going forty-five miles per hour in a twenty-mile-per-hour zone come out of comas to say good-bye to their one and only love.

She shivered at the thought and felt the rag end of loss. It was back. She just hadn't noticed.

Maybe because it had become part of her during her long sleep.

Maybe because it fueled her anger.

Or maybe both.

>—<

The books she stole from Dex's apartment were stupid. They were about things she didn't give a rat's ass over. The history of baseball. The psychology of golf. Current political bestsellers. A few fantasy novels—heavy on the fantasy and short on the realism.

She read them, anyway, and felt no closer to him. She was restless all over again and thinking about doing more work. Nia hadn't called, but that didn't mean anything.

Sometimes Kaylee got work just by showing up.

She showered, then decided she needed something new to wear, something Dex hadn't commented on. She promised herself a latte and some incredibly rich dessert if she bought two pairs of pants and three shirts.

She ended up with two shirts and one pair of pants and called it good. The coffee shop three blocks from her place had closed in the past few weeks, so she went to the other place with excellent baked goods, across the street from Armand's.

He was there, getting enough coffee for his entire staff. When he saw her, he came over and bussed her cheeks, then put his hands on her shoulders and studied her face.

"Nia said it was hard for you," he said. "I am sorry."

Kaylee shrugged. "I suspect everything'll be hard for a while."

"I would hug you," he said, "but now that you are dressed as you, I feel I must ask permission."

She half smiled. "The sentiment is enough, Armand, thank you."

"Let me pay for your order," he said. "In fact, let me pay for your next month's worth of orders."

"That's all right," she said.

"No, no, you do not understand, my friend. These potions, the commission is superb."

"Nia's worried that they're onetime and done," Kaylee said.

"That concerned me as well," Armand said. "But one person recommends to a friend who recommends to a friend. I have sold two separate lots since I last saw you."

"Lots?" Kaylee asked. "What do you mean?"

"Ten bottles per lot," Armand said. "I have sold twenty bottles, and I am halfway through the third lot."

Kaylee let out a small whistle. "That's a lot of people needing a love potion."

"A future potion; that is how I am selling it. One that heals the heart." Armand turned and gave the clerk his credit card. "You will set up an account for my friend, *de comprendre?*"

The clerk nodded, ran Armand's credit card, and then handed Kaylee a gift card.

"Hah," he said, shaking his head. "Accounts mean something different here."

She barely paid attention (although she did thank him). Instead she was doing the math.

"It's been less than a week and you've sold twenty-five bottles?" Kaylee asked. "Doesn't that seem odd to you?"

"No," he said quietly, scooping up the cardboard container with the coffee drinks shoved into their respective holders. "My customers have had a rough spring. As have you."

He kissed her again, wished her well, and then left, before she could thank him a second time.

To be fair, she hadn't thought of thanking him, not for at least ten minutes after he left, when the cinnamon roll she'd ordered arrived, dripping frosting on the china plate, a latte steaming beside it.

She took a bite, then remembered that blurred face of the man selling the potion and how he became clear only after she had breathed in the steam.

A rough spring.

The potion did give the person who used it hope for the future, a chance at rebirth, renewal.

But to have that, the person needed incentive. She needed a sense that the world did not work for her, that her past was too overwhelming to cope with alone.

She needed a great loss.

"Son of a bitch," Kaylee said, and nearly spilled her latte. "Son of a fucking bitch."

><><

She didn't run to the wharf because, first of all, there was no running, not from this neighborhood. She would've called, except no one working for Nia had a cell phone—not that Nia had one, either—and the landline probably wasn't installed yet (if it ever would be).

She could have taken a cab, but she didn't have enough cash. Besides, she wanted to get there faster than any traffic could take her. So she had the clerk box the remains of the cinnamon bun and put it in a bag. Then she grabbed that and her latte, and went outside.

And, for the first time since Dex died, she used her magic.

She transported herself from the sidewalk to the office.

Nia did not look surprised to see her, but, then, Nia never looked surprised to see anyone.

"I want you to tell me I'm wrong," Kaylee said, her hand shaking. The magic use had made her light-headed.

"Wrong about what?" Nia asked.

"Tell me they're not creating their own clients," Kaylee said.

"What do you mean?" Nia asked.

"The love-potion makers," Kaylee said. "Tell me they're not doing anything wrong."

>><<

It took Kaylee almost a half an hour to explain the idea that had come to her when she was talking with Armand. It wasn't what he said so much as what he implied.

His customers, their rough spring. Like hers.

Only *rough* was the wrong word.

Devastating. She had had a devastating spring.

Nia promised to investigate, and this time, she didn't assign Kaylee to the task.

>><<

Nia arrived at Kaylee's apartment one week later. Only this time, Nia brought a pizza and an address. It was in the West Fifties, a rehabbed brownstone that someone had poured a small fortune into.

"What am I looking at?" Kaylee asked, staring at the piece of paper.

"The sales force," Nia said.

"For the potion?" Kaylee asked.

"Yeah," Nia said.

"I'm not supposed to investigate this time?" Kaylee asked.

"That's a lot of questions for you," Nia said.

Kaylee shrugged. "It's been an odd case."

Nia nodded, one hand on the pizza box, as if she couldn't decide whether to eat or to leave.

"We investigated already," she said. "Think of the term. Sales. Force."

"They use what? Magical means—"

"No magic," Nia said. "The potion is the only magic."

"But you tested it. There's no dark magic in the potion at all."

"It's pure and elegant," Nia said. "The company is not."

Kaylee felt cold. "What are they doing?"

"Creating customers," Nia said. "Just like you thought."

Kaylee felt a growing frustration. Her brain no longer worked as well as she wanted, since half of it was still processing the loss of Dex. Grief made her slow-witted; she hated that.

"How?" she asked.

"However they see fit," Nia said. "Drug overdoses, muggings gone wrong, car accidents. First they analyze the available money, then they look for a suitable victim, then they take away the most precious thing."

Kaylee had frozen when Nia said *car accidents*. Nia did not make statements like that without a reason. But Kaylee wouldn't put it past Nia to use the phrase to motivate Kaylee, without any evidence at all.

So, Kaylee asked, "Dex? Was he—?"

"Do you have money?" Nia asked.

Kaylee's cheeks heated. "No."

"Did you offer to invest in a love potion? Were you even contacted to do so?"

The heat grew worse. "No."

"Then, no, Kaylee." The words seemed unnecessarily harsh. But Nia's gaze wasn't harsh. It was soft with empathy, even though her statements made it clear that she had used the phrase *car acci-dents* as a ham-handed attempt at manipulation.

"I only take care of the magical," Kaylee said, just because she was feeling ornery.

"Then I'll assign someone else," Nia said. "I thought maybe you wanted this one."

She headed for the door.

Principles, ethics. They belonged to Dex's world.

And Dex was dead.

"I want it," Kaylee said. "I want it even more than you know."

><×<

It wasn't quite shooting fish in a barrel. Shooting fish in a barrel wouldn't be quite as messy.

Kaylee could've just appeared in their brownstone, but she de-cided to do it the old-fashioned way. She walked up the stairs to the top of the stoop, knocked on the gigantic wood door, and waited until a man in a silk suit opened it.

"Yes?" he said politely.

"You're the sales team for the love potion Armand sells?"

"Yes," the man said, just as politely.

"I have a business proposition for you."

He looked at her, in her regular clothes—sleeveless T-shirt reveal-ing her biceps, muscular legs straining at her jeans—and said, "Um—"

"Great," she said, and pushed past him. One hand, heart, hard push, and he was sliding down the wall.

The push was a little too hard, because bits of him remained on the wall as he slid down. Fresh blood is black. Heart blood is blackish red and viscous.

It'd be hell to clean up, but that wouldn't be her job.

"Stanley?" someone yelled from the main room. Woman's voice.

Kaylee walked into that room, saw six people, beautifully garbed, and two with actual weapons in holsters under their arms.

Kaylee smiled. "He's behind me," she said.

"And you are?" the woman asked, her shoulder-length brown hair swinging perfectly as she stood up.

"Totally pissed off," Kaylee said.

Three more pushes mostly to the people in front of her. They slammed backward against the wall, leaving an even goopier trail than Stanley had. The two with the weapons—one man, one woman—unsnapped their holsters, pulled out the guns, and didn't even get to the safeties before Kaylee knocked them back.

That left three people standing near the table where they'd all been looking over some plans. Three—two men, one woman. The men were sobbing, begging. She was watching Kaylee.

Kaylee shut the men up, left the woman.

She held Kaylee's gaze. The brains behind the operation, then.

"So," Kaylee said casually. "Close to any of them?"

"What do you mean?" she asked.

"Feeling their loss yet? Because I know a great potion that'll help you feel a hell of a lot better."

Then her lower lip trembled. She knew what Kaylee meant.

"Your idea?" Kaylee asked.

"Hell, no," she said a little too quickly. "Why would anyone do that? It's so heartless."

"It's not heartless," Kaylee said. "You just need to be a person without much of a soul. The killing doesn't impact you then."

"Like you," she said.

"Two peas in a pod, you and me," Kaylee said, and killed her. Maybe a little too slowly. Maybe enjoyed it a little too much.

Kaylee didn't have to try to hang on to the bits of herself any longer. There was no Dex anymore, nothing really to strive for.

She was good at what she did.

And she never touched a goddamn thing.

She disappeared out of the room, ended up in her dingy shower. Peeled off the clothes, dumped them into the bucket of bleach she'd left for just that purpose, and then tossed them, dripping, into a garbage bag.

She showered, poured the bleach down the drain when she was done, and felt absolutely no better.

But Kaylee felt like herself again.

No lingering effects from the damn potion, no desire for a better life.

And the anger, mitigated the right way, for the right reason.

It would build up again. Nia knew that. Hell, Kaylee knew that.

She preferred it that way.

She didn't want to meet anyone, not again. No potion, no nothing, would make her ever step into those forevers again.

She couldn't bear another hospital room, another goddamn broken promise.

He said: *Forever.*

She should've said: *Fuck you.*

But she hadn't. She never had.

And she knew she would regret that little decision from now on.

Until forever.

Amen.

IMPOSSIBLE MONSTERS

A Caliban Story from the World of the Cal Leandros Novels

by Rob Thurman

*"Fantasy, abandoned by reason,
produces impossible monsters."*
—FRANCISCO DE GOYA (1746–1828)

Firstborn
(Present Day)

I changed my mind.

It wasn't something I did often. It wasn't something I did even rarely. Don't get me wrong. It's not thanks to the fact that most of my decisions—fine, all right, any of my decisions—are well thought out. Sure, I could tell you they are, but it would be a lie—not that I had a problem lying. I didn't have a problem with the truth, the hurtful kind, either. Sometimes you should lie. White lies. I know that. I do.

It's on the list.

I have two lists, if you're counting. One was given to me the moment I learned to read my first word. It was of things I should or shouldn't do, and, sadly, limited my entertainment value considerably. The second list I'd made myself. Its purpose was completely different, and its entertainment was opposite in that it was *prime*. There were no dos or don'ts on it, only names. It was also the one that might have me changing my mind, as unlikely a scenario as that has ever been.

As for the reason why I didn't change my mind often, it simply wasn't that much involved in, hell, my life as a rule or, in this case, my decision-making process. Or the lack of it. I didn't think about what I said or what I did for more than a fraction of a moment, if I thought at all. Why bother? Whatever I ended up saying, whatever I ended up doing, it came from the same place. It wasn't from my conscience. I didn't have one—or, more accurately, I *did*, but it wasn't the norm. Society wouldn't recognize it, but a lion would. In my gut, my instinct—that's where my decisions were born.

As a system, sometimes it worked out and sometimes it failed. Other times it failed spectacularly. Either way, right or wrong, I didn't second-guess myself. What was done couldn't be undone. If everything turned into a train wreck despite my giving it my best shot, well, shit happens. Why would I waste time on guilt when I could waste it on something like the newest porn mag?

With that outlook, there was no need to worry about changing my mind.

My phone buzzed for the second time.

Until now.

This time, I was second-guessing. With good reason. This was on me. This was my fault, because I *wasn't* actually second-guessing. That's what I'd done twelve years ago, by not acting on what my gut and instinct had been telling me. I hadn't had proof, but neither had I doubts. But I did have the first do-or-don't list. The Commandments, but considerably more than ten. I'd followed them more strictly at that age, whether I had misgivings or not.

Those misgivings were how the second list, *my* list, had been born. I'd written down a name, one to keep an eye on, instead of doing what I should have done. What needed to be done. Thinking a watch list was a good-enough substitute. It wasn't. That after-the-fact, second-run list only emphasized the simple truth. . . .

I'd fucked up.

The phone's alert went off for a third time, twice as loud, with the buzz-saw whine of a pissed-off rattlesnake, to remind me of how unforgivably I'd done just that.

I switched off the prompt without thought as I rested an elbow on the stained, spiderweb-cracked surface of the bar. The first alert was what had started this whole train of thought. It was my yearly prompt to myself to check my list. And I had. I dove in expecting to speed down it in minutes, same as every year, but this year that hadn't happened. Fifteen minutes had passed and I couldn't get past number one. I kept on, Googling hell-for-leather, before I'd found the end of the string and began yanking, unraveling an unholy knotted mess. Due diligence was what my brother called it. He cared about things like innocence and guilt, when, let's face it:

We're all guilty of something.

"I said, I want my fucking whiskey, you half-breed freak. Piece of shit mother—"

Rude.

Without raising my gaze from my phone or moving off my elbow, I used my free hand to shoot the Wolf twice in the throat before he could finish spraying me with spit and aggression. I had my Eagle back in its holster before the Were realized he'd been shot.

I packed a Five-seven under one arm and a Desert Eagle under the other in a double holster. It wasn't my fault that some, mostly Wolves, didn't take that as a red flag. It was in plain view, as all I wore while working besides the holster was a bar apron, jeans, and a T-shirt. Today's was black (be real: they're all black) with an invisible, impossibly wide Cheshire cat grin that showed nothing but a curving double row of far too many pointed white teeth and the slogan in dark red that read, YOU HAVE TO TAKE THE BAD WITH THE GOOD. And then below the grin: I, MOTHERFUCKER, AM THE BAD. You'd think that'd be a second red flag, but maybe this Wolf had been too lazy to read it.

This particular one, mirrored pretty well in a puddle of water I'd yet to wipe off the bar top, had wolfed out enough from the anger or the pain or both to be in half-and-half form. He had the muzzle, the fangs, the claws, the dirty cream and brown fur, and the snapping jaws, but he was standing upright like a human, with long human fingers, his eyes, filled with fury or not, a common human hazel. He swayed to one side and listed back to the other before combining a cough, a howl, and a strangled choking into a gushing spray of blood on the bar top. Then . . . *then* he finally dropped.

Figured. Rude, and couldn't take a little maiming with grace. Had to leave a mess to piss me off further. But, mess or not, I didn't change my mind over shooting him.

See how that philosophy normally worked out so well for me?

I also had no regrets and the best of reasons for that.

I'm a monster.

And, make no mistake . . .

I *like* it.

My kind, the Auphe, had been the First.

Enough to make it an official title. The first murderers to walk the earth. The first to kill for shits and giggles, not survival. The first of the perverse.

The first to be shunned by other monsters. The bogeymen to the bogeymen. And one of whom had been Daddy fucking Dearest. I came by my club membership honestly.

The Wolf was gurgling out of sight, half drowning on his own blood from the sound of it. Tougher than cockroaches, but they hate the throat shots. He would live, though. The dead don't generate much revenue for the bar, as said, and they damn sure don't tip.

Ishiah, my boss and the owner of the bar, was abruptly beside me out of nowhere. I felt a cool gust of air against the top of my head as I stayed bent over my phone. Peri, ex-angels, or whatever they wanted to call themselves, ran cold for some reason, and I refused to believe it was from floating around in the clouds and playing harps before they retired. The boss did have the smiting look to him, though—tall, blond, a heavily scarred jaw, and eyes the color of an uncertain sky, clouds a heavy threat ready to roll in and turn the world into a non-OSHA-approved water park. *WHERE it's THE END and EVERY END is the DEEP END!* For all but Noah and his SS *Minnow*, at least.

"Do you have any idea how high the rent on this place is? Do you? So, why?" You would think it would be impossible to *hear* an eye twitching in spastic frustration. You'd be wrong. "Why did you shoot the Wolf, Caliban?"

Yeah, Caliban. Mom had a helluva sense of humor, a fuzzy knowledge of Shakespeare, and a vicious glee when it came to naming her half-human, half-monster kid. She wasn't a witch, like in the play, but she had been a bitch, and that was close enough in my book to be the fucking cherry on top of that heartwarming family story.

"I'm on break," I replied absently. "And he didn't respect that."

Ah, there. The knotted Internet ball untangled and the information spooled free. Names, locations, dates. Addresses. I smirked triumphantly at the come-and-go of red sparking in the small screen. Done. Time to go.

Straightening, I stripped off my blood-speckled apron. Blowback was a bitch. Tossing it aside, I grabbed my jacket from under the bar and shrugged into it, covering up the holster, as outside the door was human territory. While no one in here cared if I carried two guns or twenty, those outside might. This was a bar for those in the know about Big Bad Wolves, the not-quite-Fallen, and a hundred other different species straight out of your average fairy tale or mythology book. You'd never find a human here, same as you'd almost never find a human anywhere who knew about any of the rest of us. "I'm taking a long weekend, boss. Take it out of my vacation time."

I jumped up and slid over the bar top, avoiding the blood. This was my last pair of unstained jeans. "Long weekend? Vacation time?" His clenched hand pounded on the bar and, unlike me, he didn't miss the blood. Fist painted crimson, he aimed it in my direction. "It's *not* the weekend, and you do not have any vacation time. In fact, you owe me close to five months' sick *and* vacation time."

"Protecting the innocent can't be scheduled. You, in particular, should know that." I waved a hand over my head in a casual farewell salute. "Remember that one time, *at monster camp*," I mocked with all the fake cheer I could gather up to push in his face, "when I saved the world, saved your life, saved everyone you ever knew or will know?" I let the cheer dissipate. "And I didn't even need a goddamn flute. You're welcome. Employee of the fucking century. Still waiting on the plaque. See you Monday."

"*Monday?* I told you already, you lazy ass. It's *not* the weeken—"

The door at the front of the bar closed, cutting off the rest of his rant. I had no time for anything but the name on my list. Checking annually or not, I suspected with this one certain name I'd been sloppy. I think I'd known all along how badly I'd screwed up, and denial makes for piss-poor research. This year I'd gotten an immediate, if vague, hit that even subconscious self-defense couldn't overlook and that made me examine the hit and everything else closer than I had the previous twelve years. It had me digging down farther, and down I did go. When I was done, I'd dug several virtual holes, all six feet deep and all filled.

All but one, and I had a name ready to slap on the marker.

I'd recognized predators when I'd been thirteen—make no fucking mistake—but I had the first list, the one my brother gave me. It was to keep the lion in me—he refused to call me a monster—safe from an inability to understand human motivations and human rules. I knew what they were, their rules; I wasn't an idiot. I just didn't know *why* they were. Sometimes I still didn't, but I had known that's precisely why the list had been made for me.

It was also why I'd let it guide me that one time, in the sweat stink of a school gym, instead of going with my gut. Since then I'd learned better. I didn't always need the human definition of "proof." I seldom did, in fact. I knew when someone lived where I did. All of the predators—the lions, the carelessly eager, the cold-blooded, the rabid—we spent our lives in the tall, tall grass. Twelve years ago, I'd recognized a wild distortion of my own reflection in the unblinking black-glass stare of a human snake, yet I let it go.

I'd fucked up but good back then. How about I didn't fuck up again?

So . . . I did it.

My once in a blue moon.

I changed my mind.

>—><—<

First Day

(Twelve Years Ago)

"Do you have your list?"

He asked me every day, but he asked twice on first days. We had enough first days that twice was closer to being the rule, not the exception.

I rolled my eyes. I was thirteen. I could still do that if I wanted. Pulling the laminated rectangle out of my jean pocket, I held it up in front of his face. "Abra-fucking-cadabra. Is this your card, sir?"

"Language, Cal." He lightly swatted the back of my head.

"I know it is. Want to hear some more?" I smirked, annoying, sarcastic shit that I was. I'd barely been a teenager for four months now, but I knew the obligations that went with it. That, added to the duties of all little brothers to drive their older ones bat-shit crazy, was going to make Niko's life hell from now on.

Who was I kidding? His life had been hell since the day he'd been born. It had gotten worse when I'd been born, for so many reasons. He'd raised me because, if I'd been smaller at birth, Sophia probably would've flushed me, goldfish style, down the toilet. He raised me starting when he was four and someone should've been raising him instead. From my very first diaper, he was my whole family and my only family. He was all I had. Which was good by me. He was all I wanted or needed.

He'd asked once when I was around seven if I missed having a real family. Did I miss having parents that made sure we were fed, warm, and safe—the kind that cooked meals, paid the bills so we had electricity and water more than half the month, who cared where we were after dark or cared if we came home at all? Did I miss that over the one who didn't know if we went to school or not; who didn't shop for food, much less cook it; who threw whiskey bottles against the walls and brought strange men home for twenty minutes before pushing them back out the door?

"She's a drunk whore," I remembered interrupting him to say, because Niko had tried to pretty things up for me. I wasn't a baby. I was *seven*. That was plenty old enough to already know what the woman everyone called my mother really was. I also remembered thinking he could talk forever when he could say it in four words, and I could go back to watching cartoons.

Although seven or not and no baby, I hadn't understood the question. Have more people? Even people with food? Why? People weren't the same as me. Niko wasn't the same, either, but he understood me, how I was on the inside, how I . . . worked. He wasn't like me, but he wasn't one of them. He was between. I liked things the way they were, him and me. It was how it should be.

I hadn't been able to explain it better. There weren't words that fit. It was the sun always rising. It was the sky being up and the ground under you being down. It was just . . . right.

Niko hadn't understood "right." He understood brothers, protecting them, caring about them, that I was his and he was mine. He'd gotten that and he was the best brother, but he hadn't been able to get the rest. How all of those things were good—they *were*—but they were . . . small. Next to right. Right was everything there was, the world, the universe, and then everything past that. Everything we didn't know about now, but was out there waiting to be found someday. I'd tried again to explain it and had given up halfway through. I didn't have the words I needed.

People hadn't made those words yet.

Right might be too big for people thoughts and people minds, but the idea of having anyone but him at seven had been weird, was still weird today. People living with us. Trying to be part of us? That had been beyond weird. Weird but not because it was wrong. Weird because it was impossible. Sharks and lions didn't live together. That was crazy. They couldn't if they wanted to, and I'd been pretty sure they didn't want to. I'd known I hadn't wanted to.

Six years later, I still didn't understand the question.

I shrugged off the memory as easily as I shrugged my backpack over my shoulder. I could hear the bus coming. *Time to go.*

"List?"

I nodded.

"Note?"

"I'm ready." I grinned at him, the grin no one but him had or would see. "Why so jumpy? It's been years since you worried about me having to put up with someone's shit or that I can take care of myself."

"First days," he said ruefully. "And, yes, it's infinitely better worrying you won't put up with someone's *crap*"—he aimed a narrow-eyed look at me sharp enough to get his point across—"and that you can take care of yourself or take care of someone else. Several someones, if you have to. Just don't, please, end up at the police station."

He couldn't fool me there about the cursing. He'd heard worse from me when I was younger than ten. Sophia was all sorts of educational when it came to any and all curse words that existed. Worrying about me, though—that wasn't fake. He did it every year on this day, the first day at a new school. There was always a new school. First days for their usual students, first days for us;

middle of the semester for them, yet still another first day for us. I'd lost count of how many schools there'd been, how many first days.

This was just one more.

>--<

The junior high school was square, brown, and ugly. All schools were. There was a giant factory somewhere stamping them out on a conveyor belt. Floor was the usual puke green tile, the walls were the shade identical to the walls in every school in every state I'd been. Nothing. They were the color of nothing. Not white, off-white, beige, or gray, not any of those yet not outside of that boring cluster. "Nothing" was the only label for it, simple as that.

The gym was no surprise, either.

The teacher? Coach? Both? He was curious though, a little. Heavy with a gut—all male gym teachers were; it was the law—he had hair black as mine although he was starting to lose it, the top of his head covered in a sparse, dying lawn. The hair on his arms was thick and coarse, though. Come Easter, little kids could hide eggs in that shit. Despite being in what I guessed was his early thirties, he had the start of a double chin and no neck; not a great combo. He looked slow and clumsy. Should've been slow and clumsy, but I watched him move back and forth through the kids playing basketball. He *slid*, quick and focused, like a hungry snake.

Like a predator.

Huh.

Halfway through the game, he pulled one guy out. He had to be in the ninth grade—it was the highest the school had—but he had to have flunked a year . . . or two. He was sixteen at least, six feet tall, and weighed 230 pounds; all muscle, more than any other kid down there. Topped his cereal off with radioactive mutagen–powered steroids instead of sugar for breakfast; ate a cow for supper and got up in the middle of the night to shit T-bone steaks and a leather jacket.

The gym teacher took him off to the side and, head-to-head, murmured something to him. After a few minutes, Godzilla straightened, gave a nasty grin—I appreciated the nasty ones as I had my own—nodded, and headed toward the bleachers. Toward me. The coach's eyes were on me, too, the bright and cold shine of black glass. Then they were back on the game. If I hadn't already suspected when I'd seen how he moved, it would've been fast enough for me to miss. And I didn't miss shit like that. Ever.

Clattering up the bleachers, two at a time, the freak of growth development gone wild bumped me hard, brutal enough to bruise. He paused in his pass and hissed, "Guess what, new kid? You're meeting me after school today for the worst ass-kicking of your puny life. If you don't, asshole, tomorrow I'll bend you over the bench in the locker room and give it to you like the pathetic little bitch you are." Then he was past me and gone.

First days.

I gave one of those nasty grins I liked so much. It was a helluva lot more fun if they went for you on the first day, made the lesson really stick, when everyone was checking out the new kid. Everyone seeing the same thing—a boy, thirteen, a year too young to be in the ninth grade, thanks to a brother's relentless tutoring. Hair shoulder length but pulled back in a short ponytail. Bet his parents are vegan hippie weirdos. Gray eyes that blended into the general gray of school life all around, making him barely worth noticing. Barely, but someone had to take one for the team. The new kid was voted for that position every time. Last, they saw someone shorter in inches, smaller and slighter in build, and pale, nearly enough to seem too anemic to live. I wondered if any of those watching me had seen the same shade in the white lining of the spread jaws of a striking water moccasin.

This was going to be a good first day.

Shocked I was not that it was this jock asshole, who was almost two of me, to be the one taking the first run. That's what jock assholes did. But I wasn't sure it was all him. He'd have gotten around to me sooner or later, yeah, but there was something that had made certain it was sooner. That whispered talk the gym teacher had pulled him into, the glance at me that had casually slipped away. Too casually. A wolf staring to the side at nothing, definitely not the rabbit crouched ready to run. Don't look at me, bunny. I don't see you. I'm not even here.

Chomp.

I didn't bother to move from where I was sitting and, as I knew he would, Goliath's juiced big brother slammed into my shoulder again on his way back down to the gym floor. He handed off a pile of towels, nice excuse if anyone was playing hard enough to sweat, to the coach. *Good doggy. Woof, woof.* The teacher—what the hell was his name? Mr. C. was all I'd caught. Mr. C. dumped them on the floor with no further need of them than an empty candy wrapper.

That was that.

I knew what he was.

Not me, but he lived hidden in the same tall grass.

Do you have your list?

Groaning at the familiar echo of my brother's voice in my head, I dug in my pocket. When I pulled it out, the note was wrapped around it. The note was what had me up in the bleachers rather than down on the floor with the other students. A doctor's note as fake as the diagnosis of mild epilepsy controlled only partially by diet and meds was met with less alarm than the one I wanted: *A thirteen-year-old borderline sociopathic half human disconnected from societal and social cues who will not only catch the basketball your* Lord of the Flies *student bully throws in his face, but then will deflate it enough with the knife he has on him at all times to shove in your best point guard's mouth, make him chew it up, and swallow every bite.*

I'd be doing them a favor, perfect for gym class. A little panic with running and screaming is good exercise. Better than pushups any day.

I tossed the note in my backpack and went on to the list. 1. *Watch for the monsters.* Check. Done it every day of my life since I was five and found out there *were* monsters. 2. *Do not bite off anyone's body parts.* He was never going to let that one go. And it had been only half an ear, not even the whole thing. If the kid grew his hair out one, two . . . four, four inches, no one would notice. Besides, if he'd been better at dodgeball, it wouldn't have happened. 2a. *Do not play dodgeball.* God. What the . . . Never mind. Just never mind. 3. *Do not bite anyone, then tell them you wanted to know how they tasted.* That had been in *kindergarten.* Although it probably didn't help when I'd told them afterward that they tasted like the really good kosher beef hot dogs. 4. *Do not bite, period.* Jesus. Okay. I got it. 5. *Do not set buildings, trailers, or cars on fire.* That— that was not fair. It had been a medical emergency. I was not taking the rap on that. 6. *Do not investigate houses when you smell dead bodies in their basement.* Yeah, whatever. Blame the victim, not the serial murderer who lived next door. That was a lesson for us kids.

The list, updated every month, had gotten long, now covering the front and back of the card in tiny print. That didn't strike me as leaving a lot I *could* do. Grumbling, I started to skim faster, since everything I'd already done I was beginning to suspect topped the list. Yep, 15. *Do not blackmail.* Victimless crime. Well, technically there was a victim, but because they'd done something bad enough to deserve being a victim. Like a nurse who lifted narcotics from the hospital. 15a. *Regardless if they are addicts who steal drugs from their place of employment.* Damn it. Resigned, I skipped an entire chunk to get into things maybe I hadn't done yet. 37. *When you are much older and certain urges become stronger, do not sexually molest livestock as a reaction to your phobia of passing on your difference by (due to birth-control failure) impregnating a girl.* That was wrong. That was so wrong. I knew that and I was *half*-monster. Did he really think I'd . . . Nope, wasn't going there. I skipped again, and there it was.

43. Do not kill unless in self-defense or the defense of others.

Fuck.

I didn't need to kill the jock asshole to take him down. And he wasn't smart enough to use other kids as personal attack dogs. He wasn't smart enough to have killed and gotten away with it, either. He was a bully and lived to hurt anyone or anything—a predator, but there were different leagues. He was an amateur. Not even JV. Barely more than a benchwarmer. Mr. C. was varsity. MVP. Playing for fun. Playing for the adrenaline rush. Playing for the love of the game. Beatings wouldn't be enough for him. They'd be a side of fries. He'd want the whole buffet. He'd want the kill. And he'd want it hands-on, no attack dogs there. If he hadn't done it yet, he would.

That's what my gut told me.

I looked away from the card and down at him. A man with a

beer gut and the soul of a snake, but no visible blood on his hands. I wasn't a killer without rhyme or reason, but I was a born predator. When I killed . . . if I killed . . . I'd have a reason. One that I could give my brother and look him in the eye when I did. That was the whole point, I supposed, to the list.

Putting it in the backpack with the note, I fished around more. Soon I had a sheet of paper ripped out of my notebook. Less soon and a crap load of cursing later, I had a pen. I started writing, beginning with a lopsided number 1.

No one said I couldn't make my own list.

><×<

Two hours later, Lord of the Flies was surprised that I was waiting in the parking lot, just as he'd told me. He was more surprised I'd found his douche-bag Lexus. Other students were already gathering. Everyone had heard, and when I asked if he had a car, at least twelve fingers had popped up to point it out to me. They either didn't like him or wanted me to piss him off enough that he'd actually tear off one of my limbs and try to beat me to death with it.

Didn't know which; didn't care. I had promptly swiveled sideways as taught by my brother and his teachers at the dojo, knocking off the driver's-side mirror with one snap kick. Picking it up, I had bounced it from one hand to the other before tucking it under an arm and giving the asshole a one-fingered wave when he showed up.

Before he could get past the disbelief of what I'd dared to do, I took him down with one sweep of a leg to both of his while avoiding a sluggish swing of his fist. The juice makes you slow. "What the f—" he began, before I cut him off by slamming an elbow into his diaphragm to drive every breath out of his lungs and render them wheezed and worthless.

That's when I did what I had done at every new school. Showed them who stood at the top of their food chain. With this dick and this school, I did it by pounding his crotch repeatedly with his own car mirror. He would have screamed for his mommy if he had breath to do it.

We'd been circled by the usual crowd. There were the identical boring shouts of "Fight! Fight! Fight!" as soon as he'd hit the ground. I thought that was hilarious at every new school I heard it. Fight?

There never was a fight.

"New kids are bitches. Isn't that what you said?" I hammered another blow directly to his balls, the bigger target, this time. His dick, what little his shorts had showed him having, had retreated for cover. A walking slab of meat, but none left over for the sausage. Sad.

"Bitches who are bent over benches in locker rooms to get what's coming to them." The next blow, number six, was the last, as his balls had swollen to elephant size, large enough to show below his basketball shorts by inches and mound beneath the rayon, making him the picture of an idiot who thought smuggling melons over the border was a great idea. He was able to get enough breath back to make *hunh-hunh* sounds, hitching in his throat. Sobbing. He'd call it moaning, if he could talk, but, as predicted, he was crying for his mommy. Without actual words, yet that was what he was doing. That, with the snot everywhere, rivers of it, made the entire deal disgusting.

You could bet I wouldn't be biting him to see how he tasted.

I leaned in and showed him an *extra*nasty grin, the type of nasty he hadn't dreamed existed. "But take away your weapon of choice, what little of it you had, and then what? I bet you've pissed off a shitload of us 'bitches.' When they get smart, they might go to a sporting goods store, buy a Louisville Slugger, thinking about you when they pay for it. Deciding they don't like how you treated them. Decide they don't like your asshole, bullying attitude. Decide they don't like how you talk shit to them while shoving them against the lockers. Decide they don't like how you walk around like you own the school, or how the teachers grade your illiterate crap like you're a college professor because you're king of the basketball team."

Moving in farther until we were face-to-face, bare inches between us, I could see the blood bursting in the whites of his eyes. His heart was in overdrive, beating too fast for the small vessels to handle. "Sooner than you think, they'll decide they don't like anything you do or say. Decide they don't even like the way you *breathe*. Notice how you're *alive*. Decide they don't like *that*, either."

There was a shifting in the crowd, and the yelling had gone to dead silence three blows in. This wasn't how things went. This wasn't how scrawny new kids acted. Was it? Now there were low and frightened but also vengeful whispers racing around the circle. And they weren't aimed at me.

"How are you going to fight back when you'll barely be able to stand? How will you run away when you can't even walk? And how long before you find out if you can ever get it up again? Or if your dick is as useless for good as your brain?" I sat back and let the mirror fall on his chest. Tilting my head slightly to the side, I aimed my unblinking gaze at his reddened, wet one. Prey, but only just. He'd turned out to be more of a bug. There's no fun in squashing a bug.

What a waste of a first day.

"Last question: Do I care about any of that? Do I care if they come for you like you came for me? Take those bats and break every bone in your body?" My new grin wasn't nasty now. There wasn't any emotion behind it. It was a functional baring of teeth with only one purpose: ripping out throats. That was how we were made, those of us who lived in that tall and endless grass. "Hell, no, I don't care. I'm not a bitch, asshole.

"I'm a fucking lion." I stood. "I hope they *eat* you."

>＜

In the First
(Present Day)

I built a gate. I tore open a hole in the world, and the world screamed in agony. It did with every gate I made. No one could hear it but me. Not that I knew. It was possible the Auphe had been able to catch it. If they had, they'd never said, but, then, the First hadn't been big talkers if it didn't involve telling you how they were going to play cat's cradle with your intestines, flay you inch by inch, and let your skin fly up and skate on the air, a homemade kite, a toy. That's all you were to them: a toy. Brand-new, bright and shiny.

And this was the beginning for you, a raw piece of meat with your guts in your lap. Just the beginning because the Auphe loved their toys. They played hard with them, but they knew how to make them last until they'd taken everything from them. They took your arms and legs and what was between them, as you had no use for that now, did you, little toy? The only thing they didn't take from their toys was their tongue, so they could scream, and their hearing, as it's no good if your toy doesn't know how much fun it is playing with it and how much longer the playing will last.

No, the First hadn't been much on talking, but when they had, you'd have ended up saner if you hadn't listened. Or less insane. It didn't matter in the end. If the Auphe had been talking to you, you were likely fucked a thousand and one times over with no way out. I'd been lucky. I hadn't been a toy. I'd been a tool. I hadn't been born, but had been intentionally *bred* like a damn dog—best in show, a half-breed experiment. I'd managed to keep all my parts, my dick in particular, which I did have use for and would've missed like hell.

I'd opened the gate as soon as I'd left the bar and walked to turn into the alley where we dumped the garbage. The gate itself was a constantly shifting circle about twelve feet in diameter, with the seething ring a roiling mix of the murky gray of a tornado-spawning storm, a slick oil-spill black, and the dark, dusky blue of a bruise with the sizzling flash of livid purple-edged lightning racing around the circumference.

This was *my* toy. If you survive being an unwilling guest of the Auphe, you deserve one incredible fucking prize. Learning how to gate was mine.

Fun and useful; I could travel from place to place, but they had to be places I'd been before, knew, or could see. That was good enough for me. I gave it the same look you'd give a well-trained pet, fond and proud, then stepped through. I stepped out more than seven hundred miles away, in Kentucky. Lots of little four-way-stop towns, but also an ocean of horse-country money. Kentucky was one was the biggest producers of two things: expensive racehorses and more pot than almost anywhere else in the country. Half the farmers, it seemed when I was thirteen, drove cars that cost more than houses. Millionaire-nice houses.

We'd lived in Lexington, a college city, racetrack city, but surrounded by velvety green fields with grazing-sleek, coated-muscle flesh. Wind captured in the body of horse. I'd seen horses before, chunky farm horses, but when I'd seen my first Thoroughbred run, I'd thought it was an entirely different animal, different species. They might not be as fast as cheetahs, but they were silk and lightning and thunder—a cyclone exploding into motion. It was amazing. Not much impressed me at thirteen, or any age, but that first run was a frozen snapshot in my mind. That the majority of them ended up as dog food when their racing days were over made me hate that place more than a good deal of worse ones where we'd lived as kids.

People: I didn't understand them, and that was one more reason I didn't feel any urge to try.

I'd gated to the parking lot of the junior high I'd gone to for a few months before we moved on—Sophia, one step ahead of the cops as usual, had maxed out her anonymous new presence with enough stealing, conning, and whoring. There was always a new city, always a new school, always another first day.

I remembered my first day here; I wouldn't have if not for the first name on my list. First days all had blended together. However, thanks to this being the birthplace of that list, thanks to Mr. C., I remembered.

Studied the school, brown, boxy, and ugly as before but older and with more grime. I smiled. I'd never done a first day over in the same place. This was the exception. This time I was getting it right. "Mr. C. Coach Lee Callahan. No more hiding in the tall grass for you."

I couldn't gate to his house, although I had to give credit to the Internet for being as invasive as kudzu with tendrils that refused to stop spreading. Thanks to it, I had his address. I had that and a damn good deal more, but there was something I wanted from the school first. Breaking in was easy. I could've gated, but I liked to keep my whole range of skills up. Bypassing simple security systems, and they didn't get any simpler than the one they had: lock picking. I'd learned those by watching Sophia. She sure as hell hadn't taught me anything on purpose. She didn't bother wasting her breath to even talk to me if she could avoid it, unless she was feeling especially spiteful, then it was an all-day monster marathon.

I was a monster, a thing, a freak, a living disease, a nightmare that had washed out of her womb and had been planted there by a worse nightmare.

That had bothered me some when I was little, and bothered me more when, at five, I'd seen my first monster peering with eyes the color of blood through the kitchen window at me. Surrounded by empty night, it had tapped the glass with a pointed black nail that contrasted with its transparently pale skin, and then it had grinned wide, wider, wider still, until I'd thought the expression would wrap around its head.

How could a grin be so big?

It had teeth that were the same as the metal needles at the clinic where my brother took me for flu shots. Bright silver needles, hundreds and hundreds. I'd run and hid under the bed, letting my brother crawl under to curl around me as I shook. In the morning when it was gone, I'd pushed the fear down, putting it in a toy box I kept in my head, and locked the lid. I'd seen the toy box in a store window once, painted bright green and blue with dinosaurs. It cost a lot. I'd wanted it, but I'd known even before then that wanting and getting weren't the same.

Instead I'd built one inside my head. When things scared me or made me feel stupid because I didn't understand, I'd locked them in the box. Like I'd done now. It let me think, and I had. I'd thought hard. Sophia had only sex stuff for money. Living with a whore, by five years old or earlier, you know something about sex stuff. She called it fucking and made it sound ugly, but Niko said to call it sex stuff.

She'd said it before, too, and I hadn't understood then, but I did now. "It gave me gold and diamonds," she'd muttered, hunched over a Scooby-Doo glass of whiskey. Whiski? "Hundreds and hundreds of necklaces and rings," she'd slurred, "but now they're all gone, and *you're* here instead. You're still goddamn here."

If I was a nightmare, what did it mean that she'd let something that was a bigger nightmare, and *looked* like one, pay to put his thing in her and put me inside her stomach?

It meant if I was a nightmare, it was *her* fault because she'd fucked one for money. "Fucked" because what she'd done, fucked a nightmare, was ugly. Ugly and wrong, but she'd done it, anyway. So she should shut up about what she called me before I got the kitchen knife and *made* her.

I hadn't appreciated at five what a cool little kid I was.

Those were the days.

Once inside I roamed around, looking for the library. A half hour later, I'd found it and everything I wanted from it. Sitting at a table with a pronounced lean, I had five yearbooks spread out. I played a small flashlight over them. I was able to get the names and bare-bone details off the Internet, but only half of the pictures, and then some of the details were too glossed-over. They didn't like to mention suicide in obituaries, and not every kid who kills himself is considered worthy of a news article. Cause of death tended to be "taken too soon." If you died between twelve and fifteen years old, the age range of these yearbooks, whether by a rope or a brain tumor, "taken too soon" covered pretty much anything.

All had dedications, and everyone had mentioned "shy," "talked so little yet said so much," "you didn't know how you depended on seeing his smiling face every day until you didn't see it again." The customary bullshit for "that geek, weirdo, freak, bat-shit kid who tried to sit by me, as if I want his crazy getting all over my new outfit, *God*, who had gone and killed himself. Now we have to come up with something nice to say for the yearbook, when no one ever talked to the loser. Let's make it short. I have cheer practice in half an hour, then I need to hit at least three stores to find a dress for homecoming. Life is so *hard* when you're popular."

The kids—the dead ones, not the ones the world would be better off for if they were—were similar. Nothing close to identical. They were all boys. Some had fair skin, some darker. Their eyes weren't the same color, but they did all have black or dark hair, and all, from what you can tell in a yearbook pictures, were on the smaller side. Either short or skinny or both. Two wore glasses. None of them were smiling but one, and it was a smile so false it shouted "misery" twice as loud as the blank faces. At thirteen, when I'd gone here, I'd have fit right in with them . . . except for their unhappy and lost expressions. I'd never had a yearbook picture. We were Rom. We lived off the grid, and we didn't do pictures, real addresses, anything that could lead someone of the lawful nature to Sophia's door. But if I had, I wouldn't have the label these kids virtually stamped on their forehead.

Vulnerable.

Mr. C. had an acquired taste, and he stuck with it. I did have access to the news article telling me where he'd acquired that particular taste. He just hadn't looked me over as closely as he should have. Sloppy for an otherwise efficient predator.

I ripped the pages from the books, which I left scattered on the table, and was outside in less than a minute. I'd walk a few blocks, steal a car, dump out the window on the road the surgical gloves I'd fished from the depths of my jacket, and pay the coach a visit.

Talk about the old days.

Say, "What about that jock asshole you sicced on me? Did his dick ever work again? No? Had to have his balls amputated. Isn't that a fucking shame?"

Good times.

>—><—<

The house was outside the city on the far edge of a smaller town. Surrounded by acres of trees and unmowed fields. If you had a hobby, a noisy hobby, no one would hear anything. And screams, electric saws, breaking bones, that sort of thing, were noisy. It was a happy man who indulged in a good hobby.

I liked mine.

Circling the house, I could see his shadow moving in a window on the second floor. It was close to ten, early for bed, but he was a hardworking teacher and coach. He was probably brushing his teeth, and twelve years after I'd noticed his thinning hair, he absolutely had a helluva Rogaine monkey on his back by now. I came through the back door. It wasn't locked, which meant no bodies in his basement, but it remained wildly naïve. It made me want to pat him on his medicated, slicked-up head or pinch his cheek—you know, before I went about shooting him in the face.

Making myself comfortable on a saggy couch, I put my feet up on the coffee table, crossing them at the ankles. The impact of the combat boots against the wood made enough noise that he couldn't miss it. I waited for him to come down, with either gun or bat. *Just move it.* I'd put this off for twelve years, and I wanted it done. I wanted it fixed. I wanted to do what I should've done then.

Put the bastard down.

A cop, a lawyer, a jury, a human: they would all call it premeditated.

Murder in the first degree.

I wasn't a human and this wasn't murder. This was taking out a rabid coyote. I was killing what couldn't be cured and protecting the defenseless herd. Also, as part of my hobby, I was removing a subpar predator from the grass. Subpar or skilled as hell, I'd kill you either way, but the subpar ones irritated me. If you're going to be a murdering dick, be the best murdering dick possible. I'd respect your intelligence, if not the monster under your face, when I pulled the trigger.

The coach brought a gun to the party.

More ambitious than a baseball bat—hallelujah for the minuscule challenge. It's the little things in life you have to learn to appreciate. Often there are days when the little things are all you'll get.

"Coach." I raised my hand and offered a lazy smile. "Long time, no see. I like your gun. That is as old-school as it comes. A Dirty Harry–style Smith and Wesson twenty-nine. Chambered forty-four Magnum? Oh shit, I get it. Coach Callahan. Dirty Harry Callahan. You are just fucking making my day. That—" I laughed. I couldn't stop myself if I'd wanted. This was not a challenge after all, tiny or not, but I didn't mind. It was the funniest shit I'd seen in forever.

"That is . . . I don't know if there's an actual term. Wait. Wait. Not calling anyone, swear. It's you and me, Coach. No one else. Just . . . Wait." I tried to hold back another laugh and ended up choking on it as I retrieved my phone. A few seconds, and I blinked. "Shit. There is a word. Obscure enough I'll bet only the British know it: Ludicropathetic. Ludicrous and pathetic. Huh."

I dropped the phone on the couch beside me, and the humor and laughter vanished instantly. "But that is you all over. Ludicrous and pathetic. Every kid killer is, but you are something special in the category. If there's one as fucking-incompetent wannabe as you, I've yet to see them."

Twelve years, but he wasn't that different. Five to ten pounds heavier, in faded navy blue sweats, less hair, as I'd already predicted, average and unnoticeable as before—if you didn't watch the eyes. The unnatural shine of black glass, and with a presence in them as shallow. He was empty of the numerous peculiar but generally harmless feelings humans have. The sole emotion I saw was less of a feeling and entirely about need. Hunger. There was nothing inside him but hunger. If you didn't see that, you'd have to depend on noticing how he moved. He was the same snake he had been, gliding, quick motions. Fast as hell and an unbreakable fixation.

I had a demonstration of that when he pulled the trigger the moment I said "kid killer." He hadn't tightened his lips, hadn't flushed with guilt, fear, or anger. Not the top of the field in killing kids or brain cells, but he was an excellent snake. No tells at all.

I had expected it, though. I'd come across too many killers to not know what would set one off. Someone revealing what they were was big. I didn't wait for any tells. I gated as I said the words, but this time I built the gate around me. I didn't need a door to walk through. I enjoyed seeing them as art lovers enjoyed looking at a painting, but I didn't need them. I could, in a manner, make myself into a gate.

I came back into the world inches behind him on the stairs. Finishing the rest of my accusation there, I'd snatched his gun and landed a vicious kick behind his knees. It sent him down the stairs face-first to hit the bottom hard, wheezing for breath. Snake or not, that extra weight wasn't good for the heart or lungs. He should've traded the gun for a treadmill. If he dropped thirty pounds, he'd be almost inhumanly fast. But "almost" was for horseshoes and hand grenades. Not serial killers.

He managed to roll over, staring at me with a nasty case of carpet burn on one side of his face and nose. "Who the fuck are you? How'd you get behind me?"

"You don't remember me? That makes me sad." I tossed the gun behind me, hearing it hit the second-floor hall. "I have filled out. Finally hit a growth spurt about three years later, to put me up there with other sixteen-year-olds. Put on muscle. I do a lot of running in my business. A lot of chasing." I grinned before adding, "I like my job. It's important to like your job, isn't it? It's important to have other outlets, too. Hobbies. But you know that." I crouched on the mustard yellow–carpeted stairs. My stairs. A lion watching a snake.

"Forget my name. Who knows if you ever knew it? I was this kid." I threw one of the yearbook dedication pages wadded into a ball at him. This wasn't SHO. I didn't have a budget for a sterile room and PowerPoint presentation of the asshole's sins. "Or this one." I tossed another ball of paper at him. "This one." The third one hit him on the carpet burn. "This one and this one." Running out, I tacked on, "Or that's what you thought."

He had sat up, black eyes flickering from me to the paper he held in his hand. He straightened out the crumpled debris of a life extinguished and stared at the photo. "I don't know what you're—"

I sighed. "Shut up. I knew when I was thirteen and I know now. I don't want alibis or character references or arguments on how suicide can't be murder. I don't care." And I didn't, not one damn bit.

"I'm pretty certain that half those kids at least did kill themselves because their lives sucked. The other students made it worse, ignored them, called them names, shoved them around.

But I'm *absolutely* certain it was you setting one of your faithful dogs on them that was the final push over the edge."

I shook a scolding finger at him. "Naughty, naughty," I said, the words casual, but the force behind them caustic enough to sear my own throat. "You had one of your brainless walking carcasses of steroid-injected beef beat them half to death. If they told their parents, a teacher, anyone, maybe someone would do something, but it would get out first. And when your dog would hear, he'd beat them the rest of the way to the morgue. Might go through with that sick rape threat your one dog liked to use to scare them out into the parking lot in the first place. They couldn't know."

I shrugged. "So, yeah, I believe they killed themselves. But you let your dogs off the leash and gave them the target. *You* were the belt, the rope, the razor blade, the overdose of drugs, the bullet.

"The others, I'm positive, were direct, hands-on. Killing vicariously isn't enough, not for long. The drowning? The alcohol poisoning?" I nodded at the far wall of his living room, with the liquor cabinet the dimension of a full-sized kitchen refrigerator. "Sympathy from a teacher who promises not to tell. Promises it won't get back to the dog. Or you didn't use your dog at all. These kids were already on the ledge. Offer them any scrap of kindness. Hell, acknowledge they *exist*, and they'd willingly crawl right into the palm of your hand with hope, not realizing you were closing that hand to crush them."

"I didn't do anything to any kid, asshole. You're fucking crazy, and I'm going to call the cops to throw your goddamn ass in prison or the psych ward." He was on the offense now and he was snarling, spittle flecking his lips, down to the level of the dogs he made out of stupid bullies. It was a mistake. Snakes are calm, cold. They can be lethal. Not Dirty Harry here, but in general.

"Those kids," I said, ignoring him. "Skinny, small kids—the

kind that bullies see as weak and vulnerable. Those kids with black hair, miserable smiles, they reminded me of your son."

"My son?" Stunned and worried for the first time since I'd showed up. Mouth hanging open, he sucked in a breath and another; then he questioned in a milder, more calculating tone, "What about my son? You don't know him. You don't know anything about him."

"Shane Callahan." I reached into my jacket pocket and pitched the last paper at him. I'd printed it off the Internet when I'd been in the library. "Nope, I don't know him. Nobody knows Shane now. Being dead doesn't make for an active social life. But I do know about him."

The article said it all. Seventeen years ago, the coach's kid runs away, steals his dad's car, and drives it to Louisville, a city a few hours away. He's fourteen but no one notices. He doesn't get pulled over. He ends up at his aunt's house, saying his dad is too strict. They don't get along. They fight all the time. It read as "fight" meaning "argue," but knowing Coach and seeing the picture of his son, in appearance a member of the society of the other dead kids, it was plain that "fight" was "fight." Add to that the physical difference in size, and "fight" was "my dad beats the living shit out of me."

Sweet Auntie May, or whatever her name was, didn't kick him to the curb, but only because she didn't let him in the house. She slammed the door in his face. Louisville's a big city. Interstates and overpasses everywhere. Shane had jumped off one of those overpasses into the speeding cars below. He was hit by five of them before the traffic managed to come to a halt. In a coma for a week before he died. A week after jumping that far and being mowed down by five cars . . . Who could say all those bruises and shattered bones didn't come from that, or if they hadn't covered up older bruises and breaks? He would've been blotched purple and black from head to toe, held together by wire and glue.

"Without Shane around, your toy too broken to glue back together, you had to get new toys. Being a teacher gave you easy access to the toy store. You could even get toys that were like your first and favorite toy. Then what was once tension release became a genuine *hobby*.

"And now here we are." I smiled wide, wider, wide enough to wrap around my head, identical to what I'd seen through my kitchen window when I'd been five.

"You don't understand. . . . You don't know what stress is like." He was inching back on his ass as I let my eyes flood red. The shade of freshly spilled arterial blood, I knew. I'd checked in the mirror once or twice.

"I understand," I assured him, and I felt my gums split and the row of teeth, hundreds and hundreds of bright silver needles, drop through to cover my human ones. "Shane and I, we both have our daddy issues."

He pissed himself, but there was none of the usual "What— What— What." They didn't often get past that to "are you?" Coach didn't manage a "what." Didn't manage a single word. And the snake in him had curled up to hide. It was what it was: a disappointment. It was that jock asshole all over again. A waste of potential entertainment. Predator against predator—that was entertaining. Predator against a bug, and now predator against what I'd thought was a snake but was merely an ill-tempered worm—that was not. I went ahead to provide assistance in getting this show over with.

"Remember when you were a kid?" I asked. It came out as a hiss. When the lion, all of him, came out, I couldn't pass for human any longer. "How your parents told you the bogeyman would come out from under your bed or slide out of your closet and gobble you up if you didn't eat your veggies? If you didn't stop pushing around kids smaller than you? If you weren't a *goood* boy?"

I prowled down the steps. "You should've listened to them. They weren't wrong. And you are not a *goood* boy." The hiss shifted into the shattering of glass and broken shards ringing against each other. "And I'm your personal bogeyman." I was on him now, close enough for his panting breath to mingle with mine. I could smell the mint of his toothpaste; the fear flowing from each pore in a waterfall of sweat; the ammonia of where he'd jacked off after instead of before he showered; the fresh, bright tang of blood from where he'd bitten his tongue and gnawed at the inside of his lip, shredding it. "Coooach." He wouldn't meet my eyes, wouldn't look at my face.

"Coooach," I repeated, the title becoming the metal warp and tearing of a car crash, "be a goood boy. I like goood boys."

I patted his cheek as he began to cry. It was inevitable, the crying.

"Coooach, telll meeee . . ."

I gave him one last pat, almost cheerful in its reassurance.

"Where do you keep your shovel?"

He didn't try to run. He did try to crawl across the avocado green living-room carpet, as god-awful as the urine color of the stairs. *He's packed on more weight than I'd guessed,* I thought as I dragged him with one hand around his neck through the house, toward the garage.

What a chore.

I could've shot him. Broken his neck. Torn open his throat. Gated him a hundred feet up in the sky and watched him fall as his son fell. But I didn't. I thought about all the graves dug because of him. I thought of lonely kids taking their lonely lives or having them taken from them, and how they were in those graves. I wondered whether they were lonely there. I didn't know. I thought Coach should have the chance to find out. It was the best way of fixing what he'd done over and over, and what I hadn't done years ago.

I dug the grave and put him in it.

I buried him.

Alive.

Then I waited by it in case the snake inside him woke up, tried to worm and wind its way out through the soil. I was curious, too. Could you hear screams from six feet under? I'd wrapped him in plastic that I'd found in the garage with the shovel. I didn't want one scream filling his mouth and airway with dirt, asphyxiating him in minutes. Kid killers don't get off that easily. I didn't hear anything, though, and he was screaming. That was unavoidable. The stench of terror on him, even through the plastic, had been profound when I'd kicked his wrapped body into the grave. Welcome to the other side. The boy you drowned. I was willing to bet he had felt the same terror.

It was a long night. I played solitaire on my phone. Marked Mr. C. off my list. Added that new word I'd learned to a file. I was a monster, but I tried to be an educated one. Now and then. Yeah, it was a damn long and boring night when I could've taken two seconds, shot the son of a bitch, and been home. I didn't regret it. Slow suffocation wasn't a comfortable way to die, but Mr. C. had earned it. Earned his own long night of screaming, and when the air finally ran out, he'd earned that agonizing trip into the infinitely longer night.

No, I didn't mind the lost hours.

I didn't regret not choosing one of the other ways to make him pay.

One with my gut and instinct, I felt good.

I felt certain.

I felt *right*.

And this time . . .

I didn't change my mind.

ABOUT THE AUTHORS

Kevin J. Anderson isn't always serious. Yes, he has published 130 books, fifty-four of which have been national or international bestsellers. He has more than twenty-three million copies in print in thirty languages. He has won or been nominated for numerous awards, and he's best known for giant science fiction or fantasy epics such as his Dune or Hellhole novels with Brian Herbert, or his Saga of Seven Suns or Terra Incognita books. They told him he couldn't be stupid, but he proved them wrong with the Dan Shamble, Zombie P.I., series. He has published four full novels in the series—*Death Warmed Over, Unnatural Acts, Hair Raising,* and *Slimy Underbelly*—and numerous short stories (many collected in *Working Stiff*), all featuring a detective who is back from the dead and back on the case. He intends to resurrect the character yet again for a new novel.

Erik Scott de Bie is a thirtysomething speculative fiction author, game designer, hand-to-hand combat enthusiast, and all-around geek. He has published novels in the storied Forgotten Realms, his World of

Ruin epic fantasy setting (*Shadow of the Winter King*, *Shield of the Summer Prince*, and the forthcoming *Mask of the Blood Queen*) through Dragonmoon Press, as well as for Broken Eye Books (*Scourge of the Realm*) and the Ed Greenwood Group, aka Onder Librum (*Hellmaw: Blind Justice*, *Storm Raven*, among others). His short work has appeared in numerous anthologies and online, and he is the author of the multimedia superhero project *Justice/Vengeance* (including fiction, spoken word, and comics), of which Vivienne Cain is one of the title characters. In his work as a game designer, he has contributed to products from such companies as Wizards of the Coast and Privateer Press, and he is a lead creative consultant on Red Aegis from Vorpal Games. He is also entirely too tall. Check out his Web site, erikscottde bie.com; he can also be found at facebook.com/erik.s.debie, and on Twitter: @erikscottdebie.

Jim C. Hines is the author of more than fifty published short stories and a dozen fantasy novels, the first of which was *Goblin Quest*, the humorous tale of a nearsighted goblin runt and his pet fire-spider. Actor and author Wil Wheaton described the book as "too f***ing cool for words," which is pretty much the best blurb ever. After finishing the goblin trilogy, he went on to write the Princess series of fairy tale retellings, followed by the Magic ex Libris books, a modern-day fantasy series about a magic-wielding librarian, a dryad, a secret society founded by Johannes Gutenberg, a flaming spider, and an enchanted convertible. He's also the author of the Fable Legends tie-in *Blood of Heroes*. Jim is an active blogger about topics ranging from sexism and harassment to zombie-themed Christmas carols, and won the Hugo Award for Best Fan Writer in 2012. He has an undergraduate degree in psychology and a master's in English, and lives with his wife and two children in mid-Michigan. You can find him online at jimchines.com.

Tanya Huff lives in rural Ontario, Canada, with her wife, Fiona Patton, two dogs, and, as of last count, nine cats. Her thirty novels and seventy-five short stories include horror, heroic fantasy, urban fantasy, comedy, and space opera. She's written four essays for Ben-Bella's pop-culture collections and the occasional book review for the *Globe and Mail*. Her Blood series was turned into the twenty-two-episode *Blood Ties*, and writing episode nine allowed her to finally use her degree in Radio & Television Arts. Her latest novel was a new Torin Kerr book, *Peacekeepers 1: An Ancient Peace* (2015), and her next will be *Peacekeepers 2: A Peace Divided* (2017). She can be found on Twitter @TanyaHuff and on Facebook as Tanya Huff, and she occasionally blogs at andpuff.livejournal.com. Four collections of her short stories as well as six of her older novels are available pretty much wherever e-books are sold.

Seanan McGuire writes a lot of things, including two ongoing urban fantasy series (October Daye and InCryptid), uncounted works of short fiction, and everything published under the name "Mira Grant." She lives in California in a crumbling old farmhouse that she shares with her enormous Maine Coons and her collection of creepy dolls. When not home, she can be found at conventions, comic book stores, and Disney Parks. We're still not sure where that last one came from. Seanan regularly claims to be the vanguard of an invading race of alien plant people, and has thus far given little reason for people to doubt her on the matter. Keep up with her at seananmcguire.com, or on Twitter as @seananmcguire.

Kat Richardson is the bestselling author of the Greywalker novels, as well as a small tantrum of short fantasy, science fiction, and mystery stories. She is an accomplished feeder of crows.

Web sites: katrichardson.com and greywalker.com
Facebook: facebook.com/Kat.Richardson.Writer
Twitter: @katrchrdsn
G+: plus.google.com/111032806480382192972

International bestselling author **Kristine Kathryn Rusch** writes under a variety of pen names, from Kris Nelscott in mystery to Kristine Grayson in romance and several others, and is a decorated writer in fiction. In 2015 alone, she won the Anlab award for Best Science Fiction Short Story, given by the readers of *Analog* magazine, for her short story "Snapshots." Her novel *The Enemy Within* won a Sidewise Award for Best Alternate History (long form). Her novel *Street Justice*, written under her Kris Nelscott pen name, was nominated for a Shamus Award for Best Paperback Original Private Eye Novel. She published a lot of books in 2015, finishing her bestselling, award-winning Anniversary Day Saga in June, and publishing three books in the Interim Fates series under her Kristine Grayson pen name. She also takes part in the quarterly *Uncollected Anthology* of urban fantasy fiction, published online. In 2016 Baen Books published *Women of Futures Past: Classic Stories*, a highly anticipated anthology featuring stories by the women of science fiction. With John Helfers, she has edited *The Best Short Mysteries of the Year* through Kobo Books. The inaugural volume has just appeared. Along with her husband, Dean Wesley Smith, she acts as series editor for a bimonthly anthology magazine, *Fiction River*. To find out more about her work, please go to kristine kathrynrusch.com and sign up for her newsletter.

Lucy A. Snyder is a four-time Bram Stoker Award–winning writer and the author of the novels *Spellbent*, *Shotgun Sorceress*, and *Switchblade Goddess*. She also authored the nonfiction book *Shoot-*

ing Yourself in the Head for Fun and Profit: A Writer's Survival Guide and the story collections *While the Black Stars Burn*, *Soft Apocalypses*, *Orchid Carousals*, *Sparks and Shadows*, and *Installing Linux on a Dead Badger*. Her writing has been translated into French, Italian, Russian, Czech, and Japanese editions and has appeared in publications such as *Apex Magazine*, *Nightmare* magazine, *Pseudopod*, *Strange Horizons*, *Steampunk World*, *In the Court of the Yellow King*, *Shadows Over Main Street*, *Qualia Nous*, *Seize the Night*, *Scary out There*, and *Best Horror of the Year, vol. 5*. She writes a column for *Horror World* and has written materials for the D6xD6 role-playing game system. In her day job, she edits online college courses for universities worldwide and occasionally helps write educational games. Lucy lives in Columbus, Ohio, and is a mentor in Seton Hill University's MFA program in Writing Popular Fiction. You can learn more about her at lucysnyder.com and you can follow her on Twitter at @LucyASnyder.

Fantasy author **Anton Strout** was born in the Berkshire Hills, mere miles from writing heavyweights Nathaniel Hawthorne and Herman Melville, and currently lives in the haunted corn maze that is New Jersey (where nothing paranormal ever really happens, he assures you).

He is the author of the Simon Canderous urban fantasy detective series and the Spellmason Chronicles for Ace, an imprint of Penguin Random House. Anton is also the scribbler of short, mad tales published in a variety of anthologies.

The Once & Future Podcast is his latest project, where he endeavors as Curator of Content to bring authors to listeners' ear holes one damned episode at a time.

In his scant spare time, he is a writer, a sometimes actor, sometimes musician, occasional RPGer, and the world's most casual and controller-smashing video gamer. He currently works in the exciting world of publishing and, yes, it is as glamorous as it sounds.

Rob Thurman is the *New York Times* bestselling author of the gritty urban fantasy series the Cal Leandros Novels: *Nightlife*, *Moonshine*, *Madhouse*, *Deathwish*, *Roadkill*, *Blackout*, *Doubletake*, *Slashback*, *Downfall*, *Nevermore*; the contemporary fantasy series the Trickster Novels: *Trick of the Light* and *The Grimrose Path*; the technothrillers *Chimera* and its sequel, *Basilisk*; and the paranormal thriller *All Seeing Eye*. The author is also included in anthologies such as Charlaine Harris and Toni L. P. Kelner's *Wolfsbane and Mistletoe*; Martin H. Greenberg and Russell Davis's *Courts of the Fey*; and Faith Hunter and Kalayna Price's *Kicking It*. For sample chapters of all books, videos, and downloadable wallpaper, or to contact the author, see robthurman.net.

ABOUT THE EDITORS

Jim Butcher is the author of the Dresden Files, the Codex Alera, and a new steampunk series, the Cinder Spires. His résumé includes a laundry list of skills that were useful a couple of centuries ago, and he plays guitar quite badly. An avid gamer, he plays tabletop games in varying systems, a variety of video games on PC and console, and LARPs whenever he can make time for it. Jim currently resides mostly inside his own head, but his head can generally be found in his hometown of Independence, Missouri.

Jim goes by the moniker Longshot in a number of online locales. He came by this name in the early 1990s, when he decided he would become a published author. Usually only three in one thousand who make such an attempt actually manage to become published; of those, only one in ten make enough money to call it a living. The sale of a second series was the breakthrough that let him beat the long odds against attaining a career as a novelist. All the same, he refuses to change his nickname.

Kerrie L. Hughes has edited fourteen anthologies in addition to *Shadowed Souls*; these include *Maiden Matron Crone, Children of Magic, Fellowship Fantastic, Dimension Next Door, Gamer Fantastic, Zombie Raccoons and Killer Bunnies, A Girl's Guide to Guns and Monsters, Love and Rockets,* and *Westward Weird* with DAW; *Chicks Kick Butt* with TOR; and *Hex in the City, Alchemy & Steam,* and *Haunted* with Fiction River. She has published eleven short stories: "Judgment" in *Haunted Holidays*; "Geiko" in *Women of War*; "Doorways" in *Furry Fantastic*; "Travelers Guide" in *The Valdemar Companion*; "Bog Bodies" in *Haunting Museums*; "Pennyroyal" in *The Courts of the Fey*; "Corvidae" in *The Beast Within 2*; "World Building: Magic Systems" in *Eighth Day Genesis: A Worldbuilding Codex for Writers and Creatives*; "Do Robotic Cats Purr in Space" in *Bless Your Mechanical Heart*; "Give a Girl a Sword" in *Chicks and Balances*; and "Healing Home" in *Crucible: All-New Tales of Valdemar*. She has also cowritten with her husband, John Helfers, "Between a Bank and a Hard Place" in *Texas Rangers*; "The Last Ride of the Colton Gang" in *Boot Hill*; "The Tombstone Run" in *Lost Trails*; "Bucking the Tiger" in *Risk Takers*; and " 'Til Death Do Us Part" in *Last Stand*. Kerrie has also been a contributing editor on two concordances: *The Vorkosigan Companion* and *The Valdemar Companion*. You can follow her at geekgirlgoddess.com, on Twitter as @kerrielhughes, and on Facebook using her full name, Kerrie Lynn Hughes.